# NOT A HOPE IN HEL

## WINTERBOURNE

## S A BAKER

*Science Fiction and Fantasy Publications*

NOT A HOPE IN HEL
S. A. BAKER

*Science Fiction and Fantasy Publications*

https://sci!fantasypublications.com

Science Fiction and Fantasy Publications is an imprint of DAOwen Publications

Not A Hope In Her / S. A. Baker

Edited by Douglas Owen

This is a work of fiction. Names, characters, places, and incidents either are the product of the author's imagination or are used fictitiously, and any resemblance to actual persons, living or dead, businesses, companies, events, or locations is entirely coincidental or used in a fictitious way.

Cover art by MMT Productions

ISBN 978-1-928094-72-2
EISBN 978-1-928094-73-9

10 9 8 7 6 5 4 3 2 1

*To the Nursing home residents who have shared their lives with me; to those who have crossed over, and those who are with us still. For providing me with endless inspiration and teaching me more about myself than I could have imagined, I cannot thank you enough. Winterbourne would never exist without any of you.*

# PROLOGUE

Elanor stood ankle-deep in the wet morning grass, dew-soaked and cold and staring skyward, hoping for something, anything more than her current situation. The breeze that pushed across her face held enough chill in it to make her wish she had a heavier coat but not enough to change her mind about moving further along. She gazed upward, away from her surroundings and back again. After a while, she decided that looking toward the horizon was better than sitting around mindless and complacent like the others were.

*Look at them, sitting, jawing away as though they'd nothing better to do.*

Walking away - just far enough from the rest to make an obvious statement - an air of superiority flowed over her. Elanor kicked at the grass and turned her face back to the sky.

*Nothing better to do. The gall of it!*

She stepped away, further now from the rest, and felt as though they were miles beneath her.

*Loathsome cows, I've a good mind to tell someone what they're up to.*

Elanor turned her face toward the breeze that began to warm in the rising of the sun, and she dared to dream of something better. A secret wish for a life beyond the wet, muddy fields. A life less ordinary. And that meant not being told when to go to bed or get up or even that it was time to eat or do anything a body should have the right to decide for itself.

*A good mind indeed. Mother used to tell me, you're meant for better things, child, and no one ever got to better things by just laying around, slack-jawed, and prattling all day.*

Elanor moved a little further still from the others, and when she had found a spot that looked suitable enough, she sat. A release, like she hadn't felt before, pushed through her, taking the stress of the morning and her disgust for the others with it. Soon, she'd mellowed entirely. If it weren't for hearing an occasional squawk from the others, she might have forgotten they were there at all. There were suddenly more important things to worry about. Things beyond the chatty little group. Dawn broke all around her and leaked out of the sky like molten cotton candy.

*Stupid, fat beasts. They don't know what they're missing. I'm not going to stay here while the rest of the world goes whizzing by me. I want to follow it. I mean to whiz right along with it. I'm moving on. I was meant for better things than this.*

Elanor was suddenly aware that she *was* moving - literally now, and without the benefit of using her legs. And, after several hundred feet of movement without effort, she decided the freedom she desired had taken her far from home and those she'd spent her entire life with. Suddenly being a part of the crowd wasn't the worst thing she could think of. In fact, being this far away from the rest, she missed them.

As quickly as it began, her momentum came to a halt.

*I can still see the others. I'll just walk back from here.*

As Elanor turned toward the group, she felt an odd pain in her left leg. It was sharp and stabbing in multiple places and came in an odd rhythm as though something had been gnawing away at the leg. She attempted to bend at the knee, trying to flex the feeling away as nothing more than stiffness at having sat too long in one position but found the leg unwilling to bend. And now the pain moved, spread wildfire like, up her left side.

*Mustn't panic. I'm sure there is a logical explanation for all of this.*

But if there were an explanation, it didn't come to her. The pain came again and again. In time, it was all she knew. Panic set in as the ground rose to meet her. She struggled to right herself.

*Oh, God, I'll bet I've had a stroke. That would explain it. Pain all down the one side, and now I can't get up. Oh, God, oh, God. I'm too young for a stroke.*

Elanor tried to stand, moving her right leg, which was now hopelessly pinned beneath a useless left. Her neck craned, and her eyes bulged against the pressure that was built from her efforts.

*No, no, no. This isn't how it's supposed to end. I should see better things, greener fields, bluer skies, but not as a cripple.*

Elanor struggled further with the same result. She called out to the others to come and help, to call someone quickly, but they were too far away. Or maybe, too jaded to do anything but continue sitting around, exercising their mouths.

*Of bloody course! Never trust a friend, that's what I say. Well, I won't go quietly. I can tell you.*

She struggled against her weight, flailing, calling out, and straining to stand. It became an awkward ballet of failure, and one that couldn't be sustained long. The old girl was tired now—more tired than she'd ever been.

*Sleep, I just need a little sleep. No, I mustn't sleep. That's the stroke talking. If I sleep, I may never get up again.*

Her eyelids felt rubbery, thick, and top-heavy, and to keep them open required a Herculean amount of strength.

*If I just close them for a moment, it'd be alright.*

And her eyes drooped shut.

*No, wake up, you fool! Mustn't sleep now. That's what it wants.*

The big brown eyes snapped open for the briefest of seconds and began to slide back closed again as quickly. Elanor knew if she let them close fully this time, there would be no getting them back open again. Her brain was too tired, and her body had given up the fight. The sleep was too inviting a prospect to reject any longer. She let go and drifted off.

"Aaah," the green thing let go a satisfied breath.

The little monster pulled his fangs from the ragged, bloody wound on the neck of the cow and felt the crimson liquid oozing down his chin. A viperous, needle-toothed grin spread across his face and threatened to extend beyond the tiny slits of his ears. He pushed away from the blanched carcass and raised himself to his full height, which would have been more impressive and menacing, had he not been slightly less than three feet tall.

He was a Necrosite. One of the vertically challenged, brutish servants of the office of Death at Winterbourne Home, the converted insane asylum that now housed the newly - and soon-to-be - deceased members of the town of Winterbourne. They were freakish in appearance, like the hybrid of a mangy chimpanzee and a monitor lizard with long, dreadlock – like spines atop their heads. Lifeless, staring, black goggle eyes encompassed most of their faces and sat above a mangled bit of flesh that could only be considered a nose if it was having an exceptionally good day. Their arms were gangly and disproportionate to the size of their bodies, and their legs were stunted appendages that seemed cut off at the knee and did little more than push the little things from place to place in a stiff-legged trot. They were vicious and nasty little things that, for the most part, did as they were told and worked around the nursing home doing the unpleasant jobs no one else wanted to do. But they had been wildly violent and successful hunters in the past, and now, the younger generations had begun to believe it was a sacred right of all their kind to continue the hunt as they pleased. That and they really did enjoy the ripping of warm flesh and the gnashing of teeth against the denseness of thick, healthy bone.

The young Necrosite wiped the blood and gore from his face

and, for an instant, felt a pang of guilt jolt through him. He had killed something - and without approval. The feeling passed as he looked at the mutilated carcass of the Holstein, and pride swelled his chest.

"Oh dear," the voice from behind him said.

The Necrosite turned and stood and suddenly found himself face to face with Mr. Richardson, the senior-most of them in the service of Death.

"Tell me you haven't done this," Richardson sighed.

"Rotfanng can explain," the younger Necrosite said.

"I'm sorry, who can explain?"

"Rotfanng. My true name."

"Dear boy," the older of the two said. "I knew your parents, and your true name is Alvin Smythe - named after your grandfather if memory serves."

"That is the name the oppressors gave my parents. The ignominy of their thralldom has been passed down to me, but my offspring will not carry the burden of my shame as I have done. They will breathe the free air and hunt on the open steppes."

"Ignominy of thralldom, hunting the open steppes? In Winterbourne? Who is filling your head with all of this dime novel rubbish?"

"The Soulreaver," Smythe said.

"Who?"

"The Soulreaver," he repeated.

"I'm not certain if I know who–"

"The Soulreaver! The greatest Necrosite who has ever drawn breath. He has shown us all the truth, and he will lead us out of the darkness of bondage into the light of freedom."

"I'm still not following who this is we're talking about. Would I know him from the office? Perhaps I've met his parents?"

"It's Barry Wilson," Smythe said, barely above a whisper.

"How's that? Didn't quite hear you."

"Barry Wilson! Barry bloody Wilson, from the–"

"Barry Wilson, from the mailroom?" Richardson interrupted,

sounding amused at the prospect of someone from the mailroom being anything beyond a delinquent wisp of air that drew an overly generous paycheque.

"He has opened all our eyes to the shame that is our lives," Smythe said.

"The real shame will be what will happen if we don't get this thing cleared away before someone upstairs gets wind of this."

"Hunters we were, and hunters we remain!"

"Yes, yes, could we remain hunters who clean up after themselves? Would that be too much to ask?"

"Oh, very well," Smythe grumbled.

"There's a good lad," Richardson said. "Grab a hold of the other end of this, young Smythe."

"Rotfanng."

"Hmm?"

"Rotfanng if you wouldn't mind," Rotfanng said.

"Oh, very well. Rotfanng, you most vicious and adept of hunters, could you kindly lend me some assistance in moving this freshly slaughtered heifer that we might secret it in the long grass and avoid any sort of reprisal from upper management?"

The two Necrosites struggled with the dead weight of the cow's carcass and managed to get the thing hidden in the underbrush.

"Well done, Sm-" Richardson stopped himself.

"Rotfanng," Rotfanng corrected.

"Ah, yes," Richardson agreed. "Rotfanng."

"Rotfanng Asswallop," the younger Necrosite said proudly.

"You what?"

Mr. Richardson looked around, past the group of cows in the clearing just beyond the long grass they stood in and was certain that no one had been anywhere near the field to witness what the young Necrosite had done.

"We'd better be getting back."

They walked out of the grass as confidently as they could on legs that were too short and seemed to hinge at the hip. And when they had made their way past the fields, past the cows, and could see the Winterbourne Home for the Elderly looming on the horizon, Rotfanng turned to Richardson.

"You must hear the words of The Soulreaver, brother. He will show you that all of your gilded bangles are the shackles that continue to keep you imprisoned."

Richardson stared at the younger green thing. A look of confusion came over him, camouflaged by the blackness of his goggle eyes. He opened his mouth to speak but was silenced by the ding of a bell. A small slip of yellow paper appeared out of thin air and floated earthward like a stray feather. It read;

*Mr. Richardson, please come to my office and bring Mr. Smythe with you.*

*Signed D.*

"Go," Richardson said wearily.

He brushed the dirt and morning dew off his lapels and out of the folds of his suit. It was unlikely to make any difference to the earful he was about to receive, but it certainly wouldn't make it any worse if he looked a little more presentable

The younger Necrosite turned to leave but paused and looked back to his elder.

"A well-dressed slave is still a slave," he said.

The bell rang again, and a second slip of paper appeared. Richardson held out a gangly arm, and the piece of paper came to rest on it.

*Now, please.*

*D.*

# 1
———

Davis Mareth walked slowly down the dimly lit hallways of Winterbourne Home, heading for room 1191. He stared at the yellowed punch card in his hand, examining the name on it - Mr. August Schuler, 11:59. His gaze turned to the clock above the nurse's station; it was 11:50

*Not much time.*

He half-jogged the last ten feet of the hallway and into the old man's room to find him sitting up in his bed, looking calm and lucid. The last thing you would expect from a man about to shuffle off this mortal coil.

"I've been waiting for you," Mr. Schuler said.

"You have?"

"I knew you'd be coming tonight. I've gotten slow, weak, and tired. So tired. I thought I'd wait up for you."

"Well, I do try to get out and spend some time with everyone who is, you know," Davis fumbled.

"Cut the crap, son, I know who you are," the old man said.

"Oh?"

"The Reaper, right? Skeleton in the dark bathrobe, big sickle, booming voice, that sound about right?"

Davis smiled.

It had been five years since he took a job on the night shift in the nursing home and found out that nothing around here was what it seemed. Winterbourne was not a nursing home, so much as it was a waiting room for the dead and a pasture for those near to dying, and *he* was the shepherd. His predecessor told him before he left on his retirement, Davis had been tapped to be the new Death. The grim reaper himself, complete with a black robe, rictus grin, and razor-sharp scythe to sever the dearly departed from their silver cord. Though, he hadn't seen any of those things in his time here.

"Well, mostly, yes. I haven't quite got the big voice down yet," Davis told the old man. "And there really isn't a robe and scythe. How'd you know?"

"Mrs. Good from across the hall, she figured it out, said she saw you with her roommate at the end. That you *helped* her along, stopped her suffering. After that, she started watching you a little more closely, said she would see you go into the rooms of anyone who was close to the end. After you came out, they'd be gone. I think she just put two and two together and figured you were something more than just the fellow running this joint. So, when I started getting sicker, I knew you'd be around sooner or later," August said.

"How many of you know?"

"A couple of us. Mrs. Good told practically everybody, but they all thought she'd gone off her nut. With her gone last month, it doesn't leave many of us who do," August said.

Davis looked at his watch; it read 11:55.

"Not to rush you or anything, Mr. Shuler, but it's just about time."

"I suppose it must be by now, but I've decided I'm not going."

"How's that?"

"I'm not going - as in staying put. As in, I will be occupying my seat on the number nine bus through this life for as long as I can. Thanks, but no thanks."

"Mr. Schuler, it doesn't work that way. We can, sometimes, choose the way that we go, but you can't just decide not to go. We all have to go in time. And it is *your* time," Davis said.

"Well, I'm deciding, and my decision is to stay. It's a nice room, it's warm, and the food is not that bad. I'm staying," the old man said.

Davis glanced at the digital clock on the old man's nightstand as it cast a red glow in the darkened room. It was now 11:57, and the minutes were slipping away. He had the old man's card, and his time was drawing to a close, in two minutes precisely, it would end – whether he liked it or not. Giving anyone more time was against the rules; it simply wasn't done. There was a balance between the living and the dead, and following procedures - the hellacious backlog notwithstanding - maintained it. It was just easier if August and the rest accepted the fact they were about to die and get on with it.

Death sensed the old man's fear - the ones that stayed awake at the end were almost always afraid. Strokes, heart attacks, aneurysms, all frightening things to stare down at the best of times, but the alternative for not going willingly was far worse. Davis heard the stories of what happened to the ones who missed their times, whether through hiding from the reaper when he came or a clerical error from the other side, and it was always a bloody and gruesome end, full of screams and gnashing of teeth and the rending of flesh. And the people doing the dying didn't much care for it either.

"Mr. Schuler, believe me, it's much easier if you just lie back and let me handle this. It will be over quickly, and we can all get on with our lives, so to speak," the younger man said.

"I'd like to help you, kid, really I would, but I've got a lot of living to do."

Davis's eyes turned back to the clock. It was now 11:58. He scanned the room, and standing in the low light of the doorway, he caught a glimpse of three squat shapes and got a whiff of the rotten meat smell that hung off them like a badly fitting sweater. He let go a

3

heavy sigh and took the old man's hand. A flash of a mind, crammed with terror, hit the younger man like a freight train.

"No, Mr. Schuler, you don't."

Davis stood and stared into the old man's eyes. He gave him a broad smile hoping it might relax him a little, and slowly dragged two fingers across his forehead. August, mercifully, gave in to the end and fell into a noisy, open-mouthed sleep, his breath coming and going slowly and infrequently. Death ducked out of the room, but not before acknowledging the Necrosites waiting in the doorway. They were always there when someone was due to depart. Waiting, watching, hoping for a chance to do what they did best - tear away the last threads of resistance to inevitability. It wasn't easy, it wasn't pretty, and they loved every gory, blood-soaked minute of it.

"Make it quick. You've got a minute left. And as painless as you can, please," Davis called out as an afterthought.

The three hissed and bounded into the room, closing the door behind them. Within seconds the room was a symphony of the screams of a tormented soul. It sounded more like a slaughterhouse on overtime than the room of a man in the last seconds of life. As soon as the noise subsided, Davis stepped in and examined the room. It was bloody and awful and made him a little nauseous to see it, but Mr. August Shuler looked peaceful and was now, officially, late of Winterbourne Home.

"Thank you, fellas. Could you get one of the others to make sure Mr. Schuler gets where he needs to go? I've got to get back upstairs," Davis said.

As a rule, he didn't like the scaly little apes - they delighted in the violence that hung off them like ugly hung off an ape, and they smelled a little like spoiled food. Frankly, they all gave him the creeps.

"Ogay?" a voice said quietly, coming from behind him.

Davis' heart leaped into his throat as he spun quickly to see Clarence Barton, one of the oldest residents of Winterbourne, wheeling up behind him in the dark carrying a handful of well-read magazines.

"Jesus, Clarence," Davis said.

The old man pressed the books toward Davis with a broad, toothless smile.

"Ogay?"

"I'll add these to the pile. We can always use new ones in the waiting room."

"Ogay," Clarence said.

The old man pushed away, blissfully unaware the waiting room his magazines were in such high demand for was populated by the recently dead. Davis wondered if he knew the truth, whether Clarence would worry or just be happy they weren't getting tossed out with the trash.

The room had been vacant since Lois Helm passed, just after he took the job. Davis had been very close to the old woman. She was his confidant and his friend, and sometimes, necessary shot in the arm. Helping her on her way to sit with the others in the waiting room had been more painful than anything he'd experienced before. After she'd gone, he couldn't bring himself to let anyone else use her room, in spite of the overwhelming number of people who needed a room at Winterbourne. He opened the closet door and touched the back wall. A pale-yellow light poured into the room, washing over Davis and forcing his eyes shut, though he held his hands up to shield them.

"I gotta fix that goddamn thing, maybe a lower wattage," he complained.

The door of the closet opened onto the staircase that led to Davis' office. They were a dank, marble nightmare of slick, sweaty twists in the dark that, with persistence and a shit-load of luck, led to his office. As he approached the room, he saw a woman with her back to the door.

He was Death, the end of all things, and could, literally, take the life from whomever he chose. Were he a different sort of person, an awful, malignant person, the world would likely be an altogether crueller place. Despite the immense power, his only desire was to scare the shit out of his girlfriend at any opportunity. Moving slowly now, silently, as only Death could, he went to her and reached out to put his arms around her. She spun around and jumped up at him.

"You're not the only dead one around here."

Jenn Henderson threw her head back and let outa laugh that warmed Davis to the underside of his feet. He had met her during his first night shift at the nursing home. She came off as all business then - she knew her job and felt a deep connection to every one of the people she took care of. She also made it clear that anyone who didn't feel the way she did about the people under their care was probably in the wrong profession. The first night, she teased and prodded and tried to scare Davis off. Shortly afterward, Jenn revealed her secret to Davis. She was dead. In fact, she had been dead longer than he had been alive, and through a clerical error, she seemed doomed to remain attached to Winterbourne.

It was Davis' predecessor who had the idea to put her knowledge of the asylum and her compassion to good use. It was a skill that couldn't be overstated in a place where people were dying, literally, and terrified of the prospect of becoming one with the void. Half the time, she walked the recently departed to the waiting room herself and made sure they each took a number and got a decent seat close to the desk.

Even when the new Death felt he could no longer do it, when he felt the role he'd taken on lacked purpose and made him feel he was just a bump on the road to inevitability, she was there. Reassuring and soothing him. Davis had lived most of his life under the impression that fate had it in for him. Jenn reminded him that even if there were such a thing, it didn't give enough of a shit about anyone to have levelled the entire universe against them. And, if there was a fate, it *had* brought the two of them together.

Davis took a seat behind the impossibly large desk he'd inherited from Nancy Seasons, the former director who had died spectacularly in a flash of electric blue flame and viscous black smoke.

"Clarence said to give you these," he said, handing her the magazines.

"These'll go over well down there. I don't think there has been anything new in a while. He's such a sweet old man. When's he due?" she asked, thumbing through the editions of National Geographic and Popular Mechanics

"Not for a while, next year or the year after, I think."

"He's like a Timex."

Davis turned to the window and went quiet for a time before he spoke again.

"How long, exactly, have you been here?"

"Exactly? I don't know, a long time. It all tends to haze together after the first twenty years or so. Why?"

"What do you think of the Necrosites?"

"I think they always seem to be underfoot and smell a little like cabbage soup, but they're alright."

"That's not what I mean," he said.

"What do you mean then?"

"I mean, what do you think of them? Do you think we really need them?"

"They have been here longer than you or me. Nearly from the beginning, I think."

"But did they need to be?"

"Your predecessor asked questions like this in the beginning," Jenn said.

"And?"

"And he stopped, like everyone before him who asked anything so stupid. He began to understand they are a vital part of what we do here."

"I just don't see it," Davis said.

"You don't have to see it. Just go along with it. The Necrosites are not going anywhere anytime soon, so you'd better settle in," Jenn laughed.

Davis turned back to the window, the sounds of August Shuler's screams ringing loudly in his ears.

"Yeah, settle in," he said quietly.

---

Mr. Richardson tottered up the staircase that led to the backdoor of Winterbourne home and hurried through into the mudroom. He rinsed his feet in the small wash sink beside the door. Davis had it installed to keep the floors of Winterbourne free of mud and to keep the elderly residents safe and upright. The younger Necrosites viewed it as just another example of how the management was keeping them subservient. The elder Necrosite saw it as a way, albeit a difficult one, of keeping his feet clean without having to take off his suit. He stepped out of the wash sink, wiped his stubby feet on the carpet, and headed up the staircase to the Director's office.

"You wanted to see me, sir?"

"Mr. Richardson, come right in, have a seat," Davis said.

The Necrosite in the grey flannel suit waddled to the chair that sat in front of the enormous desk. He stretched out his gangly arms toward the back of the seat and tried to pull himself into it. His arms lacked the strength, and his legs lacked the length and forward momentum to get into the chair. He pulled harder at the backrest, hard enough to pull himself into it, and succeeded in turning the chair completely over. It soon became an awful exercise in sweaty futility, and Richardson grew exhausted with the effort. Slowly and nonchalantly, he moved to the front of the up-turned chair and leaned a hip toward it, trying to seem as relaxed as possible.

Davis righted the chair and picked up the Necrosite, putting him onto the chair as though he were a toddler.

"It's about the cows."

"The cows, sir?" Richardson asked.

"This is the fourth one to die in as many weeks. There are folks in town who have described you guys to a T. Usually, it's after several too many over the counter at Butler's, and nobody pays much attention to it, but the fact is, it only takes one curious drunk to convince a handful of others to come up here with torches and pitchforks looking for trouble."

Richardson lowered his head.

"I will attempt to stop the hunting," he said quietly.

"I want to believe you, Mr. Richardson, really I do, but I've heard this all before."

"Yes, sir," the Necrosite began. "But this time will be different."

"Yes, yes, it will. This time your head will be the one on the block. If you can't put an end to the hunting, I'll be forced to find someone who will."

"What, another Necrosite in my place?"

"Who said anything about another Necrosite?"

"You couldn't - you wouldn't do that," Richardson gasped.

"I don't like you, Mr. Richardson, and your kind's lust for blood is more than a little repugnant to me. The only reason you're all still here is my administrator thinks I should just settle in and get used to you vicious little brutes, and I trust her judgement - for now. So, let me make something perfectly clear. Give me a reason – an excuse, just one ugly clawed toe over the line, and I will throw the lot of you out of here faster than the dead speak," Davis said.

Richardson eased himself out of the chair as gracefully as possible. Still, the distance to the floor proved too great for the stubby, little legs to reach, and he tumbled down, upending the chair and landing beneath it with a thud. He stood slowly, wiping the dust off an already tatty jacket, and headed out the door. Davis called after him.

"I trust you'll deal with this matter today, Mr. Richardson?"

"Yes sir, str...straight away," he fumbled.

He walked down the hallway toward the back staircase and descended them without glancing up from his tiny, clawed feet.

"You were a little hard on him," Jenn said. "Don't you think?"

"How, so?"

"You threatened his job."

"And?" Davis said.

"And you can't just go about threatening him with dismissal all willy-nilly. There have been Necrosites serving this office for as long as there's *been* an office. Those Necrosites have had two managers, Davis. Two – Mr. Alan Richardson and his father, Mr. Enoch Richardson. His entire existence has been spent preparing for and in service to this office. If you take that away, what will he have left?"

"He'll have nothing, I suppose, but does he - do any of them deserve any better? I don't trust them, not one of them. We'd be better off without any of the little savages as far as I'm concerned," Davis spat.

"I can't tell you what to do, but if you carry on with this, if you get rid of them, I think you are headed into a storm you won't soon steer out of."

"Where are you going?"

"I've got a nursing home to run, you know. I can't hang around all day," she said.

He wanted to keep talking, and she knew it but refused to let herself be baited into an argument.

Jenn headed out the upstairs office door and walked to the staircase leading to room 107. Davis caught a glimpse of her before she descended the stairs, and he closed his eyes for a moment. His mind was flooded with images of scaly, dreadlocked, chimpanzee things with goggle eyes, wearing poorly-tailored grey flannel suits. He knew Jenn had told him what she did to make him feel remorse or some kind of pity for the awful things. But he didn't. He wished they didn't give him the cold, trembling fear. But they did. From his first days working the night shift, when he had seen what they were capable of - what they had done to old Mrs. Nesbit - he considered them little more than perverted animals that got off on all the pain and bloodshed they could inflict.

"I've weathered some pretty heavy god-damned storms," Davis breathed.

---

*A well-dressed slave is still a slave.*

The young Necrosite's words echoed in Richardson's head. They bounced around until they found a toehold among the memories of phone numbers, dry cleaning tags, and errands he had been sent on by Davis and his predecessors. They bedded down, burrowing deep into his mind, taking root, and a tiny seedling began to grow.

*You must hear the words of the Soulreaver.*

Mr. Richardson stood by the double doors that led from the darkened, unfinished hallway into the main floor of Winterbourne home. He watched the residents for a time. They were blissfully unaware. Unaware of him or his kind and the immense amount of work they carried out. The work that went into giving these bloody people the sort of death they deserved.

"Do you think it's easy pulling a soul out of one of you quivering flesh bags?" he said aloud.

The Necrosite stared at an old woman wandering back and forth, from wall to wall, gradually making her way toward the double doors. Richardson's first instinct was to turn quickly and duck into the shadows of the unfinished hallway. But he didn't. Instead, he remained fixed to the spot, staring out the windows, goggle eyes fixed firmly on the tiny woman meandering her way toward him. She made it to the double doors, looked directly at him, and flashed a demented smile.

"Scraping a couple of fingers across the forehead, hah!, You try shuffling someone into the afterlife with a soul still inside them. See where that gets you."

The lizard-chimpanzee thing put his head back, bared his lethal needle teeth, letting loose as angry a primitive howl as he could muster.

"Kitty," the woman said and continued to smile at him. She quickly lost interest in the green thing behind the glass and drifted off back the way she came.

Mr. Richardson lowered his head and walked down the unfinished hallway to the doors that led to the back property of the estate.

"Do you think it's easy ripping a body to shreds in minutes and then having all the gore cleaned up before any of the natural world finds out? It isn't, I can tell you." He stepped through the door.

The back property of the Winterbourne estate had once been the model of wealth and means. A manicured wildflower garden around azure reflecting pools, koi ponds, filled with the fattest, happiest goldfish that had ever swum and a lawn cut with golf course precision. It had been strictly off-limits to the residents of Winterbourne from its days as an insane asylum. The inmates were constantly eating the fish and fowling the ponds and reflecting pools. All the Deaths who had come before, several of whom Richardson had served, had agreed it would be good to let the Necrosites blow off steam out there, doing pretty much as they pleased. Nobody was going to kick up much of a stink if a few squirrels and the odd raccoon or two were found dead on the property, and It did enough to satisfy their bloodlust. When Davis took over, he announced his intention to restore the backyard to its former glory and let the old folks stroll around in it as they pleased. Once the Necrosites were forbidden from satisfying their carnivorous urges on the built-in game, Necrosite eyes turned toward the town and the livestock that lived out in the open.

*If they didn't want them killed, they shouldn't have left them lying around like that,* Richardson thought.

He and took at a run-off across the lawn, snatching up a squirrel. He held the thing up to his face. Pangs of bloodlust washed over him. Cravings that made his bones hurt took hold of him. He bared his fangs and pushed them toward the clueless rodent's head. Richardson stopped short of ripping the thing to bits. The bell would surely ring if he did, followed by another slip of marigold paper from Davis Mareth. He relaxed his grip.

"I never went in for all the killing anyway."

The sun was going down. The older Necrosite would be given the night's assignments - a list of residents who they were to dispatch. Sometimes it was a single name. Sometimes, like the influenza outbreak that ran roughshod through the place a few years ago, as many as seven in a single night. There would be no praise for them in the morning, no rewards for a job well done, and there would be hell to pay at the slightest trace of them having been there at all.

"Mustn't upset the old ones, must we?"

The squirrel began to struggle in his grip, sensing the bigger thing meant to release his grasp and realizing it'd missed the opportunity for escape.

*You must hear the words of the Soulreaver.*

He brought the squirrel up to his mouth and drove his teeth deep into it, severing its head in a single bite.

*Hunters we were, and hunters we remain!*

## 2

————————

**D**avis Mareth lay in bed, staring at the ceiling. Jenn lay beside him, snoring happily, and the way she grunted and wiggled in protest when he tickled her side made him smile.

*Be your own personal Jesus.* The clock radio blared to life.

Davis slammed his hand on the top of it, hoping to silence the damned thing before it woke Jenn.

*Already?*

He sat up and felt a clap of thunder cramming its way in through the top of his head. Staying seated for a while seemed like a good plan. Nausea gurgling up through his guts agreed.

*Someone to hear your prayers.* The radio sounded again.

His hand flew, automatically, to the button to silence the overactive sleep auditor.

*Must have hit snooze.*

An attempt to stand crossed his mind and made its way, slowly, to the legs but was dissuaded from further progress by the riot currently happening behind the walls of his stomach.

*Someone who cares.*

Davis grabbed the radio and yanked the plug out of the wall. If he destroyed it in the process, he was okay with it. A broken clock was better than the wrath of a mostly dead girlfriend. And then it happened. He had to use the bathroom. Immediately. Urgently enough that he was afraid he wouldn't make it in time. He did and in time enough to avoid an embarrassing story and a mess. He finished up and stood slowly, making his way to the bathroom sink.

*Hangover. This feels like a hangover.*

He turned the tap, and the sink was soon flooded with cold water that he splashed liberally into his face. When he was sure most of the cobwebs had been washed out of his brain, he towelled off and looked at himself in the mirror. The face that stared back at him looked as whisky worn as the rest of him felt.

*How - when?*

He tried to remember a night before to equal the misery of this morning after. Had there been a celebration? Was it an exceptional Tuesday? Davis couldn't recall anything and, the fact he'd woke up in the bed with Jenn was a testament to there being no night before. At least not one worthy of feeling this awful.

*What then?*

He caught a glimmer of something out of the corner of his eye, just in the lower-left corner of the bathroom mirror. It was a pale, waifish-looking thing, huddled in the corner of the room, near the toilet. It was so close to the throne. He was amazed his legs hadn't brushed up against it when he stood up.

"Hello?"

The figure remained motionless, balled up tightly in the eighteen-inch void between the wall and the base of the toilet.

"Hello," Davis called again. "Are you alright?"

The figure began to tremble and spasm, letting out quiet whimpering sounds. Whatever fear and apprehension he felt for the thing melted away in the woeful display playing out in his bathroom. He stepped forward to offer some comfort to it. As he drew closer, the sounds coming from it became louder and clearer. Noises that were not whimpers but the slow burn of unhinged laughter from a mind that had crashed through the borders of sanity.

"What the f–"

The thing pushed its way out from beside the toilet and continued along the floor, undulating through jolts of movement broken up by spastic jerks. It rose to its full height. It was shorter than Davis pictured it - considerably shorter than Davis' own five-foot-five frame. Skin hung loosely from it, pale and dimpled, like the skin of goose, freshly plucked for Sunday dinner. Though, the oozing black lesions that pockmarked its body made it less appetizing. Ancient, deflated breasts drooped from its chest, and the briar of grubby thatch between withered legs said it was female - or had the anatomy of one. It had hair on top of its head, stringy and dripping with the same mucous glop that peppered the skin, making it look black and shiny. Its eyes stared at the white tile floor, obscuring its features behind the curtain of scuzzy hair. The thing had gone strangely quiet as it cracked and creaked its way along the bathroom floor, but now, as it stood before him, the horrid giggling resumed.

Fear gave way to sympathy, and even as the awful thing made its awful way across the bathroom floor, a swell of pity spilled over Davis at the display. But as the crying of the broken gave way to the cackling of the deranged, Davis found his sympathy shoved aside. Who was this thing to laugh at him? He darted forward and stuck out a hand to lift the things head, allowing him a better glimpse of it. As his hand made contact with the dimpled skin, a shock ripped through his arm that travelled the length of his body and laid him out in a flash of blue spark and a whiff of ozone.

"Who are you?" Davis panted.

The figure remained silent, jittering and jerking forward in a rocking motion. It stood over him, face bathed in the shadow of the stringy hair. Still, there was something familiar about it, something Davis recognized but couldn't put his finger on. He stretched out an arm and saw his hand was trembling. He was afraid to touch it. He didn't want to touch it. But he needed to. He reached for the thing again, to the same end. He lay on the floor, stinging from the shock and wanting desperately to go back to bed, leaving the greasy thing to live in his bathroom for as long as it felt necessary.

"Fine, keep your goddamned secrets. I'm going back to bed."

The thing creaked to him with surprising speed for never lifting its eyes from the floor and held out an arm to block his way.

With its other arm, the flaccid thing stretched out a hand and wrapped its bony fingers around Davis' chin, turning his face back toward the bathroom sink. The tired, ice blue eyes in the mirror stared back at him, and Davis tried to reason his way through what was happening to him.

*I'm dreaming. That's what this is. I'm having an awful dream. This thing is the result of too many drinks, or maybe too much to eat before bed. More gravy than grave, isn't that how the story went? Okay, I'll play along.*

Davis smirked into the mirror and turned his head to the thing, just in time to receive a quick smack from one of the bony hands at the end of its bony arms. And the dream came crashing down.

*Except I didn't drink anything last night.*

The fingers tightened around his chin and forced his face closer to the mirror as the other hand pointed a skeletal finger at the reflection. His eyes burned with anger, and red veins crept their way into the pale blue fields staring back at him, and that's when he noticed it. A small fault, barely more than a pillow crease just above his right eye.

Never one to leave well enough alone, his fingers groped at it, exploring the thin pinkish line - probing the edges of it looking for something to grab. When they found it, they dug in and began to pull for all they were worth. An immense pressure built up behind his eyes, and it seemed the more he dug and pulled, the greater it got until it felt like he was ripping his whole head apart. His guts churned. His knees buckled. Davis didn't know if he would puke or pass out.

When neither happened, and there was no blood or anything else leaking from the gash on his face, Davis ran the tap and splashed cold water on himself to cool the sting of the digging and pulling. A small flap of skin wiggled back and forth along the crack as he rubbed the water across his face. It caught his eye, and a finger shot up to probe it. With a little persuasion, the flap of skin peeled back and dropped away like the husk of orange, leaving a gaping, bloodless wound on Davis' face. Beneath it was scaly, thick and greyish green, like a mouldy leather hide, flecked with coarse black hair.

*What the f...*

Davis stood back from the mirror.

The radio sparked to life.

*Feeling unknown, and you're all alone.*

"Oh, come on!" he bawled, his eyes darting to the thing still standing behind him.

He moved back and stood over the sink staring in the mirror, trying to summon enough backbone to carry out what he imagined himself doing.

*Flesh and bone by the telephone.*

He closed his eyes, sucked in all the air his lungs could handle and willed his hands to move up to the hole in his face. His fingers probed along the edges and pushed deep into the jagged tear in his face. A quick, forceful exhale, and they pulled away from each other with a sound like a dull knife hacking through a watermelon.

*Lift up the receiver. I'll make you a believer.*

The huge chunk of skin tore away with a rip that sickened him but was surprisingly painless. What hit the sink looked like it was ripped off a cheap Halloween mask. A chunk of a face but there was something wrong with it, something grey and lifeless. Something dead. But underneath was something very much alive and wanting to push itself into the light. The eye was large - too large for the rest of the face - like the eyepiece of a gas mask but opaque and emerald green. It moved around in its socket, looking at itself in the mirror. It liked what it saw. There was a fiendish kind of love in that goggle-eye. Several small flecks of green-grey flesh poked through the fissure, fetid and ragged, like a disease taken root on decay. The nose, or what should have been a nose, was little more than two reptilian slits, slightly below the eyes. What the nose lacked, the mouth made up for, stretching from one side of the face to the other in a rictus grin, full of needle-pointed teeth.

*I will deliver. You know I'm a forgiver.*

The emerald eye saw the awful mouth and turned skyward, while the teeth gnashed out a dreadful rhythm and an appalling smile wormed its way between heaven and earth. The pale thing behind him released its hold on his face and raised its head. A weak attempt at a smile smeared its way across the blotchy face, and Davis understood where he'd seen it before.

"Lois?" Davis asked, sweat beading on his forehead.

"Look what you've done to me!" the Lois Helm thing screamed.

---

Mr. Richardson stood in the darkness of the unfinished hallway, waiting for the elevator that would take him to the basement and his home. He hummed a little tune, not certain where he'd heard it before, but it was stale and simple enough to occupy his mind while he waited. The ride was quiet. It felt like forever before the steel doors opened again. He stepped off into a near-empty landing that bordered the two major Necrosite neighbourhoods. A few feet in either direction, east or west, and he would be up to his elbows in his kind, going about their lives and not paying much heed to anyone. Least of all him.

The hallways were nearly always filled with them. Since the early days of Winterbourne Home, they had been there. Most of them serving the day-to-day operations of the place. Everything from pushing the paperwork through to wrenching the life away from people who just couldn't let go. In the beginning, there were so few Necrosites needed that they slept in whatever empty room happened to be available, moving on to another as they filled up. But as the resident population expanded and the nature of Winterbourne home changed, so too did the office. A demand suddenly existed for end-of-life care and assistance with residents finding their way to the afterlife. It was all so much more than one supernatural being could handle. The office of Death was created to deal with the rigours of shuffling people off this mortal coil, leaving the Omega free to attend to the cataclysmic death events like wars and religious cults checking out in the hundreds and thousands.

And the Necrosites had been there for it all. There were so many of them now that the entire basement was converted into makeshift apartments. They were clean and dry and a place they could call their own. There was a belief, in those early days, that they were on the same level - humans and Necrosites - all working for the same cause. Two equal halves of the same coin, the left and right hands of the Omega, serving the same noble cause. As time wore on, however, humans – even dead ones – began to look down on things that were different and see them as inferior. Inferiority breeds disdain, and a few of the Deaths of Winterbourne began to see themselves as overlords of the Necrosites. They were locked away like vicious dogs - let off the chain when a bloody end was the only way to get someone to the waiting room on time.

Of course, there were exceptions, and one or two Deaths tried to repair the relationship, but the damage had been done. Any thoughts of equality were pushed aside, and the Necrosites went back to their cells below the humans. They forget their former ways as hunters and killers and started to think that serving the greater purpose might have left them on the short end of the stick.

The lower levels these days looked less like the bottom floor of a nursing home and more like a block of tenements from the turn of the century Manhattan. Necrosites sitting on dirty staircases smoking and complaining about the noises from the tenants above. Bits of laundry hung from every available surface, and the overpowering smells of cooking too many different things came from all directions. As far as Mr. Richardson knew, his kind didn't need their food to be cooked for any reason - beyond them believing it might bring them closer to their pink-skinned counterparts.

"Home again, Mr. Richardson?"

"Shit," he breathed – he'd hoped to avoid this

"Home again, Mrs. Pugwash. Another day another dollar," Mr. Richardson said.

"Oh, have they started paying you now?"

She had taken the name of Mrs. Ida Pugwash to give some indication she was a female of her species. She liked the way it tumbled and chugged its way past her needle teeth, but by most appearances, there was no difference between the sexes. She wore a polka dot house dress that covered her from neck to knee and a paisley bandana that kept her spiny dreadlocks tied up and off the back of her neck, but even that wasn't a guarantee of femininity down here.

"You must hear the words of the Soulreaver," Mrs. Pugwash chuckled.

"Funny, you're not the first to say that to me today," Richardson replied.

"Someday, a rain will come," she said.

"And cleanse us all," answered Richardson. "You think this Soulreaver is the rain?"

"Not bloody likely. He's not the first one who's preached this stuff. He won't be the last. The problem with deliverers is they are always willing to deliver to the faithful, but never any of the rest of us. "

"It's a relief to hear you say that," he sighed. "I've served the office of the void most of my life, and my father served, faithfully, before me. I've never felt there was something better beyond the horizon. Sometimes Mrs. Pugwash, you just have to keep your head down and do as you are told."

He walked past her and stood by the door to his apartment, wanting to say something more to her.

"A well-dressed slave is still a slave," she said.

"Wait, what? What did you just say?"

"Someday, a rain *will* come, Mr. Richardson. A real rain and it will cleanse us all. But not of each other."

He stepped in through the door and slammed, hoping the noise might scare Mrs. Pugwash off the stoop. It didn't. Mr. Richardson took off his grey flannel jacket, hung it on a nail stuck in the back of his front door, and eased himself onto a chair in his front room. It wasn't much more than a handful of milk crates covered with a blanket, but it was comfortable enough to forget his troubles for a while. Maybe even sleep. He was tried enough. He could have slept on a fence post if he had to.

*Or I will be forced to find someone who will.*

Davis' words rattled around the Necrosite's head until they stopped making sense, leaving confusion and doubt, pressing on an already raw nerve.

*...find someone who will.*

Mr. Richardson felt his chest tighten at the thought of being removed from his position - it had meant power and respect among his people. Sure, there had been those who called him a Judas for working with the humans and turning his back on his own kind, but they lacked vision. What kind of life was rutting around in the morning dew, wet assed, and stinking of cow shit? And how long could it go on in this day and age? No, sir, a life in service of the inevitable was the way of the future. His father knew it. There was never any question of what he was going to do with his life.

"Look at everything loyalty has brought me," he said to the empty room. A swell of pride puffed his chest up.

Richardson looked around his apartment. Milkcrate chairs, scraps of found wood stacked on top of cinder blocks for a table, and a few old towels heaped on the floor to make up his bed. Suddenly the pride that inflated him began to hiss away like a punctured balloon.

*All your gilded bangles are still shackles.*

"All of my gilded bangles are made of cheap tin."

He eased himself from the chair, but with legs so

disproportionate to the rest of him, misjudging distances was almost second nature. He hit the wood like a sack of rotting meat and made his way to the bed in the corner

*You must hear the words of the Soulreaver.*

Within minutes of laying on the ratty towels, Mr. Richardson knew that sleep wouldn't come tonight. After a few awkward attempts of rolling and pushing and pulling and despite the hellacious and exhausting day he would have tomorrow, he got out of the bed. He raised the tin foil blind on his only window and saw that Mrs. Pugwash was still sitting on the stone staircase, looking like a gargoyle in a house dress. He burst through the door and spoke to her in a commanding voice;

"As a legacy employee of the Void, I command you to tell me where I can find this Soulreaver right now."

"Well, of course, you do, dear. You needn't look for him, though. In time, the Soulreaver will find you," Mrs. Pugwash said.

"Yes, of course, he will. However, in the event he can't find me, or perhaps I'm in the shower or something, why don't you just tell me where he is right now!"

"Alan Richardson, I like you, and I have known you since you were very young. Don't make me think you've forgotten your manners and make me do something you might regret," she warned.

Mrs. Pugwash began to descend the stairs of Richardson's apartment, heading for her own when she stopped and turned back to him.

"This is something else, Mr. Richardson. This isn't the piss and wind we've heard from his like before. This Soulreaver - he says things that many Necrosites are already thinking. Things they've thought for years, but few had the courage to say. Don't go looking for trouble around him. You're likely to find it."

"I don't need to go looking for trouble, I can go see it at the office tomorrow," Richardson sneered, and a smile snaked across his lips,

"You what?" Mrs. Pugwash asked.

"The Soulreaver is Barry Wilson, from the mailroom."

"And?" Mrs. Pugwash wondered, not entirely certain what he meant.

"And, when he isn't inciting all Necrosite kind to shake off the yolk of its oppression, he works as a floor supervisor. He doesn't need to seek me out. I've just remembered where he works."

"So, you have."

"I'll just go to him tomorrow. Goodnight, Mrs. Pugwash."

"When you see the Soulreaver, tell him to tell his mother to come 'round for a cuppa and a good old gab. Been ages!"

# 3

*e your own personal Jesus.* The radio blared.

B "Holy shit!" Davis woke in a panic and sat upright quickly enough. He nearly launched himself from the bed.

"What, what's the matter?" Jenn asked.

"Something's happened, something terrific," he replied.

"Well, that's good, isn't it?"

"No. Terrific, as in full of terror. I Something very bad has happened," Davis answered.

"How do you know?" Jenn asked.

"I don't. Not exactly. It's more like a bad feeling – like a nightmare just sat itself on my chest. and pushed all the air out of me."

Jenn stared at him, stunned by what he said.

"What?"

"I'm getting used to you being a little off before your first cup of coffee, what with having to do the whole Death thing at all hours, but that's about the shittiest good morning I think I have ever heard."

She laughed and pulled him back down to the bed. "Make me late for work."

They moved in different circles, or at least their circles moved at different times, with one working virtually all day and the other all night. It made meaningful connections with one another even more difficult. The upside was the sex still felt new. It felt urgent. There was hardly enough time together in the same room, let alone in the same bed, for anything to get stale. When they did manage to get together, they wasted no time. They raced into episodes of fumbling and groping that reached fever pitch and usually ended quicker than either wanted.

"Hey, wait a minute. Technically speaking, I'm your boss. How can I make you late for work when I am the one you answer to?" Davis asked.

Jenn looked down. Her eyes narrowed on him.

"You might have the robe and scythe and all, but you don't a clue how this place really runs. I know every nook and cranny, including the corners you hide in when you want to eat junk food. Incidentally, sweetie, you're Death. Sugar can't rot your teeth."

"Kind of makes you the boss if you look at it that way."

"Kinda does, kid and this boss is going to be late, and all hell will break loose if I don't get on the floor soon."

"We really should get someone to help you out, someone who could be a face for the public," Davis said.

"What's wrong with the way things are now?"

"It's been five years since I...we took over. People are only going to buy that the director is busy or on another call for so long. Sooner or later, somebody is going to come around, asking questions. Maybe we just need somebody to be a face for the families to see."

"Can we talk about this later? I really am running behind."

Jenn dressed quickly in a clean set of green hospital scrubs and hurried to the door, stopping along the way to bend low and kiss long enough to make him reach up and try to pull her back down again.

"Later, slugger," she said.

"Spoilsport."

"Don't stay in bed all day. There's a whole world out there, and we have a couple of folks who are close. They like it when you visit near the end."

"They like when Death visits?"

"No, they like when *you* visit. Most of them don't know you as anything but a nice young man with a friendly smile. You give them peace at the end. They're scared about what comes next, and you have the warmth to take that all away. Who wouldn't want that?"

Davis sat up. He had never thought of himself – new Death or not - as being anything less than a necessary inconvenience, and he was flattered that the residents of Winterbourne thought of him as something to cling to when the end came. He looked up at Jenn and flashed a slightly embarrassed smile.

"Anyway, don't stay in bed all day, get up, and do something," she said.

"Yes, dear."

---

Ginny Morrison let the screen door slam behind her and stepped out onto the back porch and into the cool, late summer air. She stubbed out a Lucky Strike and immediately sparked another to life.

"Fuck him," she hissed and puffed away at the smoke.

The him was Frank Page - her boyfriend. He'd finished his job at the Corben Mill nearly six hours ago and called her an hour after that, already sounding worse for the drink to say he was having one more, and then he'd be straight home.

"Keep it warm for me," he said.

"Sure, hon, it'll be in the oven waiting for you," she said through gritted teeth.

Ginny knew what Frank was interested in keeping warm, had nothing to do with food.

"And look after Chico," he slurred and hung up the phone.

Frank didn't love her; she knew that almost from the beginning. They met at Butler's during the summer of her 18th birthday. She'd taken a job slinging beer and fending off advances from the mill workers and river men. She saw him first, with a group of drunken rowdies from the mill, and then on his own on the few occasions, he would leave the mill for his lunch break. He spent his time drinking draft and throwing childish compliments her way, in a voice too loud and awkward to be anything other than sincere. He was big and clumsy and a little dumb, but he was easy on the eyes. If she had to guess, Ginny thought he was close to ten years older than she was. Not that it mattered. Frank Page was single and probably the best looking bachelor in a town where her choices were practically none on a good day. Her dating him was a foregone conclusion.

That summer, Ginny resigned herself to the truth - leaving Winterbourne was nearly impossible given her present situation. Around-the-clock care for her mother - a woman too crazy to work and too poor to go up the hill. At best, she could hope for a job pulling thread at the mill. At worst, she would be stuck in this dingy little bar until she was withered and old and nicotine-stained. Frank's compliments offered her a ray of hope in a downward spiral into muddled adulthood. A half-smile snuck its way across her face, and she thought of him in happier times.

Frank saw her nearly every day that summer, and though she was younger, 6 years, he found out there was something about her he couldn't let go of. He thought about her in the morning, after breakfast, and just before his ride to the mill came. She stayed on his mind and popped up for a visit just after lunch and while sitting behind number six loom pretending to work. Ginny wasn't the last thing he thought of at night, but she was right up there. Even on sober nights, the thought of her made his hand wander below the waistband of his pyjamas.

He wore her down. Daily visits and liquor-fuelled compliments turned into calf eyes and suggestive flirtations, and Ginny finally gave in and agreed to a date. Frank brought along a twelve-pack and a fifth of gin. After her first beer, she grabbed the Beefeater bottle and took a long pull from it. A second beer went down, and he told her how impressed he was that someone so young could hold her liquor, cursing under his breath that getting her drunk and getting lucky was not as sure a thing as he'd hoped. After her third can of Pabst, she was unbuttoning her jean shorts and climbing on top of him.

Ginny wasn't the prettiest thing he'd ever seen. Her hair was on the greasy side of mousy brown; her complexion still slightly spotty, and she was a little softer around the middle than he would have liked. Still, the girl was attractive enough to earn the jealous taunts and whistles from his workmates, and he bet she felt pretty good in the dark. As a bonus, she was just dumb enough to put up with his bullshit and still come back for more. They shared a handful more of these drunken nights, groping away in the back of his old Ford pickup before she decided to throw her lot in with him completely and tell him she loved him. Frank grunted something close to a response, and she nearly snapped his spine with a bear hug.

They moved in together, shacked up in one of the renovated row houses - now called modest apartments - in the middle of Parker Street. They were close enough to downtown to seem modern but not far enough away from Grey Hollow road to say the people who lived in them were anything but poor white trash. Ginny brought what few possessions she could sneak out of the house before her mother ran after her down Bluhm Street, screaming that she was a whore. Frank sat in his truck at the end of the street, prepared for the quick getaway she knew had to happen. He brought two garbage bags full of clothes, his stereo, and a handful of well-used dishes from a moist basement apartment he was glad to be out of. And Chico. Frank tolerated Ginny. He might have even been infatuated by her in the beginning - but he loved that God-damned dog. Chico, for his part, probably loved Frank right back, but he couldn't stand Ginny from the first day he met her.

He was a smallish, arthritic, yappy thing with bad breath and patchy brown hair. No doubt from the skin condition that caused it to leave piles of flaky dog peelings any place it sat for more than a few minutes. Its eyes were bluish and clouded over with cataracts, and it was nearly stone deaf, which caused the dog to bark night and day incessantly.

"Come here, Chico!"

Frank called to the dog and would not get a response unless he was practically on top of the damned thing, screaming in its ear. Chico would waddle arthritically toward the biggest shape he could, trying to make out whether it had called him or not.

"You should put him down," Ginny said. "It's cruel to keep him hanging on like this. Look at how hard he is struggling."

"What did you say?" Frank seethed.

"N-nothing, it was just a suggestion."

His fist flew, almost on its own, and connected with her face just above the jaw. If it had hit her an inch lower, he would have laid her out cold.

"Let's get one thing perfectly straight," Frank said. "If anything happens to Chico, anything at all that I am not here to witness, I will blame you. And then I will beat the holy shit out of you."

She walked to the kitchen and put some ice cubes into a towel to soothe her swelling face. That was the last time she ever suggested anything about the damned dog while Frank was in earshot. After that, she gave the dog a wide berth around the house and didn't pay it a lot of mind if she could avoid it.

"Fuck him"– she felt the cold air blow across the back porch, pushing the exhaled plume of smoke back into her face – "and fuck that goddam dog too. Hear me, Frank? Fuck your dog. That choking, fuck bag of rug pissing misery."

Ginny lit another Lucky and glanced at her watch. It was just after ten now, and Frank had been in Butler's since three or three-thirty. Even on his best day, she knew Frank didn't possess the stamina to drink recklessly for seven hours on no dinner and then get up for work the next day. He'd be home soon enough. Chico had likely fouled himself and the bed of old couch cushions he slept on since the last time since she'd looked in on him. If she hoped to survive the sting of his fists and avoid his boozy advances, Ginny knew she had to get the dog let out and fed and watered and its bed spotless before Frank stumbled through the door. She flicked away the last of her cigarette and headed into the house.

"Chico," she called out quietly, knowing it couldn't hear her.

Ginny walked closer to the back room, where his bed lay. It was an awful, smelly room that reinforced just how awful and smelly the little dog was. Chico's refusal to die of his own accord reminded her how much she hated the damned dog. She swore if Frank ever went anywhere for more than an afternoon, she would do away with the ancient thing and take the beating from him just to be rid of it.

"Chico," she called again and was again met with silence. When she entered the back room and saw that Chico was not on his bed, Ginny began to feel doubt clouding an otherwise sunny day.

"Fuck."

Ginny wasn't worried, not yet anyway. Chico must have come back in after being outside an unbearable amount of time, and she just didn't notice. He didn't make a lot of noise, except for all the barking all the time. He *must* have come in. And after several excruciatingly long minutes of not pissing anywhere. No, the little bastard would save that for after walking a pointless circle and settling in on his newly washed cushions. He *had* come in; she was sure of that. The dog was positively inside the house - somewhere. *Wasn't he?* The mangy thing disappeared before and turned up later, asleep under the sofa or tucked up in a pile of laundry, but when she searched the whole place and still couldn't find him, her heartbeat quickened. Ginny went through the house again, room by room now, and when the ratty little turd still hadn't appeared, the panic took hold.

"He couldn't have gotten back out. I would have seen him," she reassured herself.

Ginny opened the screen door on the back porch and stepped into the house.

"Chico!"

She ran back out to the porch and stood there peering into the darkness. But Chico wasn't there.

"Fuck. Fuck. Fuck!"

Ginny ran into the ground-floor apartment to find a flashlight to go look for a nearly blind, totally deaf dog.

"Fuck, fuck, fuck," she moaned and headed out beyond the porch.

Ginny made it ten or fifteen feet past the yellow pool of back porch light before she found him. She waved the flashlight in front of her like a sword. The beam caught the reflection from one of his eyes. The glare of the flashlight moved slowly across the dog's lifeless body.

"Aw shit," Ginny whispered.

# 4

M r. Richardson lay on his towels, not sleeping, when the clock radio blared out at him.

"The time is four, oh, oh A.M. it's time to wake up!"

The clock radio was a gift from Davis' predecessor. The numbers glowed an unnatural, electric red, and it talked to you. And not just for alarms. It would announce every hour on the hour if you wanted it to. It was obnoxious, and in the middle of a satisfying sleep, it was downright terrifying. The boss looked so pleased when he presented it to him. He didn't have the heart to refuse it. If nothing else, it would never let him sleep in.

Richardson woke early. There was no daylight in the basement of Winterbourne and, It would still be dark upstairs, but the sun would rise and chase away the shadows. It would never get any lighter than it already was down here. Ever. And - despite what the girl on the radio said - everything couldn't be further from sunshine and lollipops. He hadn't slept much. The nerves that rattled him from confronting Smythe and learning of the Soulreaver and being chewed out by Mareth all in the same day. Learning his job hung in the balance if he couldn't get the rest of the Necrosites into line, turned over in his head like a record catching on a deep scratch. Just as he would start to drift off, the record would skip and jolt him back awake. The gloom hung over him like a wet blanket. A long walk through the open fields of Winterbourne, in the secrecy of the dark, was just the lifejacket he needed when he was so near to drowning in a sea of self-pity. The Necrosite pulled on the grey flannel short pants and jacket he liked best, even though he knew they made him look like a schoolboy. Peering through the blind on his window, he half expected to see Mrs. Pugwash looking back at him. Richardson guessed even the worst Necrosites – like Ida Pugwash – needed. Sleep. He slipped out his door and headed out to the back property of the nursing home.

The cold and damp of the long grass felt good against Richardson's legs as he hobbled through it. Though, after a few dozen feet of tromping along, it all made him wish he owned a sweater. However, after twenty minutes of legging it across the back property, the little green thing was sweating enough that he wished he'd left the grey flannel jacket behind. Mr. Richardson made it off the nursing home's property and down across Millar's field. The Necrosite kept safely in the shadows of the abandoned houses on Grey Hollow road, but he wouldn't stay here, not feeling like this. He was low. He felt defeated and broken, and when he felt like this, he loved to walk as near Parker street as he could get. The glow of the neon storefronts that seemed to hover three feet above the sidewalk thrilled him. His dream – one day – was to stroll along the main drag of Winterbourne just as the sun began to set. To amble past the storefronts in solitude, or even better, in the company of a comely female Necrosite who dared to dream like he did.

He crested Peterson's hill, just beyond the old landfill, and sat in silence for a while drinking in the dynamo of glowing life that happened below him.

"Oh bugger," he said.

Necrosites are incredibly adept at seeing in the dark, and Mr. Richardson had no trouble making out the three young Necrosites heading toward the houses on Parker St.

"Oh, bugger. Bugger, bastard, and bother!"

The older Necrosite stood and walked down from the hilltop. In doing so, his foot plunged deep into the mix of dry long grass and living weeds and became firmly snared. The lack of mobility from below did nothing to stop the forward momentum, and the rest of him was launched ahead. After several minutes of uncontrolled tumbling, he landed at the bottom with a thud in the middle of a thicket of waist-high weeds.

The three chimpanzee-lizard things whipped around in the direction the clatter came from. They sniffed at the air and scanned the surroundings. The tallest of them looked as though he might break off from the group and walk toward the noise. After another glance toward the weeds, he turned away and continued onward.

Richardson knew to duck into the long grass and keep still as soon as he had stopped moving. For his advanced age, the head Necrosite was still remarkably fit. He felt, if it came to that, he could take out one of the younger ones, possibly two if they attacked him single file, but to tangle with all three at the same time? That was stupidity. And those kinds of thoughts stopped years ago. For safety's sake, he remained motionless in the weeds. The three Necrosites continued away from his hiding place and lumbered off in the direction of the row houses.

The older Necrosite came out of the weeds and crept slowly behind them. The long grass was thick enough to allow him perfect cover. The longer he looked, the more he recognized the younger Necrosites and knew they were up to no good.

The bigger of the three - a smug thing called Pyewackett - was a junior clerk from bookkeeping. With him were Johnston and Bunn. Both young Necrosites from the mailroom who Richardson had seen an amount of potential in, they dressed smartly, kept their heads down, and did as they were told. But now they were interested in this … this wandering around and seeking out things. Different things. Necrosite ways they all called them, wild and dangerous ways that ended in bloodshed. The sort of behaviour that had scared Richardson all his life, this generation revelled in.

The three of them rose and moved off in the direction of the back porches. Johnston cupped his hands around his mouth to amplify himself. Mr. Richardson crept closer to hear whatever it was the young Necrosite thought important enough to be heard.

"Thpzzzzt," Johnston said.

"What the hell was that?" Pyewackett asked.

"A whistle."

"No, it wasn't," Bunn chimed in. "A whistle sounds like bird song."

"It did," Johnston said.

"Oh yeah? What sort of bird did that sound like, a shit hawk?"

Bunn and Pyewackett cackled.

"It bloody did sound like a bird," Johnston griped.

"Shit hawk," Richardson whispered. "That was funny."

"Anyway, the damned thing is stone deaf and nearly blind. It ain't gonna hear no whistle," Pyewackett said.

"Tell me then, smart arse, how are we to get the goddam thing to come out here? Have you got a bit of rotting meat in your pocket?"

"Don't be stupid. It's not as though I walk around with… hang on," Pyewackett said.

He thrust a hand deep into the pocket of his ragged, black slacks and brought out a small grey lump.

"That's the ticket," Bunn crowed.

Johnston took hold of the disgusting clod of flesh and laid it out, just beyond the light spilling out from the back porch.

"You sure this is the one?"

"Shhh," Johnston hissed. "I've been watching this place for weeks. This is it."

Time slowed, almost to a stop. Even Richardson had his fill of sitting wet assed in the weeds, waiting for something to happen. He pushed himself up, and just when the old Necrosite was about to leave, the back door beside the porch burst open.

The bulb flickered and crackled to life, and the three of them stood, paralyzed by the stark, awful brightness of the back porch light.

"Hide," Johnston breathed.

"Hide?" Bunn said.

"Hide!" Pyewackettt hissed.

The three scattered toward the long grass and ducked in, mouths shut, and eyes trained on the back porch. Had they looked around, even for a second, they would have noticed the older Necrosite in a grey flannel suit, crouching in the grass, five feet from them.

The screen door whined open, and through it came a woman with mousey brown hair, carrying an equally mousey brown lump in her arms. She looked around and dropped it without bothering to bend, allowing the dog to fall to the pavement with a thud. Ginny knew the people who lived around here would be more interested in whether or not she had a cigarette than the welfare of a balding rat–dog.

"Hurry up and go pee, Chico," she said.

Chico stared, trying to focus on the three dark shapes near the lawn.

"Go pee, Chico!"

Chico did his best to do everything but hurry and go pee. He sniffed at the Hills Brothers coffee can until he discovered it was near to overflowing with old cigarette butts, the scent of which gave him a start. This, in turn, knocked the poorly functioning legs out from underneath him, and he hit the porch. Falling on the cold concrete frightened him into a tirade of angry coughs. It was the excuse Ginny needed to grab the dog's collar and haul him upward. Chico sputtered and gagged, and she let him back down.

"Fuck sake, dog," she seethed and clipped the lead to Chico's collar. "I'll be back in a minute. Take a piss!"

The geriatric dog lowered its head and foundered its way off the porch.

"Cute little bugger," Bunn said.

"Honestly, shut up. Have you forgotten why we're here?"

"Honestly, some Necrosite's children," Pyewackett moaned.

They remained crouching in the weeds, waiting for the perfect moment.

Chico was nearly blind, stone deaf, and practically lame from arthritis. But for all that, his sense of smell remained intact, and it currently homed in on an enticing aroma coming from somewhere in front of him. He put his nose to the ground and moved forward in a rush of limping and snuffling until his lips touched what his nose told him was the best thing he'd smelled in years. And then it happened. A perfect moment presented itself to three Necrosites like a neon sign that blazed Eat at Chico's.

"Now," Pyewackett hissed, and the three bolted out of the weeds.

Bunn moved in closest to the dog. Chico caught his scent and made a beeline toward his attacker. The Necrosite bent over and scooped up the dog, who practically walked into his arms.

"That was easy," Bunn said and drew back his lips into a malignant smile that bared his teeth.

"Wait," Pyewackett said.

"Wait? Wait for what?" Johnston demanded.

"This was my bloody idea. I should get first go."

"Oh yeah, your idea, was it? Soulreaver means nothing, does he?" Johnston scowled.

The three of them took hold of the dog. Chico began to growl and bark and sputter as fiercely as it could.

"Whatever we are going to do, better be done quickly. She'll be back out here in a minute if this thing don't shut up," Bunn said.

"Do it!" Pyewackett and Johnston cried, nearly in unison.

Chico didn't yelp. He didn't call out; there wasn't time for it. In a few painful, terror-stricken moments, the three of them had reduced him to a pile of blood-soaked fur and torn chunks of flesh clinging to broken bones.

"Hunters we were," Pyewackett breathed through gore-caked teeth.

"And hunters we remain," the other two panted.

"Oh shit," Richardson whispered.

# 5

Mrs. Dorothy Lauren lay in her bed asleep, drifting between deep breaths and chest-rattling gasps. Davis slipped into her room and sat at the bedside, taking her hand in his. She wasn't close to the end, not in any sense he had to worry about, but, like everyone else in here, her life *was* running out. The young man guessed she would be around for a while yet, Richardson hadn't given a mortality request for her and, so far as he knew, her name wasn't even near the top of the list.

The old woman tightened the grip on Davis and opened both eyes. The joy that appeared in them made its way to her lips, and soon, she was beaming up at him.

"I had hoped you'd come by today," Mrs. Lauren said.

"Wild horses couldn't have kept me away," Davis replied.

"That's a stupid expression."

"I think it's alright, given the circumstance."

"Really? Have you ever tried to hold a wild horse? Not as easy as all that, I imagine."

"Well, no, but I–"

"A horse is a huge animal. Must weigh over a thousand pounds.

Now give it a little bit of spirit and a taste of freedom. You try to put a rein on it and hold it down for a while? Wild horses bloody well would have kept you away and no mistake,"

She was tall. Davis remembered the day she walked into Winterbourne, tall and thin with a shock of hair as red as a freshly lit match. Dorothy was a proud woman and carried herself like she'd lived a lifetime of getting what she wanted. Mrs. Lauren had sought out Winterbourne as the one place where they would make sure you lived out your remaining days in comfort and dignity. Her remaining days hadn't stretched quite as far as she'd hoped, and health had all but abandoned her, leaving her frail and frightened.

"I'm afraid–" Mrs. Lauren began.

"I know," Davis interrupted.

He'd had this conversation many times with many residents. It wasn't that he didn't care - he did, more than most of them understood - but he had heard the words so many times that he could respond to them in his sleep. He felt like a priest in a confessional on a Sunday morning after a Saturday night off as many cardinal vices as you could squeeze in. It was wheelbarrows of guilt and thimbles of repentance. There wasn't a single person he'd encountered in his time at Winterbourne that wouldn't have traded all those nights in bed, all those lunch hours hanging off the bar at Butler's for one more day with the sun on their face. Mrs. Laurel didn't look like she was going to be any different.

"No, you don't, dear," Mrs. Lauren said curtly. "I'm afraid I have...have..."

She pulled him in close, close enough to whisper in his ear, but remained silent.

"Mrs. Lauren?"

The old woman remained seated in the bed, frozen and leaning toward Davis. Without warning, she flopped backward on the bed and began to shake up and down as if having the dust beaten out of her like an old rug. As quickly as they had begun, the tremors stopped. Mrs. Lauren's head jerked back, chin pointing skyward as her legs flexed backward, stretching in an unnatural bow that met up with the top of her head. Her eyes slammed shut, and a noise escaped her throat like the gurgling of a kettle nearly boiled dry Dorothy sat up and jabbed a withered finger in Davis' face. Her own face seemed stretched too tightly into impossible angles, sharp and unyielding. A long, crooked nose pointed down to an equally pointed chin. Her eyes, once two green pools of mischief, had blanched entirely, becoming blood-streaked orbs. Unblinking, they glared at him, never moving their gaze from his.

"Zamora, at the crossroads of the world," she moaned.

"What?"

"Zamora, at the crossroads of the world," Mrs. Lauren repeated.

"I don't follow you,"

"Wait, that message was meant for another. One moment please."

Her head bent backward again and then sharply to the left, placing her temple squarely on top of her shoulder. Mrs. Lauren held this position unnaturally long before raising it back up again.

"Moyen, at time's square," she moaned.

"Wait, what?"

"Moyen, at time's square," she repeated, the annoyance rising in her voice.

"Once more."

"Oh, for God's sake, Moyen, at time's square, already. Do pay attention."

"Yes?" Davis wondered.

"And?" Mrs. Lauren repeated.

"Do go on," he said, his interest clearly waning.

"At time's square is the way to the thin place. You must find the first one. Only then will two become one again."

Davis sat silently.

"Did you get all of that?"

"Oh sure," Davis replied.

"Did you write it down? You might want to write it down; it was a lot to get all in one go."

"I'll remember. What does it all mean?"

"What?"

"What does it all mean?" Davis repeated.

"You don't know?"

"No, not a clue."

"Well, how am I to know what it means? Do I look like an information booth to you?"

"Maybe I'd better write it down," Davis said.

He fumbled for something to write with and found a pen and a notepad from the bedside table.

"Okay, hit me with that one more time."

"Hit you with what, dear?"

"Wait, what?"

"You said you wanted me to hit you. That doesn't sound very safe."

It was her again. The cigarette rasp in a voice that was practically a croak had dissipated and returned to the soft, elderly tones of the woman he'd come to visit. But it didn't look like her. Not anymore, it resembled the awful thing that had appeared on the bed in her place, and it scared the shit out of him.

"It was just a joke, Mrs. Lauren. I'll try to stop by later, okay?"

He headed out of her room and walked toward the nurse's station, stopping to look at the charts of the residents on this ward while mulling over what Mrs. Lauren had said.

*Thin place?*

The word floated through his mind. Davis swore he'd heard that term used somewhere before but couldn't remember where or when. Creepy words and meaningless expressions flew around this place so often, odd grammar stuck out more than odd conversation ever would.

"Ogay?" Clarence asked, wheeling slowly toward Davis with a combination of his one good leg and one good arm. A kind of determined drag and push to avoid spinning in circles.

"Okay," Davis said.

Clarence stuck out his good hand, and Davis gave it a firm shake and got a flash of the man's life almost instantly. It wasn't the first time he could see Clarence some sixty years before now, standing proudly in his uniform as he boarded the train. Sometime later, he wore that same uniform, dirt-covered and tatty, as he urged his friends forward into a hail of machine gunfire. Years flew by, and now he was a proud man in a wool suit, standing in front of his business partners giving a light-hearted speech when a massive stroke twisted him and left him unable to speak.

"Ogay?" Clarence asked.

"Yeah, Clarence, she's okay. One hundred percent," Davis lied.

Davis had seen the man staring at Dorothy the second she walked on the ward. Clarence was deeply smitten and refused to talk to her, afraid she would think he was an imbecile. And now, he hadn't seen her in nearly a week. He feared she'd died without his having a chance to say goodbye. The younger man bent down and brought himself to eye level with the man in the wheelchair.

"Go see her. She'd probably like a visit. She's crazy about you, you know?" Davis prodded the old man.

"Ogay," Clarence said, turning red and glowing as bright as a traffic light, and pulled himself in the direction of Dorothy's room, trying to be inconspicuous with less than half the mobility of anyone else.

"Thin place?" Davis said.

"What?" the nurse behind the desk answered.

"Nothing, just talking to myself. Have you seen Jenn?"

# 6

Mr. Richardson crouched in front of the weeds.

*Maybe he won't know. Maybe he just won't find out, and he'll never know about this mess.*

He looked at the pile of former dog.

*Maybe I'd better get rid of the evidence before he does find out.*

Johnston, Pyewackett, and Bunn were long gone, having accomplished what they set out to do. They were, no doubt, on the way to the Soulreaver to report what fierce and savage Necrosites they were. Richardson smiled. How fierce would they seem if this Soulreaver found out they had killed a half-blind, deaf dog that was practically dead already?

*In time, he will seek you out.*

"Maybe he could hurry up a touch with the seeking me out. I could use a hand clearing away this filth before I lose my job," Richardson sighed.

If Necrosites could sweat, Mr. Richardson would have felt it beading up on his forehead and soaking the back of his neck. He scooped up what remained of Chico and stashed the bits in the long grass. For good measure, he pulled up two large handfuls of it to cover

over the gore and bent over strands of the thicker, reedier grass to be sure the secret would remain safe. He looked past the roof of the house the dog had come from. The Necrosite sighed and looked back to the porch the dog had come from. When he was sure the woman inside hadn't seen him or the other three, he looked back up the hill to Winterbourne. He was safe - for now.

The night sky was clear and vast and crowded with stars trying to outshine the lights from the city below. Richardson stared up at them, taking his time to examine the ones he could recognize. He felt small - overwhelmed by the eternity above him. And yet, it gave him a sense of hope. There were so many stars up there, and the life of one Necrosite probably didn't count for much, but there must be something better out there than hiding bits of chewed-up dog for fear of losing a job he wasn't sure he even wanted anymore. The older Necrosite could have stayed gazing at the stars until they fell and crashed around him like burnt-out skyrockets. But before too long, salmon and coral hues would begin to bleed into the sky, and the sun would start to rise and chase away the stars. Richardson could remain nearly invisible in the darkness, but if he couldn't get back to the safety of Winterbourne soon, Davis finding out about the little mangled dog would be the least of his worries.

---

Davis made his way back upstairs into the big corner office. Jenn sat behind the desk, head down, filling out reams of papers and paying little attention to him.

"What do you know about thin places?" Davis asked Jenn.

"I know they are places I am not going to enter anytime soon," Jenn laughed.

"I'm serious."

"Okay. I haven't heard that term before, but I know where to look. I'll bet there's a book. There's always a book."

"Kind of funny thing," Davis said.

"What is?"

"That there *is* always a book."

"Right?" she giggled. "You'd think people would spend less time trying to take over things all half-assed and a lot more time trying to steal the books out of this place. Maybe come up with a decent plan."

"By the way, have you seen Richardson today?" Davis asked.

"No. As a matter of fact, I haven't seen a single one of them today."

"That's odd."

"It is. I just hope word of what you said to Richardson hasn't gotten around."

"Why would what I told Richardson make any difference? Most of them don't even like him."

"But they do respect him. He inherited his position from his father, who was every bit as loyal to the office as he is. The two of them kept the peace and negotiated the services of the Necrosites for generations of Deaths, literally. Richardson has been in his position longer than many of the younger ones have been alive. He, and his father before him, carry a lot of weight in the community."

"Oh, I wouldn't worry too much about his standing," Davis said flippantly.

"And that's the problem," Jenn said.

"What's that supposed to mean?" he snipped.

"I mean, it seems like you've had it in for them since the day you stepped into the robe. What did they do? What did *he* do to make you hate all of them so much?"

"I don't hate them. I don't hate Richardson."

"But you sure don't like them much," Jenn said, trying to maintain a placid tone.

"I don't trust the little bastards, okay?" Davis said, but it was a lie.

He didn't like them, that was true, but it wasn't as simple as hate. Hate comes when love dies away, and he had never loved them to begin with. Hatred was something ugly you could keep in your pocket to take out and look at to remember all the reasons you were angry before and be angry all over again. From the first time he saw them – what they were capable of - Davis knew they were vicious, goggle-eyed little psychopaths who lived for violence and not much else. It sickened him. *They* sickened him.

"You don't have to trust them. Just trust me when I say don't do anything stupid. You know, beyond the normal stupid," Jenn joked.

When asked about it later, Davis would say he had no idea why he said what he did next. But fate has a way of moving the gears that are meant to move, for better or worse, even when they're practically rusted.

"Look, you may cook the books around this place and give the nurses a bit of a fright when they need to get their shit together, but I am the *one*, right? I was picked to be the new Death, and I'll decide whether those rotten little things deserve another day on this planet, never mind at this nursing home."

Jenn sat quietly, closed her eyes, and lowered her head. After a time that seemed to go on forever, she finally spoke.

"You're right," she said and got up to leave.

"Where are you going?"

Jenn said nothing and walked out, closing the door slowly and quietly behind her.

Davis turned and gazed at the big bay window behind him and looked out absently over the back property of the estate.

"Fuck," he breathed.

He knew then he'd just gone somewhere his mind told him it was impossible to go, with a handful of words spat out through clenched teeth and misplaced anger. Anger she didn't deserve. Words he couldn't unsay.

"Fuck."

---

Mr. Richardson stepped out of the weeds and back toward the house to make sure there was no more evidence of the dog's massacre, just as the porch light burst into life. He stood in front of the concrete slab of the porch, paralyzed. If he made for the weeds, he ran the risk of attracting the interest of whoever or whatever was coming out. The possibility of the dog's corpse being discovered loomed in front of him like a storm cloud. If he stayed where he was, the chance of being hit with a broom grew exponentially. Worse still, what if there was another god-damned dog? A younger, healthier dog with big teeth and an appetite for things that lurked in the shadows? He came to the decision that slipping into the shadows to his right, between this house and the one next door, was the safest move. It offered him the ability to remain out of sight and keep an eye on the dead dog's house in case someone came out looking for him. It was a sound plan, though, as it turned out, one that came to him a millisecond too late.

"Shoo," Ginny said.

Mr. Richardson stood still on the patch of grass just beyond the cement porch, unsure what his next move should be.

"What the fuck? Ginny said. "Is that a raccoon?"

The older Necrosite bared a mouth full of narrow, razor-sharp teeth and unleashed a hiss that would scare the piss out of anyone. Ginny Morrison, however, was not just any old soul. She lived with Frank Page. He was a brute and a bastard and could make her hands shake with terror if she was even a minute late with dinner. A balding raccoon? Even if it wore a leather jacket and came at her with a switchblade, it couldn't make her flinch.

"Jesus, you'd better not be rabid," Ginny said.

It was just another bullet point on an ever-growing list of this complete turd of an evening. The woman reached for the broom that rested against the pillar to her right and raised it high overhead before bringing it crashing down against Mr. Richardson's dreadlocks.

"Shoo, shoo!"

"Madame, please," Mr. Richardson said.

"What the f–" The broom swung again.

"I am no bloody raccoon. Now, would you kindly stop swatting me with that?"

Ginny couldn't move. She couldn't speak. The shock had taken her brain to a place where those things were games for the idle rich, and Ginny Morrison could barely afford the cab fare downtown. Her eyes moved from its gnarly, clawed feet to the crown of its bulbous head, taking in all the freakish glory, and that's when she saw it. Peaking out from beneath afoot at the end of a grey-green stubby leg, stuck to a claw, was a small, familiar bit of natty brown fur caked in blood.

"Oh no," Ginny whispered.

## 7

D avis pushed through the front door and into the smoke-stained air of Butler's and took up a stool at the bar.

"Whisky, please," he said.

He emptied the glass, and the girl behind the bar pushed another his way without having asked for it. Davis figured he must have the look of someone wanting to numb himself and took the drink. He emptied that one, and a third, and a fourth after that. The whisky quickly wormed its way into his brain, pushing out the misery that dogged him since he left the office and left glass after glass of indignation in its wake.

"I am the boss. I *am* the boss." he fumed.

"Ok, you're the boss. You want another one, boss?" she asked.

"Yes," Davis said and wondered if his face was as red as it felt. "Please."

The bartender smiled at him. He was caught off guard by it but got the message soon enough and straightened up and smiled back at her. She was cute, and she was young, probably much too young for him. But the girl was still pretty, if not a little grubby, and pale from working at Butler's. Davis thought there might have been something between them hidden in that smile. But good sense reappeared, and he knew she had hundreds of drunken fools smiling at her every day of the week. Smiling back was her way of keeping the tips coming and getting bigger with every pour. And it made him angry. Suddenly he wasn't good enough. Not for anybody, not even the pale beer slinger in a shithole like Butler'sWho was this vapid twat to smile at him? Playing for tips by trying to make him feel special. Davis seethed over the glass of whisky, trying to decide if finishing it would endear him to the barmaid or just add his name to the list of drunk assholes she squeezed for an extra buck or two at closing time.

And then the angry young man sobered considerably and glowed red with the embarrassment that follows when the fires of righteous indignation burn away. He looked back at his drink and to the floor, and everywhere else that wasn't the girl behind the bar.

"Hey... um... have you got a phone?"

The girl pointed toward the bathrooms at the back of the bar. "Over there."

Davis stood and walked toward the back of the bar without acknowledging her, feeling he'd been on the receiving end of enough imaginary heartbreak for one night. As he walked, the liquor caught up with him, raced ahead, and overtook him. It bashed around his brain long enough for the anger and resentment for the chubby dead girl to rise in him again. He would call her; he would call Jenn and tell her exactly what was what. Didn't he have the robe and scythe? Ok, they were metaphors, but they were his, and wasn't that enough? Weren't they important enough for his opinion to matter?

He hadn't exactly got the big booming voice to go right. It sounded more like the new Grim Reaper was going through puberty than heralding the inevitable, but he *was* Death. The true servant of the void. He would call the dead woman and set her straight, and then he would go back to the bar and talk to the pretty living woman behind it. And then, maybe he would walk around the bar and cut a swath of extinction from one side to the other before he asked the pale, dirty woman out for a proper drink.

The payphone was occupied by a large man who swayed and tried to stay upright as he carried on the conversation. Frank Page leaned against the wall, falling slightly forward and snapping back quickly enough to retain his balance before he tipped entirely and hit the floor. The other hand fumbled through his pockets and, when he had rummaged enough lint-covered change, he aimed it at the swaying coin slot. What began with a few giggles over repeated failed attempts quickly descended into an existential crisis large enough to bring him near to tears. Finally, an arm appeared over his shoulder and steadied his hand and guided it to its intended target.

"Thanksh," Frank slurred.

He began to speak, and from the look of it, long before the line had connected on the other end.

"Hey babe, I'm just having one...hello, hello, hello? Oh, hey babe, I'm just having one more short one, and then I'm there," he said, trying to sound sober.

The voice on the other end grew so loud that Davis could practically hear each syllable. He moved away from the man but not far enough to silence the conversation coming from him.

"Wait, what?" Frank asked.

The tone of the voice on the other end grew louder, shouting at him now, though it did little to affect his cheerfully, drunken mood or change his mind on having one more.

"Make sure Chico ish okay. What if that goddam thing ish rabid, and he gets a hold of my dog? Get him in the housh and keep him there."

He was near to hanging up the phone when he yanked the receiver back up to his face and added with frightening sobriety;

"If anything happens to my dog, you will be sorry, I promise you."

Frank zig-zagged back to the bar and spread himself onto his bar stool.

"Gimme one, Jeannine," he burped.

"Well, aren't you the loving husband, calling the wife to let her know you'll be late," Frank's workmate said.

"Shut the fuck up, Gary. We ain't even fuckin' married. The hell would you know about keeping somebody happy? When's the last time you had a girlfriend?" Frank spat.

"I know no woman would have me tied up in her apron strings. I ain't got no woman yet 'coz I never have found one that knew her goddamn place."

"Yeah, Gary, you keep telling yourself that. There ain't, but one person wears the pants in my house, and he's about to have another fuckin' shot. I've had to set Ginny right on this subject a few times. She knows better now."

He stood to get the money for his drink, and in doing so, stumbled back against his stool, lost his footing, and fell toward the floor. Davis returned to his own bar stool after a handful of unanswered telephone calls to Jen, just in time to catch the drunken man and push him back up before he smashed into the floor.

"Thanksh, buddy," Frank chuckled and sat back down.

"You're welcome."

He looked over at Frank, who had by now resumed his drunken conversation.

"Shouldn't you ought to be getting home to the little woman?" Gary sneered.

He let out a full, raucous belly laugh, his brain swearing the words that left his lips were the funniest in the history of the conversation.

"I'll go home when I'm ready."

"Sure you will, and she'll be all - Oh Frankie, you've been such a bad boy, no num-nums for you tonight."

"She'll be lucky if I let her sleep in the goddam bed."

Frank slammed his glass on the bar and gestured to Jeannine for another.

"Careful with the glasses," Jeannine cautioned.

Frank blew a kiss and tossed a handful of bills in her direction

The two sat in awkward silence for a time, and after draining glasses and ordering more, Frank turned to his workmate.

"Did I tell you what she said to me?"

"No, what'd she say?"

"Said there was some kind of fucking raccoon hanging around the back porch. She thought maybe it killed a squirrel or something 'coz there was blood all around the damn thing,"

"What?"

"Yeah, and then, here's the best part, then she says the fucking thing up and talked to her. I told her she was off her goddam nut," Frank said, and the statement hung in the air like a grotesque piñata as he drained his glass.

"Did you hear what I said?" Frank asked and clapped a meaty hand across the man's shoulder.

"You're fucking with me."

"Hand to God, that's what she said."

"And you believed her? Give me some of whatever the fuck youse two are smoking!"

"Hairless raccoon and green, no less. Fucking green."

"I think she's lost it, totally nutty. I think you need to get home and straighten that girl out," Gary said.

"Right?" Frank laughed.

The big man upended his glass and slammed it onto the bar top three times in quick succession, never once taking his eyes off Jeannine.

"Fucking green raccoon, and it talked to her. She's fucking nuts, and *this* is what I have to go home to? Fucking green, talking raccoons with fucking pointy teeth?"

Davis, listening to the two drunks discussing the finer points of relationships, pricked up suddenly at the mention of mutated raccoons. He couldn't be sure what the two of them meant, but the description had a familiar ring to it.

"Excuse me," Davis said.

"Excuuuuse me," Frank mocked.

"Excuuuuse me," Gary mimicked.

Davis carried on. "First off, let me congratulate you on a, truly, Viking-like display of drinking. I know people who have been dead inside since the civil war who couldn't drink as much as the two of you did tonight and remained upright. And I couldn't help but overhear, you said something about a raccoon?"

"Yessh," Frank slurred. "My bone-headed girlfriend says she saw some kinda mangy raccoon out back of our place."

"Oh?"

"She's been fucking drinking or smoking some shit or something. I mean, Jesus, she said the damn thing was green. Green. Huh, huh, green, and it talked to her, can you imagine that?"

"I imagine that sounds a lot less like a raccoon and a lot more like something else."

"Like what something else?" Frank said suspiciously.

"Oh, I don't know, maybe a vicious little brute that has served the office of Death for thousands of years by ripping the dying away from their mortal attachments?"

"Wait, what?" Frank sputtered.

"Or maybe a Martian?" Davis said quickly.

A beat of agonizing silence passed between the three of them. Followed by another. Davis eyed the door. The air was thick with tension, like things were about to go south quickly, and he wanted the fastest way out. He started to turn away from the bar and point himself toward the exit when the two drunken mill workers burst into fits of spastic laughter.

"I like this guy!" Gary crowed.

"Thanks for your time, fellas. The next one's on me," Davis announced.

He stuck his hand out to Frank, who happily glad-handed the man who would guarantee he'd be waiting for his ride to work hungover and nauseous.

With a flash, Davis saw the man's whole brutish life and felt a swell of pity for anyone who happened to be saddled with the big lummox. Davis also caught his address, 419 Parker St, about six blocks west of Butler's. Davis stood, stuck a hand deep into his pocket, and slapped a fifty on the bar.

"Enjoy yourselves, boys," he said and walked out into the night air.

## 8

Ginny began to pace. She figured she had about an hour before Frank spilled in through the front door. If she was lucky, he would make a pass at her, fumble his way through drunken groping and grabbing, hoping to get her into bed. If she gave in, it would be a matter of a few uncomfortable, sweaty grunts before he passed out, and she would back to whatever she'd been doing before he came in. If she was unlucky - and she always was - he would burst through the door, hollering for his god-damned dog at the top of his god-damned lungs. And he would lay into her about Chico's being gone and why didn't she look after him while he was away. Then the open hands would begin to fly. If she talked back or screamed at him to stop, the hands would clench into fists, and her eyes would blacken before he climbed on top of her to sweat and grunt anyway.

Moments present themselves. They show up when you least expect them. They show up when you're looking for something different, and they show up when you're looking for something more. Ginny Morrison's moment showed up when she was looking for the way out of a relationship that bordered on rape. And it came in the form of a dead dog. Frank was coming home, and then the dog was gone, and this seemed as good a time as any. She began to dig around the bedroom closet for a suitcase. The same suitcase she packed all her clothing in two weeks after her mother realized she wasn't coming back to stay, tail between her legs or otherwise. The small lock cylinders had been turned over, preventing her from getting into the case. Ginny couldn't remember ever owning keys for it, never mind locking the damn thing.

"Fuck."

She pulled the case out of the closet, threw it on the bed, and began to press on the lock releases as hard as she could, figuring maybe they were just stuck closed from years of neglect or moisture from the drafty old house. After several more tries, Ginny realized it was going to open. Locked by someone with a set of keys, and no amount of wishful thinking was going to unlock it. The thought of a screwdriver flashed through her mind but prying them open would probably be more difficult than she thought, and what if she couldn't get them to close the case again. Then it dawned on her.

There was a drawer in the kitchen that caught the detritus of two adult lives that pockets and handbags couldn't carry anymore. Ginny dug through the junk drawer, pulling out a forest's worth of takeout menus, rubber bands by the handful, and instructions for a toaster oven they had thrown out five years ago. The pile of trash on the counter grew, and she lost hope. The thought of stuffing everything she owned into trash bags and heading out the front door didn't seem like a bad idea. And as she grabbed the first stack of menus to replace in the drawer, she saw them. Two tiny, tin luggage keys threaded on a turquoise ribbon.

"Son of a bitch!"

She returned to the bedroom, mumbling prayers, hoping they were the right keys. Ginny got to it and sighed as the latches opened easily. Looking inside it, she understood why the case had been locked in the first place. Held firmly in place by the luggage straps was an ancient dust-covered Florsheim shoe box. She opened the straps and lifted the lid. Inside, wrapped in an old wool sock, was a pearl-handled, nickel-plated revolver. It felt heavy in her hands. It felt dangerous. She suddenly wondered what Frank had been getting up to when he wasn't home, and fear began to prickle up her back. He always had his fingers in plenty of pies, a few of which were less than legal, but he had never been stupid enough to get involved with anything that needed him to carry a gun.

"Oh, Jesus! What the fuck has he done?"

And then an awful thought dawned on her - the gun was in her suitcase. Whatever he was up to, he was trying very hard to make sure she wound up with the blame for it. Ginny turned the pistol over in her hand and looked down the barrel. She wasn't sure if it was even real; she'd never seen a gun before - apart from movies or the T.V. It looked like there were bullets in the big thing, though whether or not it would even work was another thing, she'd find out soon enough by using it to shoot the goddam raccoon before he got home. Maybe it wouldn't bring Chico back, but it might buy her a little favour with Frank if she killed the awful thing that killed his dog.

Ginny turned on her heels, suddenly feeling light and powerful, like nothing bad would ever happen to her again, not so long as she had hold of the silver gun. She even managed a smile as she stuffed the pistol in the waistband of her sweatpants and sparked a fresh Lucky. She blew the smoke out defiantly as she walked toward the backdoor, the god damned dog was dead, and no amount of smoke was ever going to bother him again.

*And good fucking riddance.* Ginny thought.

She turned gleefully from left to right and back again, blowing mouthfuls of smoke as she went. She reached for the screen door and never bothered to look at it as she opened it.

"Hello," Davis said.

"Who the fuck are you?" she screeched.

Ginny levelled the revolver at Davis' face and squeezed as tightly as she was able.

"Not as easy to shoot one of those things as it looks on T.V., is it?"

"I don't know who you are, mister, but in a minute, you're going to be very dead."

"That might be a little more difficult than you think."

———

Jenn Henderson walked out of the office, fuming. Davis was a decent guy and one of the most compassionate Deaths she had ever known. He liked people and took time to get to know them, made sure to ease their minds before he eased their passing. But Christ on a crutch, he could be thick. She wasn't a fan of the brutality most of the Necrosites seemed to love either, but they filled an important role down here. One that no one else had the stomach for. If she could find Mr. Richardson before it was too late, she could impress on him just how seriously all of Davis's posturing should be taken. And then there was the other matter. Jenn walked through the closet of room 107 and climbed the stone staircase to Davis' other office.

She sat down behind the big oak desk and opened the drawers one by one. There was a map she had seen years before, she didn't know who made it, but if she had to guess, she would lay its design at the feet of Davis' predecessor. He preferred to look like Bob Newhart, saying television personalities tended to relax people. They saw him as a slightly bumbling father figure, entirely non-threatening. Just the sort of relaxed attitude you hope for at the end. Jenn recalled seeing his actual face once, and Bob Newhart was an improvement.

His drawing the map made sense - the man had a genuine talent for getting lost within the halls of Winterbourne. However, he had lived in it nearly a hundred years already by the time she came along. It was in the bottom drawer of the desk, hiding underneath a book with a cover that read 'Do Not Read This Book.' It was practically a dare. The book was full, for the most part, with pictures of people on holiday. In the back of the big book, peeking out from souvenir drinks menus from Ricki's Island Breeze Bar, were a couple of other photographs, candid ones displaying, in all their natural glory, the men and women from the previous photos.

"Dirty, old bugger," Jenn chuckled and held up the big book. A yellowed piece of paper dropped out.

The map wasn't much more than a scrap of paper, heavily creased and nearly coming apart from years of repeated folding and unfolding. The stone staircase that came up from room 107, the laundry and storage rooms down the centre hallway, all the rooms along both basement corridors that housed the Necrosites were clearly laid out and labelled. Beyond that was a hallway or path that snaked along from the middle of the page, nearly to the bottom corner. At the end of the passage was a semicircle with ragged edges. Jenn thought it looked like a lake or drainage reservoir, though she'd never heard of anything like that in all her time at Winterbourne.

From the scale of the map and knowing what she did about the distances on it like the Necrosite tenements, Jenn realized she would be gone for most of the day. A whole day wasted trying to get to a pond with no clue what to do once she got there - that was if she could even find the way in. She thought of Davis, the way he'd dismissed her as little more than an employee and decided she might sit on this information for a while.

"Cooking the books? Hah! He has no idea how long this book might need to cool."

# 9

Mr. Richardson felt like his grey flannel suit looked – damp, dirty, and wrinkled. Like he had been balled up and thrown into a corner. He managed to make it to his desk moments before the whistle sounded. His day had begun – nearly without him. He had a mountain of paperwork in front of him that required immediate attention, and all he wanted to do was put his head down and forget about pudgy, chain-smoking hausfraus and their patchy, nervous little dogs.

"Rough night Mr. Richardson?" the voice behind him asked.

"You don't know the half of it," he answered without raising his head.

"So, I'll just leave you here to sleep it off then, shall I?"

"That is a splendid idea."

"Alright then, I'll just go," the voice said.

Mr. Richardson sighed and closed his eyes.

*Five minutes, if I just nod off for five minutes, I'll be right as raisins.*

He felt the exhaustion course through him.

"Of course, there is someone awfully interested in meeting you," Johnston's voice came again.

"Oh bugger and bother, can this not wait until a better time? Tomorrow maybe? Perhaps at my retirement party?"

The older Necrosite lifted his head slowly from the surface of his desk and, after detaching the silvery string of drool that anchored him to it, looked at the owner of the voice.

"Barry Wilson, I suppose?"

"The same. Only, he would prefer if you could refrain from using the name of his enthrallment. In time, he will also give you your true name," Johnston said.

A group of Necrosites, all younger and fitter and clearly more rested than Mr. Richardson, circled his cubicle. Richardson suddenly felt the Soulreaver wasn't inviting him, so much as summoning him.

"Oh, very well, sometime later tonight then? After I've had a chance to rest up and make myself more presentable. Say, sometime after dinner, over brandies, perhaps?" Richardson said.

"Now, Mr. Richardson," Johnston said.

He stared at the gathering brood of ape lizard things around him.

"Bit early, isn't it, for this sort of... thing?"

"The Soulreaver prefers his sermons to take place before the false deliverer or his dispossessed plaything get here," Johnston sneered.

"Oh?"

"And there are always hefty numbers of muffins in the breakroom this early,"

He detected a glee in Johnston's voice that left him feeling slightly uneasy. He wasn't sure the Soulreaver and his followers were up to, and Johnson's tone wasn't helping any.

Mr. Richardson pushed away from his desk and stood, walking toward the door automatically with head down and brain barely working. Johnston tucked in behind him, along with a growing throng of young Necrosites he hadn't noticed before. He was tired enough that he hadn't anything, apart from the exhaustion. Until they walked out of the office. A rabble of Necrosites joined them, all of them wrapped up in white bedsheets – some so filthy that to continue to call them white would have been an insult to fresh linens everywhere.

A hole had been cut in the middle of the sheets to allow their bulbous heads to poke through. The rest of the fabric was fastened round the waist by a long strip of red velvet, cut from the curtain stays by the look of it. The outfit was topped with another length of bed linen that wrapped around their dreadlocks and circled back across the forehead, with a generous leftover amount of fabric trailing behind their heads like a bride's veil. A gilded crest displaying a cat chasing a ball of yarn was emblazoned in the centre of the headwrap.

"What *are* you lot wearing?" Richardson chuckled.

"These are the robes of the Soulreaver. All acolytes wear them into the sacred meeting hall," Johnston said.

"And the picture on your hat?"

"Ah, yes, it is the mighty lion, lying in wait on the spacious veldt, anticipating the setting of the sun that he might hunt. Hunters we were," Johnston called out.

"And hunters we remain," the multitude called back.

"Looks like a cat, chasing a ball of orange yarn," Richardson said.

"It's a lion."

"You'd better hope Mareth doesn't find out what you've done to his sheets, or you'll start the day in a robe and end it on a rope," Richardson said.

"Let him find out. The Soulreaver has plans for the pretender," Johnston said. A chorus of titters went up through the crowd of Necrosites.

They walked in silence down the hallway from Richardson's cubicle, though now it looked nothing like the office he had known most of his life. The blue-grey of cheap fluorescent lighting was gone, replaced by the warm orange of cheap backyard tiki – torches stuck into house plants. Next to the torches hung banners with the same odd cat and ball of yarn that adorned the Necrosites' hats. The pair of them came to a doorway, and the throng stopped, spreading out behind them. Richardson and Johnston continued forward and walked into a cavernous room with row after row of thick, sturdy-looking oak tables. On top of each table stood a statue of the gilded cat and the ball of orange yarn.

"Oh, those are very nice. Who made them?"

"Brother Meatbag," Johnston said, the pride gushing out of him.

"Very nice, but they must weigh a ton. Where do you put them when it's time to get the office back together?"

"The front hall closet, strictly speaking, the lions are Papier Mache and stack inside one another, the rising suns are just messy balls of orange yarn until we can get Meatbag to make us some proper ones fashioned from gold or copper or what have you. When the Soulreaver is finished, it'll be the finest precious metals and glittering jewels to adorn his great hall," Johnston said.

As he approached the end of the room, Mr. Richardson could see a figure standing near to the top of a set of white steps.

"Where did you get the stairs?"

It's the stools we use to reach the tables to sort the mail, we sort of lined them up and stacked them a bit and damned if they didn't reach!"

"And all this stuff just fits away neatly in the hall closet?"

"Shhh, just a bit farther now," Johnston cautioned.

He was tall for a Necrosite, a whole head taller than Richardson and s a little different too. Maybe it was the red robes he wore that disguised his form and made him look narrower at the leg. Maybe it was his version of the headgear they all wore, it was both wider and taller, and the cat on his crest had ruby eyes to match his robes.

"My dear Mr. Richardson," he said and opened his arms as if he wanted to embrace the older Necrosite.

"Barry Wilson. Well, you've done well for yourself," Richardson said.

"I have only embraced the birthright of every Necrosite. The freedom to live as we were born. As the stalkers of the world, with dominion over man and beast. Woe to all who oppose us and all blessings to all who stand beside me and call me brother. Hunters we were," Barry said.

"And hunters we remain!"

The roar went up from the crowd of Necrosites, who now numbered in the hundreds. In the cavernous mailroom, the call of their voices was loud and fearless and sounded like there were thousands of them.

"If Davis Mareth gets wind of your little gatherings down here, you'll have to worry about more than just clearing away some paper mache cats and a few balls of natty yarn," Richardson warned.

"Why? Why should we fear him?"

"He's Death. He is the robe and scythe. He speaks for the Omega at Winterbourne, just as hundreds have done before him. It's not for us to question his methods, like or dislike. We serve the office, not the officer."

"He is a man, and like all men, he is weak and led by his emotions."

"What are you on about, Barry?"

"I mean, Mr. Richardson, that Death is cold, calculating, and exacting. It should steal your breath away in the night, not hold your hand like you were waiting in line at the movies. And wanting to do away with the blood? The ripping away of flesh? With... us?"

"Well... of course, it sounds bad when you... when you put it that way," Richardson stammered.

"What other way is there to put it? Who wants a soft Death when you can have jabs of searing pain and rhythmic crunching of bones? And the blood, oh the sticky warm rivers of it, pouring out, knee-high until nothing remains but a blanched hulk of flesh."

"I don't see how we can change any of that, Davis is in charge, and he is compassionate to a fault," the older Necrosite said.

"His compassion will be his undoing."

"Wait, just wait. Even if we could get rid of Mareth, which is highly unlikely, the Omega would show up until things are put back to right. What then?"

"The Omega has better things to do. Besides, he wouldn't interfere if Mareth had been rightfully removed."

"Removed, who could remove him? Who *would* remove him?"

"The Night Court," Barry hissed.

## 10

"Tell me about the raccoon," Davis said.

Ginny couldn't help but stare at the blue-eyed man standing on her back porch. He was tall, if not a little too thin. Maybe he wasn't as tall as Frank, but he was taller than her. His eyes were blue, so impossibly blue that no matter where her gaze moved, she found herself returning to them. His hair might have been brown, probably a deep chestnut at some point, but now flecked with enough grey, it was losing its ability to be called salt *and* pepper. There was a sadness to him - a haggard, worn down look that covered his face and made him seem older than he probably was. It was the voice that gave it away. The more the man spoke, the more Ginny was convinced he couldn't be much older than she was.

"Huh?" Ginny asked dreamily.

"Raccoon, you said something about a raccoon," Davis repeated.

"Did I?" A smile began to creep its way across her face.

Davis snapped his fingers in front of her to jar her attention a little nearer where it needed to be.

"Oh, what?"

"Raccoon."

"Oh, right. It was probably the biggest raccoon I've ever seen. It was bald. Well, mostly bald, except for little black hairs sticking out all over it. Mange can do that, right?"

"Ah... sure, I guess," Davis sputtered.

"But from all the spiky shit on top of its head, maybe it wasn't a raccoon at all."

"Shit? It had shit on its head?"

"Sorry, stuff on its head. There were things on top of it, long pointy things like the back of a porcupine only longer. And thicker, and they moved like hair. Kinda like a cross between a porcupine and Bob Marley," Ginny said.

The image of a middle-aged man in Victorian clothing, carrying a small crippled boy in his arms, flashed through Davis' mind until he caught sight of the poster of the Rastafarian on the wall.

"Anything else?"

"Nothing."

"Really, nothing else, really?"

Ginny blushed and shifted her weight back and forth, keeping her eyes fixed on the floor to avoid his crystal, blue gaze. A flirty little smile danced across her lips.

"So, I'll just go then," Davis said without moving.

She took a deep breath, paced a little, breathed a few more times deeply, walked toward the back door, and lit a cigarette.

"It talked to me," she exhaled.

"It what?"

"It talked to me, alright? I knew I shouldn't have said anything."

"No, no, it's okay. What did it say to you, if you don't mind my asking?"

"It called me madam and asked me to stop hitting it with that broom," she said.

Davis inspected the woman's face. She was not drunk; she was not delusional, and she was not lying. He knew what she described but didn't want to believe it was true.

"Can you show me where you talked to him – it?"

They walked off the porch onto the backyard, and Ginny stopped short of the threshold between the trimmed, dark grass and the tangled, waist-high mix of weeds and the reed grass beyond it.

"Here, it was right here," Ginny said, pointing at a bloodstained patch.

Davis knelt to examine the spot; it didn't take him long to conclude that something had died there violently. Though congealed and sticky, there remained a fair amount of blood on the lawn and a few remaining tufts of mousy brown hair attached to pieces of fatty tissue. Frankly, the thought of touching it at all made his stomach turn. He placed a hand on top of it and got nothing at all.

"It's not still warm, is it?" Ginny cringed.

Davis said nothing as he felt tiny electric jolts from the disgusting thing. Pinpricks of activity, like the little zips of power from tonguing the end of a nine-volt battery, beginning to shoot up his arm and tease him with crackles of light pushing through his brain. He took hold of the loathsome thing and squeezed until something stronger came his way. The image in his head flickered on and off like a television with a bad picture tube. For the first time since he discovered he could read a person by just holding their hand tightly enough, he wasn't just watching things unfold in front of him; he was a part of what he was seeing. Mareth could see, or rather he could make out light and dark and the faint outline of shapes. It was silent here, except for the sounds coming out of him – breath coming and going in wheezing gasps and a heartbeat racing in his ears. If he listened hard enough, he was sure he could hear the blood flowing through his veins. Davis felt isolated, alone and helpless and, were it not for his nose, he might have just waited for death or bedtime, whichever came first.

He could smell absolutely everything. An acrid bouquet coming from the hydrangea bushes hit him, a combination of the plant's own perfume and every cat for fifty miles using this bush as its own toilet, and he nearly let go of the piece of meat. There was a smell coming from just behind him, stale and awful like a coffee can full of wet cigarette butts. The burnt stench of it startled him enough that he jumped, toward it, trying to get further away from it. But there was another scent in the air. It was heavenly, floating high above all the others. Teasing him as it rolled along and begged him to leave the safety of the porch.

Davis' nose led him straight to it. His mouth watered at the thought of tasting this thing. It was not an appetizing smell, but it bewitched him just the same. The slimy thing moved from ground to mouth with a single, orgasmic gulp. He might have heard the three things approaching if his ears weren't useless. If he'd seen them, he might have had a chance to run back to the porch Davis had just enough time to make out the familiar sound of needle teething behind thin lips.

"No!"

Davis let go of the hairy clump of flesh and turned his gaze back to Ginny.

"Son of a bitch!"

"What, what's the matter?"

"I hate to tell you this, but your dog is dead," Davis said. "And there is going to be hell to pay for it."

Ginny sighed and tucked the pistol back into the waistband of her sweat pants.

"You don't know the half of it," she said.

## 11

"You can't be serious," Richardson said.

"As serious as tomorrow," the Soulreaver replied.

"Wait, what?"

"As serious as tomorrow, it's a common expression."

"No, it isn't. It doesn't even make sense. Tomorrow isn't here yet. Tomorrow could be full of fun and opportunity; someone might give you money tomorrow. You could have a date with one of the Necrosites from the secretarial pool," Mr. Richardson said.

"That's just it. Tomorrow has *yet* to be. The fun might be spoilt by the rain, the money might never arrive, and the secretary could have turned you down, all incredibly serious things. Yesterday, today, tomorrow, next week perfectly serious," the Soulreaver said, as serious as a heart attack.

The older Necrosite stared at the Soulreaver.

"But the Night Court? You would really do that to him? Do you hate him so much? You've heard what happens down there," Richardson said.

"Hate doesn't begin to explain it. Mareth and his kind have held us in chains for centuries, Mr. Richardson. I know exactly what happens down there, and if I had the power, I would see that the Night Court had him to the end of time."

"But the night court - isn't that a tad -"

"Brutal?"

"Extremely, from what I hear," Richardson said.

"I do hope so."

He raised a finger, stopping Mr. Richardson from adding anything else, and ascended the white stairs to the top.

"Killers. Murderers. Butchers. Exterminators," the Soulreaver said, and a low rumble began to move through the crowd like the hum of a thousand angry bees.

"Hunters!" he screamed, and the slow, steady drone became a deafening roar. He raised his gangly arms silence began to make its way through the crowd. The Soulreaver lowered his arms.

"We are ready, Mr. Richardson, as you can see. And this isn't even half of us. Two full shifts of the oppressed Necrosite working-class, loyal to the cause, are absent this morning, but they can be made ready with a word. There is only one obstacle that remains on the path to our freedom, and it must be removed," Barry said.

"But you're not talking about just removing him if you're getting the Night court in on this."

"And I know a certain someone who has the power to see it done."

"You don't want him hurt. You want him broken."

"Well, potato, potato," the Soulreaver said.

"Look, Barry, I am all for freedoms and equal rights for Necrosites and all, but you are asking me to ruin him, to destroy the robe and scythe."

"I am asking you to destroy a man. A man who despises you."

"But I swore my loyalty—"

"You swore loyalty to a position that is occupied by someone who - at best - tolerates you like a head cold. Your bed is soft and warm, and your clothes are fine, but your soul is trapped in a cage. Get rid of

Mareth, and you will be free. We will all be free. If he remains, it will be the death of all we've ever known."

"Well, of course, it will, Barry, he is Death," Johnston volunteered.

The Soulreaver shot a look at the young Necrosite that said they would be speaking later and likely behind a locked door with a hard-backed chair and a piece of rubber hose.

Mr. Richardson wondered what the Soulreaver could have said to sway Johnston and the rest of these Necrosites into doing anything except going to lunch. He suspected it had been peppered with grunting sounds and lots of words like hunt and kill. And lunch.

"I can't do what you ask. I'm sorry, Barry, but my devotion is to the robe and scythe, regardless of who happens to possess them," Mr. Richardson said quietly.

The Soulreaver placed his hand gently along the older Necrosite's chin and raised it up to meet his gaze.

"I won't say I'm not disappointed, Mr. Richardson. You are a Necrosite of immense respect. There are many in the service of Winterbourne, above and below, who would follow your lead."

"I appreciate that, Barry."

"Just the same, there are many who follow me who would like to see you torn to shreds in an agonizing end. But I do understand your position."

"Thank you. I'd like to go back to my desk now if it's all the same with everyone. I have a lot of work to catch up on."

"Of course," the Soulreaver breathed.

The older Necrosite began the long walk back to his desk. Johnston and a thick muscled Necrosite followed close behind. The Soulreaver called out to him as he neared the door. The morning sun had been steadily filtering in through moth holes in the curtains, in small beams giving the mailroom a dreamy appearance. The sunlight dotted the walls and pooled on the floors of the mailroom, casting a glow on Barry Wilson. The Soulreaver looked like he was engulfed in flames.

"When the golden pebbles you hold so tightly begin to slip through your fingers and disappear, take my hand and walk with me to freedom."

Richardson turned back to the door and walked back to his desk, trying to ignore Johnston's endless toeing of the party line. He yammered on about not shaming the white robes and equality for those that deserved it, but a very stern ripping of limbs and flesh for those who couldn't see how right their cause was. And freedom, of course. Plenty of freedom for all - except those previously mentioned. And, of course, just how amazingly stupendous the Soulreaver was at saying what they had all been thinking anyway. In time, even he would see the only Death he needed was supplied by them in steady, crimson puddles and chunks of jagged, torn flesh. The little Necrosite was a true believer; he had swallowed the bait, the hook, and was looking to the boat as the next dish in a four-course meal of second-rate propaganda.

"Thanks for keeping me company, fellas," Richardson said and took a seat behind his desk.

"No trouble at all, Mr. Richardson, sir. The Soulreaver said, you're one of us. Told us, Otto and I here, to look after you all special, like." Johnston smiled and nodded to his larger companion.

"You've done well then."

Richardson watched the two walk away. One Necrosite hobbling, one lumbering. He smiled; if they could somehow incorporate juggling, it might make for an excellent act at the office Christmas party. His mind wandered back to the Soulreaver, his parting words still ringing in his ears. The Necrosite glanced up at the mountain of papers stacked on the desk. He worked hard to clear the pile. A stream of junior clerks paraded by his desk, constantly refilling his in basket, crushing any hope of getting through this day without having to speak with Davis first.

Mr. Richardson looked at his watch. If he didn't take a break– toilet breaks didn't count – and he was extremely lucky, the old Necrosite could blast through the paperwork and make it home without being noticed. An hour into this revelation and he was starting to make strides. Halfway into the rest of his day and he could clearly see Janice from accounting, who had the cubicle across the hall. At twenty minutes to quitting time, Richardson had just four pages remaining that needed nothing more than his approval with a stamp.

Mr. A. P. Richardson, *ka-chung*. The first sheet went from desk to out basket. Mr. A. P. Richardson, *ka-chung*. The second sheet fell. He could feel his pulse quicken and gazed up at the clock – ten minutes remaining, though if he was careful enough faking a trip to the toilet, he could make it out a full five minutes early. Mr. A. P. Richardson, *ka-chung*. His hand trembled as he moved the final sheet from his desktop to the wire basket at its right top corner. He looked to the desktop with a satisfied grin and saw a post-it he hadn't noticed until now. It was small and yellow and blank. Richardson pulled it off the surface of the desk and examined it. Turning it over, he could see the note written on its underside;

**Please see me immediately,**
**Signed,**
**D.**

---

Jenn stepped off the elevator into the near darkness of the basement. It had been almost a whole day since she saw Davis. She couldn't decide whether she was still angry with him, but the map had gotten under her skin, and she needed to see for herself what was at the end of it. Then she'd decide what to share with him. If the map was right, the entrance to the twisting corridor was past the last room on the east wing, but getting to it wouldn't be easy. The Necrosites didn't trust humans as a rule, but a dead woman who refused to just be dead, poking around down here - probably because her Grim Reaper boyfriend asked her to spy on them - well, that was just going *too* far. The whispering and sidelong glances were bad enough around the office, but down in their home - their world, she imagined their reactions would be less polite.

She knew many of them had banded together in those early days. Joined by necessity more than choice. And the peace began - fight amongst themselves or come together and have a shot at prosperity with the powers that be. Their promise of loyalty was given, and they set to work in the service of Death. The place was kept running efficiently, and some of the little buggers even got to satisfy their instinct for carnage.

It started as social groups mainly, but even those had pecking orders. As the older generation died off, the cooler heads seemed to go with them, and a crop of younger, meaner, dumber Necrosites began to move into the leadership roles. In time, they broke off from the community entirely. They walked the streets of the neighbourhoods, taking what they felt they were owed by the remains of the generation that had sold them out. Extortion, intimidation, racketeering, and all-around shitty behaviour became the norm, and the young ran roughshod over those who couldn't, or wouldn't, fight back.

The Eastern Flats Heart and Soul Killers, Killers for short, prowled around the Eastern Flats like wolves looking for a snack. They were a mob of young Necrosites who walked the streets fearlessly. They wanted what they were owed. They took what they could get.

The older ones who sat on their stoops in the evening to take in the cooler air would hurry indoors when the young Turks came ankling by. They were a ball of intimidation, thirty-two of them all in torn dungarees and matching denim vests, emblazoned on the back with the words KILLERS and WINTERBOURNE, around a large golden triangle with a single, ominous black ring intersecting it.

It was a three-hundred-and-fifty-foot stretch of hallway, from the first cottage occupied by a Necrosite to the last three-level tower block of tenements, and it was all the Killer's turf. It was where Jenn

Henderson stood now and more than three hundred and fifty feet through the Killer's turf from where she needed to be.

The foyer just outside the elevator was a sort of No Man's Land, and the dead girl was fairly certain none of them would come at her here. Too many of the human staff would be horrified at the sight of them. This is precisely why the laundry and garbage facilities were straight ahead, down a short, well-lit hallway directly in front of the elevator doors. To her left, dimly lit and uninviting, the western hallway stretched out, and to her right, equally darkened, the eastern hallway – the one she needed to go down.

"Holy shit!"

She was aware they had been given most of the basement by the Death, who first convinced them to serve the void. And they had thrived, but she had no idea just how well they had gotten on down here. Her own ignorance left her believing they likely lived in cages with bits of straw and old rags for beds like animals in the zoo. This despite the fact that she knew many of them personally. Knew their spouses and the names of their children and felt pride at the smallest of their accomplishments. She hoped to show them not all humans were horrible, even the dead ones. Here, laid out in front of here, were Necrosite tower blocks lining the walls of the hallway. From the look of them, they were packing crates and shipping containers once, but the masonry and woodwork on the outside of them gave them the look of well-made, affordable city apartments.

There was a smell, not repulsive but not pleasant either. A confusing mix of garlic and baking mingling with the sweet, sickening odour of overripe fruit. But the smells didn't bother her as much as the lack of light. She knew they had an outstanding vision in the dark, but it was so dark down here, she couldn't believe anyone could find their way around other than by feeling along the walls to get where they were going. Apart from random strings of half-lit Christmas lights in a handful of tenement doorways, the only light down here came from the dull, red, emergency sconces spaced along the walls every thirty feet. It gave the whole place a depressing feel, as though keeping the Necrosites in the dark might have been part of the plan all along. The effect was not lost on Jenn. The gloom seemed to crush in and shorten her breath as she walked.

Jenn moved slowly. Not in a guarded way but trying to be aware of where she was and the possibility of something springing out of nowhere. She was aware of worried faces peering out from makeshift doors. Doors slammed as she passed by. Ragged curtains and blinds that were drawn and shut long before she had a chance to make eye contact.

A lone figure sat on the stoop of one of the apartments waiting for her to walk by.

"You're a long way from home. Where are you going, dearie?" Mrs. Ida Pugwash called out to her.

"I'm not really sure," Jenn answered.

"Oh, very good. If you don't know where you're going, how do you know it's the way you're heading?"

"Is that meant to sound cryptic?"

"Not at all. It was meant to be an honest question. Dangerous place this, are you quite sure you need to be going that way?"

"Ah, okay, yes. I'm sure I need to be going this way."

"To get to where you're not sure you need to be going?"

"Now you've got it," Jenn said.

Mrs. Pugwash changed the subject. "You'd be young Mareth's assistant, wouldn't you?"

"I've never heard it put so... delicately by a Necrosite, but, yes," Jenn laughed.

"Why on Bob's green earth would he send you slumming down here? What's he up to?"

"He doesn't know I'm down here. I don't imagine he would be too happy if he knew I was. He is not very fond of all of you."

"I had heard tell of such things but didn't believe none of it. Death not wanting Necrosites? It's not natural. Mark my words, no good can come of this. If your Mareth is that set against us, all he needs is an excuse, and we'd all be sunk, and you roaming around down in the flats like *Mrs. Death,* if you please, is likely the only reason he'd need. Especially if you managed to find some of the trouble you're up to," the old Necrosite woman said.

"I'm not exactly loving the idea of being down here, but I've got a hunch there is something important down the end of this God-damned hallway, and I need to get to it, okay?" Jenn blurted.

"Something important in the eastern flats? Not bloody likely!"

Jenn stuck a hand into her front pocket, feeling the edges of the folded map. She flicked her finger along the top of it, weighing her options. On the one hand, a Necrosite who had been down here as long as Mrs. Pugwash might be able to shed a little light on whatever it was at the end of the twisty passage. On the other hand, if she didn't like the dead girl, regardless of how pleasant their conversation was, she could lead Jenn wherever she chose.

Jenn gave in. If some kind of harm was meant to find her down here, it would happen whether she showed the map or not. She produced the ragged piece of paper and showed it to the thing on the doorstep.

"I'm going here." Jenn pointed to the curvy line on the far bottom right of the Winterbourne map.

"There, really? Why the hell would you want to go there?"

"You know this place?"

"Course I do. It's a broom closet. Not much in there, mops and nasty smelling sprays and such. Nobody goes in there much."

"I know Davis' predecessor made a map to it. Now, why would Death, the appointed servant of the void, make a map to a broom closet?"

"That old boy was potty. Never could get his ass figured from canal water," Mrs. Pugwash sneered.

"I think he knew something about that place like maybe there was more to it like maybe there were a lot of things could go on in that room, Jenn said.

"That's not exactly true. There's only one thing that can happen there, and for someone like you, it's not good. Ever," Mrs. Pugwash said.

"What do you mean someone like me?"

"When's the last time you gave blood? Or felt like you needed a nap? Ate a really satisfying meal?"

"I don't see what that has to do with -"

"There are doors, child. Doors everywhere between the worlds of the living and the dead and, for the most part, they are locked up tight. But some are guarded by things. Awful things. Ancient, ruined and angry things, much angrier and crueller than anything you or your mister have ever seen."

"But?" Jenn asked, sensing the word hanging in the air.

"But then there are a few places, thin places the old folks called them, that were more like curtains than doors. It was easier for people to get to the other side," Mrs. Pugwash explained.

"Why would someone want to go to the other side?"

"Love, mostly. But there were lots of other stupid reasons, money, missing power tools lent out long ago, birthday gifts that never received thank-you cards, that sort. But love. Ah, love was the big one —the only really good reason. Orpheus, Odysseus, Aeneas, they all went below for the ones they loved," Mrs. Pugwash said, looking dreamily to the horizon.

"I still don't see what any of this has to do with -"

"You and Davis?" Mrs. Pugwash interrupted, "Neither of you is of this side or the other, though there are many on this end of things who would wish you gone. There are twice as many beyond the veil who would like to know how you did it."

"Did what?"

Mrs. Pugwash sighed. "Stopped death, my dear. Avoided the lines on the other side and went straight through to reincarnation."

"Nobody cares about that, living or dead," Jenn quipped.

"Everybody, living or dead, that knows the difference, cares about it. You don't belong to this world. It was a mistake that kept you here.

If you was to walk by a thin place and somebody was watching, they'd likely pull you in just to pick your brain."

"Wait, what, who would be watching me?"

"All of them on that side. They are *always* watching you."

"What, why?" Jenn asked.

"Because you was the one what got away," she said. "You was the one Death forgot."

# 12

---

**D**avis paced in the big upstairs office. He was irritated, maybe even angry, but knew the best way to keep things civil and light was to keep his temper in check, despite his desire to start screaming at Richardson. Jenn was right. It wasn't the best time to do anything stupid, and she'd persuaded him to, at least, give Richardson the benefit of the doubt. Oh, he would put the fear of the reaper up him - and all the other Necrosites, but in the end, he would let him keep his job, so long as he swore to keep the others in line.

"Yup, things are going to be just fine."

Mr. Richardson brushed off the sleeves of his jacket and straightened his tie, hurrying to the big office. He stood on the landing, staring up at the stone stairs and wondered why the laundry workers and kitchen staff - the ones with fully articulated legs - had the benefit of an elevator to get them from floor to floor. It hadn't been that long ago when he and the other Necrosites had tried to kill Mareth, or at least stop him from getting up these stairs. A smile cracked on his face but faded quickly as the effort of climbing had reduced him to a bent-over, panting mess.

"Pathetic. Hunters we were, indeed."

Richardson knew he was about to be bawled out for Johnston and the other two chewing up the damned dog. He pushed on up the remaining stairs, sputtering and gasping for breath, heading for the top. All the while trying to explain to himself how the dog's death wasn't a bad thing.

*It's like this, sir, the dog was very old, and the lads must have sensed that and taken pity on the poor beast.*

It sounded stupid. Even inside his head, it sounded stupid. A mercy killing didn't account for all the blood. Putting things out of their misery by causing them more misery was what Necrosites enjoyed most of all. Especially when things weren't particularly miserable, to begin with.

*Perhaps the poor, old thing exploded from fear, sir. It's been known to happen.*

Richardson knew that lie would stink up the room the second it left his lips. And then something occurred to him. Something fiendish and horrible. Something perfect.

*The dog charged them, sir, in defence of its owner, and the lads reacted. Granted, they reacted harshly and to a tragic outcome, but I can assure you they acted purely out of self-defence. What were they doing there in the first place? I'm slightly embarrassed to say that some of the younger Necrosites have taken to horticulture, sir. It's so drab below, and many of them have taken to prettying the place up a touch. They were waiting for the right opportunity to steal some flower pots off the back porches when the dog sprung on them.*

Davis would believe it. He had to. Hell, Richardson believed it himself, and he climbed the remaining stairs with a burst of confidence. Death was gazing absently out of the bay window as he entered the office.

"Surveying all that you rule, sir?" Richardson asked, halfway joking.

"Take a seat, Mr. Richardson," Davis said without turning.

Richardson clambered into the chair and was reminded he hadn't yet slept. The nearest thing to rest he'd experienced in the last forty-eight hours was the ten minutes his head was on his desk before he was summoned to the mailroom.

"I believe you know why you're here."

Mareth's gaze remained fixed on the backyard of the estate, likely for effect and the sense of unease it gave. The Necrosite went over the story in his head, waiting for his chance.

"Sir?"

"I have always tried to give as much latitude as I could to your kind. I know you all have *desires* that need to be satisfied in your own ways. I have always turned a blind eye to the squirrels and rabbits, and the real reason there are so few wild things living around here."

Richardson remained silent, consumed by guilt. Without warning, a feeling of warmth began to creep over him, like he had just put on a warm sweater and pulled up a comfy chair beside the fireplace. Mareth's voice stopped making sense as the words melted into a steady, low drone of bees on a summer afternoon. The old Necrosite snapped forward, grabbing his hand and pinching it for all he was worth, trying to force himself back to full attention.

"But this really is the limit. A dog - and not a stray or anything like that, no. No, you jokers had to pick somebody's pet and family friend. Family fucking friend!"

Davis slammed a fist against the glass of the big bay window.

Richardson leaned forward.

*Wait, dog... he said, a dog. This is the time to tell him. Did he say it? Did I really hear it? Did I dream it?*

"And worse yet, you let one of them see you. But was that enough? No, of course not! You had to talk to her for Christ's sake!"

*Talk? Who talked? And to who... who... whom? This chair is really more comfortable than it looks.*

Mr. Richardson sat quietly and tried to remain still for as long as he could. It was either stand and move around to wake up his brain or stay sitting and give in to the sleep that was oozing through him like heroin. He struggled to raise himself from the chair, but the weight on his eyes was too much to fight off anymore. He gave in, barely noticing he had nodded off.

"Are you going to say anything? Anything at all to any of this, Mr. Richardson?"

Davis turned from the window and saw the little Necrosite fast asleep on the chair in front of his desk. A whisper of pity flashed through him, and, for a moment, he wanted nothing more than to take his underling and tuck him into a warm bed. His mind flicked back to Ginny standing on her back porch, scared for her dog. And the flash of sympathy was pushed aside by anger.

"Wake up, Mr. Richardson."

The Necrosite was motionless.

"Wake up, Mr. Richardson!"

Richardson jerked and lurched into an upright position.

"Yes, sir, sorry, sir. You were saying something about a dog?" he fumbled.

Davis took a long breath and exhaled slowly through pursed lips. He walked to the oversized oak desk and took a seat behind it. He rocked forward until he was face to face with the Necrosite in the grey flannel suit.

"You and everyone else in the basement have until month end to pack your belongings and vacate Winterbourne. Your services are no longer required."

Richardson gasped in disbelief. "But sir, you can't! Where can we go? What shall we do?"

"You are so fond of acting like animals. Why not find a nice patch of forest behind the facility, and start living like them."

Mr. Richardson ambled out of the office and stood at the top of the stone staircase. He imagined throwing himself down them. The thought of breaking an arm or a leg rather than his neck seemed more likely, so he began the slow, awkward descent. As he climbed down, he tried to find the right words to break the news to all of them that it was over - the tenements, the day jobs, the hunting parties - all of it gone in a single rush of bloodlust against a near-blind, stone deaf dog.

Richardson was no speaker. Hell, most of the Necrosites didn't like him enough to even listen. He thought about posting an announcement on some of the wash lines, hoping that enough of them would see it and pass the news along while there was still time. Then there was Mrs. Pugwash. She was like Western Union, Bell, and the post office all in one. The best way to get any piece of information from one Necrosite to another in short order was to swear Ida Pugwash to secrecy. A feeling of hopelessness closed in. It was overwhelming. No matter what he did, there was no way to save the Necrosites in the basement of Winterbourne home.

*Or was there?*

Mr. Richardson made it to the landing that led to the second-floor doorway and headed down the hallway for the mailroom. As he pushed through the double doors into the spacious room, he could see the cat statues and balls of orange string were all gone, put away in the front hall closet along with the grubby white robes. The room was alive with activity; Necrosites clawed through piles of mail and dropped them into wheeled baskets. The noise of them working was constant and deafening.

The Necrosite in grey flannel lumbered up on the stool of the first station and moved in close to the mail sorter standing there.

"Where is the Soulreaver?" Richardson whispered.

"Where is the who?" the Necrosite blurted.

"Shhh. The Soulreaver."

"I'm sorry, mister, I don't know no Soulreader, and why are you whispering?"

"Soulreaver. *Soulreaver*," Richardson hissed.

"Oh, the Soulreaver, you're looking for the Soulreaver? Why didn't you say so straight away?"

"Ah, you know him then?"

"No, never heard of him."

"Barry Wilson," Richardson said under his breath.

"What?"

It's Barry Wilson, alright? Barry, bloody Wilson. Do you know where Barry Wilson is?"

"Barry Wilson? Of course, I know Barry Wilson. You'd have to be some special kind of stupid to work down here and not know Barry Wilson."

He turned toward the Necrosite at the next station.

"Here, Jack, this fellow wants to know if I know Barry."

"Barry? What, Barry Wilson?"

"Yeah."

"You'd have to be some kind of half-wit to work down here and not know Barry Wilson," he said.

"That's what I said."

"Gentlemen please," Mr. Richardson interjected. "If we could just focus. I don't need to know him. I need to *find* him, yes?"

"Oh, yeah, yeah, yeah. He's just over there," the second sorter said.

Richardson looked at the two sorters in frustration and hurried over to the other end of the room to a figure in black casual slacks. A tailored, burgundy dress shirt and a black satin tie, lined diagonally with stripes that matched the colour of his shirt perfectly. He was hunched over one of the sorting tables, orchestrating and overseeing every bit of activity. And they all loved him for it.

"Mrs. Pendleton, this one goes upstairs, and the rest go to Resident Acquisition, yes?"

"Right you are, Mr. Wilson, won't happen again," the slender Necrosite said.

"Mr. Wilson was my father. I'm Barry," Barry said.

"Ahem," Mr. Richardson cleared his throat.

"Ah, Mr. Richardson."

"I'm ready."

"Oh? Ready for what?" Barry asked.

"To do what you asked, of course."

"Ah, very nice, hand me that bag of mail, will you?"

"What?"

"The mail, I could use a hand with the mail,"

"What about all that when you are ready to take my hand and walk with me to freedom nonsense?"

"Not here," Barry breathed.

"What do you mean, not here? If not bloody here, then where?" Richardson demanded.

"Mr. Richardson, we are in the middle of a normal day's business. It's hardly the place for the revolution to begin. Meet me in the break room in ten minutes. I think there are still a few muffins left. If you hurry, you may get some before the sorters start piling in."

He turned back to the sorting tables, leaving Richardson standing beside Mrs. Pendleton.

"Break room is over that way, dear," Mrs. Pendleton said.

"What?" Richardson asked, jerked back to reality.

"The break room. Barry said for you to meet him in the break room, didn't he just?"

"Oh, yes, I guess he did."

"It's just there."

It wasn't much more than a shipping box with a handful of chairs and a rickety table in the centre of it. For the number of Necrosites working in the mailroom, it wasn't big enough to be a break room for more than three of them at a time. Richardson entered the room, took a seat in front of the big clock on the facing wall, waiting for the Soulreaver to arrive. He looked around the drab room and understood why most of the Necrosites that worked down here were so unpleasant all the time. It was small and cramped and smelled of cabbage and stale cigarettes. There was a small serving tray sitting on the counter just under the clock in front of him. Richardson knew that those people upstairs nearing the end are given all manner of baked goods and bubbly drinks, and none of them ate a crumb of it. The leftovers made their way down here. He didn't begrudge the old folks anything to ease their passage but wondered why did you have to be a dying human to get a decent snack around this place?

Barry came into the room, followed closely by Johnston and

Pyewackett and Bunn. Two more followed close behind, and in short order, two more pushed into the small room. Soon the old Necrosite was no longer able to move his arms, let alone get up from the table.

"Is this totally necessary?"

What? Is what necessary?"

"All of the others in here sort of negates the whole let's talk in private sort of thing, doesn't it? I thought it might just be you and I having a nice chat over a cup of coffee and maybe a muffin."

"These three are my personal escort. I trust them with my life," Barry said.

"Could they not escort you from outside and give us a bit of room to talk?"

"It's break time, Mr. Richardson, and this *is* the break room."

The buzz of activity around the Necrosites in the break room reached fever pitch, and the older Necrosite became frustrated at the total lack of privacy and the inability to carry on a civil conversation without having to shout above the noise. He hoped to keep it quiet when he admitted he was ready to betray the Robe and Scythe and commit himself to an eternity of torment and suffering.

"You were saying something earlier? Something about being ready to bake a ham?"

"Wait. What?" Richardson responded.

"I like ham and all, but there might be a better use of your particular skill set," Barry shouted.

"Ham? I said I was ready to take your hand," Richardson shouted back.

"Come again?"

Mr. Richardson began to rethink his offer to betray Davis. Maybe he should just keep his head down, keep his mouth shut and accept his lot. It's what he was best at anyway.

"I am ready to turn Mareth over to the Night Court," Richardson said quietly.

Barry Wilson snapped his fingers, and the break room fell silent.

"What did you say?"

"I am ready to do it. I am ready to do whatever it takes to get him out of here."

"Why the sudden change of heart, Mr. Richardson? What happened to your loyalty to the Robe and Scythe - to Death?"

Mr. Richardson sighed and explained Davis' firing him and evicting every Necrosite from the basement, and now, if there was anything they could do, they were running out of time to do it.

"All over a dead human plaything? How absurd. Who is he to expect us to curb our natural instincts as hunters? Denying us - forbidding us the right to live as nature intended? As we are meant to be?"

"Yes... well... I told him as much," Richardson lied.

The Soulreaver went quiet, bowed his head, and hummed to himself. The tune was familiar to the older Necrosite, but not enough that he could remember its name.

"We need a plan," Barry said after a time.

"Wait. What? Wasn't it your idea to turn him over to the Night Court?" Richardson puzzled.

"Well, yes," Barry said. But I had rather hoped you would be able to help us with the particulars of that. Why do you think we were trying to get you on board in the first place?"

"He's Death, Barry. There isn't anything he can be punished for. He is the end of all things. The only thing he is forbidden from doing is changing the rules of the time cards, and nobody ever does that," Richardson explained.

"Cards?"

"Work orders. Each person who enters the walls of Winterbourne is assigned a time card, like on a job site. When their time is up, the cards come to my inbox, and then they end up in his. Death goes to see them, holds the hands and rubs their foreheads, and it's all over but for friends and relatives standing by a pile of dirt and fighting over the will."

"So?"

"So, it's the one thing, the one rule that they've all obeyed.

Nobody gets more time. When you're done, you're gone, and it's off to the waiting room."

"What if you misplaced a card or two?"

"Wouldn't do any good. Once a card gets punched by the time clock, the name automatically ends up in the big book in his office. When he helps them pass, the name disappears. Not before. I'm not quite sure how it all works, but it's always been that way."

"And who punches the cards?"

"Well, we do – Necrosites. Mrs. Levinson from accounts receivable carries a master list that comes monthly from head office that contains the names of every person who is to die within any given month. She, in turn, makes a list of names, dates, and times for the acquisitions department. Acquisitions put the cards into the appropriate slots under the big clock, where they sit until their end day comes up, and they get punched and put into the day's business file. Then I collect them and give them to Mareth to begin the day's business. Understand?"

Barry blinked, feeling as though he'd just been given the explanation for the workings of everything in the known universe and then told he didn't need to worry about it because it all smelled like the number eleven anyway.

"It would be too difficult to stop a death altogether. There are too many steps, each with a fail-safe. One step follows another. There are too many pies containing far too many fingers," the old Necrosite said.

Barry sat, contemplating all this for an uncomfortable amount of time, his head lolling back as if he had fallen asleep. Mr. Richardson started considered maybe this Soulreaver wasn't the answer to his or any Necrosite's problems and got up to leave. Without warning, Barry's face shot forward along with his hands, gripping vice-like around Richardson's own. The younger Necrosites eyes were wide and staring, his gaze never wandering from Richardson's.

"What would happen if someone went early?"

"Early, how could someone go early? The card gets stamped

when your time is up - never before that. Holy gods, the headaches that would cause if it were before," Richardson explained.

"But we do the stamping," Barry said, nearly to himself. A wicked grin began to play at the corners of his mouth.

"And?"

"And, we could punch someone's card early, Mareth would never know. The name would appear in his book, and everything would check out as far as he knew. The only one who would know, apart from us, would be the Necrosite from upstairs, and we could take care of her."

"Wait. What? I like Mrs. Levinson; she brings in banana muffins on the day she delivers the new list. No reason to do away with her," Richardson protested.

"Not take care of her like that. Just get her out of the way until this all blows over,"

"They'd know. Someone upstairs would catch on and stop it from happening."

"I'm not talking about a month or even a week early, a day, maybe two days early. What would happen then?" Barry asked.

Mr. Richardson sat silent and still as he searched for a reason why it wouldn't work or, more to the point, why he shouldn't do it.

*Your services are no longer required*

The sting of Davis's words rang in his ears, cementing all the reasons why he should.

"They would haul Mareth away," Richardson answered.

# 13

M r. Richardson stood in front of the row of card slots that spread across the entire length of the clock room's far wall and reached nearly to the top of it. Every one contained the name and information of the residents and staff of Winterbourne Home. Specifically when they were scheduled to pass from this life and in what manner. When their number came up, the card was punched by the big clock, then made its way to the older Necrosite, who, in turn, gave it to Davis. It was regimented and well maintained, so no one ever got a second more time. But no one ever looked for people going out early. The idea was absurd. Who would want less life?

"Who have you got that's close?" Richardson asked the junior clerk.

"I'm sorry?" the clerk stammered.

"Who is currently close to the end? Someone about to shuffle off this mortal coil?"

The clerk stared at Mr. Richardson and seemed to get more confused the longer he stared.

"Who's close to snuffing it?"

"Ah," the clerk replied.

He turned over a few pages on his clipboard and wandered over to the wall of cards. Running his fingers slowly along the tin slots, looking at the names and back to the sheets again. A sigh blew through his lips, and the Necrosite hobbled to the far end of the line to retrieve the moveable staircase. It was a god-awful thing of twisted and bent steel that reached to the top of the racks, and the clerk began to push it to the far end of the room. From the screeches and whines that echoed as it went, Richardson guessed it hadn't left its spot in years.

"Here," the clerk said.

"Found someone?"

"Mrs. Elsie MacGillivray, she's due out Wednesday after dinner, Thomas Gates, due out Friday after next, and Mrs. Margaret Galston, scheduled departure at 6:30 tomorrow morning. Why do you ask?"

"Give me Mrs. Galston's card," Richardson said.

"What for?"

"Just give me the damn thing, will you?"

Richardson snapped the card from the clerk's hand and stood in front of the big clock, knowing once the card had been punched, there was no taking it back - for any of them. He pushed the card slowly forward, wondering if there were something he should say, something appropriate for changing the course of his life and the world around him forever.

"Hunters we were," he said and punched three small holes in Mrs. Margaret Galston's card.

The clock let out a pained squeal. Ancient metal parts scraping to a halt against rusted springs that scraped and seized with a screech, and Richardson knew now there was no going back.

"And hunters we remain! The clerk beamed.

The Necrosite in the grey flannel suit began the long walk to the stone staircase holding Mrs. Galston's time card tightly in his hand. It was a matter of hours now – Mareth would get his, and the Soulreaver would set the world right for Necrosites everywhere. Soon they would be vindicated - soon, they would be free.

His thoughts should have been soaring. But, the second he punched the old woman's card, Mr. Richardson felt his heart was well and truly broken. He should have been hearing the cheers of Necrosites everywhere - he had delivered the blow that toppled the awful dictator. Instead, he could only hear his father's words ringing in his ears.

"Administrative assistant to the true servant of the void is not an easy role, my boy. It is a thankless job. You will be taken for granted, and you will take the lion's share of the blame for the actions of all our kind, maybe even for his kind too. But you will be the great go-between, the negotiator for both parties. If Death is the great leveller, his assistant is the great smoother over of things. Not nearly so catchy, I know, but just as important."

"But how?" Both sides hate me?"

"Yes, they probably do, but they also value you. Whether they say it or not, they both respect you for what you do. Let them hate, so long as they respect you. The balance is as close as it ever has been. Doesn't that tell you something?"

"He hates me, Papa. Death hates me, and I am loyal to him," Richardson fought back the tears.

"Loyalty is its own reward, my boy," his Father's voice replied.

"Oh, yes? Maybe tonight, then, I'll go home and pick three new suits and a Davenport from the Macy's catalogue, all bought and paid for by my never-ending loyalty."

The old Necrosite stopped outside Davis' office and stared at his reflection in the mirrors that lined the facing wall. His suit was filthy, and so was he. He looked tired, like someone whose conscience had been whispering doubt in his ear every time he started to doze off. He was sad. He was exhausted. He was lost. Standing just behind his tattered reflection, hands on his shoulders, stood his Father.

"It's not too late. Tear it up. Tear up the card."

"I can't tear it up. It exists in the book now. It'd be me hauled off to the Night Court if I destroyed a card."

"You know what happens to someone after they appear before the Night Court? You really want to do that to him?"

"I want him to feel the way he has made me feel," Richardson said.

"Needed?"

"Hated, abandoned - unwanted," Richardson sniffed.

"He needs you. They all need you."

"He hates me, hates us all."

"You need him. You need the job. Without it, you are nothing, and they will never respect you again."

Richardson gazed down at the card in his hand and watched a fat, salty tear splash down in the middle of it.

"Alan, please," his Father begged.

"I'm sorry, Papa," Richardson sobbed and opened the door.

"Mr. Richardson, I was meaning to send for you," Davis said.

"I haven't managed to deliver your message to those of us living downstairs yet, but I will see to it as soon as possible, sir."

"I wanted to tell you that I might have been a little rash earlier on."

"Oh?"

"Yes. I think it would be alright if you all were to... is that a new one?" Davis asked, plucking the time card from Richardson's hand.

"Ah, yes, well it..."

"Mrs. Galston, I didn't realize she was due to go so soon."

"She took a bit of a turn for the worse last night, I'm afraid. You know how these things can go."

"Yes, yes, sadly, we all do," Davis agreed.

The old Necrosite lowered his head, trying to avoid the man's gaze, though it did little good. He could feel Davis' eyes burrowing into his skull.

*He knows, somehow, he knows.*

His heart thundered away like a piston driving a racing engine.

Davis bent low to his assistant's level and squared up to him.

"I'll go see to Mrs. Galston right now," he said and disappeared out the office door.

"Of course, sir. Very good, sir."

*He knows. Why doesn't he just get it over with and put a stop to all of this?*

---

Davis stepped off the elevator and headed for the resident wards. He stopped to say hello to the handful of folks who were awake day and night and felt worry twist his guts like black coffee on an empty stomach. He opened the door to Mrs. Galston's room and gazed at her lying motionless on the bed, mouth open and a horrible, mucousy rattle escaping her with every breath. Her skin was a weathered grey substitute for the pink and healthy tint it had been, and her eyes refused to remain completely closed, giving the old girl the impression of having already passed. He took her hand in his.

An enormous flash hit him. A life danced before his eyes – her life. Margaret Galston was born and lived all her days in Winterbourne. She married young, like everyone did then, to a burly riverman who smelled like a wet dog most of his life and lacked the skill to do anything but offload and refill the barges that came down river all year long. Still, he loved her and spent the whole of his life trying to make her as happy as she made him.

They raised a family, two strong boys who grew up to leave the town and returned for the big holidays with wives and children of their own. As the grandchildren grew, the visits became less frequent until they ceased altogether, and then it was just the two of them again. It was in the winter, five years gone now, that she lost him. He was walking up Parker St. with an armful of groceries when a heart attack dropped him like a stone. The old boy was dead before he hit the pavement. She screamed his name and begged him not to leave her as the firemen went through the motions of trying to save his life. Margaret moved into Winterbourne Home the following spring and waited for death to come for her as loneliness and boredom took chipped away at her desire to keep going.

Davis stared into the old woman's face and felt a swell of pity for her - he did with most of them. The worst part was watching them suffer and not from the diseases and illnesses that plagued them but from the depression, the feelings of being forgotten and discarded by a world that valued youth and money over wisdom and experience. He felt even worse for the ones who felt they deserved to suffer. He knew better. None of them deserved it. He brushed the hair off her forehead.

"I'm sorry, Mrs. Galston. At least you'll see Herb again soon. The way the backlog has been lately, he may still be in the waiting room," Davis sighed.

He checked his watch, and when the time arrived, drew two fingers across her head and felt the bite of raw electricity moving up through his hand and into his right arm. Mrs. Galston sat bolt upright, choking and sputtering, eyes bulging from her head in fear and looked around the room in desperation, as though she were struggling in deep water and became horribly aware she was much too far from shore to swim.

"What have you done?" she gasped and flailed her arms, trying in vain to force more air into her lungs.

"Mrs. Galston? What the hell... it's not supposed to– "

She gripped a bony hand around his wrist.

"W... what have you done?"

A viscous slime - so red it was nearly black, oozed from her mouth and ran down her chin, staining the front of her pyjamas like a nosebleed, and pooled on the bed between her legs. She reached for Davis, bony fingers extended, and grabbed the front of his shirt.

"You," she hissed through putrid, stained teeth and pulled him closer.

The fear in the old woman's eyes had vanished, replaced by an ugly rage, focused and cruel. She flexed her hands around Davis's wrist and yanked his ear to her mouth, gurgling her final words at him.

"You have broken what cannot be undone. Only at the crossroads of time will two become one."

Mrs. Galston's grip relaxed, and she fell back on the bed. He took hold of her hand nervously and, when no more images came to him, he let go of it, certain she was dead.

---

In a grey and washed-out town square, somewhere far from Winterbourne, an ancient clock tower jutted up from the middle of an abandoned building like a lone sentry on an otherwise unremarkable landscape. The building was old. The crumbling bricks and sagging walls were testaments to that, but even they had been raised around the clock tower. Nobody remembered when it had been built or who built it, but there wasn't a time when it wasn't there. It kept perfect time and never needed upkeep, so no one bothered much about it. It was nice to look at and was a reliable landmark for knowing when to got to bed and how much time you had to get a coffee before work. A lone figure sat on a bench just below the clock tower, feeding the birds that gathered at his feet.

Without warning, the clock let out an awful wail as iron scraped along steel and parts that were meant to move indefinitely came to a screaming halt. And somewhere, deep within the hollows and empty walls, something eldritch and terrible writhed and fluttered and broke free of the bonds that held it firm for longer than there had been time. It stretched and twisted, expanded and contracted and chased away the cobwebs and atrophy of eons of immobility and moved up through the floors of the derelict structure. It made a stop along the way to inhabit a white boiler suit long forgotten, soot-covered and left hanging on a hook by the front door.

*Time,* it thought and pushed its way out the front door.

## 14

The dead girl walked in the direction of the red lights. When the faces stopped peeking out from behind curtains, and the curious stopped staring at her and moved off their front stoops, Jenn was afraid for the first time since she got down here. They might not have liked her, but as long as the Necrosites were gawking at her, she wasn't alone. Cold fingers of dread poked along the back of her neck, threatening to turn her around and send her back upstairs. A song she heard on the radio before she left the office wormed its way into her head, and she whistled it, trying to keep her mind off the nervousness that was fast becoming terror.

The glow of the first lamp faded before she'd reached the pool of light coming off the next, leaving her in near-total darkness. Jenn began to whistle louder, thinking it might stop any would-be attackers from coming closer. However, she couldn't remember anybody ever being scared off by shitty whistling. She caught a blur of movement off to her right. To the left, the sound of a large chunk of metal falling to the ground followed the skittering of clawed feet moving quickly. The woman heard voices. Many voices, whispering excitedly all around. She whistled louder though her memory of the song hadn't gotten any better.

Jenn pushed on, walking quickly, whistling loudly, and trying to make it through the basement as undamaged as possible. She could tell they were moving, the whispering things, but not which direction they were going. She kept on whistling, head down, forcing herself to walk quicker. The dead girl could see the pool of light from the next emergency lamp and broke into a run. Her whistle got louder still though by now it was little more than three or four notes - flat as a board and as shrill and loud as she could blow them.

She stretched out a hand into the pool of light but yanked it back just before a stack of wooden crates dropped down in front of her. The whistle had been reduced to a single, reedy note that warbled like a bird every time she breathed in. It would have sounded awful to her if she wasn't so scared, and it seemed to be keeping the things at bay, so she kept it up.

"For God's sake, figure out the whassname tune or pick one you know!" a voice hollered from the darkness.

"Um, you'd be the Eastern Flats club... gang... thing, I take it?"

"The same."

"Great. Say, listen, I need to make my way through here to get where I need to be going and would appreciate it if you would just me get on my way."

"What, just like that?" the voice mused.

"Why the hell not? Should I say pretty please?"

A chorus of excited whispers went back and forth in the shadows, and a voice finally spoke up.

"Not possible, I'm afraid."

"Why isn't it possible?"

"Too many things to consider."

"Such as?"

"Such as, and we might remind you that you are speaking to the gang that runs this little bit of Winterbourne. We took it with blood and kept it with fear. It's ours. Nobody goes through here unless we say so. You think they call us *killers* for the fun of it?"

"You can't actually kill me. I'm already dead, so that's already off the table. And, for the record, I do live with Death. I wash underpants. Not a lot of fear of him," Jenn said.

"Oh, right, there's that."

Jenn heard movement, like many pairs of clawed feet shuffling all around her – surrounding. While it was true she couldn't die, she could still experience pain in all its bone snapping glory. More chittering bubbled up from behind her. She was feeling vulnerable and exposed, so she turned to face the direction it came from. Wasn't it better to face your fears head-on? The voice finally spoke again.

"Alright, we'll admit the threat of death is useless now, washing the underthings of the great Equalizer and all, but what about us? We let you pass, and word gets out, then folks come and go as they please. Doesn't do much to help hold on to a bit of turf, does it?" the second voice said.

"Well, I never thought of it that-"

"Then, there's the Soulreaver."

"Who?"

"The, whassname... Soulreaver, the fellow that asked us to keep you here," the first voice announced.

"Oh, well, I'll just turn around and go back then?"

"That's no good either," the second voice said.

"Wait. What? Leaving isn't stepping on anyone's turf. You haven't gone back on anything then, have you?"

"Strictly speaking, no."

"But?"

"But the Soulreaver said we shouldn't let you leave. Ever."

A deep hollow sound rumbled beneath the ground of the Eastern Flats. Like the low growl of a massive generator turning over followed by the crack of unchecked electricity. The air smelled of ozone, and the wall beside her shook. Her first instinct was to rush between two buildings like it was an earthquake, but the tremor ended as quickly as it began.

"What the hell was that?" Jenn gasped.

"Didn't you do that, some kind of whassname, witchcraft?"

"Living dead girl, not a witch."

"Interesting."

"Oh?"

"What might be even more interesting and, it's just a thought, but if you were to go over that way and sort of, whassname, investigate that noise a bit," the voice said.

"Wait. What?"

"Sure, maybe just pop off down the hallway a bit and see what you can, whassname see, kind of thing?"

"You're kidding me?"

"Not at all, and, funny enough, that awful sound seems to be coming from a door at the end of the corridor. If your map is right, I believe that is right where you need to go," the second voice explained.

"How do you know about my – hey!" Jenn shouted.

"Sorry about that. Walter has the lightest fingers of any Necrosite I've ever seen."

"I'm going to need that back."

The map seemed to fly out of the darkness, like a paper airplane that didn't float gently to the ground so much as it flopped earthward in catastrophic failure.

"Wait, door? What door?" Jenn asked.

"The door in the wall that's marked on the bottom left corner of your map."

"That isn't a tunnel?"

Raucous laughter erupted up from the shadows.

"No, darling, it's a whassname, door in the wall of the basement. Nothing more."

"Where does it lead?"

"That's a different, whassname, matter altogether, intit? Nobody ever told us what was on the other side, only it must be something very, whassname, important. Lots of folk coming down this way to make sure the door was always in order. Yes, something very important. Or..." the voice trailed off.

"Or what?"

"Or something very, whassname."

"What? Very what? I didn't get that last bit," Jen said.

"Very dangerous, something very dangerous. Cripes, I would have thought it was pretty, whassname, obvious."

"Of course, it's dangerous. How could it not be?"

"And convenient! I mean, it's right where you wanted to go. What are the chances?"

"What *are* the chances?"

The sound came again but seemed closer now. Loud, angry air, rolling and roaring like a colossal electrical storm bearing down on them. Rattling windows and teeth as it crackled its way toward them.

"So...you'll just be going along now, then?"

Look fellas – you are all fellas, aren't you?"

"Well, yeah. All of us, apart from Wanda..."

"She's gone home," the second voice interrupted. "Something about a pain somewhere or left the iron on or some such."

"Never mind that, hadn't you better just, whassname, push off?"

"As I was about to say, I'm all for getting to where I need to go, but honestly, the thought of running toward that sound doesn't sound like the smartest thing I'll ever do," Jenn said.

The sound echoed through the block of flats again, so powerfully now that Jenn would have fallen if she wasn't close enough to one of the buildings to steady herself. The snap of electricity that followed cracked so loudly she figured it had to be lightning and the static dancing around the ends of her hair said it must have hit the ground right beside her.

"Okay, killers, let's get away from here before we're all barbecued," Jenn called out.

She was answered with silence.

"Hello? Really? It's that way? A few sparks and some flyaway hair and it's tuck tail and run? A whiff of ozone and you bastards pull up stakes?

The quiet echoed in her ears, broken by the scrambling of stubby, clawed feet.

"Eastern Flats Kittens more like," Jenn laughed. "So, down this way, then?"

She hadn't walked more than a hundred feet before she saw the first one of them pushing through the opened door. It was tall - incredibly tall - and she thought it was a male, though she wasn't sure why she thought that. As she moved a little closer, it looked like gender wasn't anything that had ever occurred to it. The thing was vaguely person-shaped and wrapped in strips of filthy muslin, moving like The Mummy in unsteady, jerky steps. It carried a length of rusted chain in its hands. The other end was firmly attached to one of its ankles, jangling as it walked.

As the thing got closer to her, she could see the muslin covered it, but not like the bandages of a mummy - wrapped around a form of withered flesh and bone. The wrappings were loosely tied around a mass of roiling black liquid, frothing and seething like a pot of coffee boiling away on a stovetop. Beneath that, Jenn thought something might have been alive, occasional glimpses of muscle and flashes of stark white bone would come to the surface, but she wasn't interested in getting close enough to it to confirm her suspicions. Its head was egg-shaped, but the similarities to anything like a skull ended there. The black froth swirling in and out of the wrappings did little to contain the bright emerald eyes that moved like a chameleon's. Each moving independently in directions no human eye could.

Jenn's heart hammered behind her ribcage like only blind panic will cause, and she decided that whatever this thing was, it looked capable of doing her no end of harm. She ducked into the shadows between two tower blocks and hunkered down low until it passed her by. The oily mummy shuffled along and stopped, sniffing at the air just in front of the shadow she was squatting in. It lumbered and stumbled toward her. Jenn covered her mouth before a scream could escape. It leaned in. Sniffing at the air. Sniffing at the shadow. Sniffing at her. The woman was close enough to touch the awful thing, and now she could see it wasn't liquid as much as it was a constantly shifting and curling ethereal black skin. She pushed back farther into the darkness, and it paused a second longer before turning away.

Jenn leaned tightly against the side of one of the buildings, forgetting they were three very large wooden boxes piled on top of one another, forcing the stack to move and let out an awful chirp of under-driven nails scraping against concrete. The swirling foam of the thing's bandaged head whipped back to the shadowed alley. The roving green eyes narrowed and homed in on the spot where she crouched. Jenn's heart raced. It was so loud in her ears she thought the thing in front of her must have been able to hear it. It snorted at the air around her again but seemed no better at locating her than it was before.

When the vaporous mummy seemed satisfied the shadow was clear, it moved back into the crimson light of the basement and continued its jangly walk to the other side of the room.

"What the fuck?" Jenn gasped.

A second thing, nearly identical to the first, pushed its way through the door, jerking along in the same spastic shuffle. When it reached the first, the two of them continued their lurching walk forward and reached a spot on the floor that seemed far enough. They both stopped. Electricity crackled, and a light flashed behind the closed door. The muslin shrouded things turned to face it, remaining as still as they were able.

Jenn strained her eyes against the darkness. A figure emerged from the door - different from the other others – looking frail and taking hesitant, meandering steps, as though time was moving beside it rather than with it. This thing was smaller than the other two but no less freakish. It was gaunt, sickly looking, and no matter how it moved, the ends of bones contorted and stretched its hide into unnatural angles. The skin hung off it like a shirt that didn't fit and was sallow and waxy grey. The basement of Winterbourne was always on the cool side. Still, the thing was bathed in a thin film of sweat. It wore a burlap covering from its neck to the tops of its thighs that might have been a livestock feed bag with holes cut into it. The thing's head looked unnaturally stretched and was sparsely covered by strands of greasy red hair. A toothless gap of a mouth – looking more like a wound in the head - perched above a whisper of a chin and below a nose that wasn't much more than two hopeful holes stabbed into the grey skin.

The redhead's eyes glared at Jenn through the darkness. Yellow watery things covered by the narrowest flaps of eyelids. They were tired eyes. They were angry eyes that had seen the rise of mankind and hated all of them. Eyes that had seen and done everything asked of them without question. And now they narrowed on the dead girl in front of them and saw a means to victory.

# 15

―――――――

"What are you doing here?" the nurse asked.

"I work here," Davis answered.

"But aren't you like the boss or something? You'd think you'd steer clear of nights now that you don't *have* to do it."

"I like the night shift, it's quiet, and it's easier to keep out of everybody's way."

"All the weird shit happens on nights. It's dark, and it's cold - creeps me out."

Davis shot her a surprised look, and she glowed with embarrassment.

"Sorry," she blushed.

"You're right. The weird shit does happen on nights," he laughed.

Something was different. It felt...off. He couldn't put his finger on what it was, but Davis had a feeling something was about to happen, and once it had, none of them would ever be the same again.

"When's the last time you saw Jenn?"

"Who?"

"Never mind," he said, forgetting Jenn Henderson could only be seen by the dead, they dying and the Necrosites. Davis, despite being dead himself, could be seen by anybody he wanted to. It made running the place easier. He'd go talk to Clarence. The man almost never slept at night and, like most of the residents of Winterbourne, could see Jenn as clear as daylight.

"I always found it was best to try and keep your mind occupied, reading or keeping a journal or something. It helps you forget how weird it can get around here at night," Davis suggested.

"I'll try to remember that," the nurse said.

"It's really cold in here. Aren't you cold?" he asked, but the nurse had wandered off.

He slipped out of the nurse's office and felt the cold air rip up through his feet, chilling every part of him. It felt familiar like he'd never really known warmth. Like he'd been teased with heat his whole life, only to have it pulled away when it began to feel good. After a few steps, Davis thought there'd never been anything but cold in the world. There had never been heat, or safety, or love. The sharp chill of the frost was all he had known and all he ever would.

Davis turned back to the nurse's station. There was usually an old sweater or blanket hanging in there he could wrap around himself to stop the cold from biting against his arms. He headed past the desk and into the back when he noticed the clock above the door. It wasn't moving.

*Dead battery?*

It wasn't unusual in this place. In fact, it was appreciated - by the residents anyway. Taking the batteries out of a clock was done a lot around the lockdown ward. It gave them a bit of hope. It was a constant they could come to rely on in a world - a mind coming apart at the seams. They might not have a clue what to do with a toothbrush when it was given to them, but out there, right by the nurse's station, the centre of activity, it was always 9:30 am, and that was alright. They still had the whole day to look forward to.

Davis walked out of the nurse's station, heading down the west hallway toward Clarence's room. He clapped his hands against his shoulders, trying to drive away the cold prickling all over his skin. He picked up his pace, nearly jogging, and his breath hung in the air like clouds. When he rounded the corner, he ran into Clarence, practically tripping over him. The old man was parked outside his room wearing only thin cotton pyjama bottoms and a V-neck undershirt. He was amazed Clarence wasn't shivering the bolts loose on his wheelchair. Stepping closer, Davis could see why.

"Aww shit, Clarence, not yet."

Clarence Mallory sat stiffly in his wheelchair. The old man's eyes were open wide. His mouth hung open, and his skin the awful blue-grey colour of sub-zero temperatures and too few clothes. Occasionally someone's number came up, and they slipped peacefully away, needing no ushering along from either the Necrosites or Davis. All that remained after was for him to free them from their body, take their hands, and lead them to the waiting room to make sure they took their place in line.

He reached out and took hold of the old man's icy hand. A flash hit him with the force of a dump truck. It was as though Clarence's life were moving in slow motion, like the third reel of a movie going at half speed through a worn-out projector, dull and crackling, full of pops and stops and blank spaces where the film had worn thin. He let go of the frozen hand and stepped away from the wheelchair, and turned toward the old man's room. The door handle had been frozen over in a solid chunk of ice. Davis had no idea why the world had suddenly become an icebox and where he was supposed to go now that he was in it but was sure it wasn't in this room. A thought struck him, and he headed back to the nurse's station and around the opposite corner, heading for room 107.

The door was closed - he expected it would be. The lights in the east hallway had been dimmed, but the entire circumference of the door glowed bright enough for Davis to see a few feet in either direction. It was bright amber and danced and flashed around the door frame like a warning light along the side of the road. Davis sighed. Swirling lights, no matter how spooky or mind-bendingly weird, weren't enough to scare him. Not anymore. Residents were a different matter. A lot of them looked normal on the outside, quiet and mild and peaceful, but they were vicious brutes on the inside whose personalities turned on a dime. He felt guilty for it, but they never failed to scare the shit out of him. There were days when Minnie Martin decided she wasn't going to do anything but try to claw the eyes out of anyone that came within three feet of her. Or Louise Keifer, a woman nearly always drenched in her own blood – the result of the overwhelming need to constantly dig and pick at any exposed skin. Strange lights? Shit, they didn't even rate anymore. Without a second's hesitation, he opened the door and stepped inside room 107.

The room was surprisingly dark for the amount of light beaming from the edges of the door. It was a mess in here but not any worse than the other rooms on the ward. A bed in the centre, headboard pushed up against the far wall, with a bedside table and a dresser. An anonymous desk lamp sat on top of the bedside table. Plain white blinds hung over the window, and a set of three white towels lay on top of the four-drawer dresser. The thing that stuck out most was the temperature. It wasn't the uncomfortably warm most of them kept their rooms and still wore thick sweaters - and complained about the cold. It was hot and wet. Like sitting in a Turkish bath in the middle of July. As though all the heat for the entire floor had been balled up inside a wet carpet and thrown into room 107.

The water hung heavy in the air, like walking into a sweaty armpit. Davis felt perspiration bead up and streak down, pooling up and soaking through his clothing. He stepped into the empty room and, to his surprise, heard the toilet.

*Foosh.*

He couldn't be sure, but he thought after the toilet flushed, he heard a round of applause and the sound of cheering.

Davis turned in the direction of the bathroom and stepped slowly forward. The pale light from beneath the door ahead of him lit a path to the closed door.

*Foosh.*

The sound of flowing water ceased and immediately resumed as the toilet flushed again. He reached for the doorknob and was surprised to find that his hand trembled as it moved to the door. Not that he was afraid. At least not afraid of whatever was behind the door, he *was* Death after all, and all things bowed to him - eventually anyway. However, he got an overwhelming sense something was off, and the reason for it was behind the bathroom door and, Death or not, if he didn't deal with it soon, he was dead meat.

*Foosh.*

"Marvelous, just bloody marvelous!" the voice crowed.

Davis's head snapped in the direction of the sound and moved toward the light piercing the darkness of room 107. It dawned on him that the owner of the voice behind the door was probably one of the residents of this ward, mind altered by dementia and obsessed with flushing. Odd, yes, but not uncommon around here. The handle of the bathroom door was moist, and the thought of how it got that way nauseated him to even touch it.

*Foosh.*

"Oh... oh dear. I don't think that was meant to happen," the voice behind the door said.

The sound of the toilet flushing crashed out again, and moments later, he found himself standing downstream from the torrent of water that poured out beneath the door.

"Sonofabitch!" Davis spat.

He may have been hesitant to meet whoever was on the other side of the door a few minutes ago, but he'd be damned if he was just going to let some maniac flood the ward by plugging the God-damned toilets.

He opened the door and barked at its occupants, "You're going to flood the goddam ward!"

Davis stopped short of entering the bathroom when he caught sight of them. Two beings stood just beyond the doorway as though they were guarding the third one. They were tall and broad and seemed as though they would have been quite muscular if their bodies hadn't been covered in thick strips of dirt-stained cloth, wrapped loosely around swirling oily black liquid. As he tried to move past, they stepped shoulder to shoulder to block him.

"You'd be Mareth?" the voice said.

And in an example of a cataclysmically bad decision – one that truly stood out in a lifetime of bad choices - Davis Mareth answered.

"Yes."

The two wispy goons stood aside and revealed a sweaty, red-headed thing in a burlap smock. She stepped forward, and what Davis saw reminded him of an amphibian. As if a frog or salamander had willed itself into human form.

"You are Davis Mareth, late of the night shift of Winterbourne Home for the aged? Now Grim Reaper and representative of His Honour, Thanatos, the True and Everlasting Void, are you not?"

"Um... yes?" Davis said.

The redheaded thing turned away and fumbled under the burlap sack. She turned back and unfolded a large piece of paper. Davis shuddered to think where she held the paper under the burlap and hoped she didn't expect him to keep it.

"Davis Mareth, you are hereby ordered to accompany me forthwith to answer the charges of which you have been accused," she said.

"Charges, what charges?"

"That you did knowingly hasten the extrication from this life of one Margaret Rosemary Galston, in violation of the Moribund Act of 1653."

"Early - who would go early? People want more time, not less."

"Nevertheless, this Galston woman departed considerably earlier than scheduled, which is forbidden by the same said act."

"This is ridiculous. I haven't sent anyone early. How could I?"

"I am no detective, Mr. Mareth. The details are inconsequential. I do, however, have this bit of paper that says I am to bring you before the courts as quickly as possible. Now, if you would just come along, please," the thing in the burlap dress gurgled.

One of the swirling oil-slick things clapped a bandaged hand on Davis' shoulder, and he felt his knees give a little under the force of it. It turned him around, so they stood face to face, never taking his hand off him. And Death became certain, feeling the pressure on his shoulder, that the gaseous thing was only waiting for an opportunity to flatten him like an empty beer can.

"Go with you? I'm not going anywhere with you," Davis said.

"Oh dearie, dearie me," the redhead sighed.

He felt the weight on his shoulder increase to impossible proportions, and his knees buckled, sending him to the floor.

"Mr. Mareth, let's not make this any messier than it needs to be. I was given a summons and instructed to bring you back by any means necessary. My two companions would absolutely love it if any means *were* necessary if you catch my meaning. But I can promise you it would be the least agreeable option for you."

The cloth-bound man hoisted Davis up and shook him like a doll being throttled by an angry child. It went on, and on and he felt light-headed and scared. He was at the mercy of these awful things - visions of being held upside down and dunked into the toilet while the three of them cheered splashed across his mind.

"Enough!" the newt thing in the dress bellowed. The oily mummy ceased his assault.

It let go and stood alongside him, nudging and poking at Davis as a reminder he was still there, waiting for the word.

"Wait, what? Instructed by who?" Davis demanded. "By whose authority are you forcing me to come with you?"

"By the authority of The Night Court," she answered.

"The Night Court? He whispered. "Shit."

Davis had heard of the Night Court before, and at first, he didn't believe it. It was a bogey man - something Jenn would scare him with to get him to do what she wanted. 'Take out the trash, or the Night Court will get you.' He didn't believe any of it until he sat in the waiting room with the Death, who looked like Bob Newhart. Bob told the new Death everything he knew about being the Grim Reaper before he departed the big office. Because Death – as an entity - wasn't an absolute but an appointed position and answers to a higher authority. Otherwise, what would stop someone from putting on the robe, grabbing the scythe, and start stomping around the terra firm a lopping souls off at the knees? Davis always assumed the Omega – the Angel of Death himself– was that authority. He isn't. That authority was the Night Court.

A body that represented the absolute control of all matters concerning the afterlife. The court's justice was swift and cold-blooded. Three immortal judges and twelve selected jurors sat in judgement of all things ethereal. Though as a rule, people avoided jury duty on The Night Court like the plague.

The three presiding justices weren't particularly fair. Nor were they particularly concerned that they weren't fair. They took bribes, looked the other way, and handed down the harshest of sentences for anyone who ran afoul of any one of the obscene number of rules contained within the Codex. The mention of their names caused paranoia and fear to ripple through a room like a football bouncing through a minefield. The judges knew it. Worse still, they liked it.

If your paperwork was late, it might garner a small fine. Payable to the clerk of the court who, as fate would have it, was also the most dishonest and best-dressed member of the passing on the process. Leaving a person trapped in a body that had passed on too long might get you temporary, in-house incarceration, but to alter someone's time? Bob Newhart told Davis that going off the clock was the absolute worst thing a Death could do. The Omega himself would stand before the Night Court if he were stupid enough to screw with a timeline. Altering times messed with the backlog. And worse, it messed with the fabric the universe is based on. We all have a beginning, so we must all have an end, and both times are predetermined and set long before someone is born.

"Has anyone ever tried it? Tried to cheat the times?" Davis asked Newhart.

"Once, I think. I heard a story that a Death a very long time ago tried to beat the big clock," Bob Newhart said.

"And?"

"And if you would be so good as to put these on," the red-haired salamander.

She handed him a pair of thick iron cuffs bound together with a heavy chain and sighed impatiently, waiting for him to put the damned things on and just start doing as he was told.

"And if I don't?" Davis asked defiantly.

The sweaty waif snapped her fingers, and the liquid goon moved on the young man. Davis could see the deep-set green eyes emerging and fading and emerging again beneath the swirling black froth and circlets of dingy cloth that made up its face. He thought he could see a trace of a smile playing across the grimy cloth before he felt the crush of the thing's arm slowly piercing through his chest, dropping him like a stone.

"We do that, and you come with us anyway," the redhead smiled.

# 16

I t was cold and damp. Cold enough that he would've seen his breath hanging in the air if he could see anything. The cold bit at him. It kept him down and forced him into a ball, trying to keep it at bay. He knew that staying here wouldn't help him. Davis sat up, trying to get his bearings, and felt an angry mule kick against the back of his brain like only too many hours in front of the bar at Butler's could do.

"Jenn?" he called out quietly, and his head thundered back with a withering reply.

*Jesus, I couldn't have had that much. I came home after the dog and I...*

Davis searched for an answer to why his head currently felt so bad and came up empty. He closed his eyes and prayed that sleep would take him again, hoping that the bad dream he was in the middle of would end.

"Jenn," he pushed out a whisper that was as close to screaming as a whisper could get.

Davis opened his eyes and struggled to focus them in the darkness. He sat up and tried to make sense of his surroundings.

There had always been a faint smell of must in their bedroom, though he could never find where it came from. They had just learned to live with the smell – it wasn't like mould in the walls was going to hurt either one of them.

But here, the dankness hung heavy in the air like fog. It felt venomous with each breath, so much that if breathing weren't still vital to his survival, he would have stopped doing it ten minutes ago. Staying put in the must-filled darkness didn't appeal to him at all, and Davis stood, arms outstretched, taking the tiniest of steps to explore his surroundings.

Davis made it to a wall in front of him and felt his way along. Moving slowly, feet side-stepping, hands flat against the stone wall, moving to the left and away from the safety of where he'd awoken. The stones were cold. And slime-covered. They made him a little queasy to touch but followed along with them until he felt an intersecting wall and kept moving to his left - coming full circle might give him some indication of just how big this room was.

In no time, Davis made it around the room as he felt the cold steel of a bed frame against his leg. His hands continued to explore and grabbed a wall sconce with a bulb sticking in the top of it. He gave the bulb a twist, and it crackled and hissed, sending little blue sparks dancing into the darkness as the lamp continued to flicker on and off like a dying neon sign. The light cast the place in a pulsing grey-green glow, and Davis could finally see it was a small room. Three or four feet wide by five or six feet long, smaller than he imagined it to be in the dark. By the look of the place. He was sure he wasn't in Winterbourne home anymore.

There was nothing in the room except two bunks at the back of it. To the right of the bunks stood a thick wooden door with a small, barred window in the centre of it. He stepped toward the window, and his legs wobbled like he was walking on an old mattress. The strobing light didn't do much to help his cause beyond threatening to bring the contents of his stomach to the surface.

For a moment, he squeezed the bars in the centre of the door and let himself go loose, hanging as limp as a jellied eel. Davis stared at a dark knot in the middle of the wooden door that provided enough of a distraction for his brain while nausea faded. He felt it was all well and good to hang there and forget everything, but he knew that someone would be coming along to remind him of exactly what it was he was expected to do. Someone always did, usually forcibly. Davis tightened his hold of the bars on the small window and pulled himself upward.

A lone figure stood in the distance - too far away for Davis to see anything, apart from it being vaguely humanoid. Davis thought about calling out to it but reconsidered when he remembered the way he ended up here. A sound erupted behind him like someone sputtering and choking on the liquid being forced into its mouth. He stumbled back in the direction of the bunks, tripping and bopping off the walls. As he stretched out a hand to guide himself to the bottom bunk, a pair of legs hung down that hadn't been there before.

It was human in shape - in that it had two arms and two legs and a head at the top of its torso - but the similarity ended there. The arms and legs both were spindly, branch-like things that ended in twigs of fingers and toes that looked far too long to be functional. The head was an amorphous blob of a thing that nearly hovered above a delicate neck. It had a mouth or rather mouths one on top of another that opened and closed, independently. Davis thought they looked like a dying fish, trying to get enough air into lungs that were starved for oxygen. It had skin - completely translucent - but gave the impression of worn leather. The creature's veins, arteries, and multi-coloured organs were entirely visible to the naked eye.

Davis could see a vicious-looking fluid, presumably the thing's blood, coursing along underneath the skin upward with each raspy breath it took. Travelling around the feet and pushing steadily upward to the chest. And that's where it ended; at least it was where the path ended. A horrible, jagged wound straight across the thin neck leaked fluid, so blue it was nearly purple, soaking the bunk it lay on. He clamped his hands over the awful gash, but the bruise-coloured liquid poured out too quickly for him to stop, and there was just so much of it to be anything but a fatal wound.

The thing turned its head to him and opened its eyes—first one set, then another, and finally the third. Six small eyes, all staring up at the man while its throat gurgled and sputtered and gasped, trying to keep from drowning in its own fluids. All six eyes, pleading with the young man to do something - anything to stop this from going any further. Davis relaxed his hold on the gushing wound and felt the tears well up in his eyes.

"What do you want me to do? Tell me what you want me to do. Do you want me to help you, or do you want me to - *help you?*"

The three mouths opened and closed in unison, maybe forming words in silence, maybe trying to get enough air past the ugly gash in its neck to keep going a while longer. For all the confusion around its mouths, there was little doubt what the eyes wanted. They were tired. Tired of fighting against inevitability. Exhausted from stopping circumstance from running roughshod over what remained of its life, when all it wanted was to close all six eyes and sleep.

For the first time since he had taken the Robe and the Scythe, Davis was at a loss. He had never ushered anything out of this life but a human and, though the thing was clearly dying, he wasn't sure anything he did would help its suffering. Davis stretched out a trembling hand and took hold of one of the things spindly extremities and found it wrapping around his hand, spreading warmth through him.

There was no flash, no startling interruption of consciousness that brought on jarring visions of this thing's life. There were sounds, interspersed with snippets of voices reaching out through white noise. A few actual words and bursts of soft white lights came through his mind like an old television with a picture tube about to give up the ghost. Flashes of half images and random sounds with nothing he could make sense of, apart from a massive clock in the centre of hundreds of crumbling buildings.

The small eyes looked up at Davis, and he placed two fingers on what he guessed was the thing's temple, moving them from one side to the other, pushing bits of gooey flesh along with them. The expression seemed to soften a little. It lifted a scrawny finger and ran it straight down Davis' face, from the top of his forehead to the bottom of his chin. And in no more time than that, the colour beneath its clear skin faded, and it was gone.

A klaxon screeched just outside the thick wooden door, and Davis pushed his face into the barred window as tightly as he could, hoping it would give him a better view out of the cell. Spotlights flared into life, blinding him and forcing him to back away from the opening. He crouched behind the door to escape the pain of the light coming in at him. The bolt-on the door let out a rusted squeal and creaked open, bumping into him as he hunkered down behind it. Without warning, the door slammed closed behind a figure large enough to block out the light from the hallway. As Davis's eyes became readjusted to the lower light, he could see that it was massive. He supposed if the dark figure wanted to, it would have been completely able to block out the sun.

Its arms were thick and chiselled logs with fingers that looked capable of pulling off one of his own arms and beating him without breathing heavily afterward. Its chest was muscled and broad and conveniently disguised beneath an abundant layer of purulent grey skin that jiggled wildly with each step it took. The head was large and bulbous and bald, and it was covered with a thick layer of greasy sweat that seemed to flow down across its face from a tap somewhere near the back of its skull. It likely had a nose once, but it had long since been burned away, leaving little more than a blackened hole in the centre of its face, directly above two milky, narrow set eyes. It stood on two thick legs wrapped in a knee-length leather kilt and ending in broad feet covered by thick black leather boots.

The thing was the same colour and appearance as the redhead he encountered back in room 107, though a much larger, brutish version. He also noticed it carried a thick cudgel, whose business end was a head that resembled its own with a gruesome, hooked steel spike where its nose should be. Davis wondered if it was a likeness of how the thing once looked before its nose had been sizzled off. He shuddered to think how vicious or strong something would have to be to burn away the nose of the gargantuan thing in front of him.

The brute stared him down, eyes narrowing and moved its face in close to his. As it straightened to its full height, towering over the man, the thing caught sight of the corpse in the top bunk. He sniffed the air and laid his free hand on top of the bloody form on the bed. With a sudden jerk, he pulled back his hand and turned to Davis. The ugly club rose, the blackened face mere inches away from Davis' own. Close enough that he could see the awful dark stains and smell the sweet stench of blood all over the head of it. The thing raised the club, lowered it, and raised it to eye level again and again and again, sticking it in Mareth's face. With the other massive hand, it grabbed hold of his neck to prevent him from escaping or even looking away as it jammed the club into his face.

To Davis' relief, the thing lowered the club, dropped it to the ground, and wrapped a second meaty hand around his neck, and hauled him up to the top bunk. The thing pushed him close enough to the lifeless body that Davis felt a little of his cellmate's blood smear across the bridge of his nose before the grey brute lowered him down again.

"It doesn't do such things, or it gets to meet Mrs. Hardmeat," it said in a nasal whine of a voice.

"Wait, what?"

The grey wall of a thing picked up the ugly club and stared at it before moving its gaze to Davis. It looked at the club and Davis' face again, back and forth between the two until it reached a solution. Mrs. Hardmeat hit the floor in favour of raising a ham-sized fist and lowering the boom in the middle of Death's forehead. Mareth felt the impact - for a moment anyway. His ears began to ring, and the awful metallic taste of his own blood filled his mouth. In seconds, the lights blinked out in his head, and everything went quiet.

When his eyes opened again, the light poured in on them so

brightly he was forced to raise a hand to shield them while they adjusted. He wasn't in the cell anymore, that much he knew, and he wasn't alone, though there were no signs of the no-nose bastard or Mrs. Hardmeat. Davis was in a room that reminded him of a bowling alley. Long, narrow, and covered in hardwood and earth tones. It even smelled of old dirty leather and older, dirtier feet. People and people-like things were spread out over the benches that lined both walls. The room stretched on, ending in huge double doors that looked a hundred feet away. He had reservations about sitting next to anyone or anything down here. His wasn't the only waiting room, and humans weren't the only things destined for the afterlife. News of his appointment as Death would have spread quickly, and it was not a popular position to be in at the best of times. Nobody likes Death.

Death is reviled by most, welcomed by a few, but loved by almost none. Death showed up at the most inopportune times - like having a splash in the ocean on the vacation you saved all year to have, only to end up a hot lunch for a large boneless fish. Or finally making past drunken fumbling and on to more serious pursuits with the lover you've been chasing all your adult life only to be felled by a heart condition you inherited through shitty bloodlines. And, though Davis' own corner of the void was a mostly, pleasant end to mostly pleasant lives - *he was Death.* There is no quicker way for a belter of a party to turn sour than to have the Grim Reaper show up and start pointing fingers around, making everyone nervous. It was a lonely life, and suddenly he felt a terrible longing for Jenn. Of all the people he'd encountered, she alone knew what he went through day after day and shared the experience with him more than anyone could. Whatever anger he had before, was gone and now he just wanted to be beside her. Even if she wasn't speaking to him.

The double doors swung open, and another grey thing, just as large and paunchy and as Mrs. Hardmeat's escort, emerged and stomped into the room. It paused briefly to flip through a large stack of paper bound to a clipboard and move its milky eyes around the room, scanning the bodies flopped out on the benches. The figures sunk further into the pews and lowered their gazes to avoid his eyes. Davis, not knowing any better, stared directly at him.

"Mareth!" the bailiff called out.

Davis looked around, wondering what the odds were of a second person called Mareth being down here with him.

"Mareth. Davis, fucking Mareth!" the thing called out again.

Davis raised his hand reluctantly.

"You're up."

"Up? Up for what?"

"Your case is up. Time to stand in front of the judges and try to explain why you shouldn't just be executed. Bloody Deaths think you can do as you please."

"Wait, what?"

"You're all the same. Think you can go around popping away lives like flicking the heads off dandelions without a minute's thought about the consequences. Honestly," he sighed.

He held one of the huge oak doors open and ushered Davis inside before stepping in himself and closing the door behind them. He led the man to a small box in the centre of the big room, locked him inside it and stepped away into the shadows. It was cramped in here, and the plank walls reached just above Davis' waist. If not for the cage covering the top of it, he would have just jumped the wall and left. Locked door or not.

The room was massive. Centred along the back wall was a towering desk as tall and wide as it was pretentious and intimidating. Hand-carved images of frightening, ugly things warring with magnificent men and women with delicate wings. All of them, angels and demons alike, brandishing swords and spears and leaping at each other with murder in mind. In the middle of the desk, looking down in judgement at all the things fighting beneath, a carving of Thanatos, the small, black-winged boy who was the true Death. Davis met him briefly five years earlier in the closet of room 107. He thought of him as an angelic little boy with a sweet disposition, but this carving made him look like a spoiled child in the middle of a tantrum because he was tired and his toys weren't playing the way he wanted them to.

Behind the desk sat three towering chairs of polished, black granite. Davis assumed this must be the judge's bench, and the caged box he was in was the prisoner's dock. He couldn't imagine anything tall enough to sit in the chairs behind this bench, let alone three of them. Above the chairs hung a sign of wrought iron that stretched nearly the length of the bench, which read, 'ODERINT DUM METUANT.'

The bench eclipsed everything else in the room. It was clearly meant to intimidate anyone who stood in front of it. The effect wasn't lost on Davis. He felt like a hyperactive kid standing in front of the teacher's desk. Something awful was coming and, no matter how hard he closed his eyes, he knew he'd have to face it. A door creaked, and the desk was suddenly bathed in white light. Three figures walked silently to the granite chairs. The judges. They were tall, though the word itself didn't do enough to sum up their colossal size. Two of them were clad in black robes, while the third wore a heavy scarlet robe trimmed in snow-white fur.

The first moved slowly, nearly creeping along, and took a seat behind the bench. A small sign in front of him read, Judge M. Leonard. His head was vaguely human in shape - in that it was oval and proportionate to the rest of his body. Still, it sat above a reedy neck that swayed slightly under the weight of the head, as if being blown by a gale-force breeze that only it could feel. In the middle of his face, between tiny narrow eyes, was his nose. It was straight, long and thin and flared out at the end, like the trunk of an elephant. Davis thought it looked more like a flesh-covered bugle than a nose.

The second black-robed judge loped to his chair and sat down behind the nameplate that read, Judge M Arthur. He was shorter than Judge Leonard but still freakishly tall. His face was skeletal and covered with gangrenous, black skin that seemed ready to slough off his face like the peel of a rotten orange. His nose was a twisted collection of flesh that gripped the middle of his face and looked like it should have fallen away years ago. There were no eyes - none that Davis could see anyway. Instead, on top of his head, three undulating appendages waved like cobras in front of a snake charmer. Moving slowly back and forth and turning, taking stock of everything that surrounded them.

The last of the three eased his way into place, like a wisp of fog seeping across an open field and moved behind his nameplate. The Rt. Hon Justice M Julius. He stood for a moment and gazed around the courtroom, eyeing everyone assembled with complete indifference. His head wasn't human, not even in the broadest terms. It seemed to be living independently of the rest of the body. The flesh that covered it was rancid like a roast beef left in the sun, greying and lifeless. The nose was very much alive, twitching and smelling a thousand things only it could detect. The eyes, expressionless and black, scanned the room, scrutinizing everything they took in. Finally, he sat, adjusted a mountain of papers on the desk in front of him, and sighed the words he had spoken thousands of times before,

"Who has business with this court?"

"Um, I do," Davis said quietly.

"Davis Mareth, you stand before us, accused of the most serious of offences, altering the timeline of a soul and shifting the balance in the process. Are you aware of the penalty for such a thing?"

"Well, no," Davis said.

"It is swift and immediate... hang on. Why are you speaking?"

"You asked a question, I answered."

"No," Judge Leonard asked. "The court doesn't mean why are you speaking. I mean, why are *you* speaking. Where is your solicitor?"

"I haven't got one."

"This is highly irregular," Judge Arthur sighed.

Judge Leonard motioned to the big grey bailiff. "You there, go and find this man's solicitor."

"Yes, M'lord."

He disappeared through the double doors and re-emerged shortly after, followed closely by a nervous-looking Necrosite in a black wool suit.

"Eustace Codswallop for the defence, M'lord," he said.

"Highly irregular," Judge Arthur said.

"How does your client plead?" Justice Julius demanded.

"If I might have a moment to confer with my client, M'lord, I've been running behind all day and haven't had time to properly depose this witness with a habemus corpuscle and whatnot," Eustace said.

"The court will allow a brief parlance."

Codswallop plonked an overstuffed briefcase on the small table provided for the defence and scraped a chair alongside the box. He struggled to stand on the chair, and, after several failed attempts and near misses, he eventually found himself face to face with Davis Mareth.

"Eustace Codswallop, solicitor and attorney at law," he said, sticking out a gangly, limp hand.

"So, I gathered. I don't recall hiring a lawyer."

"You didn't."

"Then how did–"

"I work in the legal department. Barry Wilson is my cousin, and when he heard about your situation, he thought I might be of some use to you. He suggested I go along to help you out. So, here I am,"

"Barry Wilson? From the mailroom? How does Barry Wilson from the mailroom know anything about anything but sorting and delivering memos on company letterhead?" Davis asked in disbelief.

"Oh, he knows, they all know. It's the talk of Winterbourne, I'm afraid."

"How does your client plead?" Justice Arthur asked again.

Eustace began to dig through the mountainous bloom of crumpled papers at the top of his briefcase, giving each one its due and then placing it on the table.

"Mr. Codswallop, how does your client plead?" Justice Julius demanded.

The Necrosite held up a solitary finger as though to hush the judge.

"This is highly irregular!" Judge Arthur screeched.

"Should I speak now?" Davis whispered to Eustace

"What, speak at your own trial? Of course not."

"Wait, what?"

"Shhh," Eustace said.

"Mr. Codswallop!" Justice Julius bellowed.

The other two judges gasped and quickly stood along with him.

The Necrosite continued to dig through his briefcase like someone thumbing through a shoebox full of love letters. Codswallop pulled a wrinkled sheet from the bottom of the briefcase. It stood before the three judges, a broad, satisfied smile eking its way across his lips, exposing nasty yellowed teeth.

"M'lord, my client pleads guilty to all charges and hereby throws himself on the mercy of the court and its respected and venerated judiciary."

"What?" Davis screamed.

# 17

"Can you all just come out, please?" Jenn called out and heard her words echo off the silent buildings.

"What, come out there, with you and all them, Whassnames?" the voice asked, trailing off and bouncing from the walls and windows of the tower blocks

"Yes," Jenn said. "It's customary to speak face to face when one hopes to have a mutually agreeable parlance."

"You've met a lot of them, then?"

"A lot of what?"

"A lot of, whassname, least polite societies?"

"Well, I've met some in my time."

"Cos, I reckon there aren't too many lower than us," he said gleefully. A chorus of raucous laughter bubbled up around his voice, moving along through the air like a wave and finally reaching its apex and surrounding Jenn like a hug.

"Look, if we're going to help each other out of this mess, shouldn't we do it face to face?"

"You what?"

"Help each other, all of you and all of... well... me," Jenn said.

"Oh, hang on a tic."

Jenn heard voices, many of them. Whispering excitedly and, as soon as they began, they ceased completely and left a deafening silence in their wake.

"Whattayer mean help each other? We're not in any trouble. You are. On the other hand, you look like you'd do just about anything to keep your whassname out the fire."

"I will. I will do anything. But if anything happens to me, you are all finished. I am the only thing standing between you all and Davis, pulling the whole place down around your ears. No more tower blocks, no more neighbourhoods. No more neighbourhoods mean no more neighbours to squeeze for money and food. Not much of a gang if you there aren't frightened old ladies telling everyone how fierce you are."

"Hah, shows what you know. Your man's gone, nothing he can whassname do to scare us anymore."

"Wait, what? What do you mean, my man is gone?"

She heard a chittering of nervous voices

"So here is how it is going to go. You are going to come out here, all of you, and talk to me right now," Jenn said.

"Or what?" the voice asked, the snottiness dripping from every syllable.

Jenn wracked her brain to come up with a reason - any reason that they could be made to do as she wanted when they, clearly, held all the cards.

*I could beg, hope that they took pity on me and came out to tend to my sadness.*

They were a gang of Necrosites and a notorious one at that. The living dead girl didn't imagine that pity or compassion ranked high on their list of necessary skills.

*I could threaten them.*

She pictured herself turning over the packing crates, kicking and smashing the fragile bits of junkyard furnishings that filled the insides of the big wooden boxes. Then she caught herself imagining

Mrs. Pugwash standing in front of her, crestfallen, and asking how she could have done something so awful. Jenn decided thug was not a hat she was willing to wear any more than a pitiable creature was. And at the bottom of a bucket full of doubt and self-pity, something occurred to her. She was certain the killers ruled their roost by fear like any successful gang did - like a bully would. And the best way to beat a bully was to be bigger, scarier than he was. Or a dog, a large, nasty dog, always works well for a peaceful, harrier-free walk down the street.

"Do you who my man is?" Jenn asked and clicked a leash on a foul-tempered Doberman pinscher.

"He serves the Whassname, the little man with the wings."

"That's right," Jenn cooed. "Do you know why I am with him, why he chose me to be by his side above anyone else?"

"No. Actually, we were all sort of wondering about that."

"I am dead," Jenn said forcefully enough that it felt as though the words hung heavy in the air after they left her lips.

"Yes?"

"Yes."

"No, I meant yes, as in is that all? Being dead isn't all that, whassname, impressive. Not down here anyway."

"No, it isn't, but speaking to other dead people and things? That's impressive. Especially when I call them to me to do my bidding," Jenn hissed.

"Oh yeah, like what?"

"Run roughshod over this place and take you and the rest of your gang to the other side with them, permanently."

"Pfft, do your worst. Nobody can do that, not even the little man himself."

Jenn lowered to her knees and sat back on her heels, placing her hands on her lap, palms up, and closed her eyes. She hummed as loudly and wildly as she was able. She swayed back and forth and waved her hands side to side and then wildly above her head, beckoning the heavens as best as possible.

"What's *are* you doing?"

Jenn continued humming and swaying, unabated.

"Is this meant to, whassname, scare us?"

"What if she can?" the second voice wondered.

"What?"

"What if she can really call the dead ones? That'd be us finished."

"Yeah, it would."

"Or would it?" a third voice asked.

"Huh?" the first voice puzzled.

"If we were to get her on our side, and she could really do that, really call on the dead folk and such, there could be some serious changes around here."

"We could finally get the West Side lot gone for good," the second voice volunteered.

"Bigger. The Soulreaver would have to listen to us from now on."

"Wait, woman, stop. We're coming out!"

## 18

Frank Page stumbled through the door of Butler's and into the electric glare of Parker Street. He pressed a grubby hand into a grubby pocket, fumbling for the cigarette lighter and succeeded in pulling out most of the contents along with it.

"Shit," he said, slurred and bent to pick up his change. He managed to get his fingers around thirty-five cents before the sidewalk rushed up to meet him. Frank lay there for a minute, giggling and remarking on his own stupidity at having fallen in the first place. His mind drifted back to Butler's and the cute bartender and on to Ginny and what he'd do to her when he got home. Then it switched gears, and he found himself thinking of his father. There was little doubt what the old man would have to say to him if he could see him now.

*Look at you boy, fall-down drunk – again. You'll never be nothing. A waste of Goddam skin, that's what you are. A good-paying job, security, and a future? And you piss it all away sitting behind that goddam bar every night.*

"I ain't in there every night," Frank protested.

*Oh, not every night? That's right, Butler's is closed on Sundays, right?*

"That's not fair!"

*What's not fair is the way you let that goddam whore of a woman of yours act. Walking around with her airs and goddam honours. She needs to be put in her place and no mistake.*

"Wait, what?"

*That last time she got uppity, she wore sunglasses to the supermarket for a week and still didn't learn. Get your house in order, boy. You gotta get right in there, get in between them thick ears of hers and teach her right. She'll only come around if you show her a firm hand.*

"Right, a firm hand," Frank hiccupped.

He lay on his back and rubbed his knuckles into his eyes so forcefully it felt like they might push through to the back of his skull and out the other side. Trying to will himself to sober up enough to get home and do what needed to be done, he rolled off his back to hands and knees and pushed himself up slowly. The glint of the street lights on the remainder of his change sprawled along the pavement caught his eye, and he thought about trying to retrieve it but, the idea of spending another ten minutes laid out on the ground was nearly as appealing as washing his scrotum with 40 grit sandpaper.

"Some fucker's lucky day," Frank said and stood in the glare of the streetlight, swaying like he was a ship in high seas. He managed to spark a cigarette to life between the waves and set off up the street, pinballing off buildings as he went.

Page made it two-thirds of the way to their rented house before invisible hands began to squeeze his straining bladder, reminding him just how much liquor he'd sloshed down his neck.

"One more," Frank laughed and began looking for an alleyway.

It was late enough, and he was drunk enough. His bladder was aching. He didn't much care about privacy and let it all hang out on the front stoop of Wiederson's Groceteria. Frank admired his reflection in the store window, standing in the near dark, his legs spread wide to keep him from swaying too much and pissing all over himself. Holding his own. He had never been deprived when it came to the size of things, and he never wanted female companionship because of it. Rumours spread quickly around town, and he became very popular with the female population of Winterbourne. Maybe popular was too strong a word, but he'd never received any complaints – not that it would've mattered to him if he had. The more he gazed at his reflection - at *its* reflection, the shadows playing off the image and the liquor distorting his perception, the bigger it seemed. Hell, it looked positively massive. The more he looked, the more he admired, and he thought he should have shaken off this shitty little town to chase a life in porno movies.

"Why the hell not? Have you seen the fuckers in those movies? Do they have this?" he belched and wrapped his hand around its girth.

Frank laughed at the pun and thought himself really clever for it, having just popped into his head. He imagined the people that make those kinds of movies kicking in doors to get to him, and a smile wormed across his face. The more he gawked at it in his hand, the tighter his grip got. He imagined bottle blondes with huge, fake tits fawning over him while a director yelled instructions to him from behind a camera. Suddenly, he was flooded with visions of Ginny standing in front of him, her face flushed with nervous excitement. As she knelt, he pushed her face in closer and laughed like hell as he stuffed himself fully inside her mouth, grabbing hold of her hair while she sputtered and gagged on his flesh. The tears pooled up, and he slapped her when she attempted to pull away from him - from it. Hard enough that rivulets of blood began to trickle from her nose and his excitement went through the roof. He understood why there would never be work for him behind the green door.

"A firm hand," he whispered.

He was erect and engorged, and while it wasn't the ideal place for self-love, Frank was never one to waste an opportunity for his own pleasure. His hand began to move back and forth, slowly at first, travelling the considerable length of it. He glanced around his surroundings, never stopping. Still, he kept looking around, hoping he wouldn't be interrupted. Or, if he was really lucky, a hooker might wander by and help him finish. When he was sure he was alone, Frank closed his eyes, tightened his grip, and increased the speed of his hand. The breath pushed out of him fast and ragged and matched every stroke. It wouldn't be long before he came, and Frank let his mind wander, far from Parker Street and Winterbourne. Far from his shitty job and shitty girlfriend.

Jeanine, the bartender, stood before him, completely naked. Gleaming beads of moisture trailing down her breasts onto her belly and further below. He pulled her in and grabbed a handful of hair, bending her over backward as far as she was able. Ready to receive him, completely defenceless. Completely willing. But he didn't enter her. Not yet.

Instead, he took hold of her throat, grabbing it just behind the windpipe, and dug his nails in enough he was certain the skin would break. He felt himself near to climax inside his grip. She struggled back against the pressure at her neck but didn't try to stop him. A few whimpers escaped her. Nearly silent purrs of pleasure and pain that annoyed him when they began now turned to panicked gags as he increased the pressure around her throat. His grip tightened again, and he felt the flesh beneath rupture and give way. Jeanine's blood began to flow over his hand, and he felt the end - hers and his - drawing closer. It wouldn't be long now. It never was, and when it finished, he would hurry home for the real thing or as close as he could get.

Almost there. He could feel the pressure building up behind the head and the tingling prickle the bottoms of his feet, moving up, squeezing the pit of his stomach. The image of Jeannine lying at his feet in a widening pool of red-black blood pushed its way into his head. He focused his gaze on hers, a look of terror fading from eyes that were leaving this world. He grinned and slipped inside her. Within seconds he erupted all over the front window of Wiederson's.

Frank's eyes rolled open, and he saw himself in the store window, taking it all in, from the still pulsing chunk of flesh in his hands. Up to his torso and past his chest, settling on the reflection of his face. But what looked back wasn't him, not by a long shot. The face was gaunt, warped, and stretched as though it had been turned slowly over a flame, keeping it as pliable as molten glass. Gravity pulling and stretching and distorting it with each turn of the blowpipe until it was only human by default. The skin was rank and leathery and covered by bits of sloughing flesh that dropped away like flakes of peeling paint. He recognized his eyes, bright blue, ringed with ugly red veins and wild with disbelief.

"What the fuck?" Frank screamed.

Page fell to his knees, and the cool early morning air blew across his nude bottom half. He stood and reached down to pull his pants back up and caught his reflection in the store window. To his relief, it had returned to its former, admirable glory.

"Somebody put something in my goddam drink. That's what this is," Frank said. "I'm tripping my balls off."

He remained fixed to the spot, at his own reflection, afraid to step away from it.

"There was a guy... by the... fuck, where was he?"

Frank remembered the man as being tall and thin as a reed. Though he would never let on to his workmates - they would think he was a fairy - he thought the man was really good-looking. Ice blue eyes and hair were a perfect balance of salt and pepper falling across his face just right, like somebody out of a comic book. He didn't know how but was willing to bet this good-looking man had put something in one of the several dozen drinks that sloshed down his throat.

"Wait, he bought me a drink... bought Gary a drink... bought Gary and me a drink before he left.".

He would find this good-looking fellow and fucking sort him out. Though it might prove difficult if he insisted on staying in the middle of Parker Street. Frank glanced around again and, when he was sure no one saw him or knew what he'd been up to, began to walk the three blocks home. Chilled hands fumbled for the buttons on a jacket too thin to keep out the cold already biting at him. The fog began clearing from his brain after rounding the corner onto Greyhollow road. It looked like sobriety might try to cozy up before he opened the front door. From there, it was another fifty feet before he stood on his front porch. Frank dug in his pockets, groping this time for keys. They made it into the lock with little difficulty and turned just as easily. He burst through the door and began calling for the little dog.

"Chico!"

Frank moved from room to room, calling out to him, knowing he could be standing on top of him, screaming in his ear, and the damned thing wouldn't show the slightest reaction. He moved quickly, turning over the pieces of furniture and overstuffed cushions where the dog usually hid.

"Chico!" he screamed.

Frank looked toward the room at the back of the house, the bedroom he and Ginny shared. It was silent and dark, and he guessed they could both be in there fast asleep. More likely, the dog couldn't hear a damned thing he was saying, and she pretended to be sleeping so she wouldn't have to deal with him. Both scenarios enraged him further.

"Get up, goddammit, and help me find my fucking dog," he hissed.

The light gave an ugly buzz and exploded with a blue flash. A cascade of November orange sparks showered beneath the bulb, and the room went dark again.

"Goddammit!"

"Funny thing about you lot," the voice said. "You pray to a god for deliverance and salvation when the chips are down and then curse him with the same breath when things don't go your way."

"Who is that? Who the fuck is that?"

He flicked the light switch up and down and up and down, and when it still refused to repair itself, he pulled the cigarette lighter from the pocket of his shirt and flicked it to life. He moved slowly around the room, arm thrust forward, brandishing the tiny torch.

"It would be better for both of us if you put that light out."

"Not a fucking chance, pal. I put the light out, and then you put my lights out, is that how it works?"

"If I wanted that, you'd be dead already."

"And that's my goddam point," Frank crowed.

"*If*, I did say *if*. No, I don't mean you harm. In fact, I have a proposition for you."

"Come out here where I can see you then. I feel like I'm on the fucking T.V. or something, talking to an empty room.

"No. My appearance might well boggle your mind and blacken your very eyes with madness."

"What does that even mean?"

"I look, really rather, unreal."

"Try me."

The Necrosite stepped out into the glow of the cigarette lighter. Frank was spooked by the thing standing in his bedroom, but - truth be told - he had seen scarier hallucinations waiting for him by the bathroom door after a night of blackout drinking.

"How the hell did you get in here? Some kinda trick? Can you walk through walls and that kinda shit?"

"The door was open."

"The door was open? Fuck! Where is my God damned dog?"

"I would think that depends on what kind of life he led."

Frank rushed past the thing to the dresser on the far side of the room. Specifically, the Louisville Slugger tucked behind the dresser. He moved back to the little lizard-chimp and brought the edge of the bat close enough to its face that it could smell the cowhide pressed into the wood. He seemed terribly amused by the whole display.

"Could I see that for a moment, please?"

"Are you fucking high? I give you the bat, and then you brain me with it?" Frank balked.

"I promise you, if I am going to do anything to you, it won't be with this bat."

Frank eyed the green thing suspiciously and reluctantly gave up the chunk of wood. The Necrosite scrutinized it, turning it over and around in his hands. Feeling the heft of it.

"There's nothing like a good bit of hickory," he said and snapped the baseball bat like the branch of a sapling.

"What the hell are you?"

"The monster that lives under the bed. Look, can we just get on with this? I really do have quite a long day ahead, and... what are you doing?"

"Do – you – have – a - name?" Frank over-emphasized.

"John – a - than Pye – wack – ett," he answered.

"Why are you talking like that, all loud and stupid?"

"Isn't that how you were talking?"

"I wasn't talking like I had brain damage, Jesus Christ!"

"How would you like a job?" Pyewackett changed the subject.

"I have a job."

"Ah yes, and such gainful employment too. Stuff bits of cloth into a filthy machine from the crack of dawn until mid-afternoon, and then it's off to the bar with the lads to drown your feelings in cheap beer and perfumey gin. Then a few staggering steps home, stopping along the way for a quick tug in front of the grocery store before you get home and smack the little woman around. And then the fun really begins, eh Frank?"

"What the fuck's that supposed to mean?"

"We both know that having a little fun in front of Wiederson's and then leaving the wife black and blue is all well and good, but your heart is after something much darker, yes?"

Frank lowered his head and remained silent, shame churning in his guts.

"All those years, keeping things so secret. All those bones in the backyard. Just to satisfy those urges, the horrible longing and hollowness building up in you, but it was never enough, it was it Frank? The neighbours always thinking it was coyotes and foxes chewing up their pets. If they knew what you're doing out there with the old bones and mangled bits of flesh and fur before you buried them in the backyard, what do you think they'd do to you?"

"What of it?"

He brought his hands up and covered his face, gripped by the embarrassment. Not that he felt any *real* remorse for the things he'd done – he didn't. But he felt ashamed at being called out for them. It was his God-given right to pursue pleasure for himself in whatever form it happened to take. Gratification at the expense of everything else, that was his war cry. Life was brutish and short and had to be grabbed by the throat and shaken until the last drop of joy was wrung out of it. If it meant breaking a few eggs along the way, what did he care?

"What of it? How would you like to indulge those whims creeping around in the dark corners of your head?"

"How?"

"There has recently been a change of management up the hill."

"The old folks home? I don't see how the fuck that means anything to me," Frank said.

"I'm offering you a job. At Winterbourne Home."

"I still don't..."

"Oh god, do I have to bloody spell it out for you? The old age home, where everyone is close to death, anyway?"

"Umm?" Frank puzzled.

"It's very simple. No one is going to find regular deaths suspicious if they are in a nursing home where people die all the time. How they die is a matter of personal preference," Pyewackett sighed.

"But fuck, they're all so – old."

"Up to now, your playthings haven't even been human. I wouldn't think you'd be so choosey when you can finally indulge *all* your fantasies."

A cancerous smile warped its way across Frank's face. He finally understood what the little monster was talking about, a smile that broadened and became uglier as he got what it really meant.

"What should I wear to the interview?"

# 19

"Wait, what? I haven't done anything wrong. I'm not guilty!"

"Of course you're guilty. Your attorney has just said as much," Justice Julius said.

"What am I guilty of? What crime have I committed?"

"You knowingly expedited the departure of one Mrs. Margaret Galston, late of Winterbourne Home for the aged and infirm," Judge Leonard said.

"But, I was given her card."

"The card was clearly issued in error," Judge Arthur sneered.

"How could I possibly know the card was wrong? The time cards are the foundation of the whole system. If we can't assume they are correct, what good is any of it?"

"Are you insinuating that no crime has been committed because you were unaware of the illegality of your actions?" Judge Leonard wondered.

"Yes," Davis said. "That's exactly what I'm saying."

"Ignorance of the law is no excuse!" Justice Julius roared.

"Is there any reason why this court should not pass sentence at this time?" Judge Arthur asked.

"I shouldn't think so, M'lord," Codswallop chirped.

"Well, of course, there isn't," Davis spat.

"Very well," Justice Julius replied.

He took a small square of black cloth and placed it on his head.

"Davis Mareth, having admitted your guilt and thrown yourself on the mercy of this court, and it being your first offence, though grievous beyond reckoning, this court is willing to grant you a measure of leniency. You are hereby sentenced to sixteen years in Hel."

"You're sending me to Hell?"

"No, Hel," Codswallop said quietly. "The place where all judged souls are punished."

"Right, Hell."

"No, not Hell – Hel," the Necrosite repeated.

"What's the difference?"

"As I understand it, Hel is one of the worlds beyond death. It's the place souls are judged, and the guilty are punished. The truly evil ones will live out the remainder of their time in a swirling maelstrom of rent flesh and unimaginable torment."

"And Hell?"

"Hell is a silly make-believe place where the wicked are singed and scalded in a lake of fire while being poked and prodded all day by little red men with hay forks. The whole thing is presided over by some gigantic, leathery winged goat man. Horns and all. Bloody fairy stories.".

"And I suppose Hel is governed by a beautiful woman dressed in white silk who looks at you like a mother and punishes the bad deeds but forgives anyone who shows remorse?" Davis said.

"Oh no, not at all. Last I heard, it was a large hairy fellow. Very short temper, terribly cross before his first coffee. And his belt matches his shoes."

"Are you quite finished, Mr. Codswallop?" Judge Leonard interjected.

"Quite finished, M'lord. Sorry, M'lord."

"As I was saying, you are hereby sentenced to sixteen years in Hel, to begin immediately. Bailiff, escort the prisoner," Justice Julius said

"And if I refuse, if I refuse to go along with any of this?"

"Immediate execution."

"I'm pretty sure that's the end game here anyway. Why don't you assholes just get it over with?"

"In addition, every trace of your existence will be eradicated from your particular sector, starting with the abomination that runs Winterbourne for you," Judge Leonard gloated.

"You won't touch her!"

Justice Arthur signalled, and the bailiff moved beside Davis. He produced a well-worn set of iron manacles and clapped them on Death's wrists.

"This way," the bailiff grunted.

"Aren't you supposed to shout come quietly?" Davis snarked.

"Come quietly! Happy now?"

The big guard led Davis through the double doors and back toward the cells, stopping short of them and turning to the right, facing a long, sweat-covered stone wall.

"It's through there."

"Wait, what? I haven't even mastered the big booming voice; I don't imagine I'll be able to pass through walls any time soon."

"You won't have to," the bailiff said and unhooked a large brass room key from a chain hanging around his neck. Davis looked carefully but saw no keyhole and stood dumbfounded when the grey thing tapped the key gingerly against the wall.

"Really?" Davis smarmed.

"What?"

The wall remained solid and stone.

"Um ... should it have moved around or something?"

"Just you get going."

The bailiff grunted and pushed Davis against the wall. He braced for the impact, but instead, he passed straight through the wall and was left staring at the opposite side, stretching into the horizon. His eyes were drawn to the end of the hallway, to a small white square of light barely the size of a postage stamp.

"Go toward the light."

"You're joking, right?"

"I hear it stings a little, best to just push through and get on with things," the guard said.

Davis sensed a note of compassion in the big thing's voice.

"You're not coming with?"

"Tough to believe, I know, but this is where I leave you." He turned away from the man and stomped off back through the wall, leaving Davis standing alone in the long hallway.

The air in here was alive with the stench of mould and rot that had existed long before Davis, or his grey-skinned jailer. The walls were bare stone. Gloomy, long, and greened with years of moisture. He felt almost crushed by the feeling that this hallway had seen sorrow and cruelty beyond words. Without a single torch along the walls, the only light Davis could see came from the square at the end of the hallway. It was so small, so far away from him. Yet, it was bright enough to light the whole hallway.

The thought of not moving crossed his mind. He could just stay put until the bailiff came back to push another unfortunate creature through the fake wall. Then, he might do something stupid and violent, overwhelming the bailiff and escape. The plan was solid, except for two minor details. Firstly, the bailiff outweighed him by at least two hundred pounds. Secondly, he had never been in a fight in his life. Not one - successful or otherwise - and the idea of hitting the guard and getting away scot-free seemed wishful thinking at best and downright suicidal at worst.

"I could just stand here, I suppose," he said.

It should be noted that two immutable forces govern the universe.

One is Death, which Davis was. Death is everywhere, reminding us we are alive, and one day we won't be. Despite health, fitness, and abstinence of all kinds, medicine and machinery and doing all the things we can to prolong time on this planet, we will all die. Death gives our lives meaning. The fear of Death is what it is to be alive. Revel in it or be imprisoned by it, but there is no escaping it. The other is Fate. Fate is the part in the drapes of the universe, a thumb in the eye of divine intervention. Fate is the cosmic reminder that free will is a lie. All life is unremarkable and almost entirely predetermined. You are what you are because Fate decided it should be so. Going against the grain and thinking things like *I could just stand here, I suppose,* is enough to piss off fate and earn a swift kick in the nuts.

An ominous click of well-oiled metal springs and tightly fitted mechanisms moving smoothly from one position to the next could be heard. The stone wall behind him began to lumber forward toward the square of white light.

"Are you kidding me?"

He began to walk quickly at first and then jumped to a flat-out run and soon found himself outpacing the wall by strides. In no time, he was three lengths ahead of it.

"You couldn't slow down a bit, could you?" the wall asked.

"What?"

"Slow down a little. Bert can hardly keep up. He's getting on, you know."

"The wall's name is Bert?"

"No, this fella's name is Bert. I'm Alf. I don't know what the wall is called," the wall said.

Davis stopped and turned to the wall.

"Where are you?"

"Back here," Alf said.

Davis heard a snap like lightning ripping the limb off a tree, and a crack zig-zagged across the face of the flat stone, large enough for Davis to get part of the way through. Behind the wall stood another of the sweaty grey brutes, larger than any Davis had seen before, his hands pressed firmly against the wall. Resting on his shoulders, a small Necrosite in a red, warm-up suit.

"What the hell?"

"Not Hell, Hel," the Necrosite corrected.

"Right."

"It's a trap, innit?"

The wall stretched from floor to ceiling, but what looked from the outside to be a huge, smooth, stone façade was a cleverly painted and mud-covered screen attached to a primitive sled. A length of muslin fixed to a framework of wood attached to a light and well-braced steel sleigh frame. On either side of it lay two, thickly greased stone runners, concealed entirely in the front by the length of the wood and spackle-covered brick to ease the movement down the hallway.

"Take a break, Bert," the little Necrosite said.

The big grey thing pushed back from the wall, and Davis could see that, despite its impressive size, it had not managed to find himself in a role as luxurious as a bailiff or a cell guard. It was naked to the waist; its back was scarred. Davis couldn't imagine anything powerful enough to beat down something as large as Bert.

The sweat poured down Bert's forehead and into his eyes. He pulled a dirty rag from the pocket of the ragged black pants he wore and mopped his brow. Davis noticed the big thing's nose looked burnt off, like the other two grey things. But, unlike them, Bert's eyes had also been burnt out.

"Could we get on with this? Time is money and all that," Alf said.

"Look, I could just walk down to the end; I don't need you guys to follow me. Bert looks pretty tired," Davis said

"Nonsense, it's no trouble at all. Bert is as fit as a fiddle, aren't you, Bert?"

The little Necrosite produced a thick, leather riding crop from the leg of its red tracksuit and cracked it across Bert's back. The sound of it gave Davis a sick feeling in the pit of his stomach, and he wished he'd just kept his mouth shut

"Get up, Bert, and get this fucking wall moving!"

"No, really, it's okay. I'll make my way down the hallway. No problem at all, you two can take it easy."

"Take it easy, what like not to push the wall?"

"Exactly, you could just not push the wall. Have a nice coffee or something."

"And you'd just walk down there, would you? Pull the other one, sonny. It's got bells on it. Me an' Bert have been here long enough to know when someone's takin' the piss."

"No, really. You two stay here, and I'll just walk down. I can't go through the way I came, and you two are here to stop me. Where else am I going to go?"

"It's a point," Alf said." But we just got the new spikes, you see? Wouldn't look very good if we buggered off before we got a chance to show 'em off, would it?"

He snapped the crop across Bert's back again, and the silent behemoth reached up to pull a black metal lever straight down. A dull thud, followed by the boing of a spring, echoed through the hallway, and a grin spread itself across the Necrosite's face.

"See?" Alf pointed gleefully.

Davis pulled his head back through the crack in the bricks and saw gleaming, blue steel spikes protruding from every available space on the wall.

"Say, those *are* impressive," he said.

"But you try telling the younger ones that! Rip 'em apart and be done with it. That's what they're all about. It's the blood, you see? Gets into them and warps the brain. Honestly, where's the paralyzing fright, the unnameable terror?"

The young Death pulled back through the wall and started off down the hallway toward the small blinding white square.

"Hey, what are you two waiting for?" he called out.

The Necrosite poked his head through the wall and gave Davis a confused smile.

"Come on!"

"Hear that, Bert? Time to get back to work," Alf beamed.

The hallway continued for several hundred feet, which looked more like several hundred yards. Davis noticed that the space narrowed the farther he went forward. By the time he reached the end of it, he was hunched over, chest nearly on top of his knees and knuckles scraping along the floor like a bizarre, furless ape.

"What next, fellas?" Davis asked. Silence replied.

"Bert? Alf?"

Nothing.

In front of him was the small square opening, not much larger than a bathroom window. To get through it -which, he guessed he was meant to do - he would need to hunker down on all fours, as squat as he could get, and sort of inch through it sideways.

"So, through here, then? Isn't there supposed to be a drink I swallow beforehand?"

He knelt sidelong in front of the window and felt a little like he was praying to it. In his head, he was praying that nothing was on the other side of it, waiting to rip him to shreds or even call him a nasty name. There did seem to be an awful lot of things following him around lately that wanted to do both. He stuck out a hand and pressed it into the lit-up square, and found it completely solid.

"Sonofabitch, it's a window."

Davis felt around where the frame should be, looking for a handle or a latch to get the damned thing open. It was soft and smooth around the edges, and the centre of it was hard like a window but then nothing at all like one. He placed the palm of his hand against it, expecting it to be hot - for no other reason than he thought it should be. To his surprise, it wasn't hot at all. It was cold, it might have been the coldest thing he had ever touched, and he would never feel the heat again. And then the snarl of the cold set in.

He tried to pull his hand away, wanting to shove it in his pocket or cup against his other hand and blow warm breath into it. But he couldn't. The hand was stuck tight. The harder he pulled back, the tighter it stuck. Burning and not budging, like the tongues of foolish boys on chain-link fence posts after a deep December frost. The chill moved up his arm, spreading a throbbing frostbitten agony that pulled at his skin as it went. It moved past his shoulders and was soon tearing at his neck, bending his head toward the window. Contorting him. Breaking him.

"Oh shit, burning. Really burning."

His heart began to thunder in his chest. Panic pulled up a chair, intending to stay for the whole show and the encore. In an effort to free himself, he raised his other hand and braced against the window, feeling a second hand might be just the leverage he needed to pull himself free. His other hand became as hopelessly stuck as the first, like a fly stuck in the dew-soaked strand of a garden spider's web.

The freeze seared his skin and tore its way through him, pulling him tighter to the window. Davis could feel the icy grip reaching for his face, though it was still far enough away from the window that it did little more than chill him. But it was getting worse. An awful pressure in his head, like the twist of a frozen plastic tray to free up a few ice cubes, and he was one of them. The image of him standing under a barbell flashed into his head. It'd been the one and only time he'd ever used Winterbourne's gym. Jenn made him promise to go. He did. Now, he wished he'd gone more, gotten stronger. Maybe then he could pull himself loose. It also occurred to him just how cold he was, and he wished he'd brought a sweater. Jenn would have told him that too.

An idea popped into his head. If he could brace his feet on either side of the window, he might be able to push back from the wall and free his hands. Davis moved up onto his haunches and then lowered himself to sit in front of the window, placing a foot on either side of it. As he pushed his feet downward, he felt his hands loosen. Not like they'd had been freed from the window, more like the area of the window that held them felt moved away. Looking at the window, he could no longer see his hands; they'd vanished from the forearm down. He could wiggle fingers, twirl wrists, and open and close fists, but he couldn't bring them back through the window.

"Well, shit," Davis sighed.

He could feel cool air blowing across his hands, not as cold as the window. Compared to the bite the window was giving the other end of his arms, it was quite a pleasant feeling. But knowing what he should do next and the agony he would go through took away any enjoyment of his hands being free of the window web.

Mareth pushed his head toward the window and, immediately, felt it drawing him closer. The sting of the cold bit into his forehead like ragged teeth and held him firm.

*Maybe this is it, maybe this is the punishment. Being stuck like this for sixteen years would be Hell. Or Hel.*

And without warning, his head started to pass through the window. Not all at once - slowly, with little pulls at the skin on the back of his neck. Davis imagined this was what a mouse felt like, being swallowed by a snake. Your head, plunging into hot, moist darkness while the rest of you danced free. All the while, the brain knowing the end was moving closer. Inch by warm inch. His head emerged through the other side, joining his hands in the fresh, cold air of his new surroundings. He turned his head from side to side, scanning the surroundings and saw nothing, no single landmark he recognized. He felt one more icy stab against his skin, and soon the rest of him followed his head and hands through the window.

There were trees in front of him, deep green pines tipped with the white hoar frost that crept along the ground and coated everything like a poisonous fog. To the right, a barren, snow-covered field. To the left, a dense copse of leafless box elders looking impenetrable. The pines in front looked nearly as impassable except for the rough path that cut through the centre of them. He stepped out, away from the window, afraid it might pull him back in, and saw a small box laying on the snow. The lid on the box read:

**MARETH 5840**

Davis ran his hand along the lid, tracing the numbers with a finger and felt a loose corner on the box's label. He pulled off the slip of sticky paper and found a note on its reverse.

**You have been found guilty and sentenced to time in Hel.**

**You will serve time, or time will serve you. But do not waste time,**

**time is fleeting. Good luck, and please do try the Mushu!**

"I hate Mushu," Davis breathed.

# 20

"Ogay?" Clarence asked.

"How the shit should I know? Same awful crap they give to us every morning. Shit on a shingle without the God damned shingle," Richard Walters barked.

He raised a spoonful of the earth-toned slop with a trembling hand and, what little of it remained on the spoon, ended up smeared across his chin.

"Shit," Richard said.

"Everything okay, Mr. Walters?" the orderly asked.

"Fine, just fine. Nothing the matter here."

"Ogay?"

"Because I don't need any Goddamned help. Because I am perfectly capable of feeding myself," Richard said.

"Ogay."

"Shut up, you old fool." He pushed himself up and walked away from the table.

"Good morning, gentlemen, room for one more?"

The pretty young nurse wheeled the old woman to the table and pulled a checkered bib around her neck.

"Richard, Clarence, this is Dorothy. She is going to be sitting with the two of you now," the nurse said.

"Well, well," Richard said.

"Ogay, ogay, ogay, ogay, ogay."

"Get a hold of yourself, man. You sound like an idiot."

"Good morning," Dorothy Lauren said.

Clarence forced himself back, hard against the cushion of his wheelchair, trying desperately to sit up straight. He managed a one-sided smile and stared at her, probably for too long. She was beautiful, even in age. Dorothy was beautiful, even with age softening her features. He imagined she must have breathtaking before time started catching up with her.

"Hey, don't you normally sit with an old lady? What's her name... Gallstone?"

"Galston," Dorothy corrected.

"That's her."

"She passed last night. Very suddenly."

"Heart attack? I'll just bet it was a heart attack. Lucky bugger."

"I'm sure I don't know," Dorothy answered.

"Ogay?" Clarence wondered.

"Of course, it's lucky. No-fuss, no mess to clean up in the morning. Just a little pain in the chest and then boom, hello afterlife."

"How can you t-"

Dorothy fell deathly quiet and slumped in her chair.

"I think this old broad just had a stroke," Richard sneered.

"Ogay!"

She was still and silent, and her head lolled forward. The half-smile vanished from Clarence's face, and for all the cynicism in Richard's voice, even he felt a swell of pity, fearing the worst had just happened to Dorothy. Strictly speaking, it was everyone for themself in here. Sure, there were friendships of a sort and allegiances, particularly among the older, European ladies who sat holding court and clucking away like old hens at anyone who wasn't them. But even they became cutthroat when the snack cart came by, or if a few extra desserts made it upstairs at supper time. What was understood, from day one to the last in Winterbourne, was no one should suffer anything but the quickest of deaths. Slow and lingering rot from the inside like cancer or some other awful disease was an insult nobody should suffer. Worse still was a stroke that left you half a working body with a fully working mind. Clarence knew all too well, and it looked as though Dorothy was about to find out. A breath escaped her, long and slow like steam knocking its way down a length of lead pipe.

"Darkness," she wheezed.

"I'm sorry?"

"Ogay?"

"Darkness, I said, darkness. The veil of darkness has descended over us all now that the pale man will walk along the boulevard of desolation."

"Boulevard of desolation?"

"That's right."

"Rubbish."

"Wait, what?" Dorothy asked.

"Ogay?"

"By definition, a boulevard is widened, a multilane street with some degree of landscaping and a median separating the lanes of traffic."

"Yes?"

"Well, that's not desolate. Like not even remotely desolate," Richard said.

"Well, I'm not sure really," Dorothy intoned.

"Road, road of desolation, that makes entirely more sense. Just a path between two points, really. Nothing to see in a lot of cases."

"I didn't name the bloody thing," Dorothy said.

"At any rate, darkness?"

"Yes," Dorothy said. "Darkness and a great scraping of parts un-lubricated, and the world will be bathed in the blood of the living serpent."

"Ogay?"

"Yeah, what he said."

"Oh wait... wait a moment."

Her eyes rolled back in their sockets, her jaw went slack and fell open, looking every bit like she had just expired, again. She sat motionless and quiet, and the colour seemed to drain away from her face. Almost as quickly as it had begun, it ended. Dorothy's jaw snapped shut, and she raised her head up, eyes wide and staring.

"No, that one *was* for you two. Scraping parts and serpent blood," she said.

"This happen a lot?"

"Ogay?" Clarence added.

"How the shit would I know what she means? I got here when you did."

Her eyes rolled over white once more, and her head fell back, gasping for air and spouting trippy gibberish.

"Ogay?"

"The darkness, the darkness will follow in the wake of the pale man's absence."

"Okay, we've covered the bit about the darkness. How about the pale man?"

"The pale man stalks the halls of Winterbourne. He walks eternal between this world and the next."

"So, the pale man is a janitor?"

"Ogay?"

"Oh, it could be, couldn't it? Is it the pail man? Is that right? You said he mops the halls of Winterbourne," Richard said.

"Stalks," Dorothy moaned.

"Oh, right, stalks. Umm... that makes things a little more... Oh, is it the new young doctor, the one that stops by on Wednesday?"

"Ogay?"

"It is not the new doctor. The pale man saw you first, and he will see you last."

"Well, that's the doctor, isn't it?" If you're first in line, you'll see him first, and if you're on the way out..."

"Ogay," Clarence added.

"For God's sake, do I have to spell it out for you?" the voice badgered.

"Well– "

"Fine it's-"

"It's who?"

"Ogay?"

Dorothy fell silent again and slumped forward in her wheelchair as if sleep had suddenly overwhelmed her. A long slow breath hissed its way past her lips, and she bent further forward, so now she lay with her face nearly, completely in her lap.

"She's pretty flexible for an old broad. Clarence, you should really give this one a go," Richard joked.

"Ogay!"

The old woman snapped back up and pointed her hand toward the door to the dining room without opening her eyes.

"Comes the beast," she whispered.

A slight woman with short grey hair that hadn't seen the working end of a hairbrush in years strolled into the dining room, looking like she hadn't a care in the world. She mumbled a meaningless little song and flittered around the doorway like a hummingbird choosing a lily. A thick-muscled orderly caught sight of her and backed away, giving her as wide a berth as he was able. The little woman's head darted around the room, indiscriminately, looking for something familiar to latch onto.

"Would you like to sit down?" the young nurse asked.

Most of the other staff in the dining room, orderlies, kitchen staff, care workers, and nurses all came rushing forward, trying to get the nurse to stop speaking to the old woman. It was too late, she had gobbled up the bait, and the jaws of the trap were about to slam shut.

The old woman moved quickly, reaching to take the nurse's outstretched hand but bypassed it and went straight for the thick mane of chestnut hair and grabbed a fistful of it. With her other hand, she slapped the nurse across the face with astonishing force. When she tried to duck the incoming blows, the old woman pulled tighter on the nurse's thick brown hair, forcing her to expose her face to more slaps. Soon her hand closed, and slaps became punches. The pretty nurse felt the streaks of blood flowing from her nose and mouth, and panic took her. She began to scream for someone - anyone to do something. Panic turned to dread and whispered to her in her ear. If she couldn't stop the old woman, she'd blackout, and the assault would continue until her body gave out. The idea that she might actually die sent shockwaves through her, and she struggled harder against the woman's grip. Scrapes and scratches would heal, lost hair would grow back. But the old lady was already wailing and shrieking, and the resistance only enraged her further

A handful of orderlies rushed in and pulled her off the nurse, trying to redirect the old woman to something that might calm her down. Fear and anger hung in the air like a bad smell, rattling all the other residents to a fever pitch. The residents wanted breakfast. They wanted to be warm. Some of them were too warm. The elderly were angry and confused, and they wanted somebody to make things right.

The old woman continued to pirouette around the dining room, bouncing from wall to table like a marble on a Roulette wheel. Clarence and Richard lowered their heads, trying to blend in with their chairs and avoid catching the old woman's gaze. Not soon enough. She zeroed in on Clarence's one good eye and began walking toward the three of them.

"Oh shit, Minnie Martin," Richard whispered.

## 21

"Okay, fun is fun, but come out now," Jenn said.

One by one, they began to file out from every nook and cranny and darkened pocket into the red glow of the emergency lights. They were Necrosites. But as they moved closer to her, she could see they were considerably smaller than any Necrosite she had seen working upstairs. The odd things they chose to wear as clothing and the way they all spoke led Jenn to only one conclusion.

"Kids - you're all kids."

"Kids? Kids? Ain't one of us here that ain't, whassname, under fifteen."

It was the voice she spoke to all along, likely the gang's leader, and now, having seen him, she was embarrassed he had held her captive this long and not been any older than he was.

"You the fella in charge?"

"Oh yeah, total whassname, boss, that's me."

"You got a name, boss?"

He grew quiet and, for the first time since she'd come down to the flats. Tension hung in the air like a thunderhead threatening to burst into a storm. The Necrosite lowered his head, thinking that saying his name might demonstrate how tough he wasn't and how truly, awful his name was. And, once this woman from the world above knew it, there'd be no end to how far the news would travel.

"And if I told you I didn't whatsisname, have one?"

"I'd say I don't, whassname, believe you."

"Go on and tell her, what's in a name, anyhow?" a smaller Necrosite said.

A breathless pause hung over them, waiting for the lone Necrosite to volunteer his handle or turn away and keep them standing around in uncomfortable silence. With the images of the awful salamander woman and her two mummy guards still fresh in his mind, he knew he had little choice.

"Wendell," the leader sighed. A chorus of laughter erupted from the assemblage of Necrosites

"What's wrong with that?"

"It's Wendell, isn't it? It's not rugged or tough like Steve or mysterious like Alan. It's more like, whassname, a fat kid who eats paste."

"I think it's a lovely name," Jenn said.

"A lovely name," the smaller Necrosite cooed.

"And what's your name, little one?"

"Walter," he answered.

"Two w's in the same gang, what are the odds of that, do you figure?"

"Better than, whassname."

"Oh?"

"We're all w," Walter chimed in.

"Really, all w?"

"All of us – from Wendell and Walter, to Wayne, Wyatt and William, all the way to Waylon and Walden," Wendell answered.

"And you planned it like that? Was that on the recruiting poster for the gang?"

"Course not. It's just one of them, whassnames, happy co-insidious."

"Well then, we're all just one big happy family then. Listen, fellas, it's been awfully swell, but I really need to scram out of here."

"Not supposed to," Walter said.

"Why not?"

"Big fella upstairs says we've to keep you here until he's finished getting your man out of it."

"Get my man out of what?"

"Shut up, Walter. Mustn't spill the whassname, rutabagas."

"S'alright, she's like one of us. Only less scaly and green and, whassname, way taller."

"No, no, I understand. You don't have to tell me," Jenn said.

"Besides, if we tell her what the big fella is up to, maybe he sends the whassname, Hollow Men, after us next."

"Wait, what? The who?"

"The two big, wrapped up, looking things and the toad woman from up the way. They all come from the whassname, Night Court."

"Why would the Night Court send anybody here?"

"On account of something to do with your man, something he did. How else were they gonna get him out the way?"

"I don't understand what-"

"Course it wasn't something he really did. I hear they fixed it, so one of the oldies checked out early. Wrote up a ticket or broke wind in the whassname, library or something," Wendell explained.

"Punched a card? Punched a time card early?"

"That's it!"

"After that, it was dead easy," Walter added.

"What was easy?"

"Getting rid of him, of course. The Hollow men showed up right away and, whassname hauled him off."

A gurgling blob of nausea oozed into the pit of Jenn's stomach. Roiling, churning until it made her head feel disconnected from the rest of her body. She felt feverish, and huge drops of flop sweat began to pool across her forehead and roll down into her eyes. Anger and sadness spun inside her head, and she knew if she didn't sit soon, her legs would give out. She stretched out a hand and felt the plywood walls of one of the shipping crates and eased herself down, leaning up against the walls. And it all came crashing in on her. If the Night Court really had Davis, she'd never see him again. Tears welled up and streaked down her face. She buried her head in her hands and tried to wrap her arms around herself. She wished Davis was doing it instead.

"Oh, hey, it's alright. The Soulreaver said everyone would get what's coming to them. You, Mareth, us too," Wendell soothed.

"You're not getting it. If they clocked someone out early, it will have stopped the punch clock. Or worse."

"And?" Walter wondered.

"And if we're lucky, they'll be satisfied with Davis, and that will be the end of it."

"If we're not lucky?"

"If all the clocks have stopped, then we'll have gotten the attention of more than just the god damned Night Court," she answered.

―――――――

The poisonous breath in the white boiler suit hovered just above the landing, in front of the abandoned clock tower, bobbing like rotten fruit in an oil-slick. It decided shoes on its wispy feet would be appropriate for travelling among the corporeal and moved off in the direction of an old man defending himself against hordes of winged vermin by pelting them with dried grain. The thing moved in front of the man, and the birds flew off.

"You?" the old man said.

The thing eyed him with confusion and tried to recall just who the old man was. There was a persistence of memory about him, and yet, his face was unfamiliar.

"Shoes," the thing warbled.

"What?"

The arm of the boiler suit shot forward, the black fog within it, forming a spear point fist that drove deep into the old man's chest. He gulped a mouthful of air, pitched forward, and collapsed onto the dirt.

"Shoes," it said. The smoke of its feet moulded themselves into the brown leather, rubber-soled loafers.

It walked now, in awkward steps, as it got used to moving in sensible shoes. Slowly at first, looking every bit like a child learning to walk. Within a few dozen steps, it mastered walking and headed out of the square, strolling up a narrow dirt road.

"Time," it said.

---

Mr. Richardson closed the door to his apartment. He began the long walk past the elevator onto the long marble staircase headed upward. The Soulreaver had wasted no time in taking over the big office reserved for Death. Richardson thought he should feel on top of the world like he'd won the lottery. The time of the Necrosites had come at last, and he stood at the head of the mighty wave of green-skinned heroes. He had taken his place at the right hand of the prophet, who would lead the righteous to freedom. So why did he feel so awful about the whole thing?

There was no love lost between him and Mareth. Secretly, the Necrosite had wished he would disappear from Winterbourne and end up in some awful place where they poke your legs and the fleshy bits of your arms with wooden hay forks. Something to annoy the piss out of you for all eternity but not cause any real harm. But involving the Night Court was reckless and stupid and more than a little excessive. It was sending a bull strapped with dynamite into a china shop to kill a fly already stuck to a no pest strip.

There wasn't a single being in the service of Death – Necrosite, living dead girl or otherwise - who didn't know what the Night Court was and didn't shudder a little hearing that someone had been sent to it. As Richardson crossed the hallway and headed toward the door to the Soulreaver's office, he tried to put the Night Court and Mareth's fate out of his mind. He was in charge now, well second in command at the very least, and there was a nursing home to run. Though he would admit, he hadn't the faintest clue how to run a foot race, much less a nursing home. It had been Mareth – and more to the point, his dead girlfriend who kept Winterbourne Home running efficiently.

He swung the door open, screwing up enough false confidence that he practically bounded into the office. It was trampled immediately underfoot as soon as he rounded the corner and faced the big desk. Beside the Soulreaver stood a tall, decent-looking man in a badly wrinkled suit.

"You wanted to see me, sir?"

"Ah, Richardson do come in," the Soulreaver said.

Richardson felt the fear pulling at the back of his neck, stopping him from moving further into the room. The expression in the Soulreaver's eyes said if he didn't start doing his part and walk into the room, nagging fear would be the least of his worries.

"I would like to introduce Mr. Frank Page, the new face of Winterbourne Home and, might I add, your new slave driver," the Soulreaver chuckled.

"My new... but I thought..." Richardson sputtered.

The Soulreaver crossed the room quickly and took the older Necrosite's hand.

"You thought you would assume control now that Mareth and his awful plaything have been dealt with?"

"Well...yes," Richardson said.

"And so you shall - in a manner of speaking."

"I don't understand, sir."

"Mr. Richardson, you are wise beyond your years, and there are few, if any, who know more about the workings of this position than you," The Soulreaver said.

"But?"

"But, like me, you are as ugly as the day is long. Truly hideous to behold."

"Oh, really? I've never heard that before," Richardson spat.

"My dear Mr. Richardson, the business of Winterbourne, as you know, is to house and care for the elderly until The Void comes to claim them. Do you think families would bring their loved ones to a nursing home if they knew it was staffed by... us.? Mr. Page here is to assure we have a continuous flow of available prey for the hunt," the Soulreaver soothed.

"Prey – for the hunt? Really?"

"Ah, yes, as we guide them peacefully on their way to the next world, of course."

Richardson stood in silence, unsure what his next move should be, or even if there was a next move.

"So, you're telling me I have no authority... over anything?"

"No. No, that's not what I am saying at all. Your role will remain exactly as it was and all the authority it entails. All safely intact and waiting for your triumphant return."

"Oh, right. Well, I guess I'll just go and tidy up or something then, shall I?"

"Fine, yes, excellent," The Soulreaver said.

He turned back to the man in the shabby suit. The two of them had been deep in conversation when Richardson arrived, and, now that they dismissed him, they seemed quick to pick up where they left off as he turned to leave.

"Wait, Rochester, I'm gonna need a list of all the old broads in this place who are getting ready to go," Page directed. "And their weights."

"Close the door on your way out. There's a good lad," The Soulreaver said.

"Yes sir, of course, sir, right away, sir," Richardson said.

The Necrosite crossed the threshold of the door and stopped dead.

"You bastard," he growled.

"How's that?" Frank asked.

Richardson walked slowly to Frank and sized him up as little more than a cheap thug in an even cheaper suit. He stretched out an arm and dug a long, slender claw into the thickest part of Page's thigh, the pain of which dropped the tall man to his knees. The little Necrosite bared his needle-sharp teeth. With a lurch forward, he sunk them deep into the man's throat. The blood gushed out, warm and salty and spraying in rhythm with his ebbing pulse. It filled Richardson's mouth and ran down his chin like grease pouring off a roast goose. He could feel its heat spread across his chest, soaking his shirt. The blood turning it from a crisp, pressed, white linen to a sopping, crimson rag.

"Richardson!"

The Necrosite dug his claws into the flesh of the man's face. Flaying him. Reducing his head to a crimson mess.

"Hunters we were and hunters we remain," Richardson said.

"Richardson!"

Frank moaned, low and soft. A shudder worked its way through his body like a small earthquake was erupting beneath him. It was all too much for Richardson to bear. The attack was enough to inflame desires that lay dormant for too long. The throes of this human's body as he approached his end was a final push over the cliff the Necrosite needed to reach a state that bordered on orgasmic.

"Richardson!"

"Wait, what? Yes?" Richardson panted.

"I said you may go," the Soulreaver said.

"Right. Yes, of course,"

"And close the goddam door," Page added.

## 22

Minnie Martin shuffled up to the table and took the empty chair across from Dorothy. The table mates sat silently, amazed that, of all the empty seats in the dining room, the scary old woman chose to sit with the three of them.

"Hello, Minnie," Dorothy said.

"Mm-hmm," Minnie answered.

"Ogay,"

"Mm-hmm."

"She ain't got too much to say, has she?" Richard said.

"You shut your stupid mouth, you fucking asshole," Minnie said.

The regular din of the dining room rose to near-deafening as conversations turned from how bad the food was to who in the hell was the new guy walking into the dining room. Two big orderlies came lumbering into the hall, followed by a tall man of an average build in a black suit that was a size too small for him.

"Who's that guy?" Richard said.

"Ogay?" Clarence said.

"Where's the other guy?"

"Ogay?"

"The other guy. That kid, you know, tall, skinny, looks like he has anemia, dreamy blue eyes?"

"Clarence, Dorothy, and Minnie all stared at Richard in stunned silence.

"What? He's a good lookin' kid. Needs a sandwich, but otherwise, he'd make quite a catch."

"Ogay?" Clarence wondered.

"Yeah, that's him. What's his name?"

Dorothy lolled forward again. A hollow breath escaped her lips. Richard turned his gaze to her for a moment, barely recognizing she had made a sound, and turned his attention back to Clarence.

"He met me at the door the day I came to this place. In fact, he was the first face I saw here," Richard said.

"Ogay?"

"Right? He'll probably be the last one I see before I check out, too. He's a good one, that kid."

"Oh, for God's sake," Dorothy moaned.

The tall man banged a butter knife against the top of the servery counter, and the room grew quiet as all eyes turned to him. He produced a folded piece of paper from the inside pocket of his jacket and cleared his throat noisily as he unfolded it.

"Ladies and gentlemen, if I could just have your attention for a moment. My name is Frank Page, and I took the runner's position and will be running things now that Davis Mareth is no longer with us."

A confused murmur went up through the residents. They all knew Mareth and liked him. To hear that he was gone was enough to warrant grumbles of anger and shocked outbursts from most of them.

"Davis! That's the skinny kid's name," Richard whispered.

"I would like to get to know each one of you as best as I can in my times here, and so, starting today, I'd like to meet with one or two of you in private. We can then discuss your needs and expectations for your tenor here."

Richard looked to Clarence in disbelief. Could this guy be on the level? Calling himself the runner... of things? Expections? Clarence did his best to shrug, which is a near impossibility for a man with only one functioning side. It wasn't shrug so much as it looked like he was trying to shoo away a large insect from his shoulder without using his hands.

"And where did the pale kid go?"

"Shh," Dorothy cautioned.

"Now, if Mrs. Rio or Dan and Mrs. Smith would like to come with me. We'll just pop up to my office for a nice cup of tea and some fruit pudding," Page called out.

The two women got up as quickly as they could manage and made their way over to the man in the shabby black suit.

"It's pronounced Reardin, dear," Mrs. Riordan said.

"Well, aren't you the nicest things? What I wouldn't do to you," Frank gushed.

The two women blushed and giggled and left the room with the two orderlies following close behind.

"I truly look forward to meeting each and every one of you," Page said.

He began to stroll, silently, around the dining room, eyes moving from table to table like he was eyeing up lamb chops in a butcher shop window. He ambled over to the table where Richard and Clarence sat, scanning the room as he did.

"Each and every one of you," he said and glared at Dorothy.

"Darkness has fallen," Dorothy whispered.

---

Richardson walked down the back staircase and into the unfinished hallway. The lack of light and the smell of dust darkened his already black mood as he loped along toward Jenn Henderson's office. He understood she walked the same path as Mareth and let him grope and slurp all over her in this very hallway, but, despite that, he liked her. She always had a kind word for him, and when his father lay dying in their apartment, she covered for him. She told him to take all the time he needed - to come back to work when he was ready and not a minute before. The woman had a good heart for one of *them*. Maybe it was due to her being dead for as long as she had been. Still, she had the uncanny knack of being able to see through all the weeping and wailing that circled around humans and their deaths like emotional flotsam. There was an iciness in her that occasionally pushed its way past the compassionate face wore. Death was the end. Everything dies, without exception. Crying about it was not going to change any of it, so cry your tears and get on with it. She could have been part Necrosite.

If there was some sense to be made of this, any way out of it, Richardson thought Jenn would know it. She had been here longer than anyone, including most of the Necrosites currently employed at Winterbourne. Her experience alone should offer some insight into things like this, shouldn't it?

Her office was empty and from the amount of dust on the furniture, had been for some time. A book lay on her desk. He flipped the cover open and saw a handful of inappropriate pictures of people he had never seen before, romping near the water in nothing but their skin. On the last page of the book, written in a blank, stark white square at the centre of the page, were the words: **Eastern Flats**. And suddenly Richardson knew where she'd gone. And why.

"Lost something?" Pyewackett's voice echoed.

"I have, actually. I am looking for Mrs. Levinson's list. All things run off that list, comings and goings, Joyous new arrivals and sad departures of old friends. You know, all the important bits."

"Interesting," Pyewackett breathed.

"Is it?"

"It is. It's interesting that you would come to the Henderson woman's office when you could get a copy of the list from Mrs. Levinson herself. Strange, you would come down here looking for something the woman has almost nothing to do with it until month-end."

"I am under orders from the Soulreaver himself."

"Funny, so am I," Pyewackett said.

He removed his grey flannel jacket and rolled the sleeves of his shirt up. He unbuttoned the collar and squared up to Mr. Richardson.

"Alright, old one, let's get this over with."

"You can't be serious. You don't really mean to get physical, do you? Don't you know who I am?" Richardson growled.

"I know *what* you are," Pyewackett hissed.

"Oh, and what is that, pray, tell?"

"Irrelevant."

## 23

D avis pulled the lid off the banker's box and looked inside. A neatly folded, grey wool blanket lay at the bottom. A slip of white paper with his name and number neatly typed on top sat on top of the blanket. He looked around. Something about all of this seemed like a practical joke that everyone was in on except him. But it wasn't a joke. There was no Jenn Henderson, no people to jump out and laugh. There wasn't a single thing telling Davis this was anything but the awful Hell he had been sentenced to.

*Hel.* He corrected.

To his left was a dense grove of trees. To his right was a near-identical grove of trees, and a frost-covered path bisected the two. He stood in a purpose-built clearing, evidenced by the stumps that dotted the field around him. Just to the right of the path into the trees stood a small, shoddy wooden sign. There was nothing visible on the front of it, and Davis could see that it had been covered over completely by a layer of crystalized fog. A couple of quick puffs of warm breath into the palms of his hands, and he could wipe away enough to reveal the message.

**Please Don't Wake the Baby.**

The cartoonish face of a wailing infant, soother just out of reach of an angry mouth, filled the bottom corner of the sign.

*Baby?*

The wind picked up and tinkled through the half-frozen trees like broken glass dropping on cold concrete. Davis was suddenly very aware he was wearing everything he owned, and it wasn't enough. A pair of tennis shoes and the mostly white cotton socks inside them. Blue jeans with a hole in either knee and a worn and an overstretched Motorhead tour t-shirt he bought ten years ago at a concert that was too loud to hear. He'd been too drunk to have anything but a nagging suspicion that he had a good time. His own stupidity dawned on him. Fortunately, before any real damage from the cold could make its way to his skin. He reached for the banker's box.

Davis grabbed the piece of paper and stuffed it in his back pocket. He took the blanket and unfolded it with a snap that echoed like a clap of thunder, much louder than he thought should come from a flicked wool blanket. The cold was starting to bite, and standing here wasn't making it any better. He supposed he'd better get moving. Trouble was he'd no idea where he should be going. He'd never been in trouble before, beyond getting caught pinching a few handfuls of grapes from the greengrocer's fruit stand when he was a kid. He'd certainly never been anywhere like Hel - even as one of the emcees to the Underworld.

A closer look at the blanket revealed nothing, apart from it being thick, grey and wool that was a long as he was with a wide black stripe on either end of it. The air around him was cold and heavy with the moisture of the constant freezing and thawing fog. The t-shirt gave him an air of coolness around the Necrosites – they all thought the vicious-looking, horned band logo might be some distant relative. However, it was doing little to keep out the elements. He hung the blanket over the top of his head and wrapped it around his shoulders, still feeling a generous portion of it trailing down just below his knees. It was warm and heavy and thick and managed to keep out most of the wind.

*Well, now what?*

He pulled the folded sheet of paper from his pocket, being careful not to let in too much of the cold air as he opened and read: **Mareth 5840**. The same information scrawled across the top of the banker's box.

Davis felt a scorching heat along the back of his neck and just above his knees, and, if it didn't feel so good, chasing away the cold that surrounded him, he would have thrown the damn thing away. But when the smoke started to rise around him, he realized he would have to tough out the cold from here and tossed the blanket. He backed away, fearing it would ignite at any moment. But it didn't, and he moved in for a closer look.

The blanket was intact. The only difference to it he could see, on either end, just above the black stripe, was burned his name and the same number from the letter. He wrapped the blanket back around his head and shoulders and pulled it tight. It would probably get colder soon.

The light was fading around him. The sun was setting quickly, and it left a sky in its wake that glowed with the reds and warm oranges of a dying fire. It hovered behind the trees, but Davis didn't notice the colour of the sunset. He could see another light in the distance. A different kind of light, one that looked small from here but shone as bright as a beacon in the gloom and, the way it blinked between red and blue with a steady rhythm, suggested it was not a natural light. And that meant there were probably people around it. If he kept a decent pace, he could make it there in about an hour

*Maybe.*

Davis quickened his pace as the journey went on. Partly to get to the light as fast as he could and keep up whatever heat he could manage to generate by moving. It wasn't a jog or a run so much as it was an awkward hopping step followed by vigorous arm rubs that moved him about a hundred feet from where he had begun. And then, just ahead of him on the path, he saw it. Something that looked like a child but... not quite. It filled him with dread, and he wanted to head away from it, but a sick curiosity, much like the desire to smell sour milk before pouring it down the drain, stopped him. It practically pulled him forward to get a better look and see what the little thing really was.

It was small and young, no more than a year or two. It stumbled toward him in the stuttered walk shared by toddlers and drunks everywhere. As it doddered out of the shadows and moved closer to him, Davis could see the child more clearly and the fear prickled across him with every clumsy step it took. The little one had skin the colour of cigarette ash, stretched so tightly over its tiny frame. You could see every bone threatening to rupture through it. It was flecked with black, random, blotchy patches that dotted its surface, making the baby appear scorched.

The baby continued its unsteady path toward him. He could hear the child thing giggling and muttering away nonsensically. Whatever amount of bravery Davis had, froze and cracked away in the echo of the kid's laughter. Everything about this screamed at him to run, run far from this little thing. But a small part of his mind whispered to him that it was just a child, and he should help it in every way he could. A soft, compassionate smile turned up the corners of his mouth. Davis looked down and saw it was practically on top of him.

"C-cold," the baby said. It drew nearer, grabbing the bottom of the blanket and pulled on it. "C-cold," it whined.

Davis gaped at the little thing. His eyes fixed on the blonde ringlets that covered the tiny head, and his smile vanished as the child turned its horrible little face up to him. The infant's lips were blue shrivelled things that Davis had seen before, but they were always attached to people who'd been dead for hours. It giggled and gurgled and pulled harder at the blanket. Above the lips hung a nose that still looked like a baby's nose. Round and cute as a button, but it lacked the bubble gum pink skin of a healthy child. On either side of the nose, a little too far apart were its eyes, At least they should have been. Blanched eyelids had been stretched tight against the tiny face and bound in place by four ugly sutures.

"C-cold," the child repeated.

He pulled back against the blanket but couldn't get it away from the baby. Taking hold of the top of it, he turned his back and gripped it firmly in both hands. The baby took full advantage of the new position and bit the back of his calf. Davis wailed in pain and smacked a balled-up fist against the top of the little brute's head, which inspired it to sink its little teeth deeper into the man's leg.

"Ow! Get off me, you little fucker!"

Something told him it was an awful thing to spit that kind of language at a child. For a split second, Davis felt a glimmer of guilt drift through him, though it wasn't enough to prevent him from launching another wallop at the tiny head. He leaned forward and flicked both his shoulder and his hip simultaneously. The momentum managed to free the blanket from the child's hands and removed its mouth from Davis' leg, sending it earthward, where it landed with a thud.

The little grey thing lay on its back, completely still, mouth open, and looking dead, though it looked dead before and it attacking him. It jerked suddenly and began to wriggle, trying to the right itself and stand. When it couldn't, there was only one option left. A low sound, like the tenor whir of a slow-moving propeller, escaped the ugly blue lips and began to rise in volume until it was wailing like an air raid siren.

"Mama!"

Davis moved away from the child.

"Mama, mama, mama," it sobbed.

He heard laughter echoing behind him, the careless giggling of children at play, Bouncing off the rocks. Swirling around him and disappearing on the breeze that pushed its way through frosted trees. It sounded far away, like an old record, worn down from years of play, and at the same time, it could have been right beside him. From the shadows beneath the trees to his right, they came, fifty or sixty of them. Children. All of them as grey as the first and headed his way.

Despite the stumbling and tottering back and forth, the rabble of children moved with surprising speed and was soon on top of him, biting and clawing, chewing and tugging at the blanket and tearing holes in his jeans.

"C-cold, c-cold, c-cold," the swarm rumbled.

They crawled over one another to get to him, and Davis wondered how they were doing it. Not one of them possessed the ability to see, all of their eyes had been sewn shut like the first baby. Rendered useless by someone who'd decided sight wasn't a sense these children would need. He swung wildly, bashing the awful child things from his legs, pushing and kicking them as far as he could.

"Mama!"

Davis pulled the blanket from his shoulder and twisted the end into a makeshift club. He swung it low, connecting with three of the babies, knocking them flying. That the success of the blow surprised him as much as it did them.

For everyone he flung away, two more took its place, gnawing and tearing at the flesh poking through the rips in his jeans, all the while pulling at the wool blanket draped over him.

"C-cold, c-cold."

Two of them moved in and grabbed hold of his legs. Not attacking him, but not letting go either, giggling while they held him in place. Soon another two moved in and took his right arm, immobilizing his blanket club. He let his left arm fly in an insane arc, but without the added momentum from both shoulders, it didn't do much more than making the gruesome things giggle louder. They all attacked him then - en masse. Some pulling at his arms. Some ripping and tearing at his legs. While others climbed up the shoulders of the others to kick and claw at the small of his back. In minutes they knocked him to the ground and made a final drive to get the blanket away from him.

"C-cold, c-cold."

Davis felt the little feet and hands all around him. Grabbing and shoving him, forcing his face into the cold dirt. His strength was leaving him, and he was so tired. Davis – for a heartbeat and a half –

wondered how bad it would be to just give in, to go along with the awful pain, hoping it would end quickly. He shut his eyes.

An explosion belched its way through the air, like a roman candle inside a steel trash can, lit the sky lit up like a high mass. Davis ducked, his head whipping to the right, toward the sound. No more than twenty feet from him, a large figure silhouetted against the brightness of the rising moon stood looking like someone used to saving wayward travellers from the horrors of Hell.

*Hel.*

Clutched in the stranger's hands, the outline of as gruesome a piece of weaponry as Davis had ever seen.

"Come with me if you want to live," the figure called.

The babies' turned from Davis in the direction of the stranger, and they began to roil and whip themselves into a frenzy of laughter and gnashing teeth. With withering speed, they mobilized and launched themselves at the outline in the dark. In seconds, they were on top of the figure. The babies swarming around him, clawing and biting, bubbling with laughter. Without the opportunity to reload, the stranger managed to get off a poorly aimed shot from the giant gun. The two toddlers directly in front of him fell. The noise sent a shockwave of fear through the rest of them. It didn't last. Once the others realized there would be no more loud noises, they joined the dead children that had already made it to him and moved in for the kill. Seconds fell away like hours, but not for the man with the gun. An awful shriek pierced the dusk, and Davis saw him drop and disappear in the darkness.

He thought of rushing to the stranger's aid. Maybe he could grab the gun and use it as a club, but in the time it took to entertain that thought, the agonized screams from his right had ceased, and all was quiet. The bubbling laughter dropped away for a heartbeat as the dead children turned their attention back to him and his blanket.

Davis sized up the distance between the path beyond the horde of psychotic babies. He thought if he threw the blanket far enough away, it might distract most of the little bastards. The rest, he could barrel through and leg it into the woods until they gave up following him.

The first of the dead children were already at his feet, clawing up at him, trying to rip the blanket away from him, and crying out for the others.

"Hurry, baby c-cold," one screamed out. It dug a clawed hand into the thick flesh of his calf.

"Sonofabitch!"

The grey thing was joined by a second, and then a third, and soon the searing pain drove up into his legs and threatened to drop him to the ground again. The pain was profound. He could barely think past it. But somewhere deep in agony, a tiny voice grew to a scream and ordered him to keep standing. No matter what. And then it came to him.

*The blanket!*

He reached up, moving his hands above his shoulders, and pulled it off his back. Holding it high above his head, he faked to the left, and the babies followed suit. From somewhere behind him, a clang sounded like rusted hammers beating on a worn, steel bell.

The babies, startled by the noise, stopped dead and fell silent. It clanged again, and a panic rumbled through their voices like approaching thunder. The old bell rang out again, and the babies scattered, falling on already scraped knees, only to rise again and hurry into the tree line.

The clanging continued, growing louder and moving toward him. He turned, looking for the source of it and found himself face to face with a small fat woman. She was walking toward him, banging on a rusted triangle with a crescent wrench, filling the world with the racket.

"Those things are afraid of noise?"

"Just that sound," the woman replied.

"Why that one?"

"That noise means bath time," she answered.

## 24

Mr. Richardson's eyes never moved from Pyewackett's face. The two of them circled the big desk in a ritual of bluff and bravado. Spitting and clawing at the empty air, they growled like freshly bathed cats. Each hoped it was enough to make the other Necrosite give in and avoid coming to blows. It was a time-honoured tradition - gnashing teeth, barring claws and, once upon a time, pissing on the floor of the arena. It was all for show. Someone always gave in. This time, however, it threatened to boil over to actual violence.

The elder outweighed the younger Necrosite by a good ten pounds, and with their diminutive size, ten pounds could make a world of difference. But Pyewackett was younger. Younger and faster and, Richardson knew, well-schooled in the brutality of being a frontline body ripper.

"You know, we don't actually have to–"

Pyewackett launched himself at Richardson. The younger thing just wanted him to shut up. He hit him below the chest and knocked him to the ground. He sat on the old thing and began raining blows down on him. The onslaught was quick and vicious. The old

Necrosite doubted he could hold out much longer if it kept up. And, just like that, it stopped. The fists stopped flying, and Pyewackett sat back, sucking in mouthfuls of air and wiping a gangly arm across his brow.

Pyewackett huffed. "The problem with all you old fuckers is that you always want to–"

The younger Necrosite's words stopped abruptly as Richardson smacked the bottom of a glass paperweight off the side of his head. Pyewackett grunted and pitched to his side, falling to the floor, out cold.

"You were saying?"

Mr. Richardson grabbed the book from the desk and took off toward the elevator. He knew the younger Necrosite wouldn't stay put once he came to. The ache that would be throbbing in his head would be enough motivation to finish the beating he'd begun before being brained with a snow globe. The older Necrosite ducked into the darkened hallway. He hurried into the elevator, amazed there wasn't a klaxon or anything else saying he'd got on. He had only ever been on it with Davis or Jenn and felt just riding it was terribly wrong. The ride crept along. The music droned and crackled poorly through a speaker that was little more than a wooden box with a bit of old window screen stretched across it. Richardson wished he couldn't hear his father's voice, prayed the elevator music would stop it nattering away in his head. But it was *all* he could hear.

"It might have been better if he killed you," his father's voice said.

"What, why?" Richardson said.

"You got us into this mess. Everything has fallen apart, it was trucking along nicely, and now it's completely cocked up because you listened to that Wilson kid instead of reporting him upstairs. His father was no bloody good either."

"What am I going to do?" Richardson moaned.

"What are you going to do? You are going to fix this. That's what you're going to bloody do!"

Richardson knew everything he was responsible for was damaged now – broken. Maybe beyond repair. What was good and right was complete shit and would never be good again. As he saw it, there were a handful of little problems he had to deal with; the Necrosite tenements. The broken punch clock and stopping the Soulreaver from dismantling everything. All simple things with fairly simple solutions. The real problem was none of those situations, fixed or not, would do a single thing to halt the advance of the gargantuan mess he helped set in motion. Getting Jenn back from the Eastern Flats Killers, pulling Mareth from the jaws of whatever awful sentence the Night Court slapped him with, and stopping Barry Wilson from burning Winterbourne to the ground.

The punch clock stopping was a huge problem – maybe the biggest one - it was the focal point of everything they did at Winterbourne. But without Jenn and Mareth moving the dead along, what difference did it make whether the god-damned clock worked or not?

"He has to know," his father's voice whispered.

"What?"

"Wilson, he must know she would try to find a way to bring Death back. All it would take was a clumsy trail of breadcrumbs, and he would know exactly where she was. Then he could do whatever he wanted. Or have someone do it for him. Can't be a beneficent ruler with bloodstained hands, can you?"

"He wouldn't... he couldn't," Richardson said.

"She is a problem, and he can't exactly just kill her to get her out of the way, can he?"

The elevator came to a halt on the bottom floor, and the old wooded door squealed like a wounded pig. The path into the tenements was completely black; the light from the red emergency bulbs had gone out, and fear was prickling up his back. Though most of the residents of these apartments thought he spent too much time among the humans, he was still a Necrosite. Darkness didn't scare him.

Jenn had been this way. He could still smell her. Strictly

speaking, Necrosites were more adept at finding their way in the dark by sight than by smell. They were natural masters of seeing in the dark, like a cat with night vision goggles. Their sense of smell ranked somewhere between a walrus whose nose had been bitten off by a killer whale and a corpse. But human beings sleave a stink in their wake powerful enough to be detected by every creature in existence except themselves. Like an unpleasant mingling of bacon, cigarettes, and lavender eau de toilette, and it still hung heavy enough in the air that he could follow it right to her. The trail went off into the eastern flats.

*If* he got to her, and *if* the Eastern Flats Killers hadn't done away with her, and *if* Mrs. Pugwash hadn't talked her to death, he might be able to convince her to help him find a way to put all of this to the right. It was a hellacious lot of ifs, but what choice did he have?

"Where are you headed, Mr. Richardson?"

Richardson froze. It was Pyewackett's voice, and by the sound, he was standing right behind him.

He spun, arms raised with claws bared and ready, expecting the younger Necrosite to be there, ready for a fight.

"What's the matter, old one? Alone in the dark?" the voice echoed around him.

Richardson swung blindly at the voice and felt his claws slice through the empty air to his side. A bell rang, tinny and hollow. A beam of white light erupted from the ceiling, illuminating a scrap of yellow paper that floated earthward like a feather. The older Necrosite snatched it from the air.

*You're dead!* Was scrawled across it.

"What are you doing in my office?"

"Trying it on for size," Pyewackett sneered.

"Do you honestly think I'm going to just roll over and let you take my job?"

"Do you honestly think you're going to make it out of that basement alive?"

"Wait, what? What do you mean?"

"Wasn't it fortunate you found all the hints you needed to make your way to a small room in the back corner of the basement? The only place where the woman could bring Mareth back from Hel? Seemed a bit too easy if you asked me, but the Soulreaver said it was perfect. She would hurry down there – without question - to get her man out of trouble. She's likely taken care of already, ripped apart by the Killers. If she was lucky, it was quick, maybe even easy. I don't imagine it'll be a pleasant way to spend eternity, living in pieces at the bottom of a bucket like scraps from a butcher's table, but it needed to be done. They won't be as generous with you, what with the way Mareth has treated them and you being his faithful lackey and all.".

"But why get rid of me? Mareth, I get. I even understand getting the woman out of the way. You can't kill her - even Barry Wilson doesn't have that power, and he knows it. Jenn Henderson would *never* stop trying to bring Mareth back. But why me? I don't matter. I'm a cog. I am middle management at best."

"I wondered the same thing, and I tried to have you spared, Mr. Richardson, really, I did. But the Soulreaver said you are the last remnants of the old order. You and your family have served the office of Death almost since the beginning. A new broom sweeps clean, Mr. Richardson, and you need to be swept away by the new broom of revolution. That slum of a neighbourhood is next to go. Childish gangster stand-ins and gossipy old hags have no place in the new way. Hunters we were, and hunters we remain. There can be no misunderstanding. There can be *no* dissent."

"But what about the balance? The dead will pile up like cordwood. Imagine the state the upholstery in the waiting room will get to."

"There will be no more balance. The near-dead will be prey for the pack - nothing more. The Night Court will take care of the overflows by sending them off to other Death's domains once they realize they no longer have control over Winterbourne. Our little corner will remain a free state for all Necrosite kind."

"But what about the clock? How are you going to get it going again?" Richardson wondered.

"Why would we have to get it going again? If there are no dead to worry about, why would we need a clock to keep track of their time here?"

"The clock stopped after Mrs. Galston was punched out early. It's the last failsafe."

"And?"

"And, I expect a timekeeper is already heading this way," Richardson said.

"Wait, what?"

"A timekeeper, and you know what will happen when it gets here."

"Refresh my memory," Pyewackett said.

"It will reset all of this, back to before the error occurred. And everything that is out of place in this world, living, dead - or in between - will be wiped from it."

"You don't seem too worried," Pyewackett said.

"I will pay for my mistakes," Richardson said. "I let them all down. It's not a question of if anymore, but when. I know it's coming, and I guess I'm alright with it. I deserve it. I can't say it will go as smoothly for you lot."

"I've just remembered that I–" the younger Necrosite stammered. The microphone hit the floor in a belch of static and squealing feedback.

## 25

"Now what?" Davis said.

"Now you serve out your sentence. Now you keep your mouth shut, your eyes open, and keep a firm hold on your blanket," the little fat woman said.

"The blanket? Why is everyone so interested I this god-damned blanket, is there no shelter in this place?"

"Of course, there is. There is an old mining town, just beyond the trees, about a mile, I'd say. Stick to the path. You'll get there in no time."

"And I can use my blanket to trade for food and stuff?"

"Cheese and rice, no. You mustn't lose your blanket. Don't barter with it. Don't sell it. Keep it with you at all times, no matter what. Don't ever let go of that blanket," she warned.

"I don't—"

"How long did you get, young man? How long was your sentence?"

"Sixteen years."

"Julius' favourite number," she sighed.

"And is blue his favourite fucking colour too?" Davis snapped.

"Look," she began, "There are things down here who have been given two and three life sentences by the esteemed Justices of the Night Court. There are other things - wilful and terrible things that have been locked down here until the end days."

"Oh? Davis said.

"And they would do anything to shorten their time here. 5840 days is a dawdle to something that's already spent several lifetimes locked up."

"Okay, look. I know I seem like I am in tune with Death, the afterlife, and serving the void and all, but I really don't do much more than rub wrinkled foreheads and walk folks to the waiting room. I make sure they have hot tea and fresh biscuits, and a few decent magazines. Until yesterday, I didn't even know this place existed. I still don't know what the hell you're talking about," Davis sighed.

The fat woman smiled at him and took his hand. He could see for the first time that she had a short chestnut beard, flecked with grey that framed her face perfectly. She pulled him in close and wrapped her arms around him and squeezed, but not roughly. Like a python in a fleece jacket after a full meal, the hug was forceful but not enough to hurt. A warmth washed over Davis - through him. It was the warmth he felt when he held the withered hands of those he helped depart from this world. They had no family, no friends. They were the ones who were too frightened to leave on their own but far too frail and broken to be ripped away by the Necrosites. Davis held their hands and cooed and soothed and waited with them until they slipped away, their last moments on this earth full of love and warmth.

"It's simple, really. As the days pass, they come off your sentence. They also come off the blanket. Photographs never really caught on this side of the veil. Something about them stealing souls was taken a little too literally," the fat lady said.

A laugh bubbled up from deep in her belly.

"Oh, yes, right. Right you are," Davis fumbled.

The bearded lady could see he was still struggling with all of it.

"Since there are no photographs down here, there is nothing to say you are who you are. Except this blanket. As far as anyone is concerned, Davis Mareth might as well be a colossal, winged demon with the face of an octopus, whose very countenance would blacken your mind with madness."

"Jesus Murphy, are there things like that down here?"

"Not anymore, dear. He got out eons ago," she answered.

Davis felt a chill. He pulled the blanket tight, though he knew it would do little to chase away the real source of his being cold, no woollen sheet - no matter how long or how thick the weave would rid him of that.

"Best to be heading along, it's nearly dark, and things tend to get a little rough around here after nightfall," the fat lady said.

He started down the path, managing to make it three or four steps before an overwhelming need to turn back hit him.

"Has anyone ever gotten out? I mean, gotten out before their sentence ended. Has anyone ever escaped?" Davis asked.

"Just one, and he was never the same after it."

"Where is he now?"

"He likes to sit in the square most days, by the big clock. Feeds the pigeons and, pretty much, keeps to himself."

He turned away from the fat lady and began walking through the long, dark forest ahead.

"Keep on the path and maybe jog a bit here and there. It'll get you to the other side quicker," the bearded lady called out. "But that's really the whole trick to life, isn't it? Just keeping to the path and jogging a bit here and there."

Davis walked a few more feet. He swore to himself that he wouldn't turn back around, but the warmth he felt in the fat lady's presence was almost overwhelming. The thought of carrying on by himself was terrifying. He looked back again, hoping to see her, or better yet, hear her huffing and puffing and running along, trying to keep up with him, but she was gone.

Something occurred to him, an awful something he wished had

never entered his mind, because now that it had wormed its way in there, there was no worming it back out. The bearded lady, clearly, knew all about this place. That kind of knowledge only comes with time. How long had she been here, and what could she have possibly done to get her here for that long? He didn't feel so warm about her anymore.

*The blanket. Jesus, she just kept going on about the goddam blanket.*

His eyes darted back and forth, trying to focus. He couldn't make out anything but darkness and trees, though he continued scanning the path behind him for the slightest tremor. She wouldn't catch him off guard.

*And the babies, those awful things. She called them off me. She could put them back on me just as easy... couldn't she?*

Davis quickened his pace to an awkward quickstep, pumping his shoulders while his arms held the blanket tight against him. But when it didn't move him any faster, he wrapped the blanket around his neck like a scarf and ran. He kept at it, going full out into the blackness, until his lungs burned, threatening to seize up if he didn't at least slow down a little. He stopped. The lack of food and abundance of gastric juices bubbled through his stomach. It tingled in the seat of his pants, threatening to evacuate one end or the other if he didn't. When enough of his breath had returned and the nauseating square dance in his guts finished, he set out again - at a much slower pace.

"They... can't still... she can't... she wouldn't..." he puffed.

The night had fully settled in, and the thick darkness of the forest made it easy to see the electric glow of manmade lights from the mining town ahead of him. It wasn't far, ten or fifteen minutes, he reckoned, even at the winded crawl he was moving at now.

"Hallo, Meeshter," a voice said to his right.

The nearest he could figure, Davis entered Hel around 4:00 p.m. He had been wandering around, dealing with nasty, dead babies and incredibly pleasant, hirsute mothers in clothing that resembled upholstery, for the better part of two hours. Long enough for his eyes to adjust to the lack of light in the grove. But, he couldn't see a single thing that told him whatever just spoke was anything other than a frost-covered tree.

"Ah... hello?" Davis said nervously.

The frozen fog began to crackle and snap and drop from the boughs of the Fir and Scots pines along the right-hand side of the path, twinkling starlight reflections as it fell. A thickly muscled arm pushed its way between two low hanging branches, followed by a second thick-muscled arm. A head made its appearance, and, despite the darkness around him, Davis could make out the thing's features.

It was a bulbous, melon-shaped head, wrapped in loose, scar-covered skin that looked the colour of newly rolled steel. In the middle of the face and spaced too close together were its eyes. Miniscule little holes drilled in the pale blue of its face, filled with two blanched grapes that made Davis think the thing was as dumb as ditchwater. The deep furrows cut into its forehead gave him a look that said violence would be the first and only act if it were reminded - even slightly - how dumb it was. The eyes searched the blackness, and the head cocked from side to side, trying to locate the source of the voice. Davis realized the thing's eyes were too small and too close together to be of any real use. He reasoned the sour expression was probably nearsighted squinting rather than a shitty disposition. The thing's nose was long and pockmarked, and the tip of it stretched downward, nearly covering the cleft in its lips.

The hands wrapped around the tree trunks on either side of the head and continued to pull, bringing the rest of the thing forward. Free of the undergrowth and drawing up to its full height, the head and shoulders stood atop an imposing torso that rested patiently above thick legs. The thing stood directly in front of him now, and Davis could see it was a whole head and shoulders on top of a head and shoulders taller than he was.

"See, me ish no tree. Me ish good guy. Hallo, meeshter," it said.

Davis stood still. It towered over him and outweighed him by at least three times.

"I'm Davis. I'm a good guy too."

Plainly speaking, Davis knew most of the people who confessed to being good guys were anything but. This thing was probably no exception.

"Ish dot you blanket?"

"Yes."

"Dot's a nice blanket. Maybe you give I dot blanket, and you don't go squishy."

The big brute ambled over to Davis and clapped a meaty hand across his back, nearly driving him to the ground. He realized then that if it decided to take the blanket from him, there wasn't much he could do to stop it apart from leaving a nasty bloodstain on the big bastard's knuckles.

"Oh, good guy! I ish sorry.

The big thing grabbed hold of Davis and hauled him back up.

Davis thought maybe he could leg it. Just run as fast as he could in the hope of moving himself faster than the big thing could - and reach the town. Or, at least, keep going until it gave up. It was, however, currently standing directly in front of him and blocking the path through the trees completely.

"What if I just, ugnh–"

The blow was short and sharp. It knocked Davis backward, ass in the dirt and head ricocheting off the hard ground. The thing moved in blindingly quick and stood over top of him.

"Hey meeshter, now you gonna give I dot blanket cos I just gonna take dot blanket, hokay?"

Davis lay splayed out on the rough path, bits of gravel poking and prodding the small of his back. The fog in his head managed to obscure any indication he was about to die, and so, he did what came naturally. He waved his arms and legs up and down and made dirt angels on the path. His arm struck something in the darkness. From the feel against his fingers, it was the broken end of a glass bottle. It was hard and jagged, and just enough of a neck remained for him to wrap his fingers around and drive it home into one of the big meaty legs.

The awful, grey thing howled and jumped back from the little man on the ground. It was a chance. Davis took it. He pushed up from the ground, snatched the grey blanket away from the giant thing and ran toward the light of the town. He pushed himself hard and moved fast until he could see the town coming into view. But he would have to stop – slow down at least, or he would crumple to the ground like a pile of old laundry. He slowed and caught his breath and pushed himself forward. Slowly. One foot in front of another and made it through the steel gates of the town.

"Fresh meat!" a voice screamed.

A crowd began to gather around him.

Foul, dirt-covered things. Vaguely human things gathered around him. They all wore a look of hopelessness like they were handed it on entry to Hel. All of them pushing in, grabbing at him, hoping to get a piece of the new inmate. The first blow hit Davis behind the knees, followed by a second across his back. Another harder strike landed, crashing into his gut and bent him over at the waist. He felt hands, so many of them, grabbing at him - pulling his hair and clothing and skin. Many arms groping, forcing him to kneel. A thick club came into view. An unconscious jerk rippled through his body seconds before the club thudded against the side of his temple. Davis's ears rang. He saw dozens of hands pull the wool blanket off his neck before he felt the ground under his feet rise up to hit his face. He fought to keep his eyes open. It was a losing battle.

His eyes cracked slowly open. Time had passed, Davis was certain of that, but he had no idea how much. The thudding in his head wasn't too awful. Not as awful as the blow had been in the first place. He was sitting now, but whether he got that way under his own power or someone else's, he didn't know. Though it was probably a safe bet that all of this was at somebody else's idea.

Davis looked around. It looked like he was in a gathering place, like a town square, and he was on top of a limestone platform with long granite stairs leading up to it. A well-worn wooden frame above a stone bed stood at the far end of the platform. A crowd gathered below. Things of all shapes and sizes surrounded the high stone dais. There were humans here. There were things that might be human and things that could never hope to be human on their best day. In front of the young death stood two other figures, practically human and bound at the wrists like he was. A man stepped to the three of them. An air of authority hung around his head like a bad smell. He grabbed the first prisoner in the line.

"Come swine, destiny awaits," he said.

He was tall and thin except around the middle, where he gave the impression of being six months along. His lower half was covered in filthy leather breeches. Above those was a white waistcoat stretched well past capacity. Over the waistcoat, a dark blue cutaway coat with tails extending nearly to the top of knee-high leather boots. A shirt that might have been white linen at the beginning of its life, now closer to the colour of a tobacco spit, finished the outfit and hung loose and open around a grimy neck. His hair was a tangled mess of greasy tendrils hanging close to his collar like Spanish moss.

Two other men, similarly dressed, stepped forward and took hold of the prisoner. They led him to the stone bed beneath the wooden frame and laid him on it, face down. His hands remained bound behind his back, and his legs were strapped to the stone bed with a wide leather belt. The two men stood on either side of the stone bed, facing the condemned. One pulled on a length of thick, braided rope, and when he had hauled up far enough, the other man inserted a steel pin into the wooden frame. The rope was tied to the frame, and the rope puller stepped back.

"Jesus, a guillotine!" Davis coughed out the word

"As all things begin, so must they end. Life and death are but two sides of the same coin. Tonight, he will sleep on Janus' pillow!" the ratty man proclaimed.

He nodded, and the pin was yanked from the frame. Davis

looked away, but he couldn't avoid the awful sound of the weight falling earthward and connecting with the condemned man's head. The crowd around the dais screamed their approval. In short order, the grubby man with the rodent face came for the being directly ahead of Davis. In minutes, he was strapped to the bed, the rope pulled and released. He, too, was gone.

"Ah, we've been waiting for this one for some time," rat face said.

He marched Davis to the front of the platform and stood him before the thronging mass of people and things.

"Here we have the one that would pervert the very rules our world is built on. Here is the *MAN* that would allow his fellow humans to leave this life for the next as they please. No regard for the laws that have kept time progressing since the very dawn of civilization. Does he deserve his fate, or is he worthy of Clementia's blessed mercy? What say you?"

A disgruntled rumble made its way through the assembled things and threatened to leave the greasy man without an answer until a lone voice spoke through the din of the crowd.

"Stone to bone!"

The crowd paid little attention to the noise that barely registered.

"Stone to bone!" the voice repeated. "Stone to bone!"

The noise of a thousand angry voices called out—some murmuring barely above a whisper, some shouting at the top of their lungs. A chant began and filtered its way into the sounds of the crowd until it became one roaring voice.

"Stone to bone! Stone to bone! Stone to bone!"

The head man flashed a toothless smile as his two underlings took hold of Davis and walked him to the stone bed beneath the wooden frame. As he got closer, he could see this was no Guillotine. There was no razor-sharp blade dangling from the rope above his head. It was a monstrous square stone - ugly and green and stained, with the blood and brain matter of those who had gone before. The condemned prisoner's head wasn't cut off, so much as it was crushed off its moorings.

"What the fuck is that? "Davis spat.

"Tonight, you will sleep on Janus' pillow!"

The crowd erupted with squeals and cheers.

The other two men shoved Davis into position, laying him down on the bed. They strapped his legs down and raised and secured the giant stone above his head. Though his arms and legs were securely fastened in place, his head was free, and he could turn it from side to side and face either one of his captors. While he looked from side to side, he couldn't help noticing the basket directly in front of his head at the end of the stone slab.

"Hey," he called out to the man on his left.

"Wotcher?"

"What's the basket for?"

"Wot?"

"The basket, what's the basket for? It's not as if it's going to catch my head after the massive stone smashes it to a pulp, is it?"

"Oh, that basket? S'got our lunch in it. Lunch break right after the executions are finished, innit?" the man said.

"Oh," Davis said. "Okay, I guess we should hurry things along then."

"Why all the talking? We're starting to lose the crowd. Do you think they'll throw any money once they've been bored by all this talk?" the head man said.

"Fine, right," the other man said.

"Behold the awful price of treason!" The head man nodded to the man holding the rope.

Davis closed his eyes. If this was to be the last moment he ever had, he wanted it to be a good one. His mind went straight to Jenn. The last words he spoke to her were angry, unreasonable, and he wouldn't have a chance to apologize. Or tell her he was wrong or tell her he loved her or tell her...anything. Ever. He wished there was more time. He wished she was here to wake him from this awful nightmare. He wished... for her. Death took a last breath and turned his head toward the granite staircase. If he could have anything granted to him right then, it would have been for his hands to be loose so he could rub his eyes.

Up the stairs, like the tweed cavalry, came Sgt. Joe Friday, waving an ugly black .38 revolver and screaming about the facts. The three men on the dais scrambled to get away from him, genuinely afraid of the man in the wool trench coat and black trilby hat.

"All of you savages can just keep backing away, or you can eat handfuls of hot lead. I don't give a damn either way," Sgt. Friday barked.

He rushed to the stone bed and undid Davis' straps. As the younger man sat up, he swore he saw Joe Friday's face contort and flicker like a T.V. with a bad picture tube. A small, old man in wire-framed glasses suddenly stood in front of Davis in clothes that were much too large for him. He held his breath and screwed his face up as if he were trying to push a huge weight with his mind. Suddenly his face began to warp again.

"Run for the stairs, kid," Sgt. Friday said.

## 26

"Come, brother, you know how the Soulreaver hates to have his speeches interrupted," the young Necrosite said to Pyewackett.

They rushed past him - young and old - all the true believers hurrying to the mailroom to hang off every honey-soaked word from the mouth of Barry Wilson. Pyewackett took his time getting to the great hall. He always had a prime spot during these speeches - close enough to the Soulreaver to touch him and hear every word he said perfectly clearly. Though he'd heard the speeches often enough now, he could recite them from memory if he had to. The white linens and cat statues had been removed from their closet hiding places and laid out on the sorting tables. The air was filled with the thick blue smoke of too many incense burners, which by Pyewackett's reckoning, was anything more than one. The steps had been pushed together into a stage for the Soulreaver to stand on while the throng of his sycophants adored him from below. A muscular Necrosite stood at either end, scanning the crowd, each hoping there might be something that would require a bit of yelling or bashing.

Pyewackett ambled up to the stage, sizing up the crowd as he walked. They were kids, mostly. Zealous defenders of the faith, but when it came right down to it, he wondered how many would get their hands bloody when the revolution was in full swing. He loped up the stairs and signalled to a Necrosite at the back of the room. The smaller thing swung the heavy fire door of the mailroom shut, and an excited murmur rumbled across the crowd. A hush crawled through them slowly. A chorus line of one lizard thing shushed another until there was complete silence for the Necrosite in red robes. He stepped onto the stage as though he had appeared out of thin air.

"Hunters we were," the Soulreaver said quietly.

"And hunters we remain!" the crowd screamed back in a single, deafening voice.

They erupted in a roar of cheers, and the walls of the mailroom shook. The Soulreaver raised a hand to quiet them, and the noise stopped as quickly as it began.

"My friends..." he began.

"Did you hear that? Called me, his friend," a Necrosite whispered to his neighbour.

"Shh, I can't hear him speak."

"The time for action has come at last. The untrue servant of the void and his everlasting plaything have been removed. Permanently. And it is time to throw off the shackles of oppression that have bound us to this farcical office for a millennium."

"What did he say?"

"Something about building a shack near the museum."

"You what?"

"Shhh."

"Today, we will rip and tear away the last remnants of the old ways, break the chains that have held us captive since before any of us were born. The slums that we have been forced to call our homes will splinter and burn in the flames of revolution. We will take what is rightfully ours from them, and we will, at last, be free!" the Soulreaver screamed.

He had them, all of them. If Barry Wilson told them to tear the building down, brick by brick, they would have been in the backyard of the Winterbourne estate, standing in the smoking ruin of a nursing home in a heartbeat.

"Rise up now, all of you. The time has come. A new dawn is breaking! Go to the Eastern Flats, go to the Western Path, smash and tear, break and burn - raze it all until nothing remains of the slums they want us to call home. Those who are not with us are against us and must be crushed under the wheels of Necrosite liberation!"

"Fall out!" Pyewackett yelled.

The horde scrambled for the door, seething and raging and clawing at one another to be the first to usher in the new dawn.

"A word, if you please," Barry Wilson turned to Pyewackett.

"Sir?"

"I wonder if you and the other two might go and have a word with our new director, it appears we have hit a bit of a snag."

"I'll see to it, sir."

"Thank you," he answered.

He turned to leave but stopped short when he noticed the other Necrosite wasn't leaving.

"Something further?"

"Sir, I've learned something - it may be nothing, really. Richardson mentioned it, and I would take anything out of his mouth with a grain of salt, but are you aware that while the clock has stopped, the dead will remain... that is... sort of... here... among us all, until it gets going again?"

"Aware of it? I'm counting on it. The dead wandering here like our own private game preserve, to hunt and kill whenever we choose? Once we control the clock, we control the herd, Pyewackett. They will fall like cattle in the slaughterhouse."

"Aren't you worried about repercussions?"

"From whom?"

"The Night Court, for one. Surely, they won't allow us to just stop time in our little corner of the Underworld. What would stop everyone from doing it?"

"Do you think they would come nosing around down here? Seems a bit like slumming now that they have Mareth, don't you think?"

"Richardson did mention that if the clocks didn't start again, a timekeeper would be released after a while."

"You can't be serious? A timekeeper, here? Wait, what's a timekeeper?" the Soulreaver asked.

"As I understand it, the timekeepers are a safeguard against those trying to get more life by stopping the clocks. If they are not restarted after a certain period, the timekeeper is dispatched. Everything is reset."

"Well, that doesn't sound so bad."

"All of the dead would be removed, and I should think the responsible parties would be sent to stand before the Night Court. Or worse."

"That would mean that—"

"Exactly, sir."

"Well, by the time anyone on that side of things realizes anything is out of sorts, I'll have taken over things here. They'll have no choice but to acknowledge me as the equal of every Death in their jurisdiction. We'll just have to move a little more quickly to get the big clock going before they find out".

"How?"

"I have recently learned there is someone who could restart it. We need to find her and get her to do it."

"Who is it? Say the word, and we'll round her up."

"You and the other two killed her dog earlier. Richardson spoke to her after that. Find her, and bring her here. She will start the clock and get us out of all of this."

"And if she doesn't come willingly?"

"Convince her," Barry said.

Pyewackett stood for a moment, digesting in the Soulreaver's instructions before he spoke again.

"And independence?"

"What?"

"Independence... for all of Necrosite kind, do you still intend to free us all from the bondage we have existed in our whole lives?"

"Oh... oh, yes. Yes, Freedom for Necrosites from every social stratum. Of course, the ones who run the offices and keep things ticking around here and the groups in maintenance and housekeeping will be encouraged to continue in their respective roles, but with the knowledge that now... now they will be working for the greater good of Necrosites everywhere," The Soulreaver said.

"I'm sure they'll be awash in oceans of pride, sir," Pyewackett said.

———

"Mrs. Smith, would you say you're a size seven – eight, maybe?" Frank said.

Mrs. Smith blushed. "Oh, aren't you a charmer? I'm a size thirteen."

"Excellent!"

"I'm a size 10," Mrs. Riordan added.

"I just bet you are," he said.

He grabbed a black leather valise from a closet beside the big bay window and set it on the desk. Popping the latches, he flipped it open and took out two ten-foot square, blue plastic tarps. In turn, he asked the ladies to stand and placed the tarps under each of their chairs, explaining that later that day, the office was to be fumigated. He didn't want any of the chemicals to stain the wood floors. When he was satisfied the floor was safely covered, Frank invited the women to sit back down and disappeared out the office door. He re-emerged after a few minutes of nattering between the two women with a tray full of digestive cookies and two cups of tea.

The women sipped at the tea and made polite chit–chat with him, asking about his life outside this place and did he have a wife and did he have children. All the things old women tend to talk about over hot beverages. The tea was drunk up, the cookies were eaten. The two ladies thanked the nice man in the shabby suit, telling him he was a lovely young man, and if he'd only pay a touch more attention to his appearance, he might land himself a nice girl. Page thanked them for their advice and told them their years of wisdom were a resource for everyone at Winterbourne. Frank continued to speak to them in a voice that lulled them nearly to sleep. Not long after that, Mrs. Smith and Mrs. Riordan announced it was about time they were getting back to their rooms.

"I'll just call for a porter," Frank said.

He dug in the pockets of his suit, one by one, jacket and trousers, until his hand hit a folding knife with a black handle. He flicked it open, locking it into place, revealing a gleaming, polished steel blade. An ugly serration ran along the bottom of the blade. Frank raised the cutting edge, watching it glint in the sunlight pouring in through the bay windows and stood in front of Mrs. Smith.

"Oops, nearly forgot," Frank said and walked back toward the black leather suitcase.

Frank removed his wrinkled black jacket and hung it over the back of the desk chair. He rolled his sleeves nearly to his armpits and pulled two large, black rubber gloves and an ankle-length, yellow apron from the suitcase. He put them on, never once taking his eyes off the women.

"Here is where I should say something funny and a little creepy, but I never was too good with that kind of stuff," he said.

He whistled tunelessly to himself and drove the knife into the centre of the old woman's throat. Frank left it there while he stepped out to the hallway and returned with a five-gallon bucket. He positioned it, so the handle of the knife sat just above the inside wall of the steel pail and gave the knife a quick jerk. It released with the sound of a sloppy first kiss. With it came Mrs. Smith's blood, cascading into the bucket with the force of the spray at Niagara Falls. The flow seemed to go on forever. Frank thought of timing it with his watch.

"Jesus, this old broad just keeps going," he smirked.

The gushing blood slowed to a trickle, and he was confident any excess would be blotted up in the old woman's blue cardigan or pool up on the tarp beneath her. Either way, there wouldn't be much of a clean-up when it was all done. Frank lowered Mrs. Smith to the ground and turned to Mrs. Riordan, who sat utterly stone-faced, even after witnessing the death of her friend.

"I put something in the tea to keep you here." He was shouting at her as though she were hard of hearing. She wasn't. "Momma used to give it to me when she had her special visitors come to the house, so I wouldn't make any noise while she was fucking them. Oh, I could hear it all, just like I know you can hear me, but I couldn't do a thing about it. I used to think fear alone would keep people from running away, but I learned the hard way. Fear is just enough to get people to act stupid and run. And usually call the cops. Fear isn't enough to do anything. You need terror. Real terror. Fear'll make a body shit its pants. Terror makes a body seize up and refuse to run. Fear, Mrs. Rear... Mrs. Rye... Mrs. R is a big pain in the ass. Terror is a game-changer. And you might be afraid right now. Hell, you might be crippled with fear. But you haven't experienced terror. Not yet, anyway. But you're going to."

Mrs. Riordan's eyes stared straight ahead, ringed with red, unable to convey the panic racing through her body.

Frank raised the knife to the unblinking eyes and caressed it slowly across the bridge of her nose before sticking it deep into Mrs. Riordan's throat and pulling the metal bucket up underneath. He jerked the blade out quickly and watched her blood flow into the pail. He eased her gently to the tarp as the flow ebbed and grew silent.

"If those two are meant for us, we prefer them a little less dead," Pyewackett said.

Johnston and Bunn sniggered and crowded in through the narrow doorway.

"The Soulreaver wants to see you," Bunn sniggered.

"Damn it, what does he want? I just got started here."

"To see you. I thought that was fairly clear," Pyewackett said.

"I meant, do you know why he wants to see me?"

"There is a problem with the dead," Johnston snapped.

"How can the dead be a problem, except when you can't get rid of the goddam bodies?"

"Ah, who's a clever boy? Aye, there's the rub. Before long, those two women you've skewered will get up and begin to walk around as if they had just woken up from an afternoon nap. Soon the dead will begin to scamper around the halls of this place like vermin, minus the chewing on the furniture and power lines," Pyewackett explained.

"You're yanking my chain - how can the dead not be dead?"

"The big clock is broken," Pyewackett said.

"What?"

"There is a clock, a punch clock of sorts - in the basement of Winterbourne... this facility. The moment anyone comes within these walls, as a resident or full-time employee, their name is put on a punch card, and their entry time is stamped. When it is time for them to go, they are clocked out, and the servant of the void ushers them into the waiting room where they await instructions to their final destination. However, with the big clock at a standstill, the dead remain firmly in place. *This place*," Johnston said.

Frank stared blankly at the three of them.

"Mr. Bunn, if you would please," Johnston said.

"There's a big punch clock downstairs, yeah? You punch in when you get here and punch out when you leave with us so far?"

"Gotcha," Frank said.

"Right, so the big clock is broken–"

"We had that at the mill once, the clock was broken, and everyone in the front office didn't know what the fuck to do. They ended up giving us all over time."

"So, the big clock is broken, and nobody can punch out. Now the thing about the big clock is it's the clock that measures your life here at this place. When your life's over, it's time for you to punch out, yeah?"

"Oh, okay," Frank said, and a small ember began to flicker inside his brain, threatening to grow into a matchstick-sized flame as something occurred to him.

"Wait, you're talking about death. It's some kind of death–clock... isn't it?"

"That's it!" Johnston shouted.

"Oh, wow," Frank pondered. "If the clock is broken, that would mean nobody could punch out and then–"

"I would like very much to go back to my room now, c'mon Evelyn, it's time we were going," Mrs. Smith said.

Mrs. Riordan sat up and pawed at the blue, plastic tarp beneath her.

"I don't have that sort of problem, and I've told you, people, that a million times."

The two ladies lumbered their way up from the blue tarps, stood, adjusted their clothing and, arm in arm, made their way toward the door.

"Do you want me to call someone to... uh... help you back?" Frank said.

"I'm quite sure we can find our own way back," Mrs. Smith said. The two of them trotted through the open door.

"Well then," Pyewackett said.

"Back to the task at hand," Bunn gushed.

"Yes, right. The Soulreaver is still waiting to see you," Johnston snapped.

"Right. About the clock?"

"Yes, about the cl – just starting what, exactly?" Pyewackett wondered.

"What?"

"When we came in here a few minutes ago, you said you had just started. Just started what?"

"You wouldn't believe me if I told you, and even if you did, you'd say I was off my nut."

"Try us!" Bunn blurted.

Frank's eyes darted around the room.

"What would you say if I told you I was making a suit? A skinsuit - like a suit made from human skin."

"I would say you lacked imagination," Johnston sneered.

"What?"

"Skin suit's been done."

"What, really?"

"Oh yeah, loads of people have done it," Bunn said.

"You're kidding me?"

"No, really. There was that guy in Plainfield making a woman costume, and soup bowls out of skulls, I heard. And that old lady in Dellapool, she was making hats if I remember correctly," Johnston said, nonplussed.

"And that group in Naperville reupholstered a car, I think," Pyewackett added.

"Well, sonofabitch. I figured I was doing something so terrible people'd shit themselves if they even thought of my name. I meant it to be something awful, something... evil," he said.

"Something mildly annoying," Johnston chuckled.

"At best!" Bunn chirped.

"You'll have to come up with something more revolting than just making a skin suit."

"What are your thoughts on, say, necrophilia?" Pyewackett inquired.

"No," Frank blurted. "God, no!"

"Maybe you could, you know, just not have a thing," Bunn suggested.

"What do you mean?"

"Maybe you could kill them."

"Yes?" Frank said.

"And that would be enough. Multiple murder, betrayal of a sacred trust. Angel of death kind of thing."

"I never thought of it that way. Two-faced evil bastards. Yeah. Welcome them through the front door with a smile on my face and butcher them like goddam sheep as soon as the family closes the fucking door. I could get behind that," Frank said. An odious grin clawed its way across his face.

"That's the spirit. When life gives you lemons," Pyewackett proposed.

"Do tequila shots!" Bunn finished.

"Or, if life gives you the elderly, make corpses," Johnston hissed.

"It's settled then. We'll just send along a cleaning crew to sort out all of this mess for you," Pyewackett said.

"How good are you little freaks at finding things?"

"Oh, we're the best at finding things!"

"Shut up, will you!" Pyewackett spat.

"Depends entirely on what you are looking for."

"If you were to find that bitch I live with, I could show you things that would make anyone of you call out for your momma."

"Funny you should mention her," Pyewackett explained.

"What's so goddam funny about it?"

"It turns out the Soulreaver is very interested in finding her as well,"

"Wait, what? What does he fucking want her for?"

"To get the big fucking clock going."

## 27

Ginny Morrison sat in the back corner of the bus station on a wooden bench that had been on the receiving end of so many bottoms that a permanent groove ran down the centre of it. It was old and smelled of mildew and dirty feet. She'd bought a one-way ticket to some far northern shit hole town with a name too difficult to pronounce, to see a relative who was so many times removed from her, she barely remembered her name - never mind what the woman looked like. An oversized handbag sat beside her. She thrust a hand into it and dug to the bottom in search of anything to take her mind off the boredom of waiting for a bus and felt her hand hit something big and metal.

It was a fat silver pocket watch hanging from a silver chain. She found it in a drawer in her grandmother's house when she was nine. The thing looked gigantic in her hand back then and still seemed larger than it should.

"What's this, Nana?" she asked her grandmother.

"Give that to me, child. You mustn't touch that," the old woman said. She refused to say another word about it. But, as the old woman lay dying, she took it and pressed it into the girl's hand, saying, "In time, you will know nothing but time."

Ginny didn't understand what the words meant then, and they were no clearer to her now. She held the chain aloft, dangling the watch in front of her face, nearly hypnotized by it as it twirled.

It was a godawful heavy thing, all thick silver and bevelled glass covering brass cogs and handfuls of coarse cut rubies to keep time accurate to the split second. A handmade Belcher chain hung from a loop at the tip of the watch with a small, round fob commemorating twenty-five years of loyal service hanging at the end of that. It looked to be the kind of watch a train conductor might carry, but her grandfather had worked at the mill after the war. She could never get a straight answer when she asked where it came from, and it had been so important to the old girl that when she told Ginny it was hers, she stopped asking.

"Do you accept it?" her grandmother begged.

"Umm, yes?"

"Freely?"

"Okay."

"And with an open heart?"

"Nana, you're scaring me."

The old woman pressed the watch into Ginny's hands and placed her own on top of the girl's.

"All the time in the world and all of it wasting away," she said.

Ginny felt the heat drain out of her grandmother's hands and the strangeness of flesh going cold snake into her palms, running its way up her arm and into her shoulders. It became more than just lifeless skin she was feeling; it was cold, nearly polar—ice, bitter, painful and relentless. Before long, her teeth chattered, and she tried to pull away from the woman's iron grip. She couldn't, and the cold began to sear into her flesh, biting and ripping like icicle teeth. If she'd have had a saw, or even a rusty old pocket knife, she would have hacked the old woman's hand off, freely accepted or not. But, almost as quickly as it started, the frigid assault stopped, and the old woman's hands loosened and let go.

*All the time in the world.*

It felt like a hundred years had passed since then. Ginny Morrison knew if her life was going to amount to anything, she was running out of time to do anything about it. She dropped the watch back into her purse, trying to think of something else - somewhere else. Somewhere away from Winterbourne, away from the same shitty situation, she'd found herself in time and time again. Away from Frank.

*And all of it wasting away.*

"Ma'am, may I see your ticket?" the voice behind her said.

Ginny rummaged through her purse, produced the ticket, and held it up without even glancing up at the voice's owner.

"Oh, headed up north, I see?"

"Uh, yeah, going to see my aunt Kathy," she lied.

"And will your little dog be travelling with you? Chico, that was his name, wasn't it? Poor old thing."

"Wait, what?"

Ginny leaped up from the bench like someone had just thrown scalding water at her. Standing behind her was one of the scary little things she saw the night Chico disappeared. It became clear the dog hadn't wandered off and died, so much as it wandered off and met this thing, or one just like him. The creature hissed at her and disappeared into the shadows beneath the wooden bench.

She stood and backed away from the bench, hoping some flash of brilliance might burst into her brain and show her a way out of this mess. A lone gangly arm protruded from the darkness beneath the battered wooden seat.

"Just wait 'til you see what we got in mind for you."

A dreadlocked head poked out alongside the arm and looked directly at her.

"You'll think the dog got off easy by the time we've finished."

She gazed around the vast hall of the bus station - looking for a solution, and it came to her in the form of the sign above the ladies' room door. Ginny hurried toward the bathroom and ducked inside, thinking the thing, whatever it was, had to be masculine wouldn't dare follow her in there.

"Isn't this fortunate?" a voice croaked.

A Necrosite stepped out from behind the trash can just inside the doorway of the bathroom.

"And we thought we were going to have to chase you down," a second said

"Fuck!" Ginny shrieked.

"Tsk, tsk. Kiss your mother with that mouth?" a third voice said.

"What do you want?"

"Your watch, my dear."

"Wait, what? My watch, that's it?"

"That's all. Well, there is one other thing, but the watch will do for now. If you could just pass it over," Pyewackett said.

She unfastened the pink band around her wrist and held out the small watch emblazoned with a rodent in a red dress and matching heels.

"Done, can I go now?"

"Not that watch, the nice silver one on a chain. The one at the bottom of your purse," Johnston breathed. He was trying to stay calm when all he wanted to do rip this woman's throat out and take the damn watch from her.

Ginny clutched her purse tightly. Her mind raced. Monsters weren't real, they didn't exist and – she was pretty sure if they did – they didn't need pocket watches. It was all the reason she needed to keep it away from them.

"If you hand it over, we can just get on with the other thing," Bunn chuckled.

"Shut up, idiot!" Johnson spat.

She inched away from them and, when she felt the heel of her sneaker hit the kick plate at the bottom of the bathroom door, she wheeled around and flung the door open, bursting back out to the lobby.

"There's something in the God damned bathroom!" she screamed.

The two unconscious junkies by the bus entrance didn't seem interested in this revelation, and she moved on to the ticket counter. Ginny began to jabber wildly at the man standing behind it.

"There is something in that fucking bathroom, something big. Three of them and they tried to attack me. If you don't do something right fucking now, I'll call the goddam cops!"

"Can you tell me what they were?" the man asked.

"They looked like rabid raccoons or fucking apes. Like fucking science experiment apes. No hair, like all big teeth and mutant."

"I'll have maintenance check it out."

He motioned to the man in the dark blue coveralls.

"Ray, would you mind having a look at the apes in the bathroom for this young lady?"

"What?" he squawked. "This is bullshit. I just clean this goddam place. You ain't paying me enough to be an exterminator too."

The maintenance man unscrewed the handle from a broom on his cart and headed inside the ladies' room. After several quiet and uneventful minutes, he re-emerged empty-handed.

"Nothing in there."

"You said there were three of them in there? Bald apes that tried to attack you?" the ticket asked.

"Yes, they said they needed my grandmother's watch and that they wanted one more thing from me, but they wouldn't tell me what that was. Probably to kill me."

"Okay, ma'am, you should probably just get on your way now."

"Wait, what? No, I've got to get up north, away from here," Ginny said.

"Going to see someone?"

"Yes, my aunt. I think it's my aunt."

"You don't know who you're going to see? Can I see your ticket, please?"

"Sure, it's right... wait, one of them took it. One of those awful goddam things has my ticket! It stole it just before I went into the bathroom!"

The sweat beaded up on the back of her neck. Ginny Morrison was confused and scared. She stared at the man behind the ticket counter and at the janitor when their faces said clearly what their words hadn't. Ginny lowered her eyes and stared at the floor, fear and self-loathing washing over her in huge, repulsive waves.

"Fucking junkie, why don't you just get out of here?" Ray snarled.

"Maybe you'd better go now," the ticket man agreed.

"No, I can't. I've got to get out of here."

"Look, lady, the cops are on their way. We don't want no trouble, just get going, will you?"

Ginny turned to the door. In the shadow of one of the awnings sat a Necrosite dangling her bus ticket in one of its hands.

"No!" she bawled.

As she turned to run toward the door, she caught her leg against the corner of a suitcase leaning along with one of the benches and fell straight forward. A grey-green face peered out from beneath the bench and hissed, displaying a mouth full of needle teeth.

Ginny screamed and scrambled back to her feet, turning in a wild circle, unsure of what to do or where to go.

"Now calm down, lady," the janitor soothed. He stretched his hand to rub her shoulder, trying to calm her. As he made contact, Ginny jerked and swung her arm wildly, her fist catching him just between the jaw and the upper side of his face. The janitor crumpled like wet laundry hitting the floor, and she ran toward the bathroom once more.

Waiting for her, in the shadows around the ladies' room door, a lone Necrosite stood with gangly arms wide open, and a toothy smile stretched across his face.

"That's right, come to daddy," Bunn said.

Ginny screamed again and spun around, feeling her shoes slide on the polished marble floor before she forced herself back upright. As she regained her footing, she pushed off in a run and smacked into the centre of the chest of one of Winterbourne's finest.

"Now, Ma'am, if you could just try to take it easy," the cop said.

"Fuck you, fuck you, fuck you!"

She grabbed hold of the front of his shirt and drove her foot firmly against his knee, looking like she might try to climb him like a tree when she was knocked off by a well-aimed swat from his partner's billy club.

"Just take it easy? You're too soft on these smackheads. You gotta knock some sense into them," the older cop said. He rolled her onto her stomach and snapped the cuffs onto her wrists.

"Where will you take her?" the ticket man asked.

"The only place we can take her," the younger cop said.

"Prison?"

"Worse, if you ask me."

"Oh yeah? What could be worse than prison?"

"Winterbourne Home."

## 28

The insubstantial thing clogged along in the old man's shoes, looking like a child learning to walk in stiletto heels. Walking, it decided, was an impractical mode of conveyance but one that was necessary for it to remain unnoticed among the beings it was trying to mingle with. It also noticed that none of them looked as dirty as it did. New clothes were needed—clean clothes like everyone else's. The timekeeper scanned the faces and shapes, hoping to find one alone and far enough away from others. A likely candidate leaned against the wall of one of the ramshackle buildings and practically ran after him.

"Jesus mate, you look like you could eat the arse end of an elephant and still have room for cakes and coffee," the man in the pin-striped suit said.

He clapped a hand on the back of the boiler suit. The slap made the shoulder of the garment bend and fold over and reassemble as quickly as it had disintegrated.

"Elephant," the timekeeper said.

"Right? You need to eat, and no mistake. You need food."

"Food."

"That's right, friend. I know a little place over here that will suit our needs just fine. Best food in town," the man said.

They walked across the palette sidewalks and onto the mud-caked street, stopping when they reached the front of a small brick building with a plate glass window. In the window, blinking proudly, was an emerald green sign announcing the Jade Dragon. Below it hung a small placard suggesting: Try the Mushu.

"We'll get a little grub into you, and you'll forget all your troubles." He smiled and led the way into the restaurant.

"Food," it said.

---

Mr. Richardson darted into a shadow to the right of the elevator, hoping he hadn't been seen by anyone. There were several groups of Necrosites looking for him and - worse still - if he was right and a timekeeper had been sent their way, the clock was already ticking, in a manner of speaking. And there was very little any of them could do about it. He came out of the shadows and headed into the eastern Flats.

*Where is everyone?*

The tenements were unusually quiet for a place that hadn't known silence since long before his grandfather was born. The streets were vacant like life had been sucked right out of them—nobody reclining on stoops or milling around the streets. Miles of laundry on hundreds of miles of baling twine was left unattended, hanging between buildings with no fear of absorbing the vulgar odours of stale cigars and Necrosite cooking.

"Hello?"

Richardson's voice echoed off the windows and around the buildings and up and down the closes.

"Hello!"

"Shut up and get in here, idiot. Before they hear you," Mrs. Pugwash said.

"Where the hell is everybody?"

"Gone, all of them gone."

"Gone where?"

"Anybody strong enough and dumb enough to believe the filth and lies coming out of Barry Wilson's mouth joined the cause and went upstairs," Ida answered.

"And the rest?"

"The Killers got 'em. Took them all for ransom, I expect."

"Ransom against what? There's nothing and nobody left down here. What the hell are they playing at?"

Mrs. Pugwash lowered her head and turned away from him.

"What is it?"

She remained silent.

"Ida, what... what aren't you telling me?"

"It's worse, so much worse," Mrs. Pugwash said.

"How... how is it worse? What are you saying?"

"Jenn Henderson was with them, and she was the one telling them to take all the folks out of here. She was the one calling all the shots.

———

Davis' eyes fluttered and rolled open. Nausea squeezed at the pit of his stomach, and he closed them again, hoping the sickness would pass. His head throbbed, and his body felt like he'd been sewn into a burlap sack and rolled down a hill like a wheel of Gloucester cheese. He was warm, there was that anyway, and by the crackles and pops, he assumed he was lying somewhere near a fireplace. By the smell, he could tell wood was not the first choice in heating fuel.

He felt his head and discovered two golf-ball-sized lumps just below his hairline and an ugly feeling gash that stretched from the corner of his forehead, across his nose and ending just below his eye. If it had been an inch higher, the cut would have taken his eye out. He tried to sit up, but the warmth of the fire began whispered in his ear and pulled on his shoulders, convincing him to lay back down. Hell, he might even sleep. If he still had his blanket, that's what he would have done.

"Oh shit, my blanket." He sat bolt upright, eyes wide and brain mostly engaged.

The memory of the beating and the theft of his prison blanket came creeping back, and Davis remembered he was currently in Hell.

*Hel.*

His gaze darted around the room, looking for something to tell him he was anywhere but where he was. There was nothing, not a single trace of Jenn or Winterbourne. Not a whiff of Necrosite either - a fact that made him a little happy in spite of everything else. Davis was in a small room not much bigger than a garden shed. It was made from short planks of wood that looked like they'd been salvaged from old skids. In the centre of the room, a few feet from where he sat, was a potbelly stove. Along the back wall behind the stove hung an oily piece of tarpaulin.

"Safety is clearly not job one in Hel," he said.

From the scorch marks on the floor, Davis thought the stove had one or two decent fires left in it before the whole place went up like a shoebox full of dried leaves. He pushed himself up from the floor. From there, it was a few strained pushes and grunts and groans until he was standing – more or less fully upright. A sort of calm descended on him, then A feeling that, since he was already here - though it *was* a prison - there wasn't much more that could happen to make his life any worse. At least not right now. He was safe for the moment, and there was a rumbling in his belly that said he needed food and fast. Hell, he was hungry enough to try the Mushu. Almost. He took in a huge breath, despite the rank smell seeping out of the pot-bellied stove, and headed for the door.

A gingham tea towel hung over a small window in the centre of the door. Davis lifted it, and the room was flooded with daylight that practically blinded him. It was almost enough to change his mind and put him back on the floor in front of the warm fire. He stepped through the front door and noticed something peculiar. Nobody was paying much attention to him. In fact, nobody seemed to give much of a shit that he was there at all. After the beatings he'd been handed when he got here and being robbed of the blanket, he figured there would be more of them waiting to finish the job the second he woke up. He had never actually been to Hel before, but he'd seen a good number of movies about prison and was a little disappointed that the assault that cost him his sentence blanket and nearly his life appeared to be the full extent of the hazing. Davis stepped off the porch and started walking.

The place was made up of dozens of small buildings that looked thrown together in the same lumber yard scrap heap way as the one he just left; little wooden matchbox houses, all in a row. One decent flash of lightning and the whole town would disappear in a whiff of ozone and campfire. There were several larger buildings here - sturdier ones of brick and mortar—a post office, a general store, and a Chinese restaurant whose neon sign flashed Jade Dragon. A sign hanging below it read: Try the Mushu.

"I really hate Mushu."

The road cutting through the centre of town was little more than an ancient layer of dirt, walked over by centuries of boots, feet, hooves with a thin veneer of crushed stone to give the illusion of traction. To the right, not far from where Davis Mareth walked out of the small shack, stood the stone dais with wooden gibbet that held the awful, blood-caked stone. A shudder ran up his back, and he quickened his pace to get past it.

At the end of the main road stood a red brick building that dwarfed all the others and, when the sun was directly behind it, cast a shadow that covered the whole town. Huge, multi-paned windows, including a few that still had actual glass in them, stretched across the front half of the façade. Two massive oak doors spread out from the centre of its bottom half, nearly covering the width of the building. A set of granite stairs led away from the doors and flared at the bottom as they emptied out onto a town square. An oversized, ornate fountain stretched up from the middle of what had once been the glorious centrepiece of the place. At the edge of the fountain, feeding birds and squirrels, sat a small elderly man. He stuck his hand in a crumpled paper bag and dug around, throwing bits of stale bread and nuts and seeds to the creatures at his feet. The more he threw, the more they came, and the more he cooed at them with delight.

"Nice day for it," Davis said.

"Forget it. *Forget* it!" the man moaned.

"Oh, okay. What is this place?" Davis asked.

"My father built it."

"Really?"

"Sure, five hundred years ago -maybe two. Just like that, boom, boom, boom, boom."

He made a motion with his hands, stacking them one atop the other, over and over. When he had reached what seemed a reasonable height, he stuck his right hand out toward the younger man.

"Michael Crawford. I built this town. I own it now. For five hundred goddam years, I worked, and I built it, and nobody came. Not one! But oh yes, I did it, I fucking goddam did it. Thy will be done, and the sheep will come in," he said. Tears rolled down his cheeks, and soon his body rocked with sobs that threatened to curl him into a fetal position. But despite that, he continued to stick out a hand to the younger man.

A warm smile curled across his face as he shook Davis' hand. The grip was firm but not overpowering.

"Pleased to meet you," Davis said.

He was a small man, the top of his head reached about the middle of Davis' chest. Slight was the word that came to mind, as though eating a decent meal was a pleasure that he hadn't enjoyed. His skin was tanned and wind-beaten, like someone who'd spent a lifetime outdoors, squeezing a living out of whatever fortune brought his way. The old man's hair, what was left of it, was white as midnight snow and flitted and flapped like streamers, even in the gentlest breeze. His eyes were blue - hollow and pale blue like Davis' were, and they showed the traces of a profound sadness carried for far too long. But there was still something playful in them, a glow of mischief that wouldn't be dampened.

"Wait, are you him?" Davis asked.

"Moyen, at the crossroads of time? Gah!" He winced and stuck out a hand toward Davis again. "Two become one, right?" He pointed to the giant clock tower behind him.

"Wait, what? What did you just say?"

"Forget it, forget it."

"No, wait. Are you him? You know, are you the one who... got out... is that you?" Davis scoured their surroundings, hoping nobody who could make sense of their conversation was listening in.

"Sure," Michael said.

"Really?"

"Yeah, made it out just like that. Boom, boom, boom, boom."

He piled his hands, one on top of the other, as he spoke, and after reaching his chin, he grabbed the paper bag from beside him and opened it wide. He tossed it mindlessly to the right of him and clapped and cheered as the pigeons and squirrels descended on it like vultures on a rotting elk carcass.

"Forget it, just forget it," he bawled.

The old man rose and headed away from the square.

"Come on, boy, my place is over here, and my father won't be back for two, maybe five hundred, like that. Boom, boom, boom," Michael said.

"Me?"

"You want to get out of here or not?"

# 29

Mrs. Smith and Mrs. Reid strolled into the dining room and took their usual seats, much to the dismay of their tablemates, who rose and left in a panic.

"Ogay?" Clarence said.

"Never better, why?" Mrs. Smith said.

"You're both looking a little green around the gills like you drank a skin full and then rode The Comet at Coney Island all day," Richard said.

"I think your dementia has kicked into high gear, Mr. Walters," Mrs. Reid said.

"Oh, alright then, where'd you two get to just now?"

"Ogay."

"We walked down to that nice young man's office, he's the new director, you know, and he made us some tea. I remember he asked me what size I was," Mrs. Smith said.

"Size of what?"

"Dress size, of course. What size did you think I meant?"

His mind burned. The word was on the tip of his tongue, practically daring him to blurt it out. Clarence looked at him knowingly and dragged himself toward his friend, banging into him with the footrest of his wheelchair.

"I know," Richard smirked.

"The question was a little, bloody impertinent if you ask me," Mrs. Reid bawled.

"Ogay?"

"Of course, I told him!"

"What then, did he just send you on your way, or did he want to know the size of something else?" Richard shot a look at Clarence like they were all in church, and he just farted and was waiting for the smell to creep along pew to pew.

"Yes, we had our tea and– "

"What? You had your tea, and then what?"

"I remember feeling fuzzy, out of sorts - like I was watching everything happen from a foot above my body," Mrs. Smith said.

"I could see all of it but couldn't do a single thing to stop it," Mrs. Reid added.

"Stop what, Mrs. Reid?"

"He stabbed us, dear, both of us. I felt the knife going into my throat - stung a little. Reminded me of being on a boat all day in the summer. You never seem to notice the burn until you're back in the shade. And then the pressure... oh, that awful pressure against my neck."

"Actually, I felt my skin pucker and suck up against the knife as he pulled it out. Then he held a bucket up to me while everything drained out. I felt a bit like a maple tree. Can you imagine the goddam nerve!" Mrs. Reid fumed.

"And?"

"And after that, it gets a little hazy, I think I drifted off, but it felt like more than just falling asleep."

"Agnes Reid, you've gone off your nut. I've never heard such nonsense in my life. Even from you," Mrs. Smith chided.

Mrs. Reid grabbed hold of Mrs. Smith's hand and guided it to the slick hole at the base of her throat, forcing her to probe her fingers around the awful gore-filled opening.

"What's this then, Myrna, place to keep your teabags?"

Mrs. Smith wiggled her fingers and felt around the jagged wound in her throat. Had it not already done so, the colour would have drained away from her face.

"Ogay?"

"That's what I was just thinking. How in the wholly blue fuck are you two still here?"

"Darkness has fallen. All time has stopped," the voice croaked.

"Jesus Murphy, Dorothy! You might make yourself known," Richard started.

"Ogay!" Clarence tried to push up from his chair in an awkward, startled motion.

"And the dead shall yet live, their bodies will rise," Dorothy moaned.

"Wait, what?"

"Yesterday is gone. Tomorrow has not yet come. We have only today, and it has not begun."

"Ogay?"

"Say, is there a way we could get through this without all the poetry? I mean, you can keep the spooky voice and the rolled-back eyes and all, but could you just talk plainly, without all the flashy words and rhyming? It loses something in the translation."

The voice within the old woman sighed. "Fine."

"You were saying something about the dead rising?"

"Well, yes, in a manner of speaking. The big clock has stopped, and the dead will remain until it moves again."

"Remain where?"

"Remain in the world of the living until they are touched by the hand of the void and ushered into eternity."

"Wait, what?"

"Ogay?"

"What's the matter?" Dorothy said.

"Which is it?" Richard asked.

"What? Which is what?"

"You said some big clock had stopped, and the dead would remain until it gets started again."

"Right," the Dorothy thing said.

"And then you said they'd be here until they were touched by the hand of the void, whatever that means. Which is it?"

"Well, both, really. Sort of a two-pronged thing. The big clock counts down the minutes of their lives until they run out, and then the servant of the void must usher them from this world to the next."

"Is that all? Why don't we just get the big clock going, find this servant of the void guy, and get the show on the road?" Richard wondered.

"The answers are all locked up," Dorothy said.

"Excellent!"

"Ogay!"

"I wouldn't think it was something you'd be happy about."

"You said the solution is all locked up, like in the bag, as in a certainty," Richard said.

"No, I said the answers were all locked up, as in the one who could start the clock and the servant of the void are confined to their present whereabouts."

"I got it!"

"Ogay?"

"The skinny kid, he's the one, the whattaya call it, this void thing, right?"

"Davis Mareth is the true servant of the void," Dorothy said.

"Alright, where is he?"

"The servant of the void currently resides in Hel."

"Jesus, he's dead?"

"Wait, what?"

"You said he was in Hell. I would have thought with all the good he did around here, he might have gone to the other place," Richard said.

Not Hell - Hel," Dorothy answered.

"Ogay?"

"Hel is the prison for anyone who has run afoul of the Night Court. Mareth will not set foot beyond its borders until his time is served," the voice said from deep within the cosmos that currently inhabited Dorothy Lauren.

"Well, that might make putting things to right a little difficult," Richard said.

"Ogay."

"Right. What about getting the clock going again? I suppose only the skinny kid can do that too?"

"Mareth is not the one to start the clock. There is only one who may do this."

"And? "

"She who could start the clock is now confined in room 107."

"Ogay."

"Exactly. What are we waiting for?"

"She will not be freed without bloodshed. Now, things are worse. A timekeeper has been released."

"A what? Isn't she... the timekeeper? She who could... what'd you say... wait. What was it again?"

"The timekeeper has been dispatched by the Night Court to restore order and wipe the slate clean," Dorothy moaned.

"Wait a minute, Clarence is getting all lost. Simpler language if you wouldn't mind, please," Richard said.

"Really? The Night Court released a timekeeper. They are the watchdogs of the underworld, literally. If the Big Clock stops long enough, they come and get rid of everything that doesn't belong. All the dead who should have moved on – ever."

"So that means if the clock isn't going, none of us can die, right? At least not right away?"

"Correct," Dorothy said.

Richard lowered his head beneath the weight of a sigh and knelt beside his friend's wheelchair.

"Start rounding the others, anybody whose time is a little on the short side. Anybody who can still get up and around easily. Make sure you find Minnie Martin. I've got an idea."

"Ogay?" Clarence said, slightly confused.

"I could tell you, but you wouldn't like it very much if I did," Richard said.

# 30

The door was unremarkable. It was a green fire door with a brushed aluminum handle and a sign in the middle of it that read 'storage room.' In fact, it was the 85$^{th}$, and last storage room in the entirety of Winterbourne home and Jenn Henderson was standing in front of it.

"Are you sure this is it?"

"Oh yeah, totally sure. This is the whassname, place you said," Wendell answered.

"What do you suppose is in there?"

"Dunno. That's where the whassname, night men came out of."

Jenn raised a shaky hand to the doorknob and, much to her disappointment, found it unlocked.

"Right, who's going in with me?"

"Oh, oh... uh... we should probably stay out here and make sure nobody, whassname, comes in after you, yeah?"

"I agree. All of them can stay out here and keep a lookout. You're coming in there with me," Jenn said and grabbed Wendell by the wrist.

It was a storage closet, full of brooms, mops and buckets, a floor buffer, a trash cart, and several shelves stocked with plastic bottles and jugs of pastel coloured liquids. It was small and smelled musty and slightly medicinal. It was packed full of bottles and buckets and the detritus of Winterbourne's janitors, but Jenn had a feeling there was more to it than what she could see in the glow of the emergency beacons. From the layer of the dust covering everything, no one had been down here in years

"I wish I had a flashlight," she said. She was suddenly bathed in the glow of fluorescent lighting, flickering slowly to life. Jenn scanned the room and saw, to the right of the door, the light switch Wendell had flicked on.

"Or we could, whassname, put the lights on."

Her instincts were right, and the room was much larger than it first looked. Between the two shelves of chemicals, almost unnoticeable if you looked at it head-on, was a narrow walkway that trailed off into the darkness. Jenn slid herself between the two metal racks, praying her ampler bits of her wouldn't topple a bottle or knock over a shelf. She made it through and felt a cool breeze hit her face from the back of the passage.

"You coming or what?" she asked.

"It's meant to be me giving the orders around here, you know? I am the bloody gang leader and all. This is complete, whassname."

"Bullshit?"

"What?"

"You meant to say this was complete bullshit?"

"No, no, not at all. What an odd thing to say. Why would somebody have anything to do with, whassname, cow crap?"

"Forget it."

The pathway was lit up for what she guessed was another ten or twenty feet and then continued on in the dark from there. It also appeared the ceilings lowered as the path disappeared into the blackness. They walked quickly until the light was completely gone from the hallway, forcing them to come to a stop and stand motionless in the dark.

"I can't see a goddamned thing. Got any more bright ideas?"

"Sure, follow me," the Necrosite said and grabbed her arm.

They walked along, quickly, in the dark, narrow corridor, and Jenn felt a knot tighten in her stomach as Wendell began to pick up speed.

"Wait," she.

What?"

"I can't see in the dark. We've got to slow down."

"I can. I've got, whassname, night visions."

"Wait, wait. That's what scares me. I am completely helpless in here."

"Is that it?"

Isn't that enough?"

"Pffft, if we wanted you gone, we could have killed you, whassname, ages ago. Getting Mareth back and making the Soulreaver, whassname, piss off is the only chance we got of maintaining our turf. None of that happens without you. You'll be fine. I swear it."

The woman saw him for the first time as something other than a repulsive little monster. She understood then, he was a kid whose world was about to change - for the worse - and he wanted to stop it. Desperately enough to offer his word to someone who he wouldn't trust as far as he could throw. She extended her arm.

Wendell raised a spindly arm, palm up, to meet hers. They took off down the hallway, slowly at first but within seconds, nearly flat out running. She fought hard not to let herself fall into a panic as they hurtled on into black. Like holding the reins of a spooked horse, all she could do was hang on and hope she didn't get dragged to death. The Necrosite moved at a speed that hardly seemed possible, particularly for a being that had a near-total lack of flexible knee joints. Zig-zagging along the corridor fast enough that Jenn could hear the air ripping past her and whistling through her earrings.

"I can't breathe!"

"It's true!" Wendell shouted.

"No, I can't breathe. I have to stop!"

He stopped instantly, and without the benefit of any announcement that he was about to do it, which caused the woman to snap violently forward in the direction of the wall in front of them - followed closely by the rest of her. Wendell had not released his grip, and Jenn's momentum pulled him along for the ride. The sudden, painful stop against the wall broke his grip and sent them both crashing to the floor.

"What was that for?" Wendell griped.

Jenn's face wrinkled into a look that said he may just as well have asked if the Dead Sea died straight away or whether it had been sick a while.

"Hey, there's a whassname, wall here."

"I would have never guessed," she said.

"No, I mean a wall but not a wall."

"Okay, I'll bite. What's a wall but not a wall?"

"See?"

"Oh, yes, perfectly clear."

"Here," he said.

Wendell took hold of her hand and pulled her closer to where he stood. Putting his own hands on either side of her shoulders, he turned her slightly, angling her view of the wall.

"I still don't-"

"Just give it a whassname."

Jenn guessed that with the speed of their travelling here, her eyes hadn't enough time to adjust to the dark. Though, what was there really to see in all the blackness, except more fucking blackness. She was sick of being cold. Sick of being tired and hungry and sick of being in the dark with a thing that smelled like rotten meat and boiled cabbage. And then she saw it.

It was there, but only just. If she had given up or pushed away from the wall in frustration, she might have missed it entirely, like the tiny white spot that lives on for hours after the T.V. is turned off. It was light, a tiny, dim little thing. Her eyes trained on it. After watching and waiting - staring, it grew and began to spread like molten gold over the horizon. Spilling illumination into the darkness that remained in rapidly shrinking pockets dotting the landscape beyond the storage closet wall.

"Holy shit!" Jenn blurted.

As the sun approached the tree line, Jenn could make out the grey shapes of a town. There were buildings in the places she could see, though most of them were on either side of a road that snaked away in front of her, in the shadow of a huge clock tower.

She hadn't seen anyone wandering around in the darkness, not that she *would* have seen them even if they were standing on top of her, but now that the gloom retreated from the town, bodies began emerging from the dwellings. To call them all human wouldn't have been accurate, though, for the most part, there was vague humanity to most of them. Trickling out at first and then, as the light grew brighter and the sun rose higher, they came in greater numbers.

They were dirty; they looked tired and defeated, as though the only thing that came up with the dawn was that hope had missed the bus to this town again. Jen didn't know where this place was, and she didn't know who these people were, but she knew the look of the broken and abandoned, and it was plastered on the face of every being that passed in front of her. She watched them walk by, one by one, and the pity tingled in her stomach and up her back, even for the ones she could barely look at. Why would any of them stay in such a place? What could be so tempting that it lured them? What actions so awful had damned them all to stay in this grey, rundown village?

"What now?"

"Y'got me," Wendell answered.

Jenn's gaze darted around the buildings, stopping by the flashing green sign of a Chinese restaurant just coming into view. Her eyes moved along the dirt road leading to the clock tower, and the buildings that surrounded it and back to the figures that milled around the buildings, but nothing produced any idea what she should do. A sadness settled in on her. Like a weight on her heart that sat there, a glaring reminder that there wasn't anything she could do beyond hope that this wasn't their whole world.

Hope is a funny thing. It can, and will, abandon you at the darkest of times and leave you broken, alone and full of regret. It can get lost just by entering a building. Or, when you are about to abandon it altogether, hope can come wandering down the street in dirty blue jeans and a faded concert jersey.

"Davis!" she screamed.

He walked along the palette sidewalk, being careful not to twist an ankle or step off the boards and cover himself in the mud from the dirt road. He looked different than the other faces she'd seen. She had studied every crag and every crease over the last five years with him. She missed all of them dearly, even the wrinkles he would get between his eyes that made him look old when he was trying to be angry with her. Jenn couldn't remember what the fight was about, though if she thought about it long enough, it would've come back to her. What she did remember was how awful she felt that they had parted angry. But it wasn't guilt or her love for him that made him stand out. It was that even in the crisp morning air, with steam trailing from his mouth, wearing nothing more than jeans and a t-shirt, he was beaming, and he walked along as though he hadn't a care in the world.

"Davis!" she slammed her fists against the wall.

"Is that, whassname?"

"Yes, God damn it! And I've got to get in there!"

She scoured the walls, sliding her hands along it, slapping it, punching, trying anything to get the damned thing to move. The sun had reached a height in the morning sky that cast a wide swath of illumination into the narrow hallway. But for all the light the day provided, it offered no clear way through the wall and into the dirty little town. Wendell began to emulate her movements, beating his own fists against the wall and sliding them up and down the wall.

"Umm, feels good and all, missus, but what are we doing here?"

"Davis is in that shitty little town, and he needs to get out of it.

Since he doesn't seem to be in any hurry to do that, I need to get in there and remind him of all the things he is missing out here. So, I'm looking for the goddam way in."

She pounded her fists on the wall until warm rivulets of blood trickled down her arm. She smacked the wall again, opening the cut further and reminding herself about immovable objects and irresistible forces. Jenn dropped to her knees. It was unfair, being so close but no closer to getting to him. The tears came and rolled down her cheeks like cold spring rain.

"You'll never get in like that. That door doesn't work that way," Mr. Richardson said.

# 31

The Soulreaver gazed at the back property through the bay window in Davis'office. His concentration was occasionally broken by the grey squirrels that darted around the grass and played in the box elder trees. Mareth and his plaything were gone, and the office was his, but it did little to lift his mood. The revolution had begun. All the wheels spinning in the right direction, toward better things and the Necrosite's shameful past was about to be a memory that would die out with the last of the older ones he should have been overjoyed. But Barry Wilson, the Soulreaver, was not happy.

His father brought him up here for the first time, so many years ago. As the head of janitorial services and having keys to virtually every door in the place, it meant he could keep an eye on every Necrosite employee he supervised. There was no slacking off when the elder Wilson was on the job. He ran a tight ship. He also had an incredibly short attention span and a habit of forgetting where he left his keys. As a result, he had to quickly learn to pick locks to avoid the mockery of his underlings. It was a handy skill to have, and one he taught to his only son, who used it whenever he got the chance. But not for just anywhere. There was only one place he wanted to go when the lights were dimmed, and everyone had gone home for the night. The corner office. The big office - Death's office. Barry would slink down pitch-black hallways, staying hidden in the shadows until he picked the lock on the office door.

The big office made him happy. It was wide-open spaces, and fresh air that streamed in through the window screens, not the cheek to jowl hovels pushed together underneath the grime that clung to the tenements like fog. Barry breathed deeply and felt his spirits lighten. After a lifetime of trying, he was finally free. But the elation was fleeting, and soon the blackness of his mood brought him back to where his mind tried to avoid going, right here and right now.

*Free, but at what cost?*

The faces of Necrosites in the tenements below him flashed through his mind. All running in terror from the talons of the young zealots, he'd just let off the leash. The regret hit him like a kick in the guts.

*The Western Paths, the Eastern Flats - every one of them? Should they all suffer for their lack of vision? Why do they refuse to see the truth? Or are they just stubbornly hanging on to their little bit of sod? Can't they see I'm trying to bring them freedom like they've never known?*

He looked out the window to Seonagh's woods and the horizon beyond, but his attention kept going back to the Eastern flats and the dingy home he shared with his father. He remembered the old Necrosite's words as he sat there, grey and tired, so very long in the tooth.

"We were hunters once, Barry. Great hunters. The hunter within remains. I would also very much like a little more tea and another biscuit please, it's not as though I'm dying, is it?"

And then he did.

A fat squirrel crawled out on a branch and looked up at him. It was close enough that if Barry opened the window, he could have grabbed the fuzzy little bastard and chewed its face-off. Bloodlust ripped through him like a high fever, and he knew it would not be calmed by ripping apart a squirrel.

*Hunters we were, and hunters we remain!*

"You wanted to see me, Mr... um... sir... guy?" Frank stammered.

"Ah, Mr. Page, please come in," Barry said. "You've no doubt heard we have a bit of a problem?"

"Problem, what problem? There's no problem as far as I can see."

"Ah, yes. You hadn't noticed the dead - that is, the people who have rightfully expired, some even by your own hand, seem to be lingering around a bit beyond their fucking expiry date?"

"Oh, that? Yeah, I noticed that. Those two old buzzards I took to the office sat back up twenty minutes after I stuck 'em and drained 'em. I nearly shit my pants."

"Yes, excellent, you've nailed it right on the head," the Soulreaver said.

"Weird shit, if you ask me."

"Indeed. You are familiar with Ginny Morrison, are you not?"

Frank straightened up and leaned in over the little Necrosite. His fists were clenched, body tense, and brain hanging on every syllable from the Soulreaver, waiting to determine whether he would keep following the little bastard or find something heavy enough to push his skull out through his asshole.

"Yes. Why would you ask me that?"

"I need her. It seems that the woman you spent so much time tormenting is the only one capable of starting the time clock downstairs."

"Wait, what? That useless bitch couldn't start a fire with a Zippo full of gasoline," Frank spat.

Barry stared at him blankly and wondered why humans were so quick to dismiss others as being too stupid to live because they couldn't make them do what they wanted them to do.

"Be that as it may, the woman you chased away is the last in a very long line of... well... people that can make clocks run."

"Clockmakers?" Frank suggested.

"If you like, sure."

"But what do you want me to do about it? I haven't seen her. She hates me by now, anyway."

The Soulreaver sized up the man and ambled over to him. He turned his black eyes up at him and did his best to flash something resembling a smile. Frank smiled back at the lizard-chimpanzee thing as warmly as he was able. That is until he saw the smile fade from the Soulreaver's face and felt the bony fingers wrap around his testicles and squeeze tightly.

"Ughnnn!"

"It's very simple. You will do whatever it takes to get the woman to come here. You will do anything. You will say anything. You will beg her to come back to you and promise to buy her a new car or house or ring or whatever it is you people find desirable, because - I assure you - if you haven't found her by the end of the day, I will pull off these ridiculous little bits of flesh and feed them to you one floppy piece at a time." Barry flexed a warning.

"Wait... she's... your three... unff... just gimme a..."

"How's that?"

"Your three goons are looking for her right now. I asked them how good they were at finding a person, and they took off running when I told her where I thought she might be," Frank breathed.

"Excellent. The three of them will find her easily."

Frank exhaled in relief as the little thing loosened its grip, only to suck it back in a choking gasp as the Soulreaver grabbed hold again.

"Only you'd better hope they bring her back alive and unspoiled, or the next thing they'll eat is you. Starting here."

———

"Fuck that guy. Telling *me* what to do? Do you know who I am, what I could do to you with twenty minutes and a butcher knife?" Frank snorted.

He was angry when he left the office, and by the time he burst through the double doors, he was fuming and muttering to himself, looking like someone in the throes of dementia. His swearing and stomping took him in a wild careening arc past the front desk.

"Mr. Page?" the girl behind the desk called out.

"I suppose he thinks I can just pull her out of my ass and lay her down in a god damned bed, all nice and neat."

"Mr. Page?" she repeated.

"What?" Frank snapped.

"Ah, we have a new resident, but–"

"But what?"

"She seems pretty out of it. She was hallucinating when the cops brought her in here."

"And how is that different from any of the other fucking whack jobs in this fucking place?"

"She's young, sir, like really young. Cops brought her in because they didn't know where else to take her."

"What's it got to do with me? I'm busy." Frank sneered.

"I just thought you might know what to do with here, being director and all, you must have some experience with this kind of thing."

"Right. Of course, I do. Now, where is she?"

"Room 107."

He walked down the hallway and waited by the door until the receptionist unlocked it. Frank entered the unit that held the residents with the most severe dementia. Shit flinging, pissy-pantsed loons as far as he was concerned. Any one of them might attack him, gouge his eyes out and fill the empty sockets with handfuls of their own shit if they got half a chance. If his nuts weren't hanging in the balance, he would have avoided this place like the plague.

Frank felt hot nausea rising deep of his belly and sweat beaded on his forehead, threatening to run into his eyes. Drawing a shirtsleeve across his face to stop the perspiration from reaching any further down, his other hand groped for the doorknob of room 107 and turned it. He stepped inside, as much afraid as he was disgusted by what he might find. Page hadn't the faintest idea who or what was in their room. The fact she was young only meant the shit flung at him when the sedatives wore off would be thrown with speed and accuracy.

The room was lit by a single shaft of sunlight streaming through the window beside the bed. The light gleamed off the handcuff that tethered the woman to the bed. The room stunk of urine and ancient cigarette smoke filtered through over-bleached cotton sheets and discount store nylons. Frank guessed she was so quiet because she was doped to the gills rather than the natural daze some of the old fuckers on this ward walked around in. He approached the bed confidently, knowing there was almost no chance of anything being flung at him by the figure in the bed. A sheet partially covered the woman's face. He pulled it back and nearly dropped him to his knees.

"Sonofabitch."

He moved quickly to close the curtains completely and made sure the room's door was shut tight.

"Sonofabitch!" he crowed. Frank stomped around the room in a victory dance of air-punching and crotch-grabbing.

"Sonofabitch!"

He took hold of her cheek and pinched it so hard he thought her skin might shear in between his fingers. She remained quiet and still, and a noxious smile oozed across his face.

"We're gonna have a little fun, you and me."

Frank opened the buttons of his suit jacket with trembling fingers and then groped for the belt around his waist. But something stopped him. Something that, in the normal run of things, was little, hardly worth mentioning. But this was not the normal run of things - not by a long shot. That little thing was nearly three feet high and looked like the hybrid of a monkey and a Gila monster, and it said it needed Ginny Morrison alive and unharmed or it would rip his balls off. It was all motivation Page needed to let go of his belt.

"When he's done with you after you get his goddam clock going, you and me are gonna go round and round. You can fucking bet on it."

Frank leaned in close and dragged his tongue slowly along her unconscious face from chin to forehead.

"And you're gonna fuckin' lose."

## 32

Davis followed Michael, keeping up with him while they moved slowly. But, despite his age, the old man began to pick up speed and soon, the younger of the two was having trouble staying with him. They walked down alleyways and closes, over chain-link fences - mostly low. Age may not have dulled his speed, but it gave his agility a sound thrashing. The two men crawled under a few broken gates and pulled at loose fence boards to get between houses until they arrived at something that might have been a structure once - on its very best day – which was not today.

It was a kind of lean-to. A large, oil-soaked sheet of tarpaulin stretched across the burnt-out husk of a tree with a length of rebar on either corner, holding the front half of the tarp up in a makeshift roof. Behind it stood a small hut, thrown together in desperation like the other reclaimed wood huts that made up most of the town. From the outside, oilskin veranda notwithstanding, it was identical to the hut Davis woke up in. A jagged tear ran down the centre of the tarp, the entryway to the rest of Michael's home.

"What the hell is this?"

"My father built this," Michael said.

"What, really?"

"Five hundred years ago, maybe two years ago, maybe two. And it went like that, boom, boom, boom, boom until it was all over."

He moved his hands, one on top of the other, upward from his waist until they reached just above his forehead.

"Wait, what?"

"Forget it, just forget it. I'm not staying here anymore. It's this goddamn place," Michael said and began to weep. "No more of this for poor old Michael Crawford. And those, I want no more of those fucking things. Everywhere things. I've owned this place for over two and five hundred and six one years, and now you tell me it's not even yours."

He sobbed, and tremors shook through him, visibly weakening him. Davis leaned in closer, for fear the old man would drop like a stone. And just like that, Michael straightened up and regained his.

"Ah, are you okay?"

"Come on, and just you don't," Michael said.

He lifted a side of the ripped tarpaulin and stepped behind it, disappearing into the wooden hut. Davis stood under the awning, not entirely sure what he should do. The little man had told him he could show him a way out of this place, and he wanted that more than anything, but the old boy was nuttier than a squirrel turd, and Davis was willing to bet he couldn't find the way out from behind the filthy doorway, let alone out of Hell.

*Hel.*

Davis pulled aside the tarp and followed the old man into the unknown behind the oily sheet. The inside of the hut was identical to the one he had found himself in when he first arrived. Completely constructed of reclaimed palette wood with a pot-bellied stove smoking away in the centre of the room. The only difference - this hut had a visible set of stairs just behind the iron stove. Davis couldn't see the old man anywhere and guessed he'd disappeared downstairs. He followed. It was dark and, wherever it was, it was warm. The dank odour of dirt hit his nostrils before he'd reached the bottom of the stairs. The smell took his mind back to the root cellar in the basement of the house he'd grown up in, with the added aroma of a fireplace still smouldering with hot coals. A spark flickered to life just ahead of him and burst into a flame, illuminating Michaels's face. The way it reflected off the old man's glasses gave his face a hollowed-out, empty appearance, like a skull covered by trailing wisps of silvery hair, flicking and flittering away in a breeze that constantly blew around his head.

Michael pressed a match to the nub of a candle and moved off into the darkness. He moved around the room, lighting candlesticks, hurricane lamps, candelabras until the whole place was bathed in a soft yellow glow. He grabbed a bullseye lantern off a shelf and put the match to the nub of a candle inside of it. He continued lighting sconces and lamps until the whole place was lit up like high mass. The room was huge – by any measure. It was massive, though the odd angles of it made it nearly impossible to determine just how big. Random pieces of poorly made furniture with equally weird angles were strewn around the room. The place felt like it was twisted off square. Walking a straight line was next to impossible without trying.

"I gotta sit down," Davis said. He walked the short distance to a chair near him and found the more he walked, the further away the chair felt, and he could swear it felt like he had to walk downhill to get to it.

"Yeah... yeah, there's... there's my father. Come look, come and see my father," Michael said. He thrust a small picture frame toward the younger man, and Davis stretched out a hand, refusing to stand until his head stopped spinning. The thought of vomit hitting the floor and running in a direction that defied logic nearly brought him to tears. He stared at the picture and shifted his gaze to the old man and then back again. The picture Michael had handed him was a picture of himself, and by the look of it, the photo could have been taken that day.

"Oh, I can see the resemblance."

"Forget it, forget it," Michael bawled.

"Oh, okay," Davis said.

"Goddam place, awful goddam place, anyway. He built it. Oh, that's right, he had to build it. Moyen, right here, with two hands, like clockwork. Boom, boom, boom, boom. Well, it's mine now, and this is not mine, and ooh, look at that one," the little man said. He dropped to his knees and began to grope around the floor.

"Wait, what? Did you say Moyen?"

Moyen, right here. Built it with two hands - two! Like clockwork, not a second to spare."

"I don't know what that means. That's the same Dorothy said, and I didn't get it then, either. What the hell does that mean? What is Moyen? What did he build with two hands?"

"Tired, just so goddam tired. Legs no good, body don't work, brain all broken. Tired always tired," Michael said. He began to weep and dropped down to his knees.

"Well, this has been fun. So... I'm just going to get going, Mike," the younger man sighed.

Davis stood slowly, overwhelmed and feeling defeated - convinced that coming to this bizarre place with Michael had been a huge mistake. Doubt planted itself firmly in his head and made it hard to believe there had ever been a chance of escape. Even if the old man *had* found a way out of here, it was now lost somewhere inside his fractured mind. There was a sadness surrounding him. A hopelessness that Davis could practically touch. It was heartbreaking watching this old man come unglued in front of him

An idea flashed through Davis's head. It wasn't a particularly good idea, but there was a nagging feeling that he was supposed to be here with the old fool. And he couldn't think of a single other God-damned thing to do. He leaned into the older man, took his hand, and smiled. With his other hand, he drew two fingers across his forehead, from one temple to the other. He felt the old man go limp and eased him to the ground. A swell of pity rose in him, and he felt the warmth of tears nipping at his eyes. Davis didn't know Michael Crawford from a bag of beans, had no idea who his father was or what either of them had done to make it into Hel. He knew that the old bugger claimed he made it out and wanted to tell him how he did it. And now he was a greying husk, lying on the cold stone floor of a room that hurt Davis' head just being in it.

Walking slowly around, following the mad architecture, he examined the trinkets and baubles Crawford had displayed around the room. They were shiny things, little things – marbles, bits of weathered glass and rings and bangles and delicate chains of every description. None of it gave Davis the slightest idea of how Michael escaped from Hel.

"I gotta get out of here, maybe go get something to eat. I'm hungry enough I could eat Mushu," Davis said.

"Jesus, don't eat the Mushu. It makes your brains go soft," Michael said.

# 33

"Look, we don't have a lot of time here," Richardson said.

"Time for what?" Jenn asked.

"To get out of here. From what I've heard, there is an entire legion of the Soul Reaver's faithful on their way down here, and they are not coming for the dance on Saturday night."

"There's a whassname on – "

Richardson raised a solitary finger to the younger Necrosite and shot him a look that was icy enough to wither flowers.

"I don't actually care what you lot are up to, but you've got to get moving."

"Get moving where, exactly?" Jenn asked.

"Anywhere. By the way, what *have* you been up to?"

"What do you mean, up to what?"

"Ida Pugwash said you were heading up the killers now, and you had rounded up all but the most stubborn Necrosites and taken them away somewhere."

"We're, whassname, rescuers, innit?" Wendell beamed.

"I figured, sooner or later, someone would come down here looking for trouble. We've got everybody stashed in the last house on the tenements line and in the storage rooms along the ends here. At least it might give us a chance."

"Clever, but I don't know if it'll be enough. I know what's headed this way. They're already angry. When they find the Eastern Flats empty, anger will turn to rage. Emptying the neighbourhoods might save the folks for now, but all of it will still burn. They'll be looking for somewhere to put all that rage. They'll go looking for trouble. They'll go looking for all of you. The worst of the true believers are coming. You haven't stopped them. You *can't* stop them. You've only delayed the bloodshed." Richardson sighed.

"Let 'em, whassname, come down here. We're all itchin' for a fight now anyway. S' been forever and a day since we roughed it up a bit, bout time we, whassname, had it," Wendell said.

"That's very brave of you."

"Oh yeah, we're the very bravest!"

"And very stupid. You can't possibly beat them, and every one of you, including all the Necrosites you have hidden away, will die. You should gather as many as are fit to travel, wait for night to come and head for Seonagh's woods."

A rumble of nervous whispers made its way through the assembled Necrosites.

"What?" Jen whispered.

"That place, it's, whassname, haunted."

"Nonsense," Richardson spat. "Do you honestly think that forest is haunted by the angry, vengeful spirits of our long-dead ancestors?"

"That's what they say, innit?"

"Seonagh's woods is nothing more than the boogeyman parents use to get their children to do as they're told."

"That might be true, and it is a pretty good idea to go into those woods, but for two nagging little things," Jenn said.

"Oh?" Richardson asked.

"Yes. Daylight and nighttime."

"I don't–"

"If you travel by day, you risk being seen by the people that work here —folks who aren't part of the dead and need something to do club. You know, the population of this town who would run screaming from hordes of little green monsters. If just one of them caught sight of you going into those woods, they would burn them to the ground and have the lot of you stuffed and mounted in a museum quicker than the dead speak. If you did the logical thing and travelled by night, you'd be at the mercy of all the Necrosites they sent after you. They are all a lot younger and stronger than the old and weak ones we'll be travelling with," Jenn said.

Mr. Richardson knew the woman was right but was at a loss for a better idea.

Jenn sighed and lowered her head.

"We need Davis," she said.

"What, the whassname, skinny kid from upstairs?"

"He does have a gift for this kind of thing," Jenn said.

"Abilities mean nothing if he isn't here," Richardson said.

"Wait, I've seen him!" Jenn stood bolt upright. She remembered seeing the thin young man strolling calmly on the other side of the glass.

"No doubt the dreaming of a heart longing to be reunited with its love," Richardson said.

Jenn and Wendell stared at the elder Necrosite.

"A, whassname, dreaming of what?"

"She saw him because she misses him so much. The poor woman saw The Servant of the Void because she *wants* to see him desperately."

"I do miss him–" Jenn agreed.

"You see? Nothing more to it. She misses him, and she saw him," Richardson said.

"But I did see him, through here."

"Show me."

They turned back toward the wall, all of them looking at the grubby town beyond it.

"I saw him through here just before you showed up, but I couldn't get in."

"No, no, you wouldn't be able to - you wouldn't want to get in there. Oh, they want you in there, the Night Court does, but they won't ever get you," Richardson said.

"Because no paperwork," Jenn said.

"Because no paperwork," Richardson repeated.

"So, what can we do?"

"I can get in. My father showed me the way years ago."

"Why the hell would your father show you how to get into a place like this?"

"My father said the solutions to nearly all of life's problems were simple, and sometimes the easiest way was to just open the door and look from the other side of the glass," Richardson said.

"That's deep," Jenn said.

"I thought so too until I realized he was being literal. If you stand on the other side of this glass, you can see a lot of things happening on that other side. Now, if you left the door open after you went in, you might allow things to happen that otherwise wouldn't."

He reached up behind Jenn and flicked off the light switch, leaving the closet in total darkness but for the glow coming from the town.

"It's right here near the bottom, on the corner," he said.

"Oh, I see. I thought it was just, whassname, broken."

"Be careful, Mr. Richardson," Jenn breathed.

For his part, Richardson flashed back as near a smile as any Necrosite could. The old Necrosite pushed his way through the small, nearly invisible opening and was soon completely on the other side of the glass. He waved an awkward, gangly-arm salute and headed off toward the town ahead. Jenn watched him as he moved along, hiding in the shadows of the buildings.

"And please bring back my boyfriend," she whispered.

# 34

"Nurse, would you come in here, please?" Frank called out from room 107.

"Yes, Mr. Page."

"I am going to move this woman – this very violent woman, away from the more helpless old folks, and I don't need her hitting out at anyone while I do it. I want you to give her a shot or something to keep her screwed out of her head, savvy?"

"Oh... okay... ah... we don't normally do that sort of thing around here, we try to work with them and see what their personal needs and requirements might be and then determine the best course of action for them, whether that's therapy or adjusting medications or just a warm smile and a kind word," the nurse said.

Frank eyed her, wondering how someone so completely clueless could've found the door to get out of the house this morning.

"That's really interesting," he feigned. "I tell you what, I think the best course of action right now is to give this woman some kind of goddam shot or pill or what – fucking – ever to keep her out of commission for as long as I need her to be or *my* best course of action is going to be firing your ass and writing a nice report to say you were let go because you were beating on these old fuckers in your spare time. Now go get a fucking shot!"

"Did you have something particular in mind?" the nurse sneered.

"It can be China white fucking heroin for all I care, just dope her up."

The nurse turned and entered the med room, returning in short order with a clear plastic syringe. Injected the sedative into the already sedated woman on the bed and heard a soft moan eke its way past her lips. The drug began its journey through her veins.

"Unstrap her and help me get her into this," Frank barked. He moved a wheelchair into place beside the bed.

The two of them moved Ginny from the bed to the chair. Frank carried many of his friends out of Butler's and put them into cars - passenger and driver's side both with relative ease, but lifting someone in a serious narcotic stupor was like lacing up speed skates with overcooked spaghetti. When the strung-out woman was successfully in the wheelchair, Frank told the nurse to head back to her station and, for the sake of her job, to keep her mouth shut. He kissed Ginny on the cheek. Too long and too hard before he hissed in her ear.

"Someone wants to see you. Someone dumb enough to think you're something special. But we fucking know better, don't we?"

He served up a short, sharp crack with a closed fist to the back of her head and continued to push the wheelchair along through the double doors and onto the elevator. His mind raced. The head lizard thing said that Ginny was all his once she started his damned clock, and they were close, so close.

How in the fuck would she start the clock? As far as he was concerned, Ginny Morrison couldn't manage to start the goddamn Sunbeam in time for him to have a cup of her shitty coffee before leaving for work. That thing had a fucking bright red button on it. The elevator car reached the bottom, and he stepped out, pushing her and hunching his shoulders. If something was to leap out at him, he wanted to at least be close enough to her that he could use her as a shield.

"What do you want?" the Necrosite growled.

"I want you to watch how you're fucking speaking to me. This is the fucking girl your fucking boss wants, and he told me to get her, savvy?"

"Ah, of course."

Frank pushed the chair past him and headed toward the mailroom. The two of them stood just inside the doorway, scanning the room for the Necrosite in the crimson robe.

"Looking for someone?" the Soulreaver said. His voice echoed in the empty room.

"Jesus! I just about pissed myself!" Frank belched. "Anyway, here she is."

"Excellent. She will restart the big clock, and I will kill her, thus taking her place as a master of the clock. I will show the Omega *and* the false Death - Mareth, how to truly wield the power that lies within Winterbourne. Then, only then, will the time of the Necrosite have truly begun, and we will have freedom at last!" the Soulreaver cried.

"But –"Frank began.

"Yes?"

"Y-you said she could be mine when you were finished with her, said I could do as I pleased, and I've got a lot of pleasing that needs doing," Frank whined.

"Yes. Well, I lied."

"You sonofa –"

"But I have something better in mind for you. I understand you have recently taken a liking to, shall we say, certain recreations with the elderly members of this facility?"

"I'm not building a suit or anything. It's been done to death," Frank said.

"Of course it has. Have you considered necrophilia?"

"What is it with you people and that?"

"What if we set things up so you could film it? Quite a Lucrative market for that sort of thing in the darker places of Europe, you know."

"Seriously?" Frank gaped.

"Oh yes, so much money to be made from it."

He knew the bait had been swallowed, and the hook set deep in the man's mouth. It was only a matter of time before he could convince him to do whatever he wanted.

"Really?"

"Absolutely. Anything is entertainment to the right market, especially to a man of your hidden talents," the Soulreaver explained. He gestured a bony finger in the direction of Frank's crotch.

"What the f- How could you possibly know about that stuff? It's not like you can just go to video stores or go to some of those theatres downtown and find out."

"Indeed, I could not. I am, however, very capable of using a telephone and, if one knows where to call, one can find out nearly anything. As for the – other, I have watched you a long time, Frank Page. Particularly your out-of-door activities on the way home, after a skin full of drinking and a night of gawping at the bartender's chest. When the time came to set the wheels of independence in motion, I knew I would need the right sort of person to help keep things smooth on the human side of the door. I knew in an instant that person was you. But if you don't trust me..."

"No, no, I trust you just fine. Here she is, in one piece, just like I promised. Do what you want to her, but please tell me how we can start getting this thing going."

"I'm certain there's nothing to it. We'll discover your career together," The Soulreaver said.

Frank wheeled Ginny in front of the long shelf of punch cards and looked up at the clock. Though she had made a few sounds close to moans and whimpers, Frank was convinced that she was too doped to know what a clock was, much less how to get one going.

"So... she'll just sit up and get it going or something, is that it?"

"Like this, are you stupid or something?" The Soulreaver snapped.

"I do alright."

"You've polluted her with something. Something that is dulling her wits. I need her keen and sharp, not comatose."

"By the time I got to her, she was coming to. She wasn't exactly gonna come willingly after she saw my fucking face, savvy?"

"Yes, yes. You got her as I instructed. You're a good doggie, and I'll give you a treat if you are patient. Now stand aside."

Barry Wilson stood in front of her, staring, weighing the situation. Her face was obscured by the mop of greasy brown hair hanging in front of it by a head too stoned to stay upright. A single, gangly hand raised Ginny's chin as the other gently swept the hair from her face.

"There now, pretty as a picture," he said.

"Mmphm," she sighed.

Ginny's head stayed upright. The Soulreaver stepped back and rolled up the sleeves of his robe. He stood facing the chair and grabbed her arms above the wrists. The dopey woman tried to force her eyes open, willing them to lift past the layer of wallpaper paste she was sure had been spread over them while she slept. And then there was the heat. A creeping, reptilian fever started at her wrists and moved out to all points west, scalding and searing her hide - nearly to the bone. And when she was positive the skin was melting off her bones, sloughing off in clumps beneath her, she felt the cold dig its talons into her. Cold upon cold. Frigid, worse than anything she had ever known. Abandonment, isolation, and the frost of human frailty coupled with the nostril sting of a desolate February ripped up her arm and rattled around her chest like so much infected phlegm.

The arms of the wheelchair burned against her skin. Her head swam, and a full-body shiver wracked her - starting near her feet, wriggling up and clattering its way out the top of her head. She felt disconnected, detached from herself like she was hovering above her body. Ginny wondered if this was what dying felt like and decided it might not be such a bad thing if it was. There was the cessation of... well... her, but if it meant she could walk around in the warm, thick fog that crept through her brain a while longer, then she was okay with it.

A feeling came over her - through her, really. Like she was the spout of a tea pot, and gallons of liquid was pouring out of her. A bleary-eyed glance toward her arms said it was more than just a feeling. The thing in the red bathrobe - that looked remarkably like the things from the bus station - tightened its grip on her arms. And as he did, an opaque, white liquid oozed from her arms like honey pouring from a spilt jar. His hands were cold. So cold they burned her skin, and the seeping feeling moved up her arms and into her neck. Ginny had an awful sensation, like a tickle in the centre of her brain, and she was sure the white goo was pooling in her ears. She jerked and twitched, as violently as she could, trying to shake it out.

"I've done all I can. How much, exactly, did you give her?"

"Enough to keep her calm," Frank answered.

"More like enough to keep her helpless. This had better wear off in time, or you will learn what suffering really is."

"Oh, this is good shit, Frank," Ginny cooed.

The Soulreaver shot a look at the man. This was not the first time the woman had been in this state under less than honourable intentions.

"Sometimes, a man just needs to get his own," Frank said.

"Let me make this abundantly clear. I don't want there to be any room for misinterpretation. If *that* woman is in any way harmed, assaulted, or otherwise molested before she gets *that* clock working again, you'll wish you had a tenth of what is currently swimming in her bloodstream because you and I will explore the depths of pain and misery that a man's body will withstand before he begs for death," The Soulreaver said.

"Put the record player on, Frank. I want to hear Bob," Ginny said dreamily.

"I think we need to approach this from another angle," The Soulreaver said.

Barry Wilson stood in front of the woman in the chair and sized up the best method of proceeding. He could try to force more of the drug from her system, but that would risk injuring her from the stress of it. Or he could wait it out, but he was too impatient for that. He raised her head in his left hand and smiled at her. The Soulreaver raised his right hand and cracked it soundly across the woman's face.

"Hey," Frank protested.

"Do you have a better idea?"

Barry Wilson hit her again, and when she began to make sounds that were closer to conscious speech, the two of them stood her up.

"Now, my dear, if you could just start that clock for me, there's a good girl," he said.

"Oh, Frank, is that code for something? Get my pants off, Ginny. Start the clock for me," she cackled. Her head lolled around on her neck, proving she wasn't nearly as clear-headed as they needed her to be.

"Just put the hands to the right, and we'll move this along then, shall we?" Barry said.

"Sure, any of you got the time?" she giggled.

"What?"

"Got the time, got a watch, got a match, got a cigarette?" She laughed.

"There should be a watch," the Necrosite said.

"What?" Frank started.

The Soulreaver took a deep breath and let it hiss out past the teeth.

"Where are her clothes?"

"Huh?"

"Her clothing, the things she was wearing when she was brought in. I don't imagine she was wearing a backless blue gown when she came in here. Where are her personal effects?"

"How the hell should I know? What goddam difference does it

make what she was wearing? Is she supposed to throw a shoe at the clock to get the fucking thing going?"

Barry Wilson turned away from the two humans and wondered what kind of situation he'd be in if the clock never ran again. Sure, the newly dead would be wandering around the place and getting into everything. But once the revolution was in full swing, it wouldn't make much of a difference until after the dust had settled anyway. The image of him raking clawed hands across Frank and Ginny's faces hit him suddenly. Visions of his sinking teeth into mounds of exposed, milky flesh and tasting the blood that gushed out afterward, stopping after the death of their hearts, planted itself firmly in the front of his brain. An awful thing dawned on him, and the spell was broken. *He* was the one who caused the big clock to stop. *He'd* be the one standing in front of the Night Court. Once they found out the truth, he was likely to spend the rest of his days in agony.

"I'll bet there was a watch with her when she arrived. I wonder if you might be good enough to go get it?" the Soulreaver said.

"What, me?" Frank said.

"It's unlikely the girl here will be able to go."

"Oh for f – fine, fine. I'll go," Frank whined.

# 35

"Ikil...escorted you. Why are you still here?" Davis said.

"I'm already dead. Just like you," Michael said.

"But I did the forehead thing. You dropped like a rock, like anybody else I've ever used it on."

"You can't pull out a soul that wasn't there, to begin with. My egg got a little scrambled some years back. You just unscrambled it. Might've been a bit rougher than I figured it was going to be."

"Soul?" Davis said.

"Soul, spirit, nephesh, chi, ruh, whatever cultural nomenclature you prefer, it's what you walk with to the waiting room until their number comes up."

"Huh," Davis mused. "I would've never thought."

"Huh? That's all you've got - huh? You've been given a passport to one of the most powerful forces in the entire universe, and that's the best you can come up with?"

"Wiping old ladies' foreheads and taking them to the white leather chairs so they can sit and read outdated magazines for most of eternity doesn't sound like the most powerful force in this room, let alone the whole universe," Davis snarked.

"And you think that's it? You believe that is the extent of what you can do?"

"Isn't it?"

Michael sighed and moved to the centre of the crooked stone room.

"This might take a while, haven't done it in years," he said.

The little man closed his eyes and stretched out his arms, looking like he expected Davis to come in for a hug. A deep rumble started below him and rattled around them like thunder shaking the whole building. The light around Michael dimmed until he was almost swallowed by shadow. What traces of him remained, dancing in the glow of the candles, seemed to grow from nearly two feet shorter than Davis to towering above his six-foot-two frame. The oversized flannel shirt and stained grey sweat pants that couldn't have ever fit him now looked more like they had been stolen from a child's pyjama drawer. He stepped forward from the shadows into the crooked room.

There was no skin on his face. There was no flesh covering at all and, where there should have been Michael's hooked nose, there was only the triangular hole of an empty nasal passage. The sterling blue eyes were gone, with only cavernous, black sockets staring at him. A full set of blanched white teeth reflected the glow of the candles when he turned his head just so.

**"I am the one true Death. Servant of the Omega and the end to all things. None may move beyond the veil but by me."**

His voice was beautiful. Massive and terrifying, it was alive and dangerous and shook with the vastness of the universe and the timber of a cannon fired from a mountain top. And yet, it was as if he were whispering in Davis' ears when he spoke. It was every sound that had been heard since the dawn of time and nothing ever heard before.

"Holy shit!" Davis started.

**"Not exactly the response I was hoping for,"** the skeleton of Michael Crawford said.

"Sure," Davis smarmed. "But can you fit that all on a business card?"

A bony hand extended toward the young man, clutching a dog-eared business card in its skeletal fingers. Davis read the card;

*Death – Souls reaped, brief candles snuffed, current ethereal chess champion. Weddings, parties, apocalypses. All dealings FINAL. Call: (44) 08 741 – 1968. Ask for Michael.*

"Okay, well, there's that. But technically not all final, are they? There is one who escaped you," Davis said.

The crooked room shook again from somewhere deep within it and dissipated again quickly. Michael returned to his former appearance except for a few visible bones retreating slowly into his blanched skin.

"That one wasn't on my watch."

"I had no idea.".

"I can understand how you could get distracted by all the old women fawning over you, calling out your name, giving you cookies and whatnot as you swept them away to the waiting room, but did you really think that was it?"

"Well, it didn't seem like there was too much else to it," Davis said.

"Didn't you wonder about the robe, the scythe?"

"They're a metaphor, nobody–"

"Metaphor? For the love of... what did that old fool tell you?"

Davis went silent for a moment. Why hadn't his predecessor – the Death that looked like Bob Newhart - told him any of this?

"Not much. I think he *might* have told me I was the new Death, and he did mention the back stairwell, which I had already figured out. He also showed me how to get to the waiting room before all the good snacks were gone. Oh, and he said to be firm with the Necrosites, but not too firm, that they'd respond better to a kind word than to a hand raised in anger."

"Bob wasn't too far off the mark on the Necrosites," Michael said.

"Oh? Leaving them around the place, doing as they please, has certainly been for the good of us all, hasn't it?" Davis spat, "I gave them a little breathing room and look where it's gotten me. Little bastards."

Michael sat quietly for a time. His electric blue eyes caged behind thick glasses, alternating between staring off into the space above the young man's head and the dust-covered floor. And when the silence between the two of them became nearly deafening, he broke it, zeroing his eyes on Davis' as he spoke.

"A very long time ago, I thought the way you do now. I found The Necrosites nasty, brutish little things which weren't fit for anything. Useless, mindless savages who lived only for the violence," Michael said.

"I sense a gigantic but in here somewhere."

"You see? That's why I always liked you - why I thought Newhart was right in helping you along, you always were a clever kid. Wait, where was I?"

"Um, you thought the way I do now?"

"Ah yes, right. I began to see things I didn't count on when I took this job. Things that no amount of... living could ever prepare you for. Horrifying, unspeakable things that no man... no one should endure. And I was no man. Kids, they were no more than kids, most of them around my age, I guessed, ripped apart by explosives and guns and each other. There were so many of them. Twisted, shredded, with no idea where they were or what had happened, and didn't want to go anywhere but back home to their mothers. How could I possibly send them on to the next - to the great beyond - when most of them couldn't accept they had even passed?"

"What about the scythe?"

"See? Clever. I thought about that too. I mean, what is the damned thing for if not to hurry along the stubbornly departed, right?"

"Exactly," Davis agreed.

"The thing is, slicing away the bonds of Grandma or Grandpa who've laid down for a rest and joined the choir invisible, is a whole lot easier than hacking away the silver thread of a young man cut down in the prime of his life who isn't sure he's even dead." Michael lowered his head.

"I don't–"

"There were... just so many of them. All so frightened... so broken, wandering everywhere like lost children. It was heartbreaking. It was overwhelming. Most of their uniforms were so blood-soaked, you couldn't tell what side they were on – not that it mattered - they were all looking at me like I was a monster. Trying to... crawl away from me as though taking my hand or sitting with me while I eased them along would be worse than the injuries that put them with me in the first place... and then I thought of them," he said.

"The Necrosites?"

"They were vicious, yes, but there was no malice in it. They were what they were. Hunters. They were ruthless and efficient, and they would do anything that allowed them to continue with the hunt. The fact that they moved so freely between the two worlds sealed the deal. After a while, I began to see there were just as many of them who wanted nothing to do with the ripping as there were those who did. *They* became the real power of Death, handling the paperwork and the day-to-day operations—no mean feat when you are running things out of an old delivery truck. After a few years, when an opening came up, we moved the entire operation to Winterbourne Manor, after the old man went off his nut and tried to burn it to the ground. I think you can figure the rest from there. Bringing them on offered me a kind of peace of mind and freedom."

"Freedom?"

"Yes, a measure of it," Michael said.

"No, *freedom*. You're him, right? You're the one that got out of here?"

"Yeah, that was me, but I'm not so sure it was a good idea," Michael said.

"Leaving this, not a good idea, why the hell not?"

"For starters, I had been in here for years already. I kept to myself, built most of this town. None of the serious criminals in here paid me much mind."

"You really built this town?" Davis said.

"Well, the clock tower, which used to be the post office and the courthouse, and the Chinese restaurant, of course, were already here. But the rest of it is all me. You know," he said, changing the subject. "I always thought it was odd that no matter where you go, no matter how small the town, there's always a courthouse, a post office, and a Chinese restaurant."

"I saw signs on the way into this place practically begging me to try the Mushu," Davis laughed.

"I wouldn't if I were you. It'll make your head go soft for weeks."

"It'll make my head–"

"Not like that. They put something in the Mushu to keep the inmates calm. There are a few rough sorts that find their way in here, and they're never happy about it."

"I can imagine," Davis said.

"You really can't. There are few who can. This isn't like Riker's Island or Sing-Sing, where there are a handful of thugs who run the place, shaking you down for pudding or extra smokes. The things that live here are horrors from beyond space and time. Just looking at them would blacken your mind with madness. They don't want your smokes or a nice cup of tea and some biscuits. They want to occupy their place in the universe and eradicate everything from existence that isn't them," Michael said.

"So, madness blackened mind, but my cigarettes are safe? Seems fair."

The young man laughed. The fight with Jenn and now the real possibility of never seeing her again. Those awful god-damned flesh-eating babies and the jolly, pepper pot who controlled them. The bastards that beat him up and took the only thing that reminded anyone of who he was in this horrible fucking place - the god-damned blanket - and now he didn't even have that. It all came bubbling out in nervous laughter. He couldn't explain it, and now he couldn't control it.

There are times - bleak times - when the lights have all faded and taken hope along for the ride, that laughter - genuine spastic, contagious laughter - does more to change a mood than drugs or booze ever could. Soon Michael was falling out in fits of giggles himself. As the belly laughs died away to the odd chuckle, Davis wiped his eyes and turned to the old man.

"I need to get out of here, Michael. Tell me how you did it."

" Things are different now, so different. It's nothing like when I did it."

"What do you mean?"

"I mean, they only did head counts once a year back then. There were so many escapes you could barely keep track of them all. Nothing was really locked down back then, oh sure, there were barriers, but if you knew where their weaknesses were, they were a cinch to get through."

"They must still be there. What are we waiting for, Hel to freeze over?"

"Well, that would definitely help matters," Michael said.

"That happens?" Davis asked.

"You'd think so some mornings, but no. There's more chance, however, of it happening than you getting out of here. They keep a very close watch on things in here now. It seemed a while ago, an important inmate escaped due to a lax attitude toward security. Now every name and every warm body attached to it has been written down and recorded at least a dozen times before they're even sent in. After that, they're accounted for, checked, re-checked, and given a blanket. The only way you could get out now is if someone came here unregistered," the old man explained.

"What, like came in voluntarily? Like they didn't have to be here?"

"Yeah, just like that, and who would be stupid enough to do that?'

"Well, there's a kick in the nuts."

"Maybe, you might think of better ways to use the time you have while you're here. Sixteen years isn't that long when you think about it. Though if you look at it from the beginning, it's a hellacious amount of time. Might be better not to think about it too much. It'll go quicker that way. Or it won't. Either way, you're in here for a bit. How about something to eat?" Michael asked.

"Or, and I'm just spitballing here, I could spend my every minute I have trying to get the hell out of Hel. That seems like a pretty good use of my time," Davis spat.

The old man sighed. "I promise you, if there's a way out of here now, I'll help you find it, but if you spend all of your time here looking for it, you *will* go mad. Then the others, the old and angry ones that have nothing but time until the end of time, will kill you and divide up your stuff, and your memory won't make it past lunchtime for anyone left in here. If you ever want to get out of here to see... anybody again, you'll forget trying to escape. I've seen it happen too many times before, sane men, good men, get the idea that because there are no bars, no fences, they can just walk away from this place and go home," he said.

"That's fine for you, so easy for you to say, right? You've been in here since the dawn of time, and you managed to get out once. How could you be smart enough to get out but not smart enough to stay the fuck out? What difference does it make now anyway? Truth is, if I don't get out of here, I will go mad," Davis said.

The old man rose silently and headed toward the woodstove at the other end of the crooked floor. He disappeared behind a tattered curtain of a door and re-emerged carrying a huge blackened kettle and an armful of wood.

"I thought I'd put the kettle on for some tea. There's still a few biscuits hiding around here. Best not to think about this kind of thing on an empty stomach," he said.

He stoked the coals in the belly of the wood stove and stuffed in wood, turning and pushing until they burst into flame. He hauled the kettle upward and laid it on the flat top of the pot-bellied stove with a thud.

"For the record, I came back on my own. Nobody caught me. By the time I made it out, things had changed so much... too much. Everything moved so fast. Everyone was so angry, so uncertain. Death became something to fear, something to despise, not a welcome end to pain and suffering. Once upon a time, they looked at me as a friend. Now they saw me the same way as the people they burned at the stake. Malignant and evil, they said. I had enough. I quit and came back here. Hel is where the heart is." the old man sighed.

Davis stayed quiet. He had seen it with his own eyes – everything the old man had said. It was true a hundred times over. In the five years since he had been handed this job, there wasn't a day he didn't feel like he'd been shackled to it. People gawked at him as he entered their rooms at the end. They knew him - knew why he was there, and most were terrified of him. He knew it and made a sort of peace with it. But some hated him and refused to go out without a fight. Kicking and screaming and trying to hold on to everything they ever held dear. Even after they found out that none of it meant a thing, they still offered him anything, knowing it wouldn't change Davis' mind. He'd been spat at, hit, bitten, kicked, and had nearly every bodily fluid flung his way. It left him feeling like little more than a teenaged babysitter than the ultimate power in the universe.

"Now, let's see about those biscuits. Fruit cremes, alright?" Michael asked.

As he walked toward the shelves that lined the back of the room, a flurry of knocks rattled against the wood around the tarpaulin in place.

"Bad news always knocks, and I've been here long enough that no one wants to talk to me anymore. You'd better get it," Michael said.

Davis walked uphill across the crooked marble floor and up the stairs. He stepped into the scrap wood cabin and headed for the door on the other side of it.

"You?"

"I hoped this might be where you were. You have to come with me. There isn't much time," Mr. Richardson panted.

"Time for what?"

"Time to save them."

"What? Save who? What are you talking about?" Davis demanded.

"Winterbourne... Jenn... all of them. Barry Wilson will burn it all to the ground."

# 36

"We got one here been lookin' to get somethin' to eat," the man in the suit said.

"Is that it, is it?' the man behind the counter said.

"It is, and that is a fact," the black suit answered. It was not the first time he had brought a fresh fish into the Jade Dragon. He was paid twenty-five dollars a head for each new one he brought in, and in a place where two bucks could buy you enough distraction to keep your mind off your sentence for most of a day, it wouldn't be the last. It was dark inside, and the air was thick with the smells of things cooked in ancient grease. The floor was crowded with tables and chairs covered in a thick layer of dust. There were tall bamboo stools with crushed red velvet seats along the bar, and the man in the pinstriped suit guided his guest into one of them.

"Perhaps he might enjoy a plate of Mushu," said he said.

"Pork, I'm thinking. Sir, might enjoy a nice bit of pork, or is it the shrimp Mushu you fancy?" the man behind the bar asked.

The entity sat at the bar, as still as vapour can be in a thick cotton boiler suit and remained silent.

"Food, my lad?" black suit asked.

"Food," the noxious cloud said. It had an idea of what food was, though it had no need of it. It did, on the other hand, have need of clothing that would let it pass among non-ethereal beings and knew that a stained, white cover-all was not the way to do it. "Clothes." It turned a smoky eye to the man in the black suit.

"Yes, this is what the well-dressed gentleman about town is wearing," he said. It was not his first mistake. It was his last.

The thing in the coverall stood, walking awkwardly in his old man's shoes up to the loud voice in the black pinstriped suit. It raised its arm and moved forward. The man lifted his own arm, hoping to deflect the thing from touching him, but the fog became muscle and continued its path through flesh and bone and organ and flesh and bone again. The man took a short choking breath and dropped to the floor like a bouquet of withered flowers. He was not drunk. He was not tired. He was dead. The vapour thing moved over top of his lifeless form and noticed what an excellent match the black pinstriped suit was with the shoes he got from the old man. He inhabited the suit and rose up from the floor.

"Time," it said. The vapour paused to look at the man behind the bar, who immediately came the closest he had ever been to filling his trousers with something other than himself. "Time," it said again and glided through the door.

---

"Now what? Just sit here and, whassname, wait 'til he gets back?" Wendell asked.

"Not likely, if what Richardson said is true, we need to stop the Necrosites who are on their way down here before they destroy everything," Jenn answered.

"Oh yeah, we need to get out of here then. I can get us back up to the start, but you'll have to, whassname, trust me to get us that far."

"I do," she said.

"What?"

"I always figured if I was going to say those words to anyone, they might have been a little taller."

"Any, whassname, in a storm," Wendell said.

They took off down the hallway like a bullet fired from a greased pig. Faster, it seemed, than they had travelled to get here, which was stomach-churningly quickly. The speed forced Jenn's eyes closed, and she braced against it, fearing a sudden stop at the end of the run. They arrived just inside the storage closet, and Wendell took a couple of stuttering steps to avoid the two of them flattening against the closet door.

"Jesus Murphy, how do you not lose your lunch every time you move like that?" Jenn gasped.

"Search me, I guess you just, whassname, get used to it."

A handful of East Side Killers were milling around the door when they came through.

"Hallo Walter, alright?" Wendell said.

"Alright? 'Bout bloody time you got back, have you seen the state of this place?" Walter said.

"How many are you?" Jenn asked.

"Uh... just me and my Mum, we don't like to talk about Dad and all the other," Wendell said.

"No, Killers, how many Eastern Flats Killers are there here?"

"Oh, oh. Totally different thing, that. Makes much more, whassname, sense. Walter keeps track of membership."

"At last count, we had fifty able-bodied Necrosites ready to lay down their lives for the Eastern Flats," Walter said.

"Except Warren, remember his father made him bugger off upstairs and get a job," Wendell said.

A mumble of disappointment went up from the crowd as they recalled their departed friend. "Warren," they murmured.

"And the Western path gang?" Jenn wondered.

"Where?" Wendell spat.

"No, I meant how many members have they got?"

"About the same as we do, I should think," Walter replied.

"A hundred is not a lot," Jenn said.

"Not a lot of what?" Walter asked.

"Not a lot of defence against what is on the way down here. Do you know how many Necrosites work upstairs?"

"No, not exactly. Taking into consideration all the employees of all the departments, working 'round the clock shifts, well over a thousand would be my guess."

"Richardson said the Soulreaver's army was made up mostly of the younger Necrosites. The ones who swallowed every morsel he served up. The children of the older ones holding down the everyday jobs, the awful, shitty jobs that make people angry. That anger gets taken out on their children with rough hands and even rougher words. It takes root and grows into resentment for everyone and everything above their station. It grows...it spreads," Wendell added.

They turned to him in silence, completely dumbfounded. Amazed that something so profound came out of his mouth without a single whassname to be found.

"There could be thousands of them on the way down here," Jenn gasped.

"And I don't think they're coming down here for whassname, cookies and polite chit-chat."

"Wendell, I want you to take all the Killers and go to the storage room. Wait there until we get back," she said.

"Sure, missus, where are you going?"

"I'm going to go and try to convince the other Necrosites to come down here and fight with us."

"Aren't they already on their way down here?" Walter asked.

"Not those ones, the Western Path Necrosites."

"You can't trust them, whassname, sons o' bitches. They'll never do anything but tuck tail and run."

"You don't have tails," Jenn said.

"Oh, right," Walter said. "But they are cowards to a Necrosite. He was dead right about that much."

Jenn sighed.

"The truth is, without their numbers, we don't stand any chance. But, if we meet Barry's army with our backs to the wall and the Necros beside us, they won't be able to push us back any further. We might just stand a chance of holding out until Mr. Richardson comes back through there with Davis."

Jenn ran down the hallway, out of earshot of Wendell and the rest of his gang, and kept running until she was nearly out of breath and had to stop before she collapsed. They were all walking on the edge of a cliff, and annihilation was blowing up at them like a gale. She could go back – stare down death with the Eastern Flats Killers or go forward to the Western path and risk an all-out fight with the Soulreaver's army. It wasn't much of a choice, and they were all likely to die in the end anyway. But not her.

Jenn sat on the steps of one of the smaller tenement buildings and buried her face in her hands. She wasn't crying. That would be a waste of time and a disservice to all the things which were sure to die if she couldn't get her shit together. She was overwhelmed. By the impossibility of what it was, she was trying to do. Success or failure was balanced on a razor blade. A single misstep and they'd all end up slashed and bloody.

"I didn't expect to see you again so soon. What were you looking for?" Ida asked.

"Mrs. Pugwash, you need to get out of here," Jenn said.

"Whatever for, dear?"

"There's an army on its way down here, maybe thousands of them, and they're going to rip this place apart and everyone in it."

"Pffft, is that all?"

"Aren't you worried?"

"Child, I've been living down here since before you were born or died. For that matter, I'm not going anywhere. Certainly not for Barry Wilson or his followers," the old Necrosite explained.

"What will you do? They aren't likely to stop once they've started," Jenn said.

"I've got Grandmother's recipe book."

"Oh, okay, so you'll make them lunch when they get here?"

"Sure, spicy noodles. Works every time."

"Well then, good luck with that," she said.

Jenn stood and walked down the stoop, positive she wouldn't see the old Necrosite again.

"I've got to go find the Necros," she said.

"Oh, lovely bunch of boys. Tell them I say hello," Ida said.

She moved on the fifty feet to the entrance of the Eastern Flats and into the main hallway.

*Surely her cooking can't be that good.*

Jenn rounded the corner and made it to the elevator doors when she began to hear the rolling, rumbling music of a crowd on the move. She opened the door that led to the Western Path and came face to face with a thronging mass of scaly chimpanzee things.

"You'd be the Western Path Necrosites, I hope," she said.

"The bloody same. Western Path Necros we are." the lead Necrosite said.

"I've been looking for you."

"Not too hard to find us, yeah? Didn't have to come too far in, and there we were, yeah?"

She stared at him. She was long over gawking at their freakish appearance. Still, there was something oddly familiar about him.

"You don't have a brother, do you?" Jenn asked

"Brother? Oh yeah, runs things in the Eastern Flats, yeah?"

"Wendell?"

"That's him. After M and P went their separate ways, Wendell went to live with Mum downtown, and I stayed here with dear old Dad, yeah?"

"Ah... yeah?"

"I started the Necros, to keep that little bastard and his gaggle of kids in their place. Can't let his head get too big, yeah? He can barely fit through doorways as it is."

Waves of laughter roared through the assembled Necrosites.

"Oh, yes?" Jenn said.

"Name of Keith. Keith the first," he said.

"Jenn. Are you a king or–"

The laughter was nearly deafening.

"King, yeah? Wouldn't that be a laugh and a half? I'm the first. That's Kevin over there. He was the second. Konrad and Kirk came at the same time, so they are both the third and so on. You get the idea, yeah?"

"Your names don't all start with K, do they?" Jenn asked.

"No, who would do something like that? Sounds pretty stupid, don't it?"

"Yeah, I wonder."

"See those two over there? They're called Philip and Jay."

"Right, I see. And everyone else?"

"Oh, everyone else starts with a K. It was like it was fate, yeah?" Keith beamed.

"I've come to get you," Jenn said.

"Wait, yeah? We know why you're here," Keith said.

"You do?"

Sure, old Mr. Richardson came through here a while ago, yeah? Said you might come poking around down here lookin' for us. If you did, he made us swear we'd do as you said, even if it meant doin' something totally against our nature, yeah?"

"It is."

"What?"

"It is something totally against your nature. I'm asking you to trust me and work together with someone you wouldn't dream of working together with, for the good of every Necrosite down here, on both sides of the elevator.

"Someone we wouldn't dream of, yeah? What, the Killers?"

"Yes, the Killers," Jenn whispered.

"Oh, alright," Kevin said.

"Wait, what? Just like that?" She'd planned on endless convincing to get them to help, and they agreed without so much as a grumble.

"Why not? We haven't seen them in ages. Might be fun, yeah?"

The group of them made their way to the Eastern Flats, past the elevators, past Mrs. Pugwash's stoop and beyond the tenements, all the way to the end of the hallway where the others were gathered. The Killers milled around the storage closet in silence, broken occasionally by outbursts of nervous laughter and the hollow conversation that walks hand in hand with fear.

"There they are," Jenn said.

The Killers ambled toward the approaching group a few at a time, noticing the band of Necrosites heading toward them, sizing them up, and tightening their ranks. The tension between the two gangs was palpable, and Jenn found herself directly in the middle of them. If something were going to happen, it was going to happen all over her. The two leaders stepped forward, leaving their gangs behind. Their teeth were bared, claws out and gleaming in the crimson light of the emergency beacons. They circled one another, watching, waiting for an error in judgement. The Necros struck first, Keith jabbing out a gangly clawed hand toward the other who eyed the appendage with contempt. If it wasn't for fear of all-out chaos exploding at his not returning the gesture, he might have kept his own hands in his pockets.

"Alright, Wendell?"

"Alright, Keith? Keeping, whassname, well?"

A sigh whistled through the crowd as the tension deflated. Both gangs moved in to renew friendships forged in the slums years before.

"So now that we're all here, what do we do?" Jenn wondered.

"We fight the whassnames, other ones. The ones from the mailroom."

"Well, yes, that's the idea, but it might be good to come up with something a little more like a plan for when they get here. Do you think Mrs. Pugwash would send us a signal or something?"

"No need, yeah? Left someone behind, just on the border of the Western Path," Keith said.

"That's really, whassname, clever," Wendell said.

"Thought of myself, yeah?"

"Oh, did you? Boy, you sure got a big, whassname, brainpan on top of your shoulders. You might even pass for one of them."

"One of them, yeah? Bastard, you lookin' for a snap in the snot-box?"

In an instant, the scene descended from a calm, family reunion to bedlam as Necrosite attacked Necrosite in a fury of slashing claws and snarling teeth.

"Stop it!" Jenn screamed. It did little to interrupt the carnage.

Necrosites stomped on one another for all they were worth, showing why they were enemies in the first place. Jenn attempted to pull some of them apart and succeeded momentarily, only to have them pair back up and begin beating the piss out of each other all over again. She pushed at the throng in disgust and began wading her way through them. Jenn nearly made it to the doorway to the main hall before Wendell noticed she'd gone.

"Um, where you goin'?" he called out.

"From where I'm standing, I'm the only one who seems to give a damn about this place being wiped off the map. Maybe I can't stop it, but if I'm lucky, Mrs. Pugwash will give me a little lunch before it all goes up in flames," she said.

"Lunch, what are you talking about?" Kevin said.

"She said when they came through, she would fix up a batch of spicy noodles for the Soulreaver's army."

An anxious hush fell over the Necrosites.

"What?"

The two Necrosite leaders looked up in silence as the dust from the fight settled around them. Wendell finally spoke.

"Spicy noodles ain't, whassname, food."

"What do you mean?"

"That old witch has a lot more than lunch in mind for the Necrosites stupid enough to try and knock down her tower block," Kevin said.

"Why don't you stay and help us get ready for the ones that, whassname, get through?"

"Why, what's the point?"

"What?" Kevin asked.

"What's the point? You obviously don't care what happens to this place or anybody that lives down here. You'd rather fight with each other than get ready to fight the army that's on its way and, since we're likely sunk anyway, I might just as well go see Mrs. Pugwash, lunch or not, and put up some kind of god damned fight."

"Wait, what? Don't care? That what you think, yeah?" Keith asked.

"It's the truth, isn't it?"

"Pffft shows what you, whassname, know. This *is* how we get ready for the big fight. If we can beat holy hell and then stick to each other afterward, we might just, whassname, come through all of this," Wendell said.

"Oh... oh... ah... in that case, carry on," Jenn said.

And carry on, they did. It was Necrosite vs Necrosite, on the ground, off the walls, and out into the hallway. One young Necro, who fancied himself inventive, began thumping the head of a Killer between the door and the jamb of the storage closet. When the assault slowed and broke off, the Killer crawled into the storage closet and re-emerged with a broken bit of mop handle to use as a club, which he proceeded to rap against the head of the fleeing Necro.

A cloud of dust blew up from the middle of the throng, and soon, it was impossible to discern anything - Necro or Killer, except the occasional bulbous foot or gangly arm, poking out and connecting with an equally bulbous green head. Wendell and Keith looked at each other. With little more than a knowing glance between them, they began to whistle simultaneously, and the unruly mob came to a sudden and immediate stop.

"S'nuff lads, yeah," Keith said.

"Time to get ready for the real, whassname."

"Finished then?" Jenn asked.

"Good and ready, yeah."

"That one of yours?" Wendell asked Keith.

A lone Necrosite in a black leather vest and ragged denim shorts appeared at the end of the long hallway running full tilt toward the group of them.

"What is it?" Jenn asked.

"It's my scout, yeah? Left her behind and told her to catch up if she found anything, yeah?"

The little Necro made it to them finally and stopped, hands-on-hips, gasping to catch the few laboured breaths she could before speaking.

"Got some news, yeah?" Keith asked.

The messenger held her hand up to the gang leader and waved him off while she tried to slow her breathing enough to speak. Kevin finally gripped the little Necrosite around the arm.

"Spit it out, yeah? Tell us what you saw, or I'll kill you and bloody go see for myself."

"They're here," she panted. "Just stepped off the elevator."

"How many?" Jenn demanded.

"A lot," the little Necrosite said.

"How many is a lot, a hundred? A thousand, more?"

"A lot, a really lot," she replied.

## 37

"Forget something?" the receptionist asked.

"Yes, I forgot to tell you to shut your filthy puke hole, or you can find yourself another fucking job," Frank spat.

She lowered her head, pretending to return to what she'd been pretending to do before he came in and interrupted her. Frank stomped past the front desk without another thought for the woman. Except it dawned on him then, what he might do to her if he got her alone in a darkened room with several hours to spend. He hurried on to room 107 and found several of the residents clustered outside the door.

"Something I can help you folks with?" he growled.

"Behold the usurper's lackey. Here is he who would steal time from them that would set it to the right," Dorothy intoned.

"What did you just say?"

"Don't pay too much attention to her, son. We're trying to get her to knock it off with all the spooky shit, but you know how things go in this place," Richard said. He turned his finger in a corkscrew motion around his ear and rolled his eyes back in his head.

"Well, tell her to get a hold of it. Jesus Christ. Weird old broad nearly made me shit myself."

"Ogay!" Clarence protested.

"What's up with you, mush mouth?"

"Here now, there's no need for that kind of talk," Richard said.

"What?"

"My friend here is a little sensitive about the way he talks, and we'd appreciate if you'd ease up a little."

"Sensitive about the way he talks? He doesn't fucking talk, he says the same goddam word over and over again, and he murders the shit out that!"

Clarence pulled his wheelchair forward with his one good leg, moving up close to the man in the wrinkled black suit. Frank leaned into the old man and, placing a hand on either of the wheelchair's armrests, pushed his face close enough to Clarence's that the old man could tell what he had for lunch.

"You want to add something, mumbles? Have a really nasty ogay in store for me?"

Clarence had suffered a stroke that rendered half of his body all but useless, that was true. But that was twenty-five years ago. A quarter-century's worth of learning to adapt, figuring out how to get around and take care of yourself with the resources you have left. It's also a hellacious amount of time to develop the muscles in the wrist and forearm of the still-functioning side. Clarence grabbed the younger man's wrist and held it firmly while he zeroed his gaze on the eyes in front of him.

"O–gay?" he emphasized. His grip constricted around Frank's arm like a python killing a cat.

"Ow! You sonofabitch!" Page yelped.

The old man's grip was an iron pincer around his arm, and Frank could feel his fingers going numb. The harder he struggled against it, the worse the bite of the old man's grip got.

"Now, here's how it's going to go. You're going to go your office, pack up your crap, and go back to whatever downtown, shithole you crawled out of and, you're going to make sure the skinny kid comes back here," Richard breathed.

"Wait, what? Are you telling me all of this is over the guy I replaced?" Frank grunted.

"The servant must become the master of his own house. All must be set in order," Dorothy moaned.

"What?" Frank asked.

"Don't you worry about her - and don't change the God damned subject. Are you gonna leave or what?" Richard demanded.

"Ogay!"

Frank raised his free hand and brought it crashing down across the old man's cheek. The blow connected with the force of a wet mackerel against an empty wellington boot, but the effect wasn't lost, and the old man let go.

"Now, look, you old fucks, this is *exactly* how it's going to go. I'm going to walk into that fucking room and find some goddam watch. Then I'm going to take it to the talking green bug downstairs, and he's going to get my girlfriend to start some big goddam clock with it. And once that's all done, will I get a gigantic fucking reward for my loyal service? Some little trinket maybe for having to deal with all you old assholes? Do I get to take Ginny off somewhere and make her hurt for all the shit she's done to me? And my dog? *Everything* she's done to my poor dog? No, no, I don't. I don't get shit. I get to wander around this place with my thumb up my ass, making nice for Mr. and Mrs. I don't really give a fuck!"

Richard reached out a hand to the man in the bad suit.

"Are you alright, son?"

"Ogay!" Clarence protested.

"No, I don't think so. There's something wrong with this boy's head, and he needs help."

"Help? What from you? No, what I need is for you and your coffin-dodging pals to get out of my goddam way. I've got shit to do."

"No greater measure of character is there than that of he who steps beyond the door," Dorothy whispered.

The three men turned toward her, trying to decipher how stepping through a door was a measure of anything, let alone one's character.

"Yes, that's just it, I need to get through that door, and all you want to do is stop me," Frank sighed.

"Oh, you don't want to get through that door, son," Richard said.

"I don't, you're right, I really don't, but I have to. If I don't - if I don't go back to him with the goddam watch, I'm fucking screwed."

"In days gone by, perhaps. Maybe you could get in there and poke around, really get things moving for yourself, but now? God, no, not now. You just don't want to chance going in there now, things being what they are."

"Ogay."

"He's right, you know, it really is for your own good, bad kinda crazy in that room, since the beginning, really. That's why they can't keep anybody in there. Memories floating around like a toilet full of runny shit, staining the room and everybody that goes in it," Richard said.

"And lo, the beast comes and claws away at the frailty of man's vain pursuits," Dorothy breathed.

"Hey lady, if I gave you a minute, do you think you could come up with something more meaningless and mysterious?" Frank whined.

"Don't worry about her, just you listen to me. Stay out of that room. For your own safety, stay outta 107," Richard warned.

Frank stepped back from the two of them, Richard's words ringing in his ears. It might have been fear or exhaustion, or maybe he'd just had a giant mouthful of a lot of things he really couldn't understand. The dead not actually being dead.Talking reptile-bug things that probably killed his dog. And if all that wasn't enough, shit-slinging old folks were now doing their damnedest to keep him out of rooms he had a perfect fucking right to go in. He clapped another hand, the right one this time, across Clarence's face and shot a vile look in Richard's direction that said if he took a step toward him, he would get the same.

"Alright… alright. You go in then," Richard said.

"Goddam right, I'll go in then. Why don't the three of you just carry on and go fling handfuls of shit out of your overflowing fucking diapers at the regular folks, while I just fucking go in then," Frank bawled.

The room was empty and quiet. The stillness of it all made him nervous. He saw Ginny's purse lying on the bedside table and rushed for it. After several minutes of digging, his hands hit something that could have been a watch, though if his luck carried on the way it's been up to now, it might just as well have been her birth control pills. Frank pulled it out of the purse and smiled, relief washing over him and turning his legs to jelly.

"Mmhmm," the voice announced.

Frank whipped around to see the tiny old woman behind him.

"Oh, hey, you're… ah… Minnie… right? I remember you from the dining room," he said.

"Mmhmm."

"Oh, okay, I'm just going to get going then, don't want to keep you from anything important or anything."

"Mmhmm," Minnie said. She moved out of the bathroom toward the foot of the bed, blocking his exit.

"So, I'm… the… um… new head of this place, and… um, I need to get going."

"Mmhmm."

"So, if you could just… uh… get out of the… umm… way, so I can get to doing what I need to… uh… do," Frank stammered.

"Mmhmm."

"Okay, look, you old bat. I am leaving this fucking room. If I have to fuck you up to do it, that's what's gonna happen," Frank barked.

"Mmhmm." Minnie ambled toward the man in the wrinkled suit and raised her arms to him.

"Oh, okay, do you want to dance a little before I go?" He wasn't sure if she was feeling a little frisky or if the old woman was trying to move closer in an awkward attempt to get out of his way. The truth came to him too late, and Minnie Martin was on him before he could do anything to stop her. One of the old woman's feces-stained hands found its way to Frank's face, and he thought she might be trying to pull him in for a kiss before she raked her fingernails down his neck. Frank pulled back from her, afraid she'd maim him if he didn't. It only served to enrage her further.

"Mmhmm," Minnie howled. She pushed stiff, angry fingers into the softness of his eyes.

"Jesus Christ!" Frank screamed. The pain became his whole world and dropped him to his knees.

"Mmhmm, shhh," Minnie whispered. She moved her face against his

"Ugnh." Frank gulped.

"Do you love me?" Minnie breathed.

"What did you say?"

"Mmhmm, do you love me?" Minnie repeated.

"Yes. Yes, of course, I love you," Frank choked. He was repeating everything – saying anything he could think of to appease the old harpy and make her stop.

"Mmhmm," Minnie said. She cooed in his ear, leaving soft, little kisses along the sides of his face until she felt his breath slow and the panic started to leave him.

"You fucking liar."

## 38

"Hadn't you better get packing or something?" Richardson said.

"I didn't have time to bring much," Davis answered.

"I meant that more figuratively."

"Oh, I see someone's been reading the grown-up books."

"Hey! Just you–"

"Do you two need a moment?" Michael interrupted.

"No, we don't," Davis snapped.

"Do you owe him money or something?" Michael inquired.

"He doesn't like me. He doesn't like my kind or anything about us, thinks we are all vicious, mindless, brutes in love with the violence and bloodletting," Richardson answered.

"Some of you still are. I recall you were *all* wild animals when I found you."

"Some of us have turned away from all of that."

"But why? It's in your nature to hunt, don't run from it. Run *to* it, embrace it. You can't change what you are any more than you can change the colour of your eyes, so live and revel in it."

"How can we ever get people like him to trust us as equals while we rip and tear and spill blood for no other reason than it is our nature?"

"But you aren't equal, not at all," Michael said.

"What did you say?"

"I said you aren't equal. You're talking about being on the same level as the appointed servant of the Omega, the end of all things. If life and death were sports teams, The Omega would be the town that held the field they played on, and Mareth would be the stadium the game was held in. How can you ever hope to be equal to someone with that level of power and responsibility?"

"Well, when you say it like that, it's more like– "

"You are going to find that life is a lot like walking on hot sand. Sometimes, you just need to put your head down and keep moving forward until it gets better - and it nearly always does. I've watched this one a long time, and he has a good deal to learn, but his heart is in the right place. He needs to find out, to understand the truth of what all of you really are," Michael said.

"And that is?"

"The *real* power of Death. You and those like you have always kept the wheels moving. Almost from the beginning, despite unpopular opinions and less than flattering portrayals of you."

"And look just how far it's gotten us," Richardson spat.

"Have you come so far there's no way back?"

Richardson explained Barry Wilson's rise to power. It had been easy. Davis's hatred of the Necrosites was obvious, and it divided all of them between loyalty to the job and wanting to burn it all to the ground.

"There have been other Barry Wilsons. There will be more. Happens every hundred years or so. It's all piss and wind. Mareth hasn't realized half of what he can do. Once he does - if he ever decides to really clean house - a gigantic storm will blow over the Necrosites of Winterbourne, and only those who stand with him won't coat the walls with their blood," Michael said.

"But he hates us, sir. He hates us all," Richardson said.

"He hates himself, Allan. He hates what he can't - what he's not allowed to do. His heart's in the right place, and that's the problem. Death is the end. It has a freedom all its own. But the only ones that are ever okay with it are the ones who are already dead. There is a monstrous hill of pain and suffering to climb before a reaper can usher someone out of this life. Pain and suffering that you can end but can never comfort. Heartaches you can induce but never feel yourself. It disconnects you from the world and makes you feel like you don't matter to anyone. And never will again. That you will always be on the outside looking in at life happening all around you. You spend too many lifetimes watching your loved ones fade and pass while you wade chest high in the grief you've caused. And the world will hate you for it. . He doesn't know what to do to help himself, never mind what to do to help the lot of you. It's ripping him apart from both sides," the old man explained.

"Well, I–"

"Mr. Richardson, he is not so different from a young reaper we both knew. Mareth will need your guidance just as I needed your Father's."

"Tell me again about Barry Wilson," Davis interrupted.

Richardson repeated his story, particularly the bits about the Soulreaver, his plot to remove Davis with a clerical error, and the army of weak-willed bootlickers currently marching to eliminate the tenements in the basement and everything that lived within them.

"And what about Jenn?" Davis demanded.

"I don't know that I should tell you," Mr. Richardson answered.

"Wait, what? Why not?"

"Because I don't know if you'll be saddened or completely enraged by the information."

"Try me."

The little Necrosite began to pace.

"Mr. Richardson, please." Michael pleaded.

"She's in the Eastern Flats with one of the gangs, waiting to hold off the Soulreaver's army when they come."

"How many are down there with her?"

"Not enough. They may hold out for a while, but they just don't have the numbers of surviving," Richardson said.

Visions of thousands of angry bug-eyed zealots descending on Jenn in the filthy basement of Winterbourne flashed through Davis' mind. His heart raced, his chest tightened, and the lack of anything apart from acid in his stomach beginning to exact a toll.

"I gotta–" He slapped a hand over his mouth and ran toward the door of the small cabin and found the handle a fraction too late. He buckled at the knees and began to heave. Fortunately, he hadn't eaten anything in recent memory, so the contents of his stomach consisted of little more than fresh air and a couple mouthfuls of foamy spittle.

Michael hurried to the younger man and helped him to stand up.

"Get up. This probably isn't the worst thing you're going to hear today."

"It gets better?" David gulped.

"There is a good bet if Barry Wilson succeeds in what he's doing, your girlfriend will end up in here. Permanently. The big clock has already stopped. It's only a matter of time before the Night Court comes sniffing around to find out why."

"What does that have to do with Jenn?"

"Because she is proof that the system is fallible. The administration of the underworld prides itself on its ruthless efficiency and maintaining the status quo. Her still being around is a clerical error that sticks out like a hooker at high tea. She is a black eye on the face of the Night Court, one they mean to get rid of. What better way than to lock her away in Hel for all of eternity?"

Davis stood and steadied himself against the rough-hewn wall.

"I have to get back," he said.

The older man lowered his head and remained silent for too long. He let go a heavy sigh and walked to the pot-bellied stove.

"There's a way you can do it, but it isn't easy. And it's really not going to be popular with one of us."

"What do you mean?"

"For all their efficiency, the Night Court is really pretty lax about what goes on in Hel. There are safeguards and sensors of a sort that keep track of the numbers in Hel. Thanks to my small, reptilian friend here, there is now one more live body down here with us. They don't know names, they don't know faces - they don't even know what most of us are in here for. But they do know counts. Mareth could leave, but you'd have to assume his place, Mr. Richardson," Michael said.

"So, I'm not going anywhere is what you're saying," Davis sighed.

## 39

They were close now. And they were moving, but not like an army should, like - the sound of many feet moving in rhythm as a single, orderly pair. Instead, they chugged along like a storm, thundering and rumbling in the distance and moving closer with every crack of clawed feet along ancient linoleum. It was a tempest that rolled on and rumbled with the voices of outraged young things, spoiling for a fight.

"Are we ready?" Jenn asked.

Silence answered her. A lone Necrosite stepped inside the room and considered them all with hate-filled eyes. It was followed by a second and then a third. Then a hundred more seemed to appear out of nowhere. The hallway exploded then, in the chaos of war, as the Necrosites tore into each other.

She mouthed a silent scream and stood fixed to the spot outside the storage closet. A handful of smaller, faster Necrosites broke away from the main fight, and she took off at a run. When she felt close enough, Jenn launched herself at them. To her amazement, she landed on top of the thickest cluster of the Necrosites, stopping them dead. The rest halted, frozen with fear, unsure what to do now that here was proof they weren't invincible.

She reached up and grabbed one of the few that remained standing. It reminded Jenn of picking up a small child - a very scratchy, bitey child. She tossed him to the right and watched as he thudded into the wall and slid down it - out cold. Surprised by her luck, she continued to press it and started throwing the little green things like angry sacks of wet dirt, bouncing them off the walls and chucking them to the floor. An awful smile curled her lips to a sneer. The dead girl ran toward the thickest part of the Necrosites, throwing bodies aside as she went, trying to get somewhere near to Wendell or Keith. Jenn made it a few feet toward them when pressure against the bottom of her legs slowed her progress. Very young Necrosites, smaller than the others, had latched onto her, two and three at a time, trying to bring her down like wolves on a wounded elk. She managed to remove most of them as she pushed forward, kicking and flinging them off but, for everyone she managed to shake off, two more latched on to take their place.

"Wendell!" she screamed.

The Eastern Killer spun on his heels and saw the woman was in serious distress. Without much thought, he began to claw and chew his way back to her. In doing so, he nearly flattened his brother, who turned to see what would make Wendell run from the face of such a cracking fight. When the head Necro saw the mess Jenn was in, he too turned and fought his way to her. Keith hissed and pounced on the Necrosites, holding down her right leg. Jenn crumpled and dropped to the floor like a wet tea towel, giving a perfect opportunity for the surrounding Necrosites to descend on her, and she disappeared beneath a sea of flailing arms and gnashing teeth. An anguished scream escaped Wendell as he watched her fall and the Eastern Flats Killers broke off from the fray, rallying to him. They began ripping, clawing, and tearing at the Soulreaver's forces, and in short order, they broke their hold on the woman, and she was helped back to her feet.

Jenn shook off the assault and decided then it was time to put a stop to these thugs ransacking the homes of decent folk. They would stop them, or they would die in the attempt. It'd be all or nothing from here. She grabbed hold of one of the little things and shook it like a rag doll before hurtling it into a thick group of them, knocking them down like green bowling pins. The act inspired the others, who doubled their efforts and began to beat the Soulreaver's troops down.

"That's it! We got 'em on the whassname!"

They began herding the Soulreaver's army toward the door and up the hallway. Jenn thought if this was the extent of the attack, they could hold out easily enough to drive the rest of them away.

*BOOM.*

A concussion ripped the air and shook the foundations of Winterbourne itself. They stopped then, all of them. The Soulreaver's forces and Winterbourne's alike and turned toward the door where the sound originated.

*BOOM.*

It rocked them again, and bits of plaster dropped from the walls and landed near Jenn's feet, and the Necrosites began to chatter nervously.

*BOOM.*

The sound crackled along and was joined by a long, low blast from a tinny horn that reminded her of tubas, thousands of them, all blowing the same dull note at an ear-splitting volume.

*BOOM, WAAAH!*

"This ain't good, yeah?" Keith said.

"You don't think it's, whassname, do you?" Wendell wondered.

*BOOM, WAAAH!*

It echoed off the hallways and pushed its way along, sounding nearer now than it had before.

"Almost here, Wendell. No time to hang about, yeah?"

"Got to get moving, get away from here. They ain't likely to stop," Wendell agreed.

*BOOM, WAAAH!*

It arrived.

The doorway exploded in a cloud of dust and wood shrapnel.

"What the hell is going on?" she demanded.

When the dust settled enough, she could see the doorway had been smashed clean through. A small Necrosite carrying a large rusty chain came through the opening at the other end of the chain, which was the largest Necrosite Jenn Henderson had ever seen. They were followed closely by a second pair, nearly identical to the first. Jenn was an average height by all accounts, and an above-average Necrosite barely reached past her waist. These two brutes were colossal. They stood at least a head taller than her and resembled their smaller counterparts with thickly muscled arms and the same awkward legs beneath them. Black, goggle eyes also took most of their face. Instead of small needles in their mouths, two single rows of sawblade teeth and two curved, yellowed tusks extended downward to the chin through jagged holes ripped on either side of their faces.

"The twins!" Keith shouted.

The two hulking Necrosites moved forward into the room, tugging at the leads held by the smaller ones who quickly released the chains and stepped out of the way. They both carried a thick, ugly club. They immediately began to swing, connecting with whatever happened to be foolish enough to stand in the way of it.

"Jesus!" Jenn gasped.

The twins' heads shot up, and they quickly homed in, lumbering toward her at a blistering pace. The clubs swung, clearing a path to her, hacking and smacking Necrosites aside like they were clearing brush.

"We'd better, whassname," Wendell said.

"You're right," Keith agreed.

"What?" Jenn said.

"Run!"

## 40

It had been well over an hour since he sent Page looking for the watch, and the Soulreaver grew tired of waiting for him to return. Despite the full view of the squirrels in the back property that the bay window afforded, the rage inside him was growing from a small, angry spark to a full-blown inferno.

"You there, come here," Barry Wilson barked. A young Necrosite came flouncing through the door.

"Sir?"

"Have you got the time?"

"Sir?" he repeated. The Necrosite searched through his pockets, desperate to find a pocket watch or sundial or anything resembling a chronometer.

"I'm afraid I don't," he said.

Barry Wilson thrust out an arm and gripped the younger one by the throat, his claws burrowed deep into the mottled, green flesh. The blood gushed from the gash in its neck, splattering the walls and covering the Soulreaver's bony arm. After a few final twitches, the young Necrosite was little more than a washed-out lump of greying flesh.

"It's time I went and got the watch myself."

Barry made his way to the back stairs that led to the closet of room 107 and stood at the top of them fuming, waiting for an alternative solution to present itself. When it didn't, he called out to the Necrosite standing guard.

"If Page makes it back, keep him here," he barked.

The Soulreaver could hear the old woman's voice before he made it into the closet. He opened the door slowly and peered out from the closet. The slight woman sat in the far corner of the room, rocking back and forth, assuring herself as she did. Her white, floral print, pyjamas, painted scarlet. Hands and mouth, both drenched in blood. He caught her eye, though she paid little attention as he walked into the room. Instead, she remained focused on what lay at her feet.

It was Frank Page. The poorly fitting black suit left little doubt of that. He lay on his back, feet splayed, and his left arm twisted so much that it couldn't have been anything but broken. It was the least of his injuries. The collar and upper chest of his wrinkled white shirt were completely blood-soaked, making it difficult to tell if the injury had been done to his throat or his chest. His jaw had been broken, smashed, at least twice, which left his mouth hanging open yet bent to the side at a grotesque angle. The nose had been gnawed away and not figuratively, leaving the smallest morsel of flesh dangling above a gaping, ugly black hole rimmed in crusted blood. The most disturbing sight was his eyes. They were gone for a start, but not just pulled out, not plucked from the sockets that were bloody, dark, and empty but dug out forcibly and by someone with a jagged tool. The edges around the sockets were ripped and covered with ribbons of dangling flesh and flayed skin. The Soulreaver looked at the man and felt a sudden wave of pity for him. The moment passed quickly, however.

"No less than you deserve," he said.

Frank began to sputter and groan, rolling from side to side, attempting to get up. The groans grew louder and turned quickly to keening as the pain of his injuries kicked into high gear. The wailing died away like a klaxon slowly wound down, and a muffled voice came from the floor.

"Is someone there? Help me up. I can't move my goddam legs," Frank said.

"What the–" Barry started.

The lump of flesh in the bad suit that lay in the middle of room 107 shouldn't have had a heartbeat, never mind been wailing away like a wounded child and then speaking and trying to stand up. And then it occurred to the Necrosite.

"The watch. I need the watch, or this kind of thing isn't going away."

"Mmhmmm," Minnie said.

The Soulreaver looked at the old woman and tried to shoo her away from where she sat so he could have a proper look for the damned thing. And like that, fate stepped in and pointed a flashlight into Barry Wilson's life. He saw it. A worn, silver pocket watch and chain hanging from one of the buttonholes on the old woman's pyjamas. He didn't imagine she had put it there herself so much as it ended up there during the struggle with Frank. He moved lightly and lightning fast and wrapped his fingers around both of her wrists.

"Mmhmmm," Minnie said and pushed back against his grip.

"Ah, a strong one, so much more fun when they fight back," the Soulreaver hissed.

He felt the fever coursing through him, something he had encouraged his underlings to embrace but hadn't felt himself in years. A bloodlust that crawled through him from the top of his spiky, dreadlocked head to the bottom of his stubby feet. It filled him with a soulless rage and a lust for carnage. He slowly released the old woman's arms and leaned into her, nose to nose.

"I'll take that watch now," he growled.

"Mmhmm," Minnie answered.

"What the hell was that?" Richard said.

"Ogay?" Clarence wondered.

"The blood-curdling scream from behind the door, like someone having their arms ripped out of the sockets, what did you think I meant?" Richard asked.

"Ogay."

"You need to get your hearing checked, old man."

"Ogay," Clarence snapped.

"Well, I heard it, and I'll be damned if I'm just going to wait here for, whatever it is, to come out here and do the same to me."

"Ogay?"

"No, I'm not taking off and running like a scalded dog. How could you even suggest that? I'm going to see what the hell is going on."

"Ogay," Clarence said. He raised his good arm and pointed just over the other man's shoulder.

"To go beyond the door will bring..." Dorothy trailed off.

"Yes?"

"Yes, what, dear?"

"You just said to go beyond the door will bring, and then you just, sort of, faded out. What will it bring?"

"Did I? That's a bit of an embarrassment, isn't it? Comes and goes, really. Not much control over whatever it is," Dorothy said. She gave the side of her head a smack with the heel of her hand and stayed silent.

"Nope, that's it, I'm afraid."

"Yes, well, behind the door is something, and I suppose there's only one way to find out what."

Richard grabbed the door handle and, after thinking better of it, put his ear up to the door. It was so thin, he could practically hear the heartbeats of the people on the other side of it. He opened the door cautiously and stepped in. There sat Minnie Martin, covered in blood and looking as though she'd been dead for an hour and a half. Beside her stood a small, greenish-grey thing that looked like the hybrid of a chimpanzee and a lizard wearing a red bathrobe.

"What have you done?" Richard gaped.

"She would not give up the watch, I took it from – wait, aren't you going to recoil in terror, struck dumb by the sight of me?" the Soulreaver wondered.

"Pfft, no. The first time I ever saw one of you scared the piss out of me, literally. That was years ago. I don't sleep much at night these days, and I see you little bastards prowling in and out of rooms in the middle of the night."

"And? You realized how vicious and powerful we were and thought better of approaching?"

"And I thought you were all hallucinations until I started to see you coming out of the rooms of people who turned up dead the next morning."

"How clever you must feel. You've figured it out exactly," the Soulreaver said.

"I don't get it. You things get your jollies from wasting the elderly?"

"In a way. But this isn't the time to talk about it. So much to do and so much time running out. Now, if you wouldn't mind?" Barry said.

"What if I was to say I wasn't going to let you past me?" Richard dared.

"I would say you were whistling past the graveyard. I don't actually need to get past you," the Soulreaver said.

The door creaked open and, after several pregnant moments, in rolled Clarence.

"Ogay?"

"You don't have to get past us, but you do have to go through us, savvy?" Richard declared.

"Are you trying to scare me? I can tell you, two broken-down old men... well, an old man and a half aren't enough to stop a leaky sink, and you would hope to prevent me from leaving?" Barry chuckled.

He bent down in front of the prostrate body of Minnie Martin and pulled the silver pocket watch off her.

"We don't need to stop you, just slow you down long enough. The big clock won't start itself," Richard said.

The Soulreaver stood silently, a little dumbfounded at what the old man had just announced.

"Yeah, we know about the goddam clock," Richard said.

"You're pretty smart, Mr. Walters. What else do you know?"

"Just that we can't die until you get the clock going again, so you go on, sonny, just knock it off, there's bugger all you can do to us."

"Is that what you think? That somehow you're all safe from death? The fact is grandpa. You will be every bit as dead, and you will experience a lifetime's worth of agony for every extra minute you get among the living. No one gets extra time. Ever," the Soulreaver explained.

"Do you know where you are? Every minute in this place, every awful goddam second walking among the – so-called living - is a lifetime's worth of pain. We've lost our homes, our independence, and been forgotten by families we raised to be decent people. Children that became insincere assholes and abandoned us here the first time we forgot how much it costs to mail a fucking letter. You bring on your worst. My bet is it doesn't even come close to a Saturday morning in this place," Richard seethed.

"But all of that will change. Once the clock is restarted, things around Winterbourne will change for the better. For all of us," Barry said.

"My heart tells me you might be telling the truth, and we should just let you walk, but my gut says you are a talking lizard, and you're clearly up to no good. Pain or no, you're not leaving this room with that watch," Richard said.

The closet door of room 107 burst open, and in scrambled four vicious-looking Necrosites. The Soulreaver's personal guard.

"We've come for you, sir. We feared the worst," the lead guard said.

"Excellent. Kill them, kill them both," he answered.

"Oh shit, run Clarence, run!"

"Ogay?"

# 41

One of the twins set its sights on Jenn, moving quickly to her, bashing Necrosites to the left and right as it drew closer.

"We need to stop it, yeah?" Keith announced.

"How do you propose we, whassname, stop it?" Wendell pushed up beside his brother.

"Not by just standing here, yeah?"

"Well, nobody gets to, whassname, do they?"

Their hearts were brave, but the power of their punches left a lot to be desired. The blows they rained down on the front twin fell like feathers from a torn blanket - they were gnats ambushing an elephant. The big thing got within inches of Jenn when a sharp pain in its left leg made it glance downward. Below, clinging tightly, hung a Necrosite digging its needle-sharp teeth into the soft flesh of the muscular leg. When swatting at the pest did little to dissuade it from biting further, he grabbed hold of it by the neck and pulled sharply upward. Wendell was hauled toward the ceiling and found himself nose to nose with it.

"Say, you don't know the way to Carnegie, whassname, hall, do you? Hey! Hey, I'm, whassname, talking to you, you big-"

The twin did the first thing that popped into its minuscule brain regarding the loud-mouthed little thing in front of him. That was to bash it against the closest wall until it stopped. Back and forth. Again, and again. Smashing and bashing Wendell off the wall until he stopped moving. And then once or twice more for good measure.

"No!" Jenn rushed toward the crumpled body of her friend. He was twisted and contorted into a position that a sound body couldn't be in and remain sound for long. He lay face down with one arm beneath him and the other bent at a painful angle, palm up. His legs were twisted in ways that defied logic. Wendell's head was turned on its side, looking over his right shoulder and thin rivulets of blood trickled from his ears.

"You sonofabitch!" Jenn threw anything she could lay her hands on at the hulk in front of her. The big thing closed the distance between them in a couple of steps and clapped a huge, meaty hand around her arm and hauled her straight up. Strictly speaking, she wasn't afraid to die. In fact, she was pretty sure she couldn't - being already dead for some time now. However, the thought of spending eternity as a perpetually living collection of broken bones and seeping wounds scared the shit out of her. If she hoped to avoid that, she'd have to stop him. She kicked the big thing, hoping his anatomy was similar enough to humans and that a well-aimed boot to the breadbasket might make it let go. It wasn't. And the kick did little more than giving the twin greater determination to stop her. It raised its other hand and landed a heavy, thudding blow across Jenn's face that left her light-headed but didn't prevent her from trying to escape his grip.

"No good," the twin grunted. It clopped another bell-ringing fist across her head.

Jenn remained still, thinking there might be a better way to go. She didn't think she could remain conscious if he hit her again. Once the twin seemed satisfied she was through struggling, it started dragging her back toward the entrance.

"Not going to be easy, yeah?" Keith said.

"If he gets out, he'll head for the tenements. They both will. They'll kill everyone over there," Jenn gasped.

She motioned for Keith, hoping he would move the rest of their forces into line to stop the larger twin from leaving. But she forgot about the second twin. It grabbed hold of her legs and began to pull. The pain shot through her like a chunk of steel being driven into the small of her back. Jenn felt the twin at her feet pull harder. The lead twin, confused by the slowing of its progress, pulled harder forward. It became a tug-of-war between two mindless titans. And she was the rope. Suddenly, the idea of being a heap of broken bones wasn't so bad compared to be pulled apart by two large Necrosites too stubborn to let go. The pain seared through her, and soon, it was all she knew. When it all became too much, a muffled scream escaped her, and she blacked out.

A strange sensation washed over her. She was falling in a loop, with no end. Her head spun, and she felt that she might puke if she couldn't find solid ground soon. She opened her eyes and, when nausea rocketed through her stomach, she slammed them back shut. But closed eyes didn't stop the waves of heat that drenched her forehead. She imagined this might have been what her death felt like, and she didn't like it a bit. Jenn's eyes opened slowly and frantically searched the room for someone she could cry out to for help. And then she saw it.

A lone figure in black emerged from the storage closet and stood in the shadow of the doorway. He was tall and, though the black robe covered him from head to toe, there seemed a gauntness to him. A thick, braided, silver chain hung around the neck of his cowl. At the end of it hung a small hourglass. The black robe extended well past the fingertips of his left hand, so it appeared there was none. In his right hand, he clutched an upturned mop. He raised the cleaning implement and brought it down silently. When nothing happened, he raised it again with a little more speed and brought it back down fiercely. Still nothing. He looked to the mop and shook his cowled head. The robed figured disappeared back into the storage closet.

"What the hell?" Jenn said. The two Necrosites loosened their grip, distracted by the solitary figure standing outside the storage closet.

The being in black came through the doorway again, careful to remain in the shadows until he was certain he possessed all the tools he needed. In his right hand, he now carried a gleaming silver scythe. The head resembled a great raptor with a vicious, sharp beak ending in the point of the blade. The handle extended downward from the head, black and twisted, like stained fruitwood. Whatever distraction he caused earlier, passed and the Necrosites went back to doing what they'd been doing before he showed up, beating the hell out of Jenn and the two gangs. The hooded figure glanced around carefully at the scene, and when he decided the time was right, he raised the scythe a fraction of an inch and tapped it against the floor.

An explosion tore the air like an erupting volcano. The battling forces immediately stopped and gazed at the robed figure. The twins dropped Jenn and walked toward the storage closet. The figure in black moved forward out of the shadows and into the light. He glanced around the room and noticed two gigantic figures lumbering toward him, raised the scythe again and tapped it against the concrete. The force of the blast drove them to the floor. The figure in black lifted the bottom of the handle and examined it. He lowered it again, very slowly. He stepped fully into the room now and pulled back the hood of his robe, revealing a skeletal face, though not a skull. It was moribund and withered, though still very much alive and, perched on the smallest amount of a bridge of a nose, black framed sunglasses with blue mirrored lenses.

"Davis!" Jenn shouted.

# 42

---

"Mr. Richardson, you can't do this. I won't let you," Davis said.

"You don't have a choice. I can't do anything to turn this mess around. And let's be honest, Mr. Mareth, you're no fan of mine," the Necrosite said.

Shame and guilt twisted Davis' guts like a greasy supper churning around, leaving him sweaty and nauseated. Richardson was right. He didn't like them. Any of them. The man may have even hated them and didn't feel he owed the little abominations anything. The sooner they were gone from Winterbourne, the better. But now... here was one of them, willing to trade his freedom for the Davis'. Unconditionally.

"We don't have a lot of time," Michael said.

"What do you mean? You said the big clock isn't running, and everything is on hold until it starts again, right?"

"Yes, for the most part, that's true, but the thing is, if it doesn't get started again after ten or twelve hours, they'll send out a timekeeper, and he'll wipe the slate clean. Take it all back to the beginning."

"A wha–"

"They'll just move everybody along to the waiting room, no questions asked—everyone who is dead. *Everyone*," Michael said.

"If they moved everyone on, no questions asked, that would mean they could–"

"You'd never see her again," Richardson said.

"Then let's go." Davis headed for the front door.

"Wait a minute, you're going to need a couple of things first," Michael said.

He led them downstairs and across the crooked floor to an oak door with leaf-covered branches carved along the outside edges of it and a likeness of old man Winterbourne directly in the centre of it.

"Hey, is that?" Davis smiled.

"Yeah, it is. My father stole this door years ago," Michael answered.

The room was small, not much bigger than a broom closet, and looked to be a storage room though the amount of dust and tarp-covered boxes around Michael's home said the whole place might have been a storage area. The old man disappeared into the room and began to root around through pile after pile of boxes, emerging triumphant after a time, carrying a folded square of black cloth. The fabric was blacker than anything Davis had ever seen. So black, it seemed to draw other colours into it, absorbing and blanching them out as Michael moved along with it. The cloth was black within black within black, and Davis was mesmerized by it and had to force himself not to stare at it. Michael held it up. It was a hooded black robe that looked to have been made for him. Passing the robe to Davis, he continued to dig around the boxes and under tarps. Without looking up, he passed back a scythe that was only slightly taller than the old man was. Davis grabbed it and held it at a distance while he looked it over. The head looked to be solid silver cast in the shape of a vulture's head - the sharpened blade forming the length of its hooked beak. It should have weighed a ton but took no effort at all to lift. Beneath the head, a twisted handle of black, oily wood extended down.

"What's this?"

"It's the robe and scythe," Michael answered.

"The robe and... I really thought that was just a metaphor."

"And you wonder why your area is in such a mess? Your predecessor should have told you all of this, but he always was a little too laid back for his own good."

"Told me what?"

"That you're Death," Michael said.

"Is that all?" Davis chuckled. "He did tell me that, told me all about the thousand years and retiring to a nice warm island somewhere."

"No, you're not getting it, son. You are *Death*. The duly appointed representative of the Omega. The end of all things - for your particular area, of course."

"You're still not telling me anything I don't already know."

"Apparently, I am. You wield the greatest power in the universe, and your house is completely in ruin," Michael said.

"Wait, what?"

"For shit's sake, boy, you're Death. The Grim Reaper. You are the end - great and terrible, yes, but you are what gives life purpose. Death's constant lurking inspires the creation of beauty and truth and love and hate and the unexplainable drive to finish a delicious meal when you are too full. From the first sensible thought that enters their heads, everyone knows that no matter how rich or smart or talented they are, life will end, and there is nothing they can do about it. Life is a glorious thought that chugs along until it's just a memory in somebody else's head. That is where the Reaper exists. Between thought and memory lies Death. There is no power more awe-inspiring or terrifying. All who stand before you will fall away."

"What do I need to do?"

"Take the robe and the scythe. Go clean house."

Davis looked at the scythe's wooden handle. To say it felt unlike anything he'd ever felt before suggested he'd touched a lot of otherworldly things. He hadn't. But the feel of the wood against his skin was familiar and frighteningly alien at the same time. There was a warmth to it, and it felt good against the skin of his hand, causing him to grip it tighter. However, the heat began to wear away, leaving him with cold pushing into his hand that bordered on painful. The tighter he held it, the worse it got. When the old man handed it to him, the scythe was the size of a Kaiser blade. It towered above him now.

"Try the robe," Michael said.

"You're a foot shorter than me. It'll never fit."

"Clothes make the man, give it a go."

Davis pulled the cloak over his head. To his amazement, it went on easily, stretching and fitting itself to him. It moved along his body, covering it from head to toe.

"Have a look." Michael pointed Davis to an ornate, floor-length mirror near the door of the storage room.

He had changed, grown taller somehow. There was a cadaverous, pale face that looked back at him from the mirror. Skeletal was the word that immediately came to mind. Apart from his liquid, blue eyes, he would have taken his own reflection for a corpse if he didn't know better.

"You'd better go. You've no time to waste," Richardson said.

"But how?" Davis said. His voice echoed and shook the walls of the crooked room

"Well done! Best not to talk too much until you need to. The big voice takes a lot to keep going. Try not to blow your fuses all in one go," Michael said.

Davis nodded.

"Now, really, get going," Richardson implored.

"Right, just walk into the mirror," Michael said.

The head of Davis' robe whipped around toward the old man. A noise of muffled shock shot out from beneath the shadow and fabric.

"It's fine - really. Just close your eyes and run if you're worried. Oh wait, take these. The eyes never work out the first time around." Michael handed him a pair of sunglasses.

Davis put the sunglasses on, closed his eyes, and walked toward the mirror, arms outstretched. Where he should have felt glass and solid wood, he touched a thick substance like gelled gasoline - viscous and ethereal. He felt something grab his arm and start to yank him into the mirror. It was terrifying. And it got worse. The further in he went, the more he felt like a grape being ripped from its skin by a chain attached to the slug fired from an elephant gun.

He arrived in a small dark room with a thud, scraping what little skin remained from his hands and sending the scythe flying off into the blackness. Davis stood and waited for his eyes to adjust to his new surroundings. After a time, he began to grope along the floor for the sickle. He felt his fingers brush against the handle and grabbed it. Davis headed for the outline of the door. Even before he opened it, he could hear the voices of hundreds of things pressed together in an area too small to contain them.

*I weild the greatest power in the universe,* he reminded himself and stepped through the doorway.

Davis surveyed the room and saw the chaos spread out in front of him. He tapped the bottom of the scythe to the concrete floor. Nothing happened. A second tap also produced a less than spectacular result. His gaze turned to his right hand, and he saw the mop.

"Oh shit." He headed back into the closet and re-emerged, carrying the scythe and tapped it against the concrete floor. A shockwave erupted from it. A wicked smile crossed his face and seemed to cement itself there as he stepped forward to the crowd.

## 43

"Wake up, miss," the Soulreaver said.

There wasn't much time left. If he couldn't wake her, couldn't get her to start the miserable clock, he was as good as gone with the rest of the dead weight. The figure in the chair wasn't moving. In fact, she hadn't moved from the time she had been brought in here. He shook her, hoping to jar her back to consciousness, but when he saw that it only moved her closer to fall out of the chair, he knew he needed something more drastic. The Soulreaver propped the young woman back up in the wheelchair and let one of his gangly arms fly, connecting with a stiff slap across her face.

"Jesus Christ!" Ginny pitched forward, falling on the floor.

"Ah, you're awake." The Soulreaver smiled.

"Fuckin' right, I'm awake. What the hell was that for?"

Ginny tried to rub the sleep from her eyes but still felt the effects of the morphine lurking behind them, waiting for an opportunity to force her back to sleep. She caught sight of the Necrosite in the red bathrobe and remembered the trio of awful things that killed Chico and tried to end her at the bus station. A scream built up in her throat. As she opened her mouth to let it out, Barry Wilson raised a spindly finger to silence her.

"Yes, yes, horrified by my appearance? Or my speaking? Or by the crimson robes of my office, but terrified all the same, yes? Now can we just get on with it? We're nearly out of time," he sighed.

"Out of time for what?"

"It would take too long to explain, and you wouldn't understand anyway. Suffice it to say that the big clock over there isn't working, and no end of unspeakable things will be arriving soon if you can't get it running in the next, oh, twenty minutes or so."

"What do you want me to do about it? Do I look like a clock repairman to you?"

"No. You are, however, the owner of this wretched thing, and as such, you should be able to use it to start the fucking clock." Barry held up the silver watch and waved it in front of her face.

"My grandmother's watch? That thing doesn't even work. It was broken when I got it," she said.

"Excuse me a moment, would you?"

He walked out of the room and back into the big hall of the mailroom.

"You there," he called to a Necrosite walking past. "Where is Mr. Pyewackett?"

"He is leading the troops through the Eastern Flats, along with Bunn and Johnston."

The rage building in the Soulreaver grew like an angry blue knot after a sharp blow to the head. It was palpable in the air around him.

"Find him, find all of them, and bring them back here. I don't care how many others you need to take with you but go get them. Now."

Barry stomped to the backroom, looking from the clock to the young woman and back again.

"Here is exactly how things are going to go. You will start the clock now, or I will kill you," he scowled.

"What?"

"Yes, kill you - and not quickly. I will peel the flesh from your bones, inch by inch, and in the end, you will beg for death."

"Don't get your fucking hopes up."

"What did you say?"

"I'm going to say no to the whole no more flesh on my bones thing. Sounds like kind of a drag. I am going to bet that you can't really kill me. Not yet, anyway," she said.

"Aren't you Frank's clever girl? So why don't you use some of that very clever brain and just get the clock going?" the Necrosite said.

"I stopped being Frank's girl the second I let your friends eat his goddam dog. He just don't know it yet. And I told you before I can't fix your goddam clock."

Barry Wilson sidled up to her, uncomfortably close, their noses nearly touching. Ginny could smell the rot on his breath.

"Remind me then, why I am keeping you alive?"

---

The first of the twins made it to Davis - close enough to touch him with an outstretched hand and swung his club wildly. The robed man side-stepped the blow, but in doing so, allowed the club to knock the scythe out of his other hand. It was the opportunity the two massive Necrosites were waiting for. Rushing at the figure in black, one toward either side of him - clubs extended and running full out, the twins gave each other a knowing look before moving in for the kill.

"Look out!" Jenn screamed.

His mind raced. He could drop and fumble around for the scythe, but the chances of him getting to it and back up again in time to take out both of them was laughable. This wasn't a movie - at least not *that* kind of movie. In the end, he decided that the twin in front of him presented the greatest threat and thought a well-aimed boot to the crotch would impede his progress. His realization that the twin to his rear was the bigger threat came too late. He felt the thickly muscled arms wrap around him and squeeze like pythons. The breath was leaving him. Giddiness slithered into his brain. Davis could swear his head had popped off as a thick, opaque fog seeped into his mind. The tiniest of white lights began to flicker and dance happily around him. As quickly as the pressure constricted around him, it dropped away and then subsided entirely. Davis turned his face to his assailant and was shocked by what he saw.

The titan Necrosite turned the colour of a dry suburban lawn, like damp straw after the last of the snow has melted away, blanched and lifeless. His skin wrinkled and shrivelled and contracted against his bones. One of the large tusks dropped from his face and puffed into a desiccated cloud as it hit the floor. Dead.

The smaller of the twins attempted to stop his assault on Davis. Seeing his brother wither up and die left a bad taste in his mouth, and he considered that maybe the life of a thug wasn't all it was cracked up to be. But the speed he was moving, coupled with his sheer size, created enough momentum to carry him forward. His free hand touched the sleeve of the black robe, and in less time than his next heartbeat, he was a dried-out husk, blowing along the floor like a broken corn stock—the second glorious martyr in the cause of The Soulreaver.

*Holy shit!* The words echoed through the cowl of Davis' cloak.

He picked up the scythe and stepped forward. Jenn rushed over to him but stopped short for fear of touching the robe.

"I want to hug you, but-"

Davis stretched out a skeletal hand and took hers, pulling her close in an embrace that was too long overdue. It felt good. But there was a strangeness - not unwelcome - but different. A coldness that didn't come from his heart but a chill that seemed to encompass him now. At least this form of him.

"Would it make much difference if I said I was sorry?"

He pulled her tighter, and Jenn felt the saline tears prick at her eyes.

"Wouldn't you like to say something to me?"

Again, Davis pulled her close but stayed silent.

"If that's the way you're going to be about it, Davis, then to hell with you," she blurted.

Davis raised a hand and pressed a bony finger to her lips. With the other hand, he pulled back the hood of his robe and pulled off the sunglasses. His face was gaunt, nearly skeletal. Delicate skin stretched tightly across the bones as though he had known only hunger his whole life. His nose had nearly vanished, though enough sinew remained to perch the sunglasses on. His eyes remained. Blue. Past azure. Beyond aquamarine. Deeper than cobalt, cerulean, or beryl. Blue, like every perfect summer day she could remember. Laughing under warm beach-side skies with her parents when she was still small enough, her father had to carry her to the water.

Davis removed the finger from her lips and pointed to the pandemonium of Necrosites. He moved toward them, one measured step at a time, but stopped early enough to avoid any contact with them. He turned back to her and winked before putting the sunglasses back on. His mouth opened slightly, the faintest of sounds making their way past the whisper-thin lips. It was low and soft and grew in strength and volume the longer it went on until it became deafening, a danger to hear. It was all sound as it was no sound ever heard on earth.

**"I am Death,"** Davis said. **"There are none who may claim dominion over me. I am the great equalizer."**

"The robe is a bit of a give-away," Jenn whispered.

The Necrosites continued fighting. They wouldn't be deterred from such a cracking fight by a slightly larger than a normal human in his father's bathrobe.

Jenn shook her head.

**"Knock this shit out now, or I'll wipe the floor with the lot of you!"** the big voice boomed.

Jenn looked up at him.

The fighting ceased, and all of them flopped to the floor, quaking with fear. A solitary Necrosite in a white robe strolled forward, unconcerned with the consequences of his actions.

"Your time is past. You are a fraud, little more than a big dog on the front porch of an absentee landlord. You are finished here, Mareth. Now comes the time of the Necrosite. We will not yield, not to you nor any man that follows you. The Soulreaver has shown us the door to our freedom, and now, we step through it," Pyewackett said.

Bunn and Johnston rose from their positions on the floor and stood alongside him. Davis remained silent, glaring at the three of them through blue mirrored lenses. The two ape things looked to each other and then to Pyewackett, who showed no signs of giving in. Davis looked the Necrosite up and down, admiring him for his refusal to back down. He was brave, and his desire to help his people was genuine, but his fanatical devotion to the mail clerk was fanatical. And wrong.

**"Yield!"** Davis's voice shook the walls of the basement.

"Never," Pyewackett replied. He took another step forward.

Davis raised the scythe from the floor and replaced it slowly. The sound mutated, bending and twisting into the deafening roar of air being shredded by an explosion. The shockwave travelled forward, hitting Pyewackett at chest level. He remained upright, though that was the best he could hope for. A gigantic crack opened in the centre of his chest, and blood sprayed out of in a crimson fountain. The colour left his skin, the blackness drained away from his eyes, and he was gone. Johnston and Bunn saw what became of their comrade and leader and dropped to the floor immediately, hoping to avoid a similar fate.

"Where is the Soulreaver?" Davis demanded.

# 44

The t cloud in the pinstriped suit moved away from the Chinese restaurant. It breezed past the beings walking along the palette sidewalk, and none of them paid it any mind at all. It smiled a vaporous smile and stutter-stepped its way toward the gateway it knew existed just beyond where it stood. The front door was unlocked. It willed itself to become solid long enough to turn the knob and open it - through the vapour thing could have entered under the door or through the keyhole. It sat for a time in the small wooden room. The heat from the pot-bellied stove made it feel stronger, more confident. Powerful.

It gazed around the room and spied a set of stairs that curled down to a large room. It clunked along awkwardly in the old man's shoes and felt the unevenness of the floor underneath it. The thing passed a smoggy arm through the keyhole and unlocked the door from the other side, letting itself in. The room was filled with dust-covered boxes and blanket-covered objects, treasured enough to someone to secure them away like this. On a small wooden table lay a pair of leather gloves. The malicious breeze liked these gloves and inhabited them with little thought. In another box folded neatly was a black silk handkerchief. The thing smiled and assumed the scarf as its billowing face. There would be little to differentiate it from any of the other beings around this place now, it thought. It returned to the search.

The vapour carried on that way for some time, digging through boxes, looking for something of use as it moved to the back of the room. Something came into view that made it stop. Before the timekeeper stood a large, ornate mirror, and he knew his search was over.

"It is time," the timekeeper said. It stepped through the mirror into the basement of Winterbourne.

---

The building was quiet as Davis walked through the double doors toward the nurse's station.

"Maybe you'd better go first," he said.

"What for?" Jenn said.

He motioned to his appearance. The idea of Death coming for a visit with the friendly and courteous staff of Winterbourne home would go over as well as a fart in church.

"Oh, right."

The desk was deserted, which was not unusual for this time of day. Jenn walked into the break room and screamed. There were two of them in there. Both were nurses she had known since they started at Winterbourne, and they were standing motionless, in positions that said something was very wrong with the world. They weren't frozen, a touch of a stiffened arm confirmed they were still warm, and the colour of their skin was pink and healthy. It was as if they had just stopped - everything had just stopped.

"Davis, you'd better get in here!"

"I was afraid of this," he said.

"Afraid of what? What is all of this?"

"The big clock in the basement has stopped. The only things moving around here are going to be dead."

"But the Necrosites aren't dead. They're still moving around."

"Long story for another time. Necrosites don't count... not like that," he explained.

"What does it all mean?"

"We need to get the clock going again. It's just a matter of time before someone from the Night Court shows up and resets it all."

"That doesn't sound so bad," Jenn admitted.

"Anything not living will be sent to the waiting room where they will stay until their number is called. Until the end of time, if necessary. Anybody else will end up in Hel. Guess who that means?"

"They wouldn't," she said.

"You have no paperwork Jenn, you'd have a front seat on the bus ride there."

"Well then, fuck that. What's the plan? What do we do to fix all of it?"

"Head to the time clock behind the mailroom and hope we don't see too many people walking around," Davis said.

"The big clock is the time clock in the mailroom?"

"Yeah, why?"

"I just expected something a bit more...I don't know... impressive. An ornate carving of dragons or something, maybe an image of an hourglass or Father Time? Anything but the grubby old punch clock down there."

The quickest way to the mailroom was through the double doors and onto the elevator. But something was gnawing at Davis, whispering in his ear, telling him to turn around and take the stairs through the closet of room 107. As he rounded the corner, he saw what the something was—all three of them.

"Aw shit," he sighed.

Richard Walters and Dorothy Lauren stood outside the door of room 107, hovering over Clarence, who was laid out on the carpeted floor. The pair of them would have had more luck flying a brass kite than getting the old man off the floor and into his wheelchair. A danse macabre of the bungled and botched in full bloom.

"Ogay, ogay, ogay, ogay," Clarence babbled.

Dorothy held him under the left arm but suddenly released the hold and let him drop.

"Ogay!"

"What the hell?" Richard snapped.

"Someone comes on swift wings."

Davis walked up to the three of them. He saw the extent of what they'd endured. They were blood-soaked, and bits of ragged flesh hung from open wounds on their faces and necks. Richard's right eye dangled from its socket like an over-ripe grape. Clarence hadn't fared any better. Four deep gashes crossed his head, leaving terrible peaks and valleys of gore from forehead to chin. Dorothy seemed the least worse for wear, though the gaping wound in her throat, frothy with spittle and blood, told a different story.

"I'm so sorry this happened to you," Davis said.

"Don't sweat it, kid, we volunteered," Richard replied.

"Ogay?"

"Who did this to you?"

"The one that would steal time," Dorothy moaned.

The three men turned to the lone woman.

"Creepy old broad has been going on like this all god damned day. Can't make head or tail of what any of it means. Does it mean anything to you?"

"Yeah, yeah, it does," Davis sighed.

"It ain't good news, is it?"

"Look, I have to go do something that's going to put everything back to right," Davis said.

"I'm sensing there is about to be a bit bigger than this old gal's-"

"Ogay?"

"But as soon as I do, it's all going to end for you. Time will begin again, and I'll have to take everyone who has died away. All of you will have to go."

Richard Walters lowered his head and remained silent for a time.

"Promises," he said.

"What?"

"Take my hand," Richard said. He stared directly into the sunglasses.

Davis got a flash of the man who stood in front of him, a man who had spent his life taking the easy road. Though he had done no harm - no serious wrong to anyone - his was a life of little consequence to anyone but himself.

"I never married. I have no kids. Nobody to mourn, nobody to give a shit about me after I'm gone. If dying today helps to put everything back the way it should be, I guess my life will have meant something. But here it is. The day I walked into this place, I met you. You *promised* me that I would never be alone again. You swore that you and everyone that lived here or worked here would be my family. That you would be here for me when nobody else could. *You* would remember who Richard Walters was. It looks like your check has come to the table now, son. I'm holding you to what you promised."

"I have remembered all of you. From the very first one of that I took to the waiting room, to the very last I will ever help cross over, I remember. I will carry all of you with me until time is no more," Davis said. He felt his lip tremble, suddenly flooded with the memories of Lois and everyone else who he'd help leave this world.

"So... does that kinda talk come with the fancy bathrobe, or did they give you a book of creepy shit to say when you took this job?"

Davis beamed at the three of them. An unlikely army, but they had been a secret weapon. Certainly, one the Necrosites hadn't counted on.

"Get going, kid, we'll hold down the rear,"

"Ogay," Clarence agreed.

Davis pushed open the door to room 107.

"Be careful. Minnie Martin is in there," Richard added.

"Oh shit," Davis breathed.

He walked into the room, fear chewing away at his insides.

Minnie Martin broke the silence. "Mmhmm."

"A little help here," Frank Page said.

Davis knelt beside him, nearly tripping over his own robes as he bent down. Frank snorted at the other man's clumsiness.

"Where's the girl?" Davis demanded.

"What girl?"

"Look, there are things on their way down here that don't give a damn about you. They are going to kill the shit out of you and everything and everybody in this place just to set things back in order. You will spend eternity living in a filthy little shack in the middle of nowhere, eating Mushu pork until it's coming out of your god-damned ears. But if that doesn't sound bad enough for you, you've got *her* to contend with right now. I have seen Minnie Martin in a blind rage that lasted for four days. She was a lot calmer then than she is right now."

"Mmhmmm."

"Now, where is the girl?"

"He has her, the green thing. The head fucking green thing in the red bathrobe. He said he needed her to start some stupid clock. He's wastin' his time if you ask me."

"But it isn't going yet. The big clock isn't going yet," Davis said.

He headed through the closet door.

"Minnie, keep him company until I get back."

"Wait, what?" Frank choked.

# 45

"What do you mean, gone?" the Soulreaver said.

"All of them, sir. Gone over to the other side. Except for Pyewackett - he... he is no more," the young Necrosite said.

"How can that be? Who could sway all of them away from me?"

"Him," Smythe answered.

A lone figure in black stepped through the swinging doors of the mailroom. He seemed to defy logic as he moved, and in a heartbeat, he had crossed the room and was bearing down on them.

"Quickly, quickly, get back inside the door and lock it," the Soulreaver barked.

"Sir, I don't imagine a locked door will– "

"Just do it!"

The two of them pushed into the small back room that held the time clock and the young woman in the wheelchair, making the already cramped space claustrophobic.

"That was close. He was there, just outside the door," Barry said.

"Just in time, who knows what he would have done if he got in here," Davis said.

The Soulreaver whipped around and stood, chewed up nose to chewed up nose, with the man in the black robe.

"Who are you? Someone new working for the Night Court? Come to see that I get what's coming to me?"

"I go by many different names."

"Oh?"

"Yes," Davis said. The thunder beginning to lazily weave its way through his voice, building to a cannonade.

"Yes, well, could you share one or two of them with us? It might help to move things along a little."

**"Perhaps this will help."**

He fished around the folds of his robes until he found the silver-headed scythe. The handle had shortened considerably in the folds of his robe, but it lengthened quickly as he held it and now stood well above the top of his head. The figure in black, scythe in right hand, stood before the two Necrosites, looking every bit the Grim Reaper he was.

**"How about now?"**

"Father Christmas?" the younger Necrosite beamed.

**"Father, what? No,"**

"How about a hint?" The Soulreaver said.

**"Oh, for the love of - yes, fine. Look, long black robe, scythe, very grim expression?"**

"Oh, right, right," The Necrosite said.

**"Yes?"**

"Nothing, I've got nothing. Maybe if you took off the sunglasses," he added.

Davis pulled back the hood and removed the sunglasses.

**"Still not ringing any bells?"**

"It's you," the Soulreaver said.

**"Yes, Barry, it's me."**

"I don't understand. How can you be here?"

**"That's not important. Well, actually, it's very**

**important how I got here after what you did, but there are more important things to worry about. Like the clock.”**

“I know all about the clock, and once I get it running again, things will change around here. You’ll go back where you belong,” the Soulreaver said.

**“I’m offering you a choice, stop this now, it’s not too late, and we can undo most of the damage that’s been done.”**

“Can you switch that off, the booming voice? It’s a tad on the too much side for this small of a space.”

**“Wait, what?”** Davis boomed. The walls of the small room began to rattle beneath the awesome timber of his voice. **“Oh, I suppose yo**u’re right. How’s this?”

“Yes, much better. Now, you were saying?”

“I was saying stop all of this,” Davis repeated.

“Or?”

“Or face what’s coming. I can stop this - *we* can stop this - but I can’t stop what’s on its way here. Either way, we’re running out of time.”

“Stand outside the door. It sounds like he has help on the way,” Barry said. Smythe turned and walked out, closing the door behind him.

“*We* can fix? Tell me again what *we* can fix, won’t you? Can we fix the thousands of years my people under your kind’s oppression? Can we fix the fact that you and all your elders live in the splendour of this palace while we’re crammed - sometimes two families to a crate - in the dark regions of this place like garbage? How can we hope to fix anything when my children will never know the decency even your pets are afforded?”

Davis lowered his head, shame squeezing at him like poorly fitting shoes. The Soulreaver was right, and if he could have hidden inside his robe to avoid the Necrosite’s gaze, he would have. They may have been equal parts of the same whole, as Michael told him, but it was obvious now that some parts were much more equal than others.

"I was wrong. My kind has always been wrong. We think that because we made things like post-it notes and colour televisions and we know enough not to eat food that's gone bad, that it makes us d clever. So clever that we've decided we are superior to everything that hasn't done enough to attract our immediate attention. Humankind thinks all culture that isn't our own is primitive and stupid. We hate it, and we strive to subjugate it. People fear what they don't understand and want to poison and destroy everything they fear. It's what we do. It's what we've always done. But we can change. I can change. We are spokes on the same wheel, Mr. Wilson. The wheel that turns this place. We need each other. If that wheel stops turning, we'll all suffer the same fate," Davis said.

"Pretty words, but little more than lip service from master to slave," the Soulreaver said.

Davis got down on his knees, being careful this time not to trip on the folds at the bottom. He took hold of one of the gangly, clawed hands and looked Barry Wilson in the eye.

"You might want to see this, sir," Smythe said, opening the door and thrusting his head inside.

"Not now."

"If you are willing to fight for your people's freedom, fight now to keep them alive and safe," Davis pleaded.

"Sir, you really ought to come take a look at this," Smythe said again.

"Not now, Smythe!" Barry howled.

A gale-force wind blew against the door of the clock room and rattled its hinges like someone on the other side of the door was wiggling the lock. The hinges creaked, and Davis saw the door bend inward from the top. It was only a matter of time before the barrier gave way, and whatever was on the other side would be in the room with them. The door let go with a groan before an awful crack split it and sent shards of wood hurtling across the room. A being entered, taller than Davis by a whole head and nearly triangular from its broad shoulders, tapering down to the narrowest of hips. It wore a black pinstriped suit and filled it out well, though there appeared a constant ripple of movement beneath it. Its hands were covered in black leather gloves, constantly opening and closing into fists. The face was covered by a length of black silk that fluttered like a steady breeze was blowing directly in front of it.

"Time," it whispered. The timekeeper scrutinized Davis and decided he was not the one he was looking for.

"Time." The timekeeper floated to the Soulreaver, sizing him up.

Smythe, sensing a threat to his leader, leapt quickly in front of him - shielding him from whatever was to come. It was a valiant and completely selfless act. The black-gloved hand penetrated deep into his chest, cauterizing as it went. As the appendage emerged out the other side, it remained dry and clean. It did, however, carry a heart in it that was also completely dry. The Necrosite hit the floor before he'd even realized what just happened to him.

"You bastard!" the Soulreaver knelt beside the fallen guard.

"Time must go on," the-wisp in the wool suit said. It drove two misty hands through the chest of the little Necrosite in the red robe. Barry Wilson let out a strangled gasp and dropped to the floor.

"Stop!" Davis swung the gleaming scythe in the direction of the pinstripes.

It immediately rounded on Davis and fired a gloved hand into his chest. He felt the fist as it burned its way in, like the sting of the first glass of top-shelf whiskey. But it was not painful, not in the way the thing had intended, and when it removed the hand from his chest, it was little more than the uncomfortable feeling of flatulence and indigestion after too much of a good meal. The thing tried to push a hand into him again, a second time, and again a third, always coming up with the same, confusing result.

**"My heart is already dead,"** Davis grinned. His words cutting the air like a finger of lightning.

He raised the scythe slightly above the concrete and brought it down slowly, expecting the crack and the following shockwave to burst out and bowl this arrogant bastard with the handkerchief face over. The fruitwood hit the cement with a thud, and Davis was left staring vacantly at the wispy thing in the black suit. He raised the scythe again, higher this time, and brought it down with force against the hard floor. The handle splintered, and the heavy, silver head hit the floor with a clang.

"Time must go on," the thing said.

**"Wait, what?"**

The outline of the thing's mouth curled into an awful smile beneath the silk scarf. It glided around the back of the wall to where Ginny sat tied to the chair, still wrestling with the drugs in her system. The black handkerchief of its face moved close to Ginny and seemed to be smelling her.

**"Get away from her!"**

"Time must go on," it said and fired itself at Davis like a missile.

Davis felt it pass through him. All of it. The pain seared him, violating its way along. Every vaporous inch of the timekeeper moving forward. In the seconds before his mind went blank, he understood what a needle and thread must feel like from the needle's point of view. His body crumpled to the floor in a heap.

Ginny opened her eyes., She was still tied to a wheelchair in a dingy basement. Struggling to free herself from the ropes and the grip of the morphine still trudging its way through her bloodstream. She pulled at the straps on her arms and legs and thought one of them was coming loose when she felt it. The pressure hit her chest like a pile of cinder blocks had been set on top of it. If that wasn't bad enough, it was followed by a warmth that began as a foot moving slowly into a warm bath but quickly seared like the skin of a hot dog held too close to a campfire. Worry turned to panic, and she felt the skin of her chest blister and slough off.

"Stop it, stop it!" She was screaming but couldn't tell if it was out loud or just bouncing around her head.

"Stop!" The pressure continued to increase, and she strained to free herself from it.

"Shhh," the billowy voice cooed in her ear.

The pressure subsided a little, and she thought the assault had ended, but it returned. And with greater force. Ginny tried to scream but couldn't catch her breath enough to produce the sound.

"Shhh," the voice whispered again. Ginny was sure it wanted her to just let go. There was a safety in the whisper. An end to all the pain. She closed her eyes and surrendered to the whisper. And, without warning, it stopped, all of it. The stabbing pain, the awful pressure and the heat burrowing its way through her chest ebbed away. Ginny's head was still buzzing with the drugs. Sounds made their way to her, from far off and echoing, like a speech through a plastic traffic cone. It wasn't the whisperer she heard, not the voice in the darkness that had soothed her into this place between life and death. It was something smaller, almost trying not to be heard. And it was full of hope.

"Get the girl, I've got his, whassname," the voice said.

"That's all very well and good, yeah? You at his legs and me up here, yeah?"

"Just you two hold him down and give it a rest," Jenn said. She bashed a thick table leg through the black silk face and brought it crashing back across the suit, sending the clothes in a multitude of directions. The timekeeper floated off toward the other side of the room. For the moment, they had confused it enough to render it immobile.

"She's still pretty mickeyed," Jenn said and slapped Ginny.

"What the f–" she protested.

"What I wouldn't give for a hot shower and a cup of coffee."

"I would like a nice bit of braised pork just now, but there's no time for that, yeah?" Kevin hollered.

"Not for me, idiot, for this one."

She smacked the girl, trying to drive as much alertness into her as she could.

"Stop it. Jesus, I'm awake."

"Not yet you're not." Jenn smacked her again.

"Alright, goddamit, I'm awake," Ginny said with a clear voice.

"Good, you need to start the clock."

"Wait, what? I told that thing I don't know how to do that."

"It's a clock, you set it, and it goes," Jenn explained.

"I'm not stupid, lady. Not that stupid, anyhow. If it was that simple, don't you think I would have done it by now?"

Jenn thought about this and realized the girl had a point.

"W-watch..." the Soulreaver wheezed.

"What, what did he say?" Jenn said.

A trembling gangly hand held out an old, silver pocket watch attached to a thick, silver chain.

"Wa-watch..."

Jenn bent down to him. She knew this Necrosite. He had been the cause; the deaths of so many at Winterbourne home, the fight between her and Davis, his imprisonment. All of it. She wanted to hate him for it, wanted to see him die, slowly and painfully, so he could experience some of the grief he'd caused. But as he lay there sputtering up mouthfuls of black blood on the concrete floor, she pitied him. Barry Wilson struggled to lift his head and turned his eyes to her - eyes filled with pain, and she wanted the pain to end quickly.

Jenn took his hand and stroked his head tenderly, hoping he would pass quickly if she kept him calm, wishing Davis was there to ease him through it.

"I'm sorry, Barry," Jenn said.

"Too," he whispered.

"No, it's alright, it's–"

"Make sure," he struggled to get out.

"What? Make sure what?"

He drew in a huge breath, large and rattling as it went through him. She knew it would be his last.

"Free," he exhaled.

Jenn took the silver pocket watch from the Soulreaver's hand and gave it to Ginny.

"Start the clock, get us out of this," she said.

"That watch hasn't worked since I got it. How am I going to start a broken clock with a broken watch?"

"Time must go on," the timekeeper said. The silk handkerchief fluttered back into place like a sail in high winds. It shot a black-gloved hand out toward Ginny's throat.

Jenn jumped to stand between the two of them.

"Get him, you two, keep him busy!" she barked.

Wendell and Kevin sprung to life and launched themselves at the figure in the pinstriped suit, knocking the smoky stuffing from the folds of wool again. It was all the time Jenn and Ginny needed.

"Have you wound the watch?"

"What?"

"Wound it, have you wound the watch? You know, back before you were born, watches need to be wound to work," Jenn explained.

"Really?" Ginny said.

Jenn grabbed the watch away from the girl and examined her own. She quickly adjusted the time on the pocket watch and gave the crown a handful of turns. It began to tick along loudly, and from deep within Winterbourne, a metallic clang rang out as if some long silent mechanism had suddenly sprung back to life. The thing struggled against the hold of Wendell and Kevin, thrashing and driving gloved fists at them in turn. For all its effort, the Necrosite brothers would not allow it to move and gather itself fully in the clothing again.

Ginny Morrison took her grandmother's watch and stepped toward the punch clock. Gazing at the time on it, she took hold of the long metal hands of the big clock. The power flowed into her, surrounded her, and without warning, she became time. The world revolved around her and moved at her command. There was nothing but time. Time to eat, time to sleep, time to go to school and to the dentist. More time than anyone could use in three lifetimes. And it all bent to her will. A tremor hit her as she adjusted the hands to match the pocket watch. A bell rang out from the big clock; a mechanism clicked into place and started running. Though no one said a word, it felt as though everything had shifted, and everything resumed moving along exactly as it should.

Wendell and Kevin let go and stepped away from the timekeeper. It was every bit as menacing in appearance but seemed to have lost some of its bite.

"We could use you now," Jenn said. She jiggled Davis' sunglasses.

"What, what?" he yawned.

"I need you to eighty-six the guy in the gangster suit, you know - your way." She smiled.

Davis stood and adjusted his sunglasses. He stretched out an arm, and the pieces of the broken handle shot toward him, re-assembling as they moved. By the time they reached his hand, they were restored, and the scythe was whole again. Massive waves of white electricity shot forward, knocking the Necrosites back and blowing them a safe distance from the timekeeper. The black silk of his face fluttered uncontrollably, trying desperately to remain in place in the face of the storm raging against it. He withheld the gusty onslaught and moved closer to Davis.

"Time must go on," it said.

He moved, raised his arms, and pushed the palms of the black gloves toward the man in the black robe.

"I am time. Without me, the world stops," the timekeeper said.

Davis took a deep breath, raised the scythe, and drove it against the concrete floor. Blinding Rings of flame, wreathed in sparks, shot forward toward the thing in the pinstriped suit. He raised both arms, and a gigantic set of tattered wings erupted from his robe.

**"I am the void. Time and tide may pass, but *none* can avoid my grasp."** His voice shook the foundations of Winterbourne.

He raised the scythe again, and another blue flame ring - smaller, burning hotter and twice as bright as the first - scorched its way toward the timekeeper. The heat danced in a wave behind it, blowing the black handkerchief from his face across the room. As it floated earthward, empty and devoid of life, the black woollen suit followed, and the timekeeper dissipated.

# EPILOGUE

"No, just the pertinent stuff," Davis said.

The young Necrosite was helpful, there was no mistake about that, but he was no Richardson.

"Just go," Davis said.

The Necrosite moved with a fearful jerk and headed for the door.

"Wait."

The gangly young lizard thing stopped and turned back toward his boss.

"You're doing a good job, Steven. See you tomorrow."

The little thing spun gleefully on its heels and headed out the door.

"You're too hard on him," Jenn said.

"He's so bad. Richardson might have creeped me out a little, but Goddamn, he ruled this office," Davis said.

"It would be nice if we could get a message to him, let him know we haven't forgotten him."

Mr. Richardson walked along the wooden pallet streets, feeling pretty good about himself. Sure, he was stuck in the most awful place he could think of, but his sacrifice had saved them all.

"Nice to walk around in the clean air, no?" Michael asked.

"Yes, yes, it is. But still," Richardson said.

"But what?"

"I snuck in here. I am a necessary body in this place, but there is no record of me. Effectively, I am stuck here until the end of time, right?"

"You made a choice and not an easy one at that. It was for the greater good, which is easier to say than it is to live with. We all appreciate it, but when all is said and done, it's you that *must* live with it. At least we can keep each other company." The old man smiled.

Richardson sighed as the two of them walked on in silence.

Michael finally broke the quiet. "Should we get something to eat?"

"You've been here from the beginning?"

"Near enough, yes."

"Is it always so fucking cold?"

Michael laughed and handed the Necrosite a square of folded, plain brown paper wrapped in string.

"Take this and come on."

The Necrosite took the package and unfolded it. Looking at it, a broad smile crossed his face, displaying his needle teeth. He wrapped the blanket around his shoulders, the thick, black stripe stretching across his back. Written below the stripe we the words: Mareth, 5832.

"How many years *can* Mushu make you forget?" Richardson asked.

# S. A. BAKER

S. A. Baker is a healthcare worker and recovering professional musician who spent eleven years touring around North America and despite popular opinion, he really does know how to smile.

From early on, he excelled at telling stories and won several local writing awards before being bitten by the rock and roll bug.

He currently lives in a small town in Ontario with his wife and two children and two of the dumbest cats that have ever drawn breath. When not writing, Mr. Baker plays bagpipes competitively (no, really) and thinks about learning to fly fish. Not A Hope In Her is S. A. Baker's third novel in the Winterbourne saga.

## ALSO BY S A BAKER

Winterbourne

Faun Song

Life, The Universe, and Isobel